COLOMBA

ALBA

(White Dove)

By

Julius Charrett-Dykes

Cover art by Julius Charrett-Dykes.

Published in Great Britain by the author.

www.charrettdykes.com

The birds they sang at the break of day
Start again I heard them say
Don't dwell on what has passed away
Or what is yet to be.
All the wars they will be fought again
The holy dove, she will be caught again
Bought and sold and bought again
The dove is never free.

Excerpt from "Anthem" by Leonard Cohen

PROLOGUE

"The problem is sin," Antoine insisted, "Things go wrong because of unconfessed sin in one's life." The light lit Antoine's face from below, making his eyes glitter intensely. The gathered audience, grim-faced and serious, nodded in silent agreement.

Within the seated ranks, Faith felt Fatima's silent sob wrack her neighbouring body, and was glad that her friend's tears could not be seen by the feeble light of the room's solitary candle.

Antoine continued, "We are called to be perfect beings, to leave our sinful and lustful ways behind us. If an eye offends, we should pluck it out, if a hand offends, we should cut it off!"

Faith tapped her brother's forearm to get his attention and nodded silently, her eyes turning down to draw his attention to the crumpled form of Fatima at her side, "Let's get her out of here," she whispered.

Together, the siblings helped Fatima to her feet. "Sister Fatima is feeling a little unwell," Faith explained to the speaker and his audience.

Antoine, his intense eyes still afire, continued addressing the group as the three rose and made towards the door, the audience's eyes were full of reproach for the trio who made the interruption, "It is the unconfessed sin in our lives that will prevent our ascension into the heavenly realms!"...

OCCITANIA / PAYS D'OC / LANGUEDOC

Before it was conquered and became part of France, most of the southern part of the modern Republic was known as Occitania or 'lo Pais d'Oc' where Occitan (Langue d'Oc) was the primary language.

When Charlemagne's Frankish Empire divided on his death in the Ninth Century into three discreet regions; the most southerly, Occitania was split into different self-governing kingdoms, duchies and counties with its own bishoprics and clergy.

Although the region was never subsequently politically reunited, a common culture grew across and between these fluid, ever-changing boundaries. Under the protection of powerfully independent dukes and counts whose feudal loyalties to nominal European sovereigns were tangled, the peculiarly Occitan culture grew and flourished. A hotbed of ideas; Occitan troubadours famously conceived and exported concepts of chivalry and courtly love embraced by the royal courts of medieval Europe.

One powerful county was that of Toulouse; ruled by a Count who, though technically a vassal of the French crown, was in reality an autonomous ruler of a region that, in the Twelfth Century, stretched from Toulouse in the west to the Rhone in the east, and was known in common parlance as the province of Languedoc.

Toulouse and its other Occitan neighbours were also under a different code of Law from the rest of Northern Europe, its had been inherited from Visigoth and Roman Laws, and under it women enjoyed legal rights and protection that the fairer sex would only realise elsewhere in the Twentieth Century. They could inherit land and title and manage it independently from their husbands or male relations, dispose of their property in legal wills if they had no heirs, and women could represent themselves and bear witness in court by age 14 and arrange for their own marriages by age 20.

Resenting the region's autonomy and the strong influence of the Counts of Barcelona the French crown was quick to prosecute a proxy crusade in the Languedoc on the behalf of the Catholic Church whose own power in the region was being eroded by another branch of Christianity, conveniently proclaimed heretical, known as Catharism. And so, it was that the province was ravaged by a 20-year war that effectively exterminated a rival religion to the Holy Empire of Rome, and also served to realign Toulouse to France.

By 1500 the whole of Occitania was assimilated into France. So, it was, that from the Thirteenth to the Seventeenth Centuries, Occitan culture was gradually eroded by its conquerors. By the end of the Fifteenth Century, Occitan nobles and gentry were speaking French and in the Sixteenth Century the administration, by order of the French King, was conducting its business in the Gallic tongue. But the area's ancient language was only finally eradicated by a directive from the French Minister of Education in 1880, to punish children who used Occitan in school, in a protracted process known as the 'shaming'. Even so, French only got the upper hand in the Twentieth Century.

10th June

The mattock made a hollow 'pop' as Marc brought it down into the debris in the sump. He stopped working and called up to Gilbert, "I've hit something!"

Gilbert, the foreman, grunted in acknowledgement and moved the portable light-stand closer, so that the lamp shone into the ditch. Now, when Marc lifted the blade free, it was plain to see that it had made a hole in something spherical and terracotta coloured.

Marc hoped it was something interesting this time, some Roman pottery from the ancient castle up there in the darkness above them – a treasure trove of old gold coins that would see he and Gilbert amply rewarded for their nocturnal service to the Commune.

More likely some old camping bowl though, with our luck, he thought.
He bent down, his orange plastic overalls rustling as he scraped away at the mud with a gloved hand. He suddenly recoiled in shock as his fingers ran over two hollows in the object, and the black strands he'd taken to be plant roots were clearly hair. "Merde!" he swore as he bolted in fright right out of the trench.
"What is it this time?" asked an unfazed Gilbert.
"A skull, a human skull." replied the frightened youngster.

The first gendarmes arrived, bleary-eyed, some minutes later and parked across the road to block the passage of non-existent traffic, their blue flashing light joining with the idling council truck's orange beacons, to wash the area in strangely hypnotic light. They walked to the side of the lorry's well-lit and warm cab, in which the two workers awaited them, reading the local papers and sipping coffee from their vacuum flasks.

Gilbert wound down his window to address the nearest one, "Salut Renaud! Sorry to get you up so early, but my young apprentice here thinks he found a skull in the ditch we were clearing."

Renaud shrugged, "Last time it was a fox's! Still, best to be sure eh?"

"Yeah, I suppose," said Gilbert reluctantly folding his paper and placing his mug on the dashboard.

He stepped down from the cab, "The boy's a bit spooked," he explained as he led the two officers around to the kerb side of the lorry. They looked down into the ditch, and it was easy to see the skull from the dark wound the mattock had made in its crown.

"Get your gloves and boots on Pratt," ordered Renaud of his younger companion, "We need to be sure."

While the reservist gendarme returned to the squad car to change, Renaud and Gilbert leaned against the warm throbbing flank of the truck.

"Think it is human then?" asked Gilbert.

Renaud nodded, "Looks like it," he affirmed.

A few moments later Pratt reappeared clad in blue coveralls, Wellingtons, and nitrile gloves. He carefully lowered himself into the ditch as the others stepped to its edge and monitored his movements. He shone his torch at the sphere and moved mud away from its base, to expose a little more of it. Dark strands of hair were still attached at the back, the hollows were eye sockets. "Definitely human!" he called up.

Renaud pulled a radio handset from his jacket, "Better call for the cavalry then!"

By dawn, further gendarmes from the nearby town of Rivesaltes had set up a roadblock to prevent any traffic access to the site, on the single-track road that led to the ghost village of Périllos. They allowed access to a forensics team from Perpignan and an unmarked police car, also from the regional capital, driven by a young raven-haired beauty who, much to their surprise, volunteered Lieutenant Detective's credentials.

This detective took confident charge of the men at the scene, and after speaking to the forensics team, she interviewed the reporting officers – Renaud and Pratt, who she promptly stood down and allowed to return to their station. She'd call on them if need be, she said, before she turned her attention to the two council workers.

Gilbert and Marc could scarcely believe that the attractive woman who interviewed them, was old enough to be a police officer, let alone a detective. Her face was long, her cheekbones high and she had almond shaped, brown eyes, so dark that they appeared to be black under thick shapely eyebrows. Her head was held erect and proud on a long neck and when she looked at them her regard was strangely calm and piercing.

Her broad smile was disarming, "Bonjour messieurs," she said, as they looked up open-mouthed from their coffee mugs, "I'm Detective Babayan, I'd like to ask you a few questions."

Gilbert, who Marc normally found to be a little dismissive of women, especially those of middle-eastern origin or appearance, cast an approving eye over the shapely detective - who he later said reminded him of Cleopatra - began, of his own accord telling her all about their discovery, of events prior to it – how they'd been routinely maintaining drains and culverts on roads around Opoul-Périllos since April, as employees of the Department.

As he listened Marc, with a jolt, realised that they had not yet informed their superiors about the incident. He wondered whether he should get his mobile phone out and ring to inform them, or would it make the detective suspicious? He squirmed uncomfortably, as he waited for the foreman to finish his increasingly lengthy and detailed statement, the earlier fright and the coffee making him need to pee. But, as if sensing that he was becoming increasingly stressed, the woman turned her eyes upon him and seemed to emanate a signal to calm and his panic abated.

Lucine recognised the tell-tale signs of autism, "Do you need a moment?" she asked.

Marc nodded and she allowed him five minutes, so long as he stayed close to the truck. While Gilbert, continued telling her how Marc would clear heavy debris from the bottom of drains onto the kerbside, and he would then load it onto the lorry's grab, Babayan noticed the young council worker urinate against the rear wheel of the truck and begin making calls on his mobile. "Is he easy to manage?" she asked, nodding towards the youngster.

"Oh yes, he's harmless. Gets worked up and panicky sometimes. You need to tell him things a hundred times before it goes in, but he's a nice lad, works well..." said Gilbert reflectively.

With a faraway look the detective nodded, "I've got your details, I think you need to get him home."

Gilbert looked up, to see that Marc was sitting on the rear fender of the truck, rocking backwards and forwards and weeping as he blubbered to someone over his mobile phone. "That'll be his mum," explained Gilbert, getting to his feet and walking towards his young charge.

Lucine watched the orange truck chug away down towards the village of Opoul. She noticed that Marc, sat high in the passenger seat, kept turning his head to look back at the scene he was leaving. Then she walked across to the tents of the forensics team. The lead technician stepped away from his companions and pulled her aside as she approached, he obviously had some news. "Ah Lieutenant Babayan! There appears to be more than one body in the drain," he said.

She nodded in understanding and withdrew her mobile phone from her jacket pocket.

Maury tapped the thermometer that monitored the outside temperature, the needle was at 26 degrees and rising. He was glad of the climate control in the office, today would be another scorcher, summer had arrived with a vengeance. He wondered, as he stepped into his adjutant's adjoining office, if the garage had yet managed to fix the air conditioning on his official car? Gardien-de-la-paix Martinez was speaking agitatedly on the phone, his ridiculously thin moustache bristling as he gesticulated wildly for his invisible audience. He covered the receiver when Maury raised his eyebrows in query, "I'm talking to the garage now Sir. They say there's something wrong with the control module and the car will have to be returned to Citroën under warranty," he explained. He also pushed a yellow post-it note across the desk at his superior and went back to berating the mechanics from the motor pool. The note simply said, "Contact the Perpignan office ASAP."

Maury returned to his own office and picked up the phone, pressing the fast-dial button for a direct line to the satellite office. Someone picked up the phone immediately. "Allo. Commandant Maury here, I have a message to ring."

"Hello sir. This is Captain Guillot, thanks for ringing back. We've got a little manpower problem here, and I wondered if you could spare one of your senior detectives for a while?"

"Ah Guillot! No, we have no-one spare here. You know how it is at this time of year, everyone's taking their leave because of the summer ban. You've got Verdier there, why can't you use him?"

Guillot went quiet. When he spoke again it was in a conspiratorial whisper, "There's history between him and the junior detective I've put on the case. There's a bit of bad blood down here and they're both better off being elsewhere."

"Then why don't you swap them over and put Verdier on the case instead?" asked Maury.

"I can't, Babayan witnessed him assaulting a witness, she's the detective on the case, and Verdier's at home on sick leave until the matter is resolved."

"What about you then Guillot?"

Guillot laughed, "We need a detective not an administrator…"

"Why do you need to assign a senior detective anyway?" asked Maury.

"Because, the forensics team on site tell us that they're dealing with more than one deceased."

It was protocol to assign a high-ranking officer to incidents involving more than one victim. Maury quickly looked over his open desk diary, it was covered in appointments for him to attend strategic meetings, seminars, and conferences. He saw his chance to escape, "Then I'll come down myself."

When Maury emerged from his office with his laptop bag over his shoulder and his jacket in the crook of his elbow, Martinez looked up in shock, "Are you off out, Sir?" he asked.

"Yes. I'll be working out of the office for a while. I'm needed down at Perpignan. Only contact me if it's a dire emergency, otherwise just email me. Have you got me a car sorted?" asked Maury, looking once again at the outside temperature display. 28 degrees and still rising. He made a mental note to pass by home on the way and pick up some short-sleeved shirts and lighter slacks. He noticed that Martinez was squirming a little in his seat, "What's the matter man?" he asked.

Martinez pulled a car key from his drawer and passed it across the desk, "All the new Citroens and Peugeots have been recalled for a software upgrade," he explained apologetically.

"What've you given me here then?" asked a puzzled Maury looking down at the little key with the prancing lion logo of Peugeot on it.

"An undercover car Sir."

Maury nodded, "That'll do. As long as it's got air conditioning."

In the basement Maury pushed the key-fob's plip and the lights on a dark red hatchback, parked carelessly in full sunshine, flashed in response. As he drew closer, he could see that almost every panel on the ancient car was dented. The paint was peeling from the roof and bonnet in unsightly blisters where it had suffered the ravages of ultraviolet exposure. He pulled open the door and was immediately hit by a furnace-like heat from its basic interior. He noticed the old manually wound window winders and realised why Martinez had gone so quiet, open windows would be the closest thing to climate control that the old car could provide.

He tugged open a rear door, it squeaked in complaint, and put his things on the rear bench seat, then he went to each door and wound every window right down. Returning to the driver's seat he put the key in the ignition and turned it. The starter motor engaged noisily, and the engine turned over but refused to start. What am I doing wrong? Maury asked himself. Then he noticed the little orange coil light on the dashboard and realised that such ancient diesel-engine cars need to pre-heat. He went through the rigmarole again, and this time the engine clattered to life and a cloud of acrid blue smoke filled the garage.

By the time he reached home he was quite enjoying the old car, it was less claustrophobic than newer cars, there was more room inside and it had nice big windows which gave it an airy feel. Marie-France came to the door to meet him and giggled as she told him she thought it may be a neighbouring farmer who had come to call.

"By the way, Elisabeth called. She wants to come with the children," Marie-France shouted after him as Maury went upstairs to prepare a day bag.

Maury's heart warmed, it would be good to see their daughter and the grandchildren now that they were settled into the place.

"When?" he asked as he pulled shirts from a drawer.

"Tomorrow!"

"But I'm working," Maury protested.

"No, you silly, they want to come for a holiday...a couple of weeks."

A couple of weeks! Usually Elisabeth stayed for a couple of days at most. But that was when they were living in Lozère, now they lived in Aude and things were much different. Not just the house, but he and Madame Maury had changed – for the better. Maybe their perceptive daughter picked up on the new positive optimism of their lives?

"That'll be alright won't it?" asked Marie-France, her voice betraying a little concern.

He came to the top of the stairs buttoning his shirt over his ample and hairy belly and looked down at his wife, smiling broadly, "No, it's not alright. It's fantastic news! Anyway, I'll be back every evening."

Marie-France beamed back, "Do want a coffee or a bite to eat before you go?"

"No, you get the rooms ready. I'll get something en route."

He left, his wife happily preparing the rooms for their very important guests, and he waved up at her as he stepped back into the car and cranked it over. Marie-France mouthed something from the window as he began turning the car around, he frowned and shrugged to indicate that he'd not heard. When he switched off the rattling engine she shouted and giggled at her own cheekiness, "That car suits you Commandant!"

Maury drove south on the old Route Nationale, rather than the parallel-running motorway, enjoying the vista that opened up of the Plain of Roussillon, as the road skirted the eastern edge of the Corbières. To the east, the etangs, those salt-water lakes, with their strange grid-work patterns of oyster beds, sparkled in the sun and beyond them glinted a dark-blue Mediterranean and the white apartment blocks of the resort towns. And there, to the south were the smoky flanks of the Albères, that part of the Pyrenees that met the sea. Above it all, shimmered the conical snow-white head of the volcano-like Canigou Mountain.

At Salses, he left the main road and headed upward and westward through the little village of Opoul, on a poorly surfaced departmental road towards Périllos. He reached the roadblock, where two bored and sweltering gendarmes waved him down. On production of his Warrant Card, they saluted smartly and allowed him to pass, telling him that he could not miss the incident site.

They were right, the orange shelter, next to a large white van, was easy to find. He parked alongside a compact black Renault and stepped out of his car. Above the site was a rock bluff, and along its crest he could make out masonry, that indicated that it was the remains of a long-ruined castle. A petite, neat, and dark-clothed young woman walked confidently towards him from the garish orange of the shelter, "Bonjour Monsieur, can I help you?" she called.

Her dark wavy hair had bluish highlights, her skin was olive, her nose aquiline and her lips full. Maury approved, by her professional deportment, this young woman was quite obviously Babayan, the detective from whom he was taking charge, "I'm Commandant Maury," he replied.

The pretty mouth momentarily fell open in shock, and the girl stuttered, as her eyes passed over the old banger in which he'd arrived, then as she composed herself she offered a good firm handshake, "Hello Sir, I'm Lieutenant Babayan the detective assigned to the case. Follow me, and I'll get you up to speed."

As she turned to lead him to the forensics shelter, Lucine groaned inwardly, she felt she'd already made herself look a fool in front of the regional boss. Maury followed in her wake, appreciating her form, and looking around about him at the lay of the land.

The lead forensics officer, a Sous-Brigadier, his white disposable overalls drenched and semi-translucent with perspiration, took them through what his team had discovered so far, "There are three bodies, all are badly decomposed, two female and one male. They were at the bottom of a sump designed to prevent debris entering a culvert that diverts water-flow from one side of the road to the other."

"Any evidence of foul play?" Maury asked.

"There are broken bones and they're all tangled up, I'm no expert - they could have got damaged post-mortem, the Coroner is the person to ask. We'll be sending the remains to him as soon as my men have recovered all they can."

"How long do you think they've been here?"

"My guess is, about a year, Sir."

"Okay. Carry on..." Maury paused and dug into his pocket to extract a twenty Euro note, that he pressed upon the protesting forensics man, "Here, buy your men a cold beer when you're done."

Maury was glad to be out of the sweaty confines of the plastic shelter, in which the poor forensics team had to work, it was hot enough outside. He stopped and wiped condensation from his spectacles.

"What now Sir?" Lucine asked.

"How about a little walk around?" Maury suggested, already heading off along a pathway that would lead them up to the castle ruins.

Lucine regretted her morning's choice of footwear, as she followed the senior detective on semi-high heels through the thorn, privet and rosemary, that edged the precipitous and rocky little path. She was amazed that an overweight, middle-aged man could move so fast, but then she heard his wheezy rasp and knew that his pace could not be sustained.

As they reached the rocky crest a panting Maury exclaimed, "I'm getting too old for this!"

From their high vantage point, they saw the plain swimming in heat haze south of them, the forensics shelter and the land sloping down to Salses, the etangs and the sea to the east, and the mountain range of the Corbières running away north and west behind the abandoned village of Périllos with its forsaken buildings.

They stopped for breath and a welcome breeze cooled them a little. The place was wild and starkly beautiful, and as Lucine looked around in awe from their high vantage point, Maury slowly and methodically scanned through three hundred and sixty degrees looking for anomalies, something out of place. The area was a heathland, a virtual desert – wild and windblown. He pointed at a large, blackened area of garrigue near a ravine to the south-west.

Shielding her eyes against the brightness she looked in the direction his outstretched hand indicated, "There's been a wildfire by the looks of it, but not recent, the Canadairs always seem to be out here, it may be because the military have shooting ranges on those hillsides," she explained.

Maury continued scanning clockwise, and could see why flying fire engines were needed, there were unmade tracks and ravines running away to the south-west, few metalled roads and little sign of human habitation, apart from the abandoned village of Périllos, with its church tower and ruined feudal keep to the west.

"And what's that?" asked Maury, now facing north-west and pointing to a small building, nestled among cypresses.

"I have a map in the car… I should've brought it," Lucine rued.

Continuing his rotation, Maury spied a large detached farmhouse, a Mas, with green swimming pool and recently re-tiled roofs at the north foot of the spur on which they stood.

"You interviewed the workmen who found the first body?" he asked, his eyes still carefully scanning the landscape around them.

"Yes sir. Well actually I only interviewed the one. The second seems to be prone to panic attacks."

"Have you got your notes?" asked Maury.

Babayan dug for her notebook from her jacket pocket and passed it to the senior detective, who looked over her entries carefully through his old-fashioned glasses. "What's your feeling?" Maury asked, passing back the notes, removing his glasses and turning his attention back to the scenery.

For a moment, Lucine wondered what the middle-aged detective was talking about, then she realised that he was asking her for her first impressions. She measured her words carefully, "We don't know how they died. But what business could have brought them here? Or maybe they were dumped?"

Maury nodded, as if in approval, "How many big cases have you worked on?"

"I've worked on several murder investigations, mostly domestic, some robberies and a kidnapping."

"Did you solve them all?"

"Not personally, but I was part of the team that did... Except for the kidnapping, we brought the perpetrators to justice in every case."

"What's your area of expertise?"

She wanted to sound assured and competent, but not crow about her abilities, "I'm good at getting background information and taking note of little details."

"I can see that," said Maury, referring to her detailed notes, "I think your skills are going to come in handy."

When they returned to the incident site, a plain black ambulance was collecting the bagged remains from the forensics team. From her car, Lucine extracted the map from the glovebox and opened it out on the bonnet. She quickly oriented herself, and identified the building Maury had seen from the hilltop on the map, "The building you pointed out is a chapel!" she called after Maury, who was walking along the road looking carefully at the verges.

Maury called back, "We'll work out of the Gendarmerie in Rivesaltes. From what your Captain Guillot tells me, it might be a good idea for you to be out of Perpignan for a while."

"Yes Sir." Lucine conceded, wondering what her superior had told Maury of the case.

"We'll make our way there," Maury stated.

He turned back to look at Lucine, and could see that mention of Verdier had made her withdraw into herself, her face was set and there was a tic in her cheek, "Are you alright?" he asked.

Babayan pulled herself together, it was a relief to be away from Perpignan, but she'd have liked to have toughed it out with the chauvinistic pricks in the office. Now, they could talk behind her back, and make her feel even more isolated and unaccepted than before, when she returned. She put her mobile away and looked levelly at the Commandant, "I'm fine."

"When it comes to casework," Maury warned, "We can have no secrets, we put it all out there, our maddest ideas and theories, our inklings and ideas. If this thing with Verdier affects you, then I need to know..."

Maury gave contact details to the forensics men and got into his beaten-up old car and led Lucine in her modern black hatchback towards Rivesaltes. He stopped at the roadblock to talk to the gendarmes ,who had erected a garden gazebo and now sat at a table in its shade, "You're well installed," joked Maury, "Where's the Pastis?"

They laughed back, but then got to their feet in concern, as the echoing sound of a high-powered car being driven fast up the hill rolled towards them. Then, with a screech, a dirty yellow Porsche came into view about one hundred metres away and pulled to a hasty halt. Reverse gear was selected with a crunch, and the car was spun in the other direction, and driven away at the same insane velocity with which it had arrived.

"Got its registration?" one gendarme demanded of the other.

"Yep!" his companion said, unclipping his radio and calling for support from other local units and giving then quick details of the fugitive car, which could still be heard being manically driven away south-east, towards Rivesaltes.

"Joyriders?" asked Maury.

"More like something to do with Jimenez," said the first gendarme.

"Who is Jimenez?"

"He's the pimp who owns that Mas just up the road from here."

"The one at the foot of the castle?"

"Yes, that's right."

"A pimp you say?"

"Yeah, he runs brothels at Perthus and La Jonquera on the Spanish border."

The second gendarme, his radio communications now concluded, joined in the conversation, "It's been said that he entertains his more exclusive clients out here."

"At the Mas?"

The two gendarmes nodded.

"So, what's the connection with the Porsche?" asked Lucine, who'd stepped from her car to join the group.

"Probably a Go Fast … a drugs courier," the first gendarme stated, "We'll get them. They'll probably head back onto the motorway, but we've got a team already working down at the toll station."

"Good work," said Maury.

The Gendarmerie at Rivesaltes was already buzzing with celebratory excitement when Maury and Babayan presented themselves there. The Desk Sergeant happily boasted about his comrade's involvement in the apprehension of the drugs couriers. "We've been aching to bust that Jimenez for ages. I hear they're raiding the house as we speak."

"The Mas at Périllos?" queried Maury.

"Yes, that's the place."

"Who's in charge of the operation?" Maury asked.

"It's an Interpol operation, a joint operation with the Spanish authorities. The French liaison is a chap from Toulouse, a Captain in the Vice Squad called Wittmeyer."

"Can you give me a contact number?"

"Of course," said the sergeant, tapping keys on his laptop.

"Then I'd like to speak to the station commander," Maury added.

The Major in charge of the station was pleasant and accommodating, he saw to it that Maury and Babayan were allocated a small, fully-equipped incident room and two local gendarmes; Renaud and Pratt, who had been the first responders, to assist with the investigation. Maury immediately sent them on a task, "I need a statement from the other council worker who found the bodies."

"Marc Belcourt?" suggested Renaud.

Maury nodded, "Yes, that's the one. Go easy, Lieutenant Babayan thinks he might have been a little spooked."

"I know the family Sir," said Renaud, nodding at Lucine as he and Pratt took their leave.

"What do you want me to do?" asked Lucine.

"See if you can rustle up something to eat and drink, while I get hold of Wittmeyer."

When she returned, with pre-packaged sandwiches and a flask of coffee, Maury was waiting and eager to leave, "Wittmeyer says we can look over the Mas, as long as we don't get in the way of the investigators on scene." He grabbed a sandwich, unwrapped it and began chewing upon it as he led his way down to the parking area. "We'll take my car," he said reaching into his pocket for the keys.

"Maybe it's nothing," Maury explained between mouthfuls of ham, cheese, and bread, as he drove back into the heathlands towards Périllos, "but this Jimenez Mas is the nearest habitation to where the bodies were found."

"Do you think there's a connection?" the Lieutenant asked.

Maury noticed a smell like Turkish Delight in the car. Babayan smelled of middle eastern confectionery...

"Drugs, sex, criminals...violence..." Maury mused, "More than likely!"

The Jimenez Mas was crawling with uniformed and plain-clothes officers, a tall, sandy-haired man in his mid-thirties detached himself from a group of smokers in animated discussion, in front of a beautiful scarlet Ferrari in the triple garage and introduced himself as Wittmeyer, "You want to have a look around, right? Be my guest."

Maury thanked him and led Lucine into the renovated farmhouse. Its transformation was startling, its interior Spartan and ultra-modern with white tiled floors and bespoke fittings. "What are we looking for?" Lucine asked.

"Everything... Nothing in particular." Maury replied enigmatically.

The house was laid out around the large swimming pool and terraces at its centre. There were stainless steel kitchens and sitting rooms on the ground floor, and an annexe where staff appeared to be accommodated. Upstairs, there were generous en-suite bedrooms, all decorated and equipped according to a particular sexual fetish. The attending police officers seemed particularly drawn to a S&M themed room with its shackles, its leather accessories, and other paraphernalia. They all looked suggestively at Lucine as she entered, and Maury quickly moved her on to other parts of the house. He caught her sweet scent again...

In the stairway Maury asked a detective if the house staff were still on-site, "Yes, they're sat in the summer house," replied the man.

"Where's that?"

"There's a door in the wall on the far side of the pool which leads out into the garden," said the man with a wave.

No, not Turkish Delight... Babayan smelled of Rose Water!

They found the door without trouble, and found themselves in a fragrant and shady courtyard with a Mediterranean-style garden, with old potted olive trees and herbs at one end, and a water garden with tall reeds and other semi-aquatic plants at the other. A path led to the summer house, a single storey building, simply equipped with a bar and dominated by French windows, that gave a panoramic view of the village of Périllos and the far ranges of the Fenouilledes and the Pyrenees proper beyond.

Three small dark people were sitting glumly together on a sofa, under the bored eye of a plain-clothes officer sat sipping a tall glass of icy liquid on a bar stool. "Do you mind if I have a word with these people?" Maury asked.

"Who are you?" the officer asked.

Maury reached into his pocket and extracted his credentials, "Commandant Maury from the Regional CID."

The officer waved at the people on the sofa, "Of course, Sir, help yourself."

Maury approached the three on the sofa, a compact greying middle-aged couple with the dark slightly oriental look typical of Filipinos and a stocky younger woman who looked to have a family resemblance, he introduced himself.

In poor French, the man replied that they only spoke Spanish, Maury looked to Lucine who shook her head. "What about English then?" he asked.

The man nodded his head vigorously, "Yes, we all speak English. I am Irlo Malit, this is my wife Alesha and our daughter Grace. We are from Manila in the Philippines"

"Do you all work here?"

"Yes, we keep house for Señor Jimenez"

"How long have you worked here?"

"Nearly three years now."

Maury paused, wondering how to phrase his next questions in English, but was saved by Lucine who asked, "What exactly do you do here?"

"I look after the garden and grounds," Irlo replied, "My wife Alesha does the cooking and laundry. Grace cleans and keeps house."

"You know what goes on here?" Maury asked, looking directly into each of their faces. The Filipinos all looked at the floor.

Irlo Malit looking uncomfortable, spoke for his family, "Yes," he admitted.

"But Señor Jimenez is very good employer!" Malit's wife suddenly interjected, "He looks after us very well."

The daughter Grace, still silent, was nodding her head in agreement at her mother's words.

"Okay. Has anything strange happened while you have worked here? Any fights or parties that got out of hand?" asked Maury.

"No," replied Irlo emphatically, "It is always very civilized."

Thinking about the rooms upstairs and what obviously went on in them, Maury thought this a bit of a contradiction, "Has anyone got hurt in a sex game?"

"It is playing! Not real... it is a game," Alesha protested.

Maury noticed that Grace still said nothing, her mouth appeared clamped shut. "Is that true Grace?" Maury asked, suddenly switching his focus to the girl.

Grace shook her head, "Sometimes the girls get hurt."

"Badly?" Maury pressed.

"Cuts and bruises usually. But, one girl had her jaw broken," Grace conceded.

"What happened to her?"

"Señor Jimenez took her to the doctor."

Maury was surprised, "Did he take her himself?" he asked.

"Yes."

"What happened to the man who did it?"

Grace's brows knitted, "It was not a man, it was a woman. Señor Jimenez, asked her to leave."

"Did she?"

"Yes."

"When did this happen?"

"About a year ago."

"Is it only girls that work here?" Maury asked the family.

"Usually." replied Irlo.

"Any dressed as pilgrims?"

The Malits looked at one another in unfeigned astonishment. Irlo shook his head, "No, we have never seen that."

"Okay, thank you for your help," said Maury, indicating to Lucine with a nod that it was time to go.

"What are you thinking Sir?" asked Lucine as they walked through the garden back to the house.

"Just an idea. Fast cars, narrow roads, drugs and substance abuse..."

"Ah!" Lucine exclaimed in comprehension, "You think our three unknowns may have been hit by a car!"

"Maybe, we'll have to see what the Coroner says." replied Maury.

Back at the Gendarmerie in Rivesaltes, Renaud and Pratt were waiting to give them a report on their interview with the young council worker Marc Belcourt. "Nothing different to the foreman's report really. They've been digging out debris from ditches and drains along all the roads in the area starting with the main roads and gradually working along the minor ones. The road to Périllos is one of their last ones.

"Poor buggers have been at it every day, for nearly a year, as last summer's weather was so terrible. Marc says he was in the ditch digging in the sump when he put a hole in what turned out to be a skull. Course it freaked him out, his mum says he's sensitive and will probably have nightmares for a couple of weeks now. He's not all there — a bit retarded, his mum says," Renaud reported matter-of-factly.

"OK, record it and stand down for the rest of the day. Babayan and I will be visiting the Coroner in the morning to see what the autopsies tell us. Be here ready for a nine O' clock start," said Maury.

As the gendarmes turned to enter the witness statements onto the computer Maury turned to Lucine, "I think you can stand down for the rest of the day too Lieutenant. Text me your address and I'll pick you up at around 7.30 tomorrow morning, there's no point in using two cars."

Maury's route home led him past a large out-of-town shopping complex. On impulse, he pulled in at a large toy store in order to buy his grandchildren something to enjoy in the garden. Nothing in the warehouse-sized space caught his eye, until he came upon the ride-on pedal tractors. There were two Renault versions, one larger than the other, but otherwise identical. He quickly decided that they'd be great for the kids to enjoy the garden, he might even get them to help, if it became a game. He found a morose assistant, who reluctantly carried one boxed tractor to the checkout while Maury carried the other.

At the checkout, he was surprised to find Babayan in the queue ahead of him, buying children's armbands and swimming costumes. She smiled in recognition and arched her eyebrows at his purchases. "For the grandchildren," he explained, as Lucine was called forward by the cashier.

Once her purchases were made Babayan smiled back at her boss and gave a little wave as if to say, "See you tomorrow."

The cashier, obviously itching to see her queue reduce, so that she could sit idle, rolled her eyes at the spotty colleague who'd helped Maury to the checkout. "Have you explained to Monsieur that we can't deliver on Tuesdays?"

The floor assistant, seeming to not care less, dumped his carton on the counter and walked away, "I'm going on my break now," he said, as he walked off between the aisles.

The cashier now turned to Maury and looked at him as if he was an idiot. "We don't deliver on Tuesday's, I doubt that you'll get two in your car," she said. Her voice was slurred, her face too heavily made-up — without the foundation and attitude she might be passably pretty, thought Maury.

"I'll try," said Maury.

This remark seemed to confirm the checkout girl's opinion of the idiot customer in front of her. With a sigh, she scanned the barcodes and demanded payment. As he fumbled for his wallet, Maury pulled his shirt up, inadvertently exposing his holstered pistol and the tricolour police shield on his belt. The effect of this action was as if he'd got a full house on a one-armed bandit. The girl suddenly became polite and accommodating, ringing a bell as she took his credit card and processed his payment, "I'll see if someone can help you take these out to the car, sir."

"Thank you," said Maury, "You have a pretty smile."

A fat, mousy-haired man dressed in the ubiquitous cheap suit of a store manager approached, and the now gushing checkout girl explained that 'Monsieur l'agent' had purchased two toy tractors and would like assistance getting them out to the car.

"Oh, no need sir." said the manager, "I'm sure we have a van going out in your direction. Where do you live?"

Maury explained, as the manager beckoned for assistance from other shop staff. He noticed that the checkout girl was transformed, she was all smiles and manners with the next customers in line.

Next, stop to get some bottles of Fitou from a vigneron, and a couple of bunches of flowers for the ladies in his life. "I'm looking forward to the drive," he thought.

And this evening they'd need to make sure the vegetable patch was saturated. The cloudless sky seemed to indicate that tomorrow would be another scorcher and he feared that the tomato plants may well begin to wilt.

CATHAR COUNTRY

The modern Languedoc region lauds its Cathar heritage in glossy magazines and web sites. by featuring the astonishing citadels and fortresses of the modern Department of Aude. Their local moniker is apt, "les citadelles du vertige", literally the vertigo-inducing citadels, they sit atop the fangs of mountains dominating and overlooking the vineyards, sleepy villages and meadows of this mountainous region, stretching from Aude, southward into the Pyrenees-Orientales, north-westward to Herault, west and south-westward into Ariege and Hautes-Pyrenees.

From the top of one set of battlements can been seen the battlements of another castle, and it is hard to imagine that anyone would be foolish enough to attack their vertical flanks, while the defending garrison sat atop their thick stone walls and rained down missiles upon their attackers. But, in actual fact most of the ruins now visible today replace earlier fortresses that saw battle and destruction in one of the most bloody and hard-fought holy wars of medieval Europe.

These earlier castles, were the sites upon which the Albigensian Crusades, a twenty-year ethnic and religious cleansing by the armies of the French crown, under the direction of the Roman Catholic Pope and Bishops, took place in the early Thirteenth Century, pitting Christian against Christian and French subject against nominally French subject. Under the incumbent Pope Innocent III, the spiritual leader, the Roman Catholic Church was engaged in a power struggle with the secular Kings of Western Europe, over whom he claimed suzerainty, and he was determined to wrest back lands where Roman Catholic influence was waning. These areas included the Languedoc, where the Cathar church was beginning to thrive, the Pagan North of Europe, Moorish Spain and the Holy Land.

Of the Cathars in Languedoc relatively little is known, they were exterminated, and history was written by their exterminators. We do know that they were professing Christians, who espoused a counter-doctrine based on Gnosticism, which was highly reformist, evangelical and steadily gaining popularity and adherents in Occitania.

During the first four hundred years of Christianity's existence, Gnosticism was just another co-existing branch of that Faith. It is thought to have originated with the Coptic mystics of Egypt, and moved steadily westward into the Roman Empire, the Persian Empire and the lands of the Arian Goths.

Gnosticism became the enemy of orthodox Christianity when orthodox Christianity was embraced by the Roman Empire, and an organised church came into existence. The Gnostics held the view that the soul can only find salvation through gnosis – esoteric or intuitive knowledge – a 'deep revelation' of the divine nature (many are called, few are chosen). The Orthodox Church though, held that salvation was obtained simply through a declaration of faith, and the act of baptism. And while the 'catholic' church set up a hierarchy of priests, bishops and archbishops, the Gnostics held to the simple belief that every true believer was already a 'son of God' and therefore a priest in his (or her) own right.

When orthodox Christianity became a state-sponsored arm of the Holy Roman Empire, through adoption as the Roman Catholic Church, the doctrinal differences and the shunning of ritualised worship by the Gnostics, and subsequent loss of income, became problematic and Gnosticism quickly and conveniently became identified as 'heretical' - 'the Church of Satan' - by the Church Fathers.

To escape persecution the Gnostics simply went underground, their ideas still evolving and adapting - taught by individual ascetic priests who set few guidelines - gaining foothold in disparate areas of Europe: the Paulicians of Armenia and the

Eastern Byzantine Empire, the Bogomils that emerged in Bulgaria as a synthesis of Paulician and Bulgarian Orthodox reformation and spread throughout Europe, until finally surfacing several hundred years later, under the guise of Catharism in northern Italy and Languedoc.

The Gnosticism of the "Good Men" as the Cathars were then known, seemed attractive to the Occitan people, a counterpoint to the excesses of the Catholic Church, which common Occitans seemed to have seen as an evil political beast, at odds with true faith. The Good Men, by contrast, were simple, devout, with attractive views on the evil nature of the material world in which the medieval peasantry lived and the assurance that every man, and woman, of any status could attain salvation and 'oneness' with God – their doctrine was evidently seen through their actions within, and service to, the little communities of the Languedoc. Their clinics and schools, the free discussion of scripture and the dissemination of ideas and ideals made a real-life utopia seem possible. The Cathar message even attracted their feudal overlords to publicly identify with them, and as a result Catharism began to flourish, and undermine the grip not only of the Roman Catholic Church in the territory, but also that of the Languedoc's remote liege Lord, the King of France.

11th June

The Coroner worked from the city morgue in the basement of Perpignan's Centre Hospitaller, an angular grey building at odds with the warm red brick of the small city's predominantly Catalan architecture. Maury and Babayan were met at the door by the Coroner himself, a tall neat man in his fifties who introduced himself with a rustic accent, at odds with his urbanite appearance. He led the detectives through the building, and after a long descent in a lift, into a brightly lit room where the remains of the three bodies from the ditch were waiting, shrouded with cloth on separate stainless-steel trolleys.

He pulled the shroud from the first, to expose a dark leathery skeleton, loosely laid out on the shiny metal, "The on-site forensics team approximated that these persons died around one year ago, I concur…

"This first subject is male, aged around twenty-five years, of black African origin." The coroner pointed at the sightless skull, "There are orbital fractures and minor fractures to the right-hand cheekbone and jaw."

The coroner continued, using an outstretched finger to indicate what he was reporting, "The clavicle is fractured, as is the left tibia. And here on both forearms, is evidence of third degree burns on the lower parts of each forearm. All these injures were incurred shortly before his demise but were not the cause of death."

Brusque and business-like, the Coroner pulled the shroud from the second body, and although damaged, lightly boned, evidently female to even the inexpert eye, "Subject two is female, also of black African origin. In fact, a DNA analysis indicates that subjects one and two were siblings. She too, shows signs of perimortem trauma: sternal fractures, broken femur and deep third degree burns to both lower legs."

Babayan stole a glance at Maury, who looked back, his mouth and jaw grim.

The coroner turned and pulled the shroud from the third body, this time with less haste, almost gently, and his voice softened, "Subject three is Semite – most likely an Arabic woman of around nineteen years of age. She suffered no fractures but shows evidence of third degree burns to the backs of both her legs and her buttocks, like the others her injuries were incurred perimortem." The Coroner now looked up, "However, she was with child and about six-months into her pregnancy at the time of her demise.

"All three adult victims died from drowning, in freshwater. All three were wearing white cotton garments, that seem on closer inspection, to be a little like nightshirts. All three wore leather sandals and cotton underwear. And all three were each wearing a gold pendant on a thin gold chain from their necks."

He looked up, as if expecting comment from the detectives, but both were silenced and inverted by the bombshell news that the three appeared to have died from drowning and that there was an unborn child among the casualties.

Professional, business-like, the coroner continued spewing facts, "It will be problematic identifying them. None have any fillings or dental work and the DNA samples seem to indicate that the siblings are from central Africa and the other young woman is from North Africa. I suspect that they are immigrants. The child is of mixed race, however, the father can safely be assumed to be Caucasian, mostly likely French."

"I cannot easily identify the trauma that all three adults suffered prior to their deaths. The burns seem to have been made by some sort of chemical; analysis seems to indicate molten nylon. The man's relatively minor bone injuries are consistent with those inflicted by airbag deployment in a car crash."

The coroner pulled the shrouds back over the pathetic forms and reached under one of the trolleys to produce vacuum-sealed bags containing the garments, footwear and undergarments, "You can access a full technical report online." he said, passing the bags to Babayan.

"Oh, one more thing, the contents of their stomachs seem to

indicate that all three were vegetarians." With these words the coroner appeared to be dismissing the policemen, but Maury took charge, "I want their skulls scanned, so that a forensic artist can produce some three-dimensional facial reconstructions."

"Of course," said the coroner, "I'll have that data uploaded by the end of the day."

"Could they have been hit by a car?" asked Lucine.

The coroner looked at her in silent contempt for a few moments, before answering, "Except for subject two, who suffered a broken femur, their injuries are inconsistent with those inflicted by impact with a motor vehicle."

Maury's theory about them being run down by a car from the Jimenez Mas appeared to have evaporated.

"Merde!" Maury exclaimed as he sat down in the driver's seat. Next to him Lucine, her mouth still a tight grim line, looked blankly ahead into space. Both seemed oblivious of the cauldron-like heat of the car, where it had sat exposed to the morning sun. The senior detective exhaled, "We'll pass the clothing to forensics for examination," Maury turned in his seat, pulled an evidence bag from the back seat and held it aloft, "We'll start with these." In the bag were the pendants.

Lucine expressed her puzzlement, "How the hell did they drown out there? It's almost a desert..."

"Maybe, they died elsewhere," suggested Maury.

"You think that they were dumped out there?" asked Lucine.

"Well..." Maury said, as he cranked the old car over and it clattered to life, "That's what we need to find out."

Back at Rivesaltes, Maury brought Renaud and Pratt up to date with developments. The two gendarmes were as astonished as the detectives had been at these latest revelations. "So, according to the evidence, it looks as if they were subjected to some sort of trauma, including being burned, before they eventually died by drowning. We can't be sure whether the injuries were accidental or inflicted by a third party. We need to keep an open mind. It would seem logical to first identify them."

"I want you to find out, if there were any incidents recorded in the vicinity of Opoul-Périllos, between ten to fourteen months ago," Maury directed. "I'm hoping that soon we'll have facial reconstructions of the three adult victims. When we have, then we'll start some good, old-fashioned door-to-door to see if anybody recognises them.

"Then I want you to access the missing persons database, to find out if there are any possible matches with our victims, it's a long shot, so let's narrow the search to the past two years."

"I'll start on the database," said Renaud. "You can see if there were any incidents in Opoul-Périllos, or within a twenty-kilometre radius," he added, speaking to his junior colleague.

As the two gendarmes sat trawling through data on their desktop computers, Maury and Babayan turned their attention to the pendants. The pendants themselves were identical, though the chain on each was of a different weight. They were small, appeared to be gold, oval shaped, and embossed. The obverse design appeared to show a naïve figure of a laughing Christ on an Occitan cross – anciently the symbol of the Counts of Toulouse – with a small stylized dove, in the top right-hand corner of the design. The reverse design varied from pendant to pendant, though the common design was the same, it seemed to depict a constellation of twelve minute five-pointed stars, the difference between them being that each had one star in the constellation slightly larger than the rest.

"The cross is commonly known as the Cathar Cross around here," Maury remarked, "But it goes on everything in this region. The little dove motif is Cathar too."

"Maybe they are monks," suggested Lucine, "They were wearing the sort of clothes that monks wear, habits, sandals, pendants..."

"Cathar monks?" asked Maury aloud.

"Something like that," Lucine agreed.

"They're probably Grail hunters," Renaud muttered, with thinly disguised contempt, from the corner of the room.

"Grail hunters?" repeated Maury pensively.

"Yes Sir, Périllos is somehow connected to the legend of the Holy Grail," Babayan, who'd obviously been doing her homework, explained, "Apparently, the landscape there corresponds with a model commissioned by Abbé Saunière, the infamous priest of Rennes-le-Chateau, it's supposed to indicate where the Grail was hidden in the Middle Ages."

"Those types are always around here. It's not just the model though, there are a couple of paintings, they always go on about, that they reckon show Périllos in the background," commented Renaud.

"Poussin's 'Shepherds of Arcadia' and Tenier's 'Temptation of St. Anthony,'" Pratt added knowledgeably.

Maury exhaled, "Right, then we need to contact Miviludes, to see if they know of any Cathar cults to which these people might have belonged."

"I doubt it Sir," Pratt, who was obviously well-informed, opined. "Miviludes are only interested in monitoring Cults who may have large amounts of capital to sponsor terrorism or have enough adherents to be a source of concern. Cathars take vows of poverty and reject materialism."

Maury looked sternly at the young officer who, seeming to realise that his opinion had not been sought, quickly added, "I'll get on to them as soon as I can. Want me to check on other local sects too?"

"Maybe send them a picture of the pendants, let them do the legwork," suggested Maury, with a wry smile. He liked Pratt's insight; he had the makings of an excellent police officer.

"There are experts on this sort of thing up at Périllos itself," Lucine remarked, "A couple of them run a mystic website."

"I thought the village was abandoned."

"They run a sort of shop and tea rooms there most days," explained Lucine.

"Worth a visit, even if we only get a coffee." Maury suggested.

On their way back towards Périllos from Rivesaltes, the road climbed up from the area's famous Muscat grapevines, passing by the old military base with its sorry history as a wartime concentration camp. With Lucine happy to drive the old Peugeot, Maury could enjoy the scenery as the road rose into the mountains, the air from the open windows blew over them, relieving them of some heat. The surface of the narrow road shimmered ahead and Maury marvelled as they passed an ancient racing cyclist, his brown skin like baked leather, his legs rotating slowly as he propelled himself up the merciless gradient in an impossibly high gear.

Soon, they turned onto the Périllos road, passing the spot where the bodies had been found, now demarcated by fluttering red and white tape, then Jimenez' Mas, a strange memorial on the hillside, and a small well-maintained chapel, until eventually the road petered out at the abandoned village of Périllos itself. They parked in the shadow of a large fig tree, waited for the cloud of dust, raised by their passing, to settle, then stepped from the car and looked about at the place.

Most of the buildings looked to be beyond repair, but some were surprisingly well preserved, their roofs intact, the walls sound. The village was dominated by two vertical structures, the teetering quoin of an ancient castle or tower built on a rock outcrop, and the bell-tower of a church just below it. Little unmade roads ran among the buildings and the detectives followed one of these towards a house near the church, which had poorly executed hand-painted signs proclaiming it to be the café they sought. They entered a courtyard, sheltered by another enormous fig, and a figure standing in the open cafe doorway greeted them.

"Are you serving coffee?" Maury asked.

The tall elderly man with neatly trimmed white goatee stepped aside and beckoned them into the cool, dark interior.

"No, I've never seen a pendant like this before," said Jean-Baptiste Vincent over his bifocals at Maury, "Though the triumphant Christ is also thought to be Cathar, it comes from a sculpted cross in Cassés, near Carcassonne." His thin liver-spotted fingers turned the pendant over, and he bowed his head to look at the reverse design carefully. "I've no idea about the design on the back, I'd suggest that it's maybe a constellation of stars."

Behind Maury, Lucine was thumbing through the books on display on the bookstall. Now that he wasn't absorbed by the pendant that he now placed on the table between himself and the senior detective, Vincent watched as she opened books and pored over the contents of one select title, "That's an interesting one..." he observed.

Maury turned in his seat, to see that Lucine was holding a weighty paperback in her hand entitled, 'Crusade Against the Grail' by Otto Rahn. "Isn't there a connection between this place and the Grail?" asked Maury.

"That's one theory," Vincent agreed, "Abbé Saunière of Rennes-le-Chateau had a diorama made which is supposed to indicate the location of Christ's tomb in Jerusalem, except the model isn't of Jerusalem at all, it's of here."

Vincent got his tall, spare frame out of the chair, shuffled over to a windowsill, and reached among the items there. The square of intense outside light that framed him, made the white-washed interior of the house look gloomy in comparison. The amateur historian returned with a plastic replica of Saunière's original plaster model and placed it on the table in front of Maury. "Saunière seemed obsessed with this topography, a few more replicas have since come to light and they differ only in the smallest details, he even had his garden landscaped to look like this."

Vincent was in his element, his eyes glittered earnestly as he spoke, "Only one place on earth can match this exactly... Périllos! On the model are several features of note, these tombs..." his finger hovered over two small oblong features on the model, "Were labelled, to indicate the locations of the tomb of Christ and the tomb of Joseph of Arimathea. A deliberate red herring or a code perhaps? Because the bible says that Christ was buried in Joseph's tomb."

"Are these tombs real places in the village?" asked Lucine, who had wandered over to look with interest at the model.

"Maybe," Vincent replied enigmatically.

"Would Cathars come here looking for their treasure?" Maury asked, not really wanting to get embroiled in some discussion about ancient legends and artefacts.

Vincent paused, "Not usually, they tend to go to Montsegur. Some say, that the Cathars were custodians of the Grail and spirited it away during the Albigensian Crusade, to some secret place, and that Abbé Saunière got rich because he found it, and may have buried it here in Périllos. But their idea of the Grail and our idea of the Grail aren't the same."

"*Our* idea of the Grail?" queried Maury.

"I should say, a more likely idea of the Grail is that it isn't an artefact, it is a bloodline..." Vincent explained.

Maury breathed out as the historian continued his theory, "There's more evidence to suggest that the King of France is a direct descendant of Christ..."

Vincent was on a roll, Maury let him expound on a number of inter-related conspiracy theories which somehow had this mysterious village at their centre; tales of the ancient Lords of Périllos, the Knights Templar, an entrance to the Underworld, strange alignments of buildings, the Illuminati, and of course the Priory of Sion.

From Vincent's passion it was clear that he was himself convinced of these stories' veracity. Maury said little, sipping coffee as he listened to theories that, he was sure, would unravel if a forensic eye were properly cast over them.

"I think that one of those 'so called' tombs on the model could be that little chapel, we noticed from the hill yesterday, and passed on the way in," remarked Lucine as they stepped from Vincent's cafe.

The village, ruined and dusty, crumbled in the glaring sunshine, stark pillars of masonry and wooden staircases stabbing upward into the pale blue sky, offering little shadow or shelter from the pitiless sun. The heat assailed them as walked through narrow unpaved streets back towards the car. Maury turned and looked back at Vincent, whose grey whiskered face was at the window watching them go, "Shall we go and have a look then?" he suggested, "Do you want me to drive?"

Babayan nodded, the steering and clutch on the old car were both heavy to operate, and she passed the keys. Once at the old Peugeot, they opened the doors and windows, waiting for some of the stifling heat to disperse, before buckling up and driving off.

It was a short drive to the little building. The chapel was in good order, well-cared for, with a fresh bouquet of flowers on the font and a little visitor's book, that Maury asked Lucine to photograph the pages of.

While she used her mobile to do his bidding, Maury stood framed by the glare of the doorway, looking out at the forgotten village of Périllos. "Were they coming or going?" he wondered aloud.

Lucine understood that he was wondering about the victims.

Just then, Maury's mobile phone vibrated — a message from the Narbonne office, requesting his presence on the morrow. "Let's get some lunch and see how Pratt and Renaud are getting on," he suggested, putting his phone back into his pocket.

While Maury drove them back to Rivesaltes, Lucine decided to tackle a display that flashed annoyingly on the dashboard. She noticed small holes and correctly deduced these to be the reset buttons, so using the nib of a ballpoint pen, she pressed it into the upper hole. Immediately, the flashing ceased, to be replaced by a read out that demanded to know the required language and date format. She chose French, by scrolling through the options by pressing the lower button, then adjusted the calendar and clock. The operation was fiddly but satisfying, and job done she raised her head to see that they were approaching the shimmering form of the small town dancing through the heat-haze.

"Merde!" exclaimed Maury.

Lucine looked at her superior in surprise, what had caused him to utter the profanity? Had he had a brainwave or forgotten something?

Maury tapped the display that she'd just fixed, it was now displaying the outside temperature, a crushing 44°c.

In the air-conditioned comfort of the little Incident Room, Renaud and Pratt were looking dejected. Their enquiries had drawn a blank, as had matching descriptions of the deceased to the National Missing Persons Database. So, now they were laboriously trawling through an extensive list of incidents, reported within a twenty-kilometre radius of Opoul-Périllos, ten to fourteen months previously. "Seems to be mainly routine stuff," reported Renaud, "Domestics, breakdowns, a couple of burglaries, a murder in Estagel, and a whole lot of weather-related incidents."

Babayan was toying with one of the evidence bags containing a pendant, "I could take one of these to a jeweller, maybe he could tell us where they're from," she suggested.

Maury nodded, "That's a good idea. Do you know someone?"

He was surprised when she said that she did, as she did not wear jewellery herself, and didn't seem the type to need to further advertise her innate attractiveness, "I know someone in Perpignan."

"What news on the facial reconstructions?" Maury asked of the gendarmes.

Pratt tapped at his keyboard and squinted at the display on the monitor, then shook his head, "They're not ready yet."

"Okay. Extend your search radius by five kilometres," Maury instructed the gendarmes, "the Lieutenant and I will visit the jewellers."

Maury let Lucine drive the car into the regional capital, after all she was familiar with its streets and one-way systems. He watched the dusty scenery slip by and the temperature read-out climb by two whole degrees, as they entered the airless cauldron at Perpignan's centre, and he was relieved when she opted to park in the cool of an underground car park.

They had a short walk through scorching sunshine, the heat and glare intensified by reflection from the pale slabs of the pavement. Lucine led the way to a modest jeweller's shop with anonymous window displays. Inside, they paused in the sudden cool of the air-conditioning unit blasting cool air down at the doorway. Then, from where she sat, behind a high traditional counter, a trim elderly lady in a trouser suit greeted them. She smiled in surprise as she recognised Lucine, she opened the gap in the counter and stepped through to embrace her warmly, "How are the children?"

"They are well, Mikel is starting guitar lessons..."

"With the little guitar his grand-pappy bought him?" asked the delighted old lady.

Lucine smiled happily and nodded, "...and Samara wants to do ballet."

Lucine became more serious and made the introductions, "Madame Mayeur, this is Commandant Maury. I'm afraid we are here on official business. Is Monsieur Mayeur in?"

Madame Mayeur nodded, "Yes, come through, he's in the workshop."

Maury followed Lucine through the gap in the counter and whispered, "Enchanté," as he passed the old lady.

He was led through a well-concealed door, behind heavy drapes, into a workshop that smelled of machine-oil and burning. The walls were lined on all sides with grey metal strong-boxes, and racks of strange-looking, highly-specialist, tools. There were work-benches with gleaming metal surfaces, lit by extremely bright angle-poise lamps and equipped with vices, tiny lathes, burnishers and other contraptions. From behind one of these, a small, bald man rose and removed thick loupe spectacles to reveal quick and intelligent grey eyes, that lit up when they recognised Babayan.

"Oh, my dear!" he exclaimed, "How are you?"

"Very well," replied Lucine, stepping aside so the jeweller could see the shirt-sleeved Maury in her wake, "This is my colleague, Commandant Maury, we'd like your help please."

The old man's face straightened, as he realised that this visit was official. Lucine reached into her jacket pocket, withdrew, and offered the polythene wrapped pendant, "What can you tell us about this?"

Taking the bag from Lucine, Mayeur started pulling the bag fastener apart, then stopped, "May I?" he enquired, looking past Lucine at Maury for permission.

Maury nodded assent and with deft fingers the jeweller pulled the pendant from the bag. He rubbed the golden disc and weighed it in his palm, before holding it under the white glare of a lamp and pulling his eyewear down to give it a detailed examination. "Gema Abraxas," he stated.

"Gema Abraxas," Lucine repeated, "What is that?"

"A generic name for a gnostic symbol," the jeweller explained, "The pendant seems to be hand cast. Not professional work. Hand tooled former I imagine. Quite nice though. The chain is cheap, mass-produced, it deserves better!"

"What about the reverse?" asked Maury.

The jeweller examined the constellation of stars, "Pressed into the surface, except for the larger, which seems to have been deliberately punched, to make it stand out."

Mayeur looked up at the detectives, his grey irises and black pupils huge through his lenses, "It appears to have been made from unalloyed gold. Its provenance may might give us some idea of who made it and where. But first, let's give it an even closer inspection."

So, saying, he laid the pendant on the bed of a large machine, and with the flick of a switch bathed it in even more intense blue-tinged light. Another deftly flicked switch, activated a screen and a high-resolution image of the super-magnified pendant came into focus.

First the face was examined, the metalwork, so fine to the naked eye, seemed coarse and poorly executed at such high magnification. Then the reverse was scrutinised, and the pendant gave up an unexpected secret. The larger star was not a star at all, it was a tiny abstract Cathar dove like the larger one on its face. Lastly the jeweller examined the edge which appeared to have been hand-filed.

"As I said, artisan made. No assayer's mark, so it probably had more symbolic value to its wearer than actual worth," Mayeur reiterated.

"How can the gold's origin be checked?" asked Maury.

"Can you leave it with me?" asked the jeweller.

"If you give us a receipt," said Maury.

In one of the city's modest suburbs, Maury dropped Lucine outside her apartment block, confident that the investigation would be in good hands during his temporary absence. Babayan seemed a bright, self-assured and observant young woman, rather like his own daughter Elisabeth.

Elisabeth! She'd be at home now with Marie-France and the grandchildren! Maury cursed at the heavy traffic snarling up the exits of Perpignan and headed home.

THE SUN AND THE MOON

Lotario dei Conti di Segni, adopted the name Innocent III upon his election as Pope on the 8th January 1198. The thirty-seven-year old Roman, was determined to wrest very real political control of Europe from secular powers, by making them subservient to the Roman Catholic's spiritual power.

"The Lord gave Peter the rule not only over the universal Church, but also the rule over the whole world." "No king can reign rightly unless he devoutly serves Christ's vicar." "The priesthood is the sun, the kingdom the moon. Kings rule over their respective kingdoms, but Peter rules over the whole earth."

So determined was he to exert the Church's power over secular kings, that Innocent promoted this doctrine from the moment he took the Papal reins, underpinning his claims through the (mis)use of Holy Scripture

"Just as the founder of the universe established two great lights in the firmament of heaven, the greater light to rule the day and the lesser light to rule the night, so too He set two great dignities in the firmament of the universal church..., the greater to rule the day, that is, souls, and the lesser to rule the night, that is, bodies. These dignities are the papal authority and the royal power. Now just as the moon derives its light from the sun and is indeed lower than it in quantity and quality, in position and in power, so too the royal power derives the splendour of its dignity from the pontifical authority.... "

If then, the Pope was the Sun, who were the Moons?

Within Innocent's sphere of influence ruled the Emperors and Kings of medieval Europe, including the first King of France, Philip II, whose predecessors had been known as the Kings of the Franks.

Philip's France was a relatively small feudal state, and he set out to expand its territories and influence, bringing it into long and bitter conflict with the Angevin Empire of the English Plantagenet kings, his nominal vassals. After some twelve years of struggle, he wrestled control of John Lackland's (King John of England) continental possessions, with the exception of Gascony, by defeating the English and their German and Flemish allies in the Battle of Bouvines, earning the moniker 'Augustus' as recognition of his success. Under his ambitious rule France was fast establishing itself as the powerhouse of Western Europe.

In the region of the Languedoc then, Innocent was the sun and Phillip Augustus the moon, but their light shone dimly...

12 June

Maury was looking forward to the coffee-break. The seminar in which he sat, was little more than a gathering of highly-paid senior officers crowing about their achievements to an audience of their peers. No-one was fooled, everyone knew real police work was done by lowlier ranks – improvements in crime prosecution rates came about when, contrary to their instincts, officers on the ground were ordered to pursue misdemeanours that they'd otherwise let pass with a caution. He wondered how someone figured his attendance at a back-slapping ceremony was more important than finding out how the poor pathetic creatures in the ditch had met their demise. Still, it was an opulent venue, this five-star hotel, and there might be a biscuit served with the beverage and looking out through the French doors to the sun-bleached outdoors, he was glad of the air-conditioning.

He was sore where he'd worked his lower back pushing the grandchildren around the garden on the toy tractors, and his head ached a little from the wine that had been imbibed in celebratory conversation, with his grown-up daughter the previous evening. Thinking of the garden, the tomatoes were looking strong, he was glad that he'd resisted the temptation to feed them in the days before this present heatwave, but the water-butt would need replenishing tonight.

A hand on his shoulder stopped his reverie. Around him uniformed officers were rising from their seats and heading towards the foyer. Maury looked around to see who had disturbed him. When he saw it was his old friend Pierre they embraced warmly. There was no formality between the Inspector General and the detective, Lafitte asked after Maury's wife Marie-France, and led Maury by the elbow toward the eagerly awaited coffee. In a private corner, their conversation became more serious, "I'm sorry Maury, I'm going to have to pull you off that Perpignan case. The Procureur General doesn't deem the case worthy of pursuit."

"The Chief Prosecutor? But we've only just started our investigation," Maury protested.

Pierre nodded sadly and knowingly at his friend, "Yes, I know. There's something fishy going on down at Perpignan."

Lafitte had said little, before being tapped on the shoulder by another high-ranking officer who demanded his attention, just "Look into it, if you can".

Maury read between the lines; Pierre had effectively asked him to dig into the affair on the Inspector General's behalf. As a scowling Pierre was turning his attention to the interrupter, Maury quickly invited his old friend to a soiree, "Elisabeth is down with the grandchildren and staying with us for a few days. Perhaps you and Jeanette would like to join us for a meal one evening?"

Pierre brightened, "We'd love to," he said.

Martinez looked up in surprise as Maury entered the office, "Hello Sir, back already?"

"Mm," Maury growled, "Can you get Guillot from Perpignan on the line for me?"

"Of course, Sir," said Martinez.

There was something different about his aide, he looked cleaner and younger. "I see you got rid of the moustache Martinez," Maury remarked, as he passed by the aide's desk to enter his own office, taking his habitual glance at the thermometer as he went.

His desk phone rang, almost as soon as he reached his desk, "Maury speaking," he said, as he put the receiver to his ear.

"Guillot," his compatriot from Perpignan greeted him.

"Ah yes. What's the latest down there?" asked Maury.

The Captain hesitated, "We've been ordered to close down the investigation into the three bodies found on the Périllos road," he reported.

"Can you tell me why?" Maury wanted to know, as if surprised.

"I had instructions from the Procureur General's office. We sent our daily report in yesterday, and they got back to me early this morning, saying that we don't have the resources to investigate what is probably just an accident involving illegal immigrants."

"Is that their exact wording?"

"Near enough," Guillot admitted, "Hang on, I've got an email that says near enough the same thing."

"Can you forward me a copy?"

"Of course," said the obliging Captain.

"Thanks."

desk-diary was open in front of him, a list of afternoon appointments with various people seeking audience. A name on the list caught his eye and an idea started forming, "Can you get a folder and put together a dossier from all the stuff I'm about to print Martinez?" he shouted to his aide through the open door.

He just hoped that Babayan and the Rivesaltes gendarmes were up to date with their paperwork, as he accessed the Police Database on his desktop computer.

His third visitor of the day was the one he hoped would not cancel, as the previous two had done, and he was pleased when Martinez announced her arrival in the anteroom.

Mademoiselle Petit did not look like an investigative reporter, she looked more like a hillwalker, in her khaki blouse and shorts, with dusty, well-worn espadrilles on the end of long and sinewy legs. She was severely thin, with her greying blonde hair tied up into a ponytail. She looked a bit like an old hen, thought Maury, with her scraggy neck, her bottom-heavy body-shape and quick green eyes looking over wire-framed bifocals, as she rooted in her massive leather satchel, as she sat waiting. Maury guessed her to be in her late fifties or early sixties, with a reputation that preceded her of being awkward and anti-establishment.

He opened the door and greeted her warmly, "Bonjour Mademoiselle Petit, I am Commandant Maury, I believe you made an appointment? Would you like to follow me through into my office?"

Petit looked almost dismayed at the cordiality of Maury's greeting, she was more probably used to being cold-shouldered, than made welcome by policemen. She stood up tall, from the waiting room chair and hoisted her obviously heavy bag onto a shoulder, and followed the detective as requested. Maury sat her on one side of his desk, and sat down to face her over it. She exchanged brief pleasantries, then pulled a dog-eared notebook from her bag, "You were involved in a celebrated case in Lozère, shortly before you were transferred to Narbonne."

Maury nodded, "That case is well documented," he remarked.

"Yes, but you have never spoken publicly on the subject."

"There's nothing to tell."

The journalist gave him a sideways look that said, "I don't believe you."

"I could give you a little more background, I suppose, but really you need to speak to Inspector Gadret, it was he who broke the case," offered Maury.

As Mademoiselle Petit nodded and opened her notebook, Maury rose from his chair, "How rude of me. I should have offered you a cool drink. Can I get you a lemon-water or something before we begin?"

Once again, Petit looked taken aback at the courtesies he was extending, then she smiled brightly, "Lemon water sounds lovely," she said, "Do you have ice?"

"I'm sure we do", said Maury heading for the office door, "Please excuse me for a few moments."

When he returned some minutes later with two tall glasses balanced on a tray, he saw that the journalist had made herself at home. She had a notebook, voice recorder and digital camera laid out neatly on her side of Maury's desk. With yellowed smoker's fingers she took a glass of sparkling water and gulped down half its contents. "Thank you," she said gratefully.

Maury sat down slowly and asked, "Where shall we begin?"

"Shortly, after your team had solved the 'Cannibal' case, there was an incident involving the serial killer Paul Guy. Were the two cases connected?"

Maury wondered if she was grasping at straws, or had really joined the dots, "No, it's just that the crimes both happened on our patch. If the Paul Guy incident had occurred just one kilometre further west it would have been a Midi-Pyrenees case."

Petit looked poised to immediately ask another question, when she was interrupted by a buzzing sound from her handbag. "Excuse me," she said, digging into it, to extract her mobile phone. An indistinct voice spoke at her when she answered.

Saying little except, "Okay, I'll be right there," she replaced the phone with a sigh of regret.

"I'm afraid something has come up. Could we reconvene some other time?" she asked, picking up her stuff from the desk.

"Yes," said Maury, rising to his feet, "I'm sure we can reschedule."

She smiled and took his hand, "Thanks so much for your time, and the drink," Petit said, slinging her bag over her shoulder.

"The pleasure is all mine," said Maury.

"I'll see myself out."

Once Petit had left the office, Maury looked down at his desk. The Périllos file he'd left in his pending tray, appeared to have moved. He smiled in satisfaction, she'd taken the bait, now he had only to wait.

Looking at his watch, Maury decided that the rest of the day's administration tasks could wait. If he hurried, he could join the family on the beach, at least on the coast of the Mediterranean there was bound to be some movement of air.

ZEAL versus ZEAL

The first weapon used against the Cathars by Pope Innocent's Catholic church was an austere and humble Spaniard from Castille. Of medium height, thin, handsome with reddish hair and beard, Dominic de Guzman was an envoy of the Bishop of Osma, and had travelled with his patron through Languedoc, to secure a Danish bride for the Castillian crown prince.

A self-flagellant, who stayed up at night weeping for those he tried to convert to Catholicism, Dominic had a severe attitude towards heretics. To him they were worse than the infidel Moors, from whom the Spanish had gradually been wresting control of their own country. If the Moors were the enemy without, he saw the Cathars as the much more dangerous and subversive enemy within. Their heresy attacked God by denying him to be The Creator, attacked Truth by denying the church 'catholic'. But, much as he hated their heresy, he longed to convert individuals.

On their return to Spain, the Bishop and his envoy planned a return to Languedoc to convert heretic Cathars back to Roman Catholicism. So, the pair instigated public debates, where they argued with Cathar preachers about the merits of their own church, and the error of the Cathars, in the vast County of Toulouse. The meetings had little success, a handful of converts were made, and Dominic concluded that a new type of evangelist was needed.

Ten years later, Dominic returned to Languedoc with a handful of hand-picked men who demonstrated sanctity, humility and asceticism. The fledgling organisation adopted much of the Cathar's ways; they served the community, educated children and adults, and subjected themselves to a monastic ritual of prayer, penance and preaching. Their renouncement of worldly pursuits and devotion to spiritual work was a new thing to the Roman Catholics, and directly reflected what the Cathar clergy had been practicing from the beginning. The Catholics expected great things of this new order, the Dominicans, but although it had massive success elsewhere, its mission failed in its birthplace, the Cathar lands of Languedoc.

But, then again, the Dominicans were up against perhaps the greatest Cathar orator of the age, a local man called Guilhabert de Castres.

Guilhabert was a member of the Cathar priesthood, whose ministry was based around Fanjeaux, between Carcassonne and Toulouse, the place where Dominic had decided to base his own operations. Such was Guilhabert's intellect and oratory prowess that he had a large and fervent local following, who knew him as the 'Bonus Homo de Castris' or the Good Man of Castres. (Cathar ministers were given the name Bonhommes or Goodmen rather than any title or rank). His 'diocese' ran from Toulouse to as far south as Usson and the Sabarthes, including the citadel of Montsegur, in Ariege.

At Montreal, a small town two hours walk from Fanjeaux, Guilhabert and Dominic came face-to-face in public debate. The local audience came to cheer on their respective champions. By all accounts, these discussions were serious affairs and debate was at times, hostile and fierce.

We cannot know what passed between the two men, but we do know that Dominic soon retreated from the scene. Where Catholics had to prove 'truth' to the audience, the Cathars had no mystery to their church, their arguments appealed more to common-sense and life-experience.

Dominic's parting words to some gathered Cathars were telling, "For several years now I have spoken words of peace to you. I have preached to you, I have besought you with tears. But, as the common saying goes in Spain: where a blessing fails, a good thick stick will succeed. Now we shall rouse princes and prelates against you; and they, alas, will in their turn assemble whole nations and peoples, and a mighty number will perish by the sword. Towers will fall, and walls will be razed to the ground, and you will all of you be reduced to servitude. Thus, force will prevail where gentle persuasion has failed ..."

13th JUNE

The sun rose, climbing over the Mediterranean, casting yellow light and blue shadow on the foothills that bordered it. It entered the half-open shutters of Mas Maury, bringing with it the scent of mint and fennel. The crickets and birds began their chirruping choruses, and from somewhere the hollow sound of a woodpecker at work echoed from the woodlands, making Maury stir from sleep. So, he and Marie-France rose early to enjoy the cool of morning before the white disc's heat radiated from ochre rocks and limestone walls. They watered the garden and tended the more delicate plants before breakfasting together on the terrace of the sleeping house.

Maury's phone rang. The call, from Inspector General Pierre Lafitte was not entirely unexpected. "Allo?"

"Allo Maury? Pierre here. Have you seen the early papers yet?"

"No."

"Well, suffice to say that I had a phone call from the Procureur's office in Perpignan asking us to reinstate our investigations into those three bodies found up near Périllos. I don't know how you did it...I don't want to know what you did, but I trust that you know what you're doing?"

"I think so," said Maury. He looked across at Marie-France, who was looking at him over a bowl of cafe au lait with a furrowed brow. "Pierre," he silently mouthed. His wife smiled and mouthed something back.

"Don't forget your invitation to dinner Pierre," Maury reminded.

Fabienne Petit's article entitled 'Bodies in Ditch Low Priority' was clever and well-written, it suggested that there may be racial motives for dropping the police investigation into the deaths of three, seemingly illegal, immigrants and an unborn child. It asked if French citizens would accept the same treatment, from a foreign police force, and if French justice really did apply equally to all? Maury read with grim satisfaction, regretting that it had taken underhand methods to get the investigation back on track.

He wondered who in the Procureur General's Office had pulled the plug in the first place, and if the motive had been financial, racial, or otherwise? He sat back from the table enjoying the bitter taste of an unhurried espresso, wondering where the investigation would next lead. In front of him lay Petit's 'reliable source', the Périllos case file he'd had Martinez assemble the day before. It was open at the Coroner's Report. Cause of death - death by drowning.

If they drowned, where did they drown? A large-scale map lay open, and Maury scanned it, looking for water sources in the area where the bodies had been found. No streams, no pools, no wells, no springs immediately adjacent to the site. The nearest water was at Jimenez's Mas, the pimp's swimming-pool. There was also a well-spring, south of the village of Périllos, some three kilometres as the crow flies. He'd detail one of the gendarmes to get samples of water from each. He was about to call when his phone began vibrating. "Allo, Maury here."

"Bonjour Commandant, its Renaud here. I just wanted you to know that the facial reconstructions are ready and wondered if you had any orders for today?"

"Did you complete examining that list of local incidents?" Maury asked, impressed at the gendarme's professionalism.

"We were on it all day yesterday."

"Really?"

"Yes Sir. There may be a few things worth following up. I'll have a shortlist on your desk ready for you."

"Who put you back on the case?"

"I beg your pardon?" asked Renaud.

"Who put you back on the case this morning?"

With a slight hesitation and obvious puzzlement, "But we haven't been off the case Sir," Renaud replied.

God bless the French policing system, thought Maury, one hand doesn't know what the other is up to, the Gendarmerie had obviously been oblivious of the Prefecture's instruction to the Police Nationale to close the casefile!

"Okay, I'll explain later. For now, I'd like you and Pratt to get water samples from Jimenez's pool and any other water source within a five-kilometre radius of where the bodies were found."

"To find out if they were drowned somewhere then dumped?"

"Precisely. Take the facial reconstructions with you, and start some enquiries locally."

"Yes Sir."

"Very good, I shall be along to Rivesaltes shortly."

Jimenez. Maury couldn't escape the feeling that the Spaniard had some sort of involvement in the affair. It would be worth showing him, and his Filipino staff, the facial reconstructions. He'd ring that detective from Toulouse to see if it could be arranged. What was his name again? Wittmeyer. Without identities the bodies would be reluctant to give up their secrets. Let's give Mademoiselle Petit a little more background to her story!

How about the pendants? Had Babayan had any more luck tracking down the gold's origins? He heard the patter of feet on the carrelage floor of the kitchen, the whoop of delight from Marie-France as she was accosted and cuddled by their two grandsons. Maury closed the folder and waited for the boys to catch sight of him.

The Gendarmerie at Rivesaltes was quiet, Renaud and Pratt, according to the desk sergeant, were circulating in the Opoul-Périllos area, as instructed, to get water samples and to show locals the facial reconstructions.

The revised list of incidents lay on Maury's desk, he glanced at the pages, and noticed that Renaud had highlighted some items of interest; a racist incident in Salses, another in Tautavel, an assault in Vingrau and lots of car breakdowns. Nothing immediately piqued Maury's interest. Looking at the empty chairs of the field office, Maury wondered if Babayan had been told they were back on the case. Perusing his notes, he picked up the phone and asked the switchboard to be connected to the Commissariat in Toulouse. Once connected, he asked for Wittmeyer and was soon speaking in person to the liaison officer.

"I'm sorry," Wittmeyer told him, "The Jimenez case is being

handled solely by the Spanish."

"Ah?" muttered Maury in surprise.

Wittmeyer explained, "It seems Jimenez had two types of operation going on. Here in France, the Périllos Mas was like a high-class brothel with an exclusive clientele. While in Spain his operation was altogether less high-brow."

"Was he involved in people trafficking, do you know?" asked Maury.

"Not from outside the EU as far as I'm aware, he seems to favour girls from Eastern Europe."

"Any black or Arabic girls?"

"Not that I'm aware."

"What actually went on in the Mas at Périllos?"

"Seems he offered a discreet high-class service, to the better-off. You saw the place, sadomasochism, latex, leather...that sort of thing."

"Were there any girls there when you raided the place?"

"No. It seems like he lived there with a couple of his own personal favourites. He brought girls in from La Jonquera and Perthus, on the nights the place was used."

"So, how often was the place used?"

"Every weekend, by the sounds of it."

"If I need to interview Jimenez, where can I find him?"

"He's on remand in Figueres, the detective in charge down there is Suarez. He seems like an upright type of guy."

"How come the case was taken off you?"

"On the orders of the Procureur General's office in Perpignan," Wittmeyer stated.

Somehow news of interference from the Perpignan Procureur's office came as little surprise.

"Yours is the missing person's case plastered all over the front page of the Midi-Libre isn't it?" Wittmeyer asked.

"Yes," Maury confirmed.

"Mm. I read the article. Is it true that they were dressed in chemises?" the Toulousain detective asked.

"Yes, why?"

"It's just that I remember a suicide around here a few months ago and the poor sod was dressed in similar sort of clothes."

"Where was this?" asked Maury, his interest piqued.

"It wasn't my case. It happened in Ariege at a place called Roquefixade."

Maury had heard of the place, a small mountain village, under an imposing ruined castle, "The castle?"

"That's, right, jumped off the battlements, I think. I could send you the details if you like."

"I'd appreciate that," said Maury, thanking the Toulousain investigator.

That was interesting, another Cathar link. If memory served, Roquefixade was one of the sect's last strongholds in the Albigensian crusades. Maury rang off and turned back to his mental to-do list. There was still no sign of Babayan.

He rang the Narbonne office of the Midi-Libre and asked for Mademoiselle Petit. They made a few moments of awkward small talk, her stand-offish, as if expecting to be bawled out for accessing the file, he had purposely left on his desk for her to find.

Maury kept his tone friendly and business-like, "I have received facial reconstructions of the three victims found up at Périllos. Do you think your paper would be interested in publishing them, our investigations in the local area seem to be drawing a blank?" he asked.

Realising the call was far from hostile, Petit answered in the affirmative and provided an email address for the images to be forwarded. Maury thanked the journalist, concluded the conversation, and sent the images as instructed.

Where was Lucine? Perhaps the Perpignan office could shed some light on the Lieutenant's whereabouts. He rang and was connected almost immediately to Guillot. "Bonjour Guillot! You've heard the latest I suppose? Could you tell me if you've reassigned Babayan to the case?"

"Yes, of course," the Captain confirmed, "But there's a Disciplinary Tribunal over Verdier's misconduct, so she's not available."

"Oh? So, she's likely to be off for the next couple of days?"

"Yes, I suppose so," Guillot confirmed, "She'll be at the Tribunal all day tomorrow."

"Tell me Guillot, did you know who in the Procureur's office pulled the plug on this investigation?" asked Maury.

"A lot of good it did them, the regional press and civil rights groups have been baying for blood since this morning's Midi-Libre hit the news-stands...Hang on, I've got the written instructions here somewhere on my desk. Ah! Yes, it looks like the Procureur General himself signed the order."

Maybe the Procureur had signed the order, but Maury guessed that he just signed papers that someone else slid in front of him. Perhaps, the motive had been to simply save money and resources. So, who in the Prefecture had oversight of police budgets in Perpignan?

Maury thanked Guillot for his help and decided to make an incident board. He printed out the facial reconstructions and looked at the faces of the dead looking back at him. The siblings, flat-nosed, broad foreheads and large eyes, and the finely boned Arab girl, all young, all with lives still to live. What a waste, he thought. Add to that the life of an unborn child and it was a Racinesque tragedy. Why the hell did someone in the Procureur's Office seem hell-bent on stymieing the investigation?

He looked at those dangles, those clues that remained to be chased up. The clothing, the shoes, and the pendants...

The pendants. He wondered if Babayan had made any progress in ascertaining the origin of the gold. He sent her a text inviting her to visit his home with her family, for that very evening. Then he rang Marie-France to tell her that they would have additional guests.

He felt all but done here but looking out at the beige scenery swimming in heat beyond the windows of the police station, Maury was reluctant to leave its air-conditioned comfort and expose himself to the endless heat. He returned to Renaud and Pratt's incident list.

The racist incident at Salses. French itinerant workers assaulted North African immigrants in a squabble over piece rates for harvesting apricots for the local Co-operative. Two men charged for grievous bodily harm - one young Tunisian hospitalised.

The incident at Tautavel. A black stallholder verbally abused by another street vendor. More a case of business competition boiling over into violence, than an outrightly racist incident. Both men cautioned and bound to keep the peace.

An assault in the sleepy village of Vingrau. The local boy-racer assaults a middle-aged man in the village, accusing the man of 'touching up' his girlfriend. The girlfriend's first statement seemed to imply that she and the middle-aged man were having a liaison behind the cuckold boyfriend's back. The man, a retired doctor, refused to talk. However, under caution, and away from the boyfriend in the offices of the local Mairie, the girlfriend changed her story, admitting that she met with the doctor to arrange the termination of boy-racer's unwanted pregnancy. A search of the boy-racer's car meanwhile resulted in the discovery of a substantial amount of controlled substances and the boyfriend was charged with battery and possession of Class A drugs with intention to supply.

What things happened here in the middle-of-nowhere, thought Maury. However, the break the present investigation so desperately needed would not come from this list. It wouldn't need any further Machiavellian machinations, from the politicians and lawyers of the Prefecture to close down the case. Without some viable line of inquiry, Maury would have to close down the case himself. There was no more to do here, it was time to go home.

Maury had managed to potter about in the vegetable patch and assemble a fresh salad from home-grown produce, and marinade lamb steaks by the time his happy solitude was invaded by the returning family. Marie-France and Elisabeth wore pretty summer dresses and looked more like sisters than mother and daughter. The two boys, Joel and Maurice, ran to their grandfather like puppies, demanding his attention, before getting distracted by the toy-box in the cool of the house. Maury embraced his wife and daughter who were intrigued at the dishes he was preparing. "You'll see, you'll see," he told them as he shooed them giggling from the kitchen.

The women had just laid out the dining table on the terrace when Babayan's little Renault crunched onto the gravel drive. From the kitchen door, Maury waved in greeting, as Lucine alighted and set about extracting two children from their car seats. Elisabeth, her motherly instinct cutting in, stepped forward to help her. Soon the two petite women, one blonde, the other dark, both in figure-flattering dresses, were leading two doe-eyed children towards the house. Elisabeth and Marie-France made their own introductions and called for Joel and Maurice. The boys came trotting, and soon took Babayan's little boy with them back to the toy-box. The little girl clung shyly to Lucine and looked up at Maury as he emerged from the kitchen with a decanter of home-made lemonade.

The adults sat together enjoying a long cold drink, in the shade of the fig trees that protected the terrace. Maury was glad to see that the women seemed to take to one another, they were already chatting on familiar terms about children and their respective domestic arrangements. Finishing his drink Maury returned to the kitchen to continue preparing their meal.

As he busied himself, he became aware that he had silent company, Lucine's little girl had come into the kitchen and balanced herself on a chair to observe him. "Hello," Maury said, "What's your name?"

"Samara," the little girl told him. "I'm five," she added, gravely.

"Can you help me make these plates look pretty?" Maury asked.

Samara nodded, as Maury passed her some slices of tomato.

The meal was a minor triumph. Young and old ate everything that was put in front of them, and as the children left the table to have one more play, the adults sat chatting over coffee. Knowing that her husband and Lucine had official business to discuss, Marie-France suggest that she and Elisabeth see to the dishes.

"How did it go today?" Maury asked.

"At the Tribunal you mean?" Lucine said, her face suddenly serious. Maury nodded.

"They don't give anything away. I gave my evidence and that was it, everything else happens behind closed doors," said Lucine.

Maury nodded in understanding and changed the subject, "How did you get on with the pendant?"

Babayan smiled, "Ah! I think that maybe you'll like what the assayer had to say about the gold's provenance. A complete analysis of the metal was made, and apparently it comes from the Ariege."

"The river or the Department?" Maury asked.

"Both actually. From the River Ariege, near its source in the Ariege department. Which ties it in nicely with the Cathar theme. That got me thinking about the chemises they wore, I wondered if cloth has a provenance too..."

"And has it?" queried Maury.

"Actually, it does. The chemises are artisan made in Ariege too, from the town of Lavelanet. They are sold in markets everywhere in the department," Lucine reported. "The same goes for the sandals, artisan made in St. Girons, and sold at market, just like the chemises."

"Then, we might safely say that our victims are likely to have come from somewhere in Ariege?" Maury ventured.

Lucine nodded.

So, what were our four poor unfortunates doing in the middle of nowhere, over a hundred kilometres from their presumed point of origin? Silently, the two detectives pondered the implications.

Maury told Lucine about Wittmeyer's suicide at Roquefixade – the similar clothing. The Ariege connection now seemed very strong.

"Let's wait, until Wittmeyer's file arrives, before we jump to any conclusions," Maury cautioned.

The quiet arrival of Samara onto Lucine's lap signalled that the soiree was over. Children were gathered, bundled into pyjamas, and ushered towards bedrooms or the back seat of the car. Then, with the little Renault's departure, the house returned to quiet.

"She's nice," remarked Elisabeth of Lucine as she enjoyed a night-cap on the terrace with her parents. Marie-France nodded in agreement, "and very pretty too," she added.

Knowing that his response was being monitored, Maury nodded in silent agreement.

A Good Thick Stick

Before Innocent sent Dominic to Languedoc with his blessing, there had, in fact, been several attempts to supress the Cathars by force. Innocent's predecessor Pope Alexander III had pronounced the Cathars to be 'burnable' or anathema in 1179.

With the Cathars in their sights, several Catholic bishops attempted to deal with the Cathar 'problem' but found that the nobles of the Languedoc were unwilling to persecute their own countrymen on the bishopric's behalf. They did manage to single out individual Cathars, every now and again, and get them to recant or find them guilty of some mortal sin for which they could be condemned, tied to the stake, and burned. But, these 'successes' were few, and far between.

If it was to succeed in eradicating the heresy, the church had to organise. In 1203 two stern and authoritarian figures, the Papal Legate Peter of Castelnau and the Abbot of Citeaux, founder of the Cistercian Order, Arnaud Amaury, took to the roads of Languedoc to convince Cathars to convert. They met with the Cathar clergy and engaged them in public discussion, as Dominic would later do, but the contrast between the Catholics and the Bonhommes was summarised like this, by one observer.

"Their God always went by foot – yet today his servants ride in comfort. Their God was poor – yet these missionaries are wealthy. Their God was humble – yet these envoys are loaded with honours."

The Catholic envoys must have made threats of impending violence, because in the same year as this abortive attempt to convert them, the Cathars requested that the Lord of Puivert reconstruct the fortress of Montsegur (the secure mountain) to serve as their administrative centre, a refuge and their treasury for the funds being donated to their cause by the region's richer classes.

With Dominic's failure the Catholics had to regroup and reconsider their strategy in Languedoc. They tabled a plan put forward by Arnaud Amaury, the checked missionary, to convince the local barons to hunt out the heretics on their lands by force or risk excommunication.

Excommunication, in those days, was a very big deal. The excommunicate would be prohibited not only from ceremonies of worship, but also from conducting some of their administrative offices, such as the exercise of governance.

But Raymond VI, the Count of Toulouse, the most powerful lord of Languedoc refused point blank to join the hunting party. Without their liege lord's blessing, his vassals, the other barons of the region would not take up arms against the Cathars either.

All looked lost for the Catholic call to arms, until on the 15th January 1208 some of Raymond's knights, incensed at him being excommunicated, vented their frustrations upon Peter de Castelnau, Thomas à Beckett style, cutting down the Papal Legate as he crossed out of Languedoc into Provence at St Gilles.

This tragedy gave Innocent the pretext he needed to prosecute a proper crusade against the Cathars. In that same year, 1208, the Pope declared a crusade and promised its prosecutors the lands of any Cathar heretic they exterminated.

So, they came from all over Europe and gathered as an army at Lyon in the summer of 1209. They numbered 10,000 – mercenaries, chancers, and religious bigots (or defenders of the faith – according to your view) under the supreme command of Simon de Montfort an Anglo-French nobleman (father of the infamous knight who forced King John of England to sign Magna Carta) dispossessed of a large portion of his lands by that same King John.

Described by his peers as a man of unflinching religious orthodoxy, de Montfort was deeply committed to the suppression of heresy. As a general he was ruthless, daring, brutal and wholly committed to regaining lands for his family's estate.

His right-hand man was a Catholic clergyman with a personal grudge against the Cathars, the Abbot of Citeaux, Arnaud Amaury, once a failed missionary, now a 'holy' soldier.

14th June

Maury accessed his emails, before leading the family on an expedition to the African Park at nearby Sigean. A note from Wittmeyer with more details of the suicide at Roquefixade was intriguing, it bore many similarities to their own Opoul-Périllos case. In this incident, the deceased was a young man thought to be in his early twenties, clad in white chemise, sandals and cotton underwear. He'd been seen to jump, his arms outstretched, from the highest point of the ancient castle ruins at the very moment the battlements were illuminated by the rising sun. He'd fallen, his arms still held out like wings, to his death on the rocks far below. Recovery of the body had been difficult, as the sad creature had burst asunder on impact. Due to his horrific injuries, he could not be identified from dental records. His fingerprints were not on file, and he had no distinguishing marks, but DNA testing had revealed him to be a West-European Caucasian, most likely French. A photo-fit had been circulated and compared to missing persons databases, but there had been no positive match. His remains had been buried, in an unmarked grave, in a Pamiers cemetery, his effects stored in the military camp nearby. A full file was being held at the Gendarmerie in Pamiers.

Maury decided to formally request the file and to send Babayan to examine or collect these artefacts on Monday. The weekend was beckoning, he shut down his computer and locked his work phone in his desk.

15th June

The heatwave was in the news, the South of France and the Midi-Pyrenees were sweltering in temperatures more commonly seen in high summer. As he was wont to do, Maury checked the temperature gauge on an upright of the terrace, as he returned from giving the garden an early morning watering.

"Twenty-eight degrees," he called out softly.

"Already!" exclaimed Marie-France bringing the breakfast tray to their outdoor table, "It's barely seven!"

As he sipped his coffee Maury wondered what the day would bring. The investigation still needed a breakthrough. Wittmeyer's suicide case might give it more impetus, but until then the two Rivesaltes gendarmes would have to continue circulating the e-fits and trawling through case files.

His reverie ended with a beep, signalling an incoming text message, on his mobile phone. He picked it up and read a message from Guillot, "Babayan suspended. Verdier reinstated. I am putting him on your missing person's case. Sorry." Included were Verdier's contact details.

Sensitive to her husband's change of mood, Marie-France noted his furrowed brow and asked him what was wrong. He read her the text, as an idea formulated in his mind.

"That's terrible," Marie-France remarked.

Maury just nodded

"What's Verdier like?" she asked.

"I don't know," admitted Maury, his fingers busy on the phone's keypad, "I'll soon find out, I'm arranging to meet up with him now."

This new development troubled Maury, he liked Babayan and she'd already demonstrated her competence and reliability. He decided to defer meeting up with the new detective, Verdier, and do some background checks from his office in Narbonne first. He'd access the transcripts of the tribunal - if they'd been entered on the database. Maury had not had any concerns about Lucine's professionalism, so why had she been so suddenly and unceremoniously suspended from duty?

He sat watching the speckled sunlight flood the garden through the poplars that lined the drive, his hand entwined with his wife's, her warm head upon his shoulder until he felt it was time to go.

The dossiers were interesting. The tribunal had dismissed the charges brought against Verdier, but not before it had been firmly established that he had a history of heavy-handedness when making arrests or questioning witnesses, particularly if they were from immigrant stock. Babayan alleged an assault on a young man from one of the poorer areas of Perpignan's ugly urban spread. However, to everyone at the tribunal's surprise, the boy himself had been produced at the hearing as a defence witness and claimed that he'd fallen down a stairwell and sustained injuries to his cheek and eye socket as a result of accident rather than assault.

The panel were not convinced that the boy's new testimony was true, they felt that given Babayan's record, she was likely to be telling the actual truth. But then, in order to undermine Lucine's credibility, Verdier's legal team had shown the panel her official personnel file, in which she stated that she was single and had no dependents. The panel members, all serving police officers in Perpignan, were astounded, it was well-known that Babayan had two small children. The panel had little choice, her credibility undermined, it suspended Babayan and dismissed all charges against Verdier.

Maury mused as he drove back down to Rivesaltes to rendezvous with Verdier. He wondered how the defence team had managed to access restricted personnel files, and who had represented Verdier at the tribunal? According to the car's temperature gauge, the heat had risen again, the landscape danced in haze and mirages, as if the distant road were a troubled sea. Even with the windows fully open and the cooling fans roaring at top speed, his head was wet with perspiration, his shirt clinging uncomfortably to his sweat-drenched back.

On arrival at the Gendarmerie, Maury went first to freshen up before entering the office. Renaud and Pratt were busy at their desks, opposite them - sat at Maury's desk and busy fiddling with the stationery - was a compact young man, clothed in dark blue suit trousers, white shirt with shoulder holster. The man's hair was mousy and thinning on top. He was clean-shaven and well-kept, wearing a black tie despite the heat. This must be Verdier, Maury guessed, as he turned first to the gendarmes for an update. Both shook their heads regretfully. "Nothing so far Sir," Renaud reported.

"Keep looking," Maury instructed, "and let me know if the Pamiers office try to make contact."

Maury turned to Verdier, still comfortable at his desk, and introduced himself without offering a handshake. "You must be Verdier?" Verdier nodded in assent, "I am Commandant Maury."

Verdier looked surprised, and rose up quickly, from his superior's chair. Maury waved him back down, "I assume you're up to speed on the case?" he asked.

"Three drowned people in a ditch, on the side of a road towards Périllos," Verdier answered.

"So far, we're following up on a few leads but seem to be getting nowhere. Have you any suggestions?" Maury asked, testing the new detective, to see if he had any creativity or ideas.

Verdier looked blank, "I haven't read the case file in any great detail yet," he admitted.

Maury drew breath between his teeth, "Then I suggest you do," he said, "I'm off to Perpignan to see a jeweller about a pendant. When I get back maybe you could suggest a new line of inquiry."

As he passed them, Maury turned to Renaud and Pratt, "Okay, if there are any developments, you can get me on my mobile. Give Verdier some of the incident logs to look at once he's gone over the case file."

Madame Mayeur recognised Maury immediately he entered the shop. She called for her husband, and made polite small talk until the jeweller emerged from his workshop, with the pendant in its evidence bag, "I'm afraid I didn't come up with anything else," he apologised.

Maury took the gold piece from him, "Your help is really appreciated, thank you."

"No Lucine today? Is she not well?" the jeweller asked, noting the empty shop behind the detective.

"Shh, Albert. It's probably one of the children that's under the weather or something..." Madame Mayeur scolded.

Their obviously genuine concern touched Maury, and he wanted to allay it, "It's official business," he explained.

Looking satisfied, the jewellers wished Maury goodbye as he stepped back into the cauldron that was Perpignan's city centre.

He stopped on the doorstep, something nagging him. How did the jewellers know Babayan? He turned and re-entered the shop. The jewellers look at him in surprise, "Have you forgotten something?" Mayeur asked.

"Could I ask how you know Lieutenant Babayan?"

The Mayeur's faces saddened, "She is our son-in-law's sister," Monsieur Mayeur explained.

"She is looking after our grandchildren," Madame added.

His business in the departmental capital was not yet finished, Maury drove into the grey suburbs in Perpignan's north. He found a parking space amongst other aged and battered automobiles, in the shade of a Plane tree and walked towards a faceless apartment block. The streets were silent, but for the domestic sounds emanating from the buildings that lined them. Washing hung from lines on small balconies, baking in the blazing white sunshine. Sweltering heat reflected from every surface, and Maury was glad to pass into the relative cool of an external stairway. He climbed, until he reached the anonymous floor he was seeking, and knocked upon a heavy wooden apartment door. Feet slapped across uncarpeted floors and stopped on the other side of the portal. A woman's voice, heavily accented, challenged him, "Who is it?"

"Madame Nassim? This is Commandant Maury from the Police Nationale," Maury replied, "There's no need to worry. I wondered if I might have some words with your son Mankour?"

"He did as he was told yesterday. Can't you just leave him alone now?" There was obvious distress in the woman's voice.

The door remained closed and locked, and Maury realised that they'd reached an impasse, "Okay. I'll pass my card under the door. If Mankour would like to speak to me, get him to call my mobile number."

He knelt down and was passing the card when an aggressive voice from the top of the stairway challenged him, "Who the f*ck are you? What do you want?"

Maury stood up slowly, showing the palms of his empty hands at a snarling Arab youth dressed in faded jeans, a 'Barca' football shirt and backwards baseball cap. "Hello. I've come to speak to Mankour. I'm Commandant Maury from the Narbonne Police." He hoped that the hint that he wasn't local would reduce the obvious animosity.

"Narbonne? What the f*ck do you want with my brother?" The youth's tone was still aggressive, but his shoulders had relaxed, his body language was less hostile.

"I understand that your brother was assaulted by one of my subordinates from Perpignan..."

"Verdier!" spat the youth.

Maury nodded, "Yes, that's right. But your brother testified yesterday that no such assault had taken place..."

"Of course, it took place!" shouted the boy in exasperation, as the apartment door opened and his mother, stout and middle-aged, swaddled in hijab and gown scolded him, "Be quiet Ali! We don't want any more trouble!"

Maury nodded at the woman in acknowledgement, "I'm just trying to find out if the detective who testified against Verdier at the tribunal was lying," he explained.

Mother and son went silent, then the youth shook his head, "Lieutenant Babayan? No, she wasn't."

"Ssh," said the mother.

Her shushing seemed to make her son even angrier, "No mother! Mankour lost an eye because of that *rsehole!"

On the periphery, Maury noticed movement behind the mother, a slender boy had come to stand behind her. He was tall and handsome, though his face was marred by an ugly wound to eyebrow and cheek, and he had one white, sightless eye as a result. Maury guessed this to be Mankour.

Sight of Verdier's victim strengthened Maury's resolve, he ignored mother and elder brother, looked directly at Mankour, and spoke softly, "Did Verdier do this to you?"

Again, mother, and elder son fell quiet, as they awaited Mankour's response. The boy nodded.

"Can I come in please Madame?" Maury asked the mother. The woman paused for a moment, then stood aside to let him enter the doorway.

The flat was gloomy, the curtains and blinds pulled closed against the pitiless sunlight. It was hot, despite the best efforts of a ticking, off-balance, ceiling fan to stir the air. Maury was ushered into the sitting room, where carpets adorned the walls rather than floors in true middle eastern style. The floor itself was tiled, the furniture heavy and ornate, and Maury sat down at one end of a three-seater sofa. The mother remained standing, hovering, her hands restless, unsure what should happen next. Mankour sat himself near the policeman on an armchair, his belligerent brother at the other end of Maury's sofa.

"Take your hat off in here Ali," said the mother. Ali complied immediately, though he scowled.

The younger brother, Mankour looked like a rabbit caught in headlamps, stock-still and frightened. Maury sought to reassure the boy, "It's alright, you're not in any sort of trouble. I just need to ask you all a few questions."

"Okay," said the boy in a whisper.

The police had come to interview a neighbour, living in an apartment on the floor above, about petty thefts and burglaries. On their arrival, Verdier, who had a reputation in the quarter as a racist bully, was recognised by youngsters in the street. The news of their impending visit beat the detectives to the suspect, who hid on the flat roof, while the detectives rapped on his front door. He'd then run, clattering, down the common stairway, in order to evade them.

Hearing him, the two detectives launched themselves in pursuit.
Mankour, who'd been sent to the local supermarket, was returning
to the flat when he was passed, on the first landing of the stairway,
by the fleeing suspect. Hot on his heels came Verdier, followed a
little later by a more composed Babayan. Mankour said he heard
Verdier stumble and shout out in frustration when he reached the
outside and found the suspect had lost him. Verdier had then burst
back up the stairway and caught up with Mankour, as he continued
to ascend the stairs. He grabbed the boy, making him drop his
groceries, and demanded to know where the suspect would be
hiding. Mankour, frightened and concerned for the foodstuffs that
had escaped from his shopping bags and were tumbling down the
steps, said he did not know. This reply enraged the already seething
detective who simply lashed out, grabbing Mankour by his head and
smashing his face into an angle of the wall. This was witnessed by
Babayan, who was climbing back up the stairs with the dropped
shopping in her arms.
The sad story was recounted by both Mankour and his distressed
mother. It tallied with accounts given at the tribunal. "So, why did
you change your story?" Maury asked, cutting straight to the chase.
Mother and son looked at each other in silent collaboration, but Ali
who'd been squirming in his seat while the story had been
recounted, got up and crossed to a shelf and picked up a business
card which he pressed into the detective's hand, "Because this
bastard came along and threatened us!"
"Watch your language!" snapped the mother.
Maury looked at the card, it was from the Legal Department of the
Procureur's Office in Perpignan, a staffer called Eric Dubois.
Somehow, the Commandant was not surprised. He'd follow this up
later, but right now he wanted to know what pressure had been
exerted on the little family. "How did he threaten you?" he asked.
"Mankour needed medical attention for his injuries. This man said
that our paperwork wasn't in order, and that if we didn't change
our story, we'd be liable for all the costs of his medical care..." the
mother began to explain.
Ali butted in, "Non, non maman! Mankour is underage, his

healthcare is free. I kept telling you."

The mother's eyes began to well, "But he said, we'd lose the flat and our benefits, because our permits aren't up to date."

Maury turned to Mankour, who was looking uncomfortable as his family squabbled, "How old are you Mankour?"

"Fifteen."

"Are you a French national?"

The boy nodded.

Maury had heard enough, he spoke with quiet authority to the family, "If Mankour is only fifteen then his healthcare is free."

"I told you!" exclaimed Ali.

"And how long have you lived in France, Madame?" Maury asked the mother.

She made a quick calculation, "About thirty years," she said.

"So, both boys are French?"

Madame Nassim nodded.

"Then, you have automatic rights of residence, Madame."

The mother looked wide-eyed; the boys were jubilant.

"I need you to complete new witness statements, which explain everything you've told me," Maury said, looking closely and earnestly into each of their faces, until, overcoming their fears, they nodded in assent.

As Maury walked back to his car, Ali ran after him clutching a wad of papers, "Commandant! A moment please!"

He thrust the papers at Maury, who expected them to be documents proving the family's legal status, instead he was looking at beautiful sketches and drawings of landscapes, portraits of animals and people. "Please don't forget about us Monsieur," said Ali as Maury admired the handiwork, "Mankour has...had, a gift."

Maury was astounded, the drawings showed such competence and maturity, that he could scarcely believe they were the work of a teenager. He looked up at the young artist's older brother, moved to see that the proud street-savvy youth was wiping a tear from the corner of his eye. Maury handed back the drawings, squeezed Ali's forearm and said, "I won't forget."

"Wait!" commanded Maury, as Ali turned back for home. He reached into his pocket and recovered his mobile phone. He pressed a quick-dial number as the youth, his brow furrowed in puzzlement, looked on.

"Allo Commandant," came a voice on the receiver.

"Busy Martinez?"

"Normal stuff sir. Your in-tray is beginning to fill."

"Mm," replied Maury, aware that his absence from the Narbonne office would mean a backlog to tackle on his return. "Listen Martinez, fancy a trip down to Perpignan to take some witness statements for me?"

"No problem Commandant," the aide replied with some eagerness. "What's the address?"

Maury, looking at Ali as he spoke, gave the Nassim family's names and address. "How long to get here?"

"Say an hour?"

"The family will be expecting you. I'll be at the Commissariat in Perpignan, meet me there when you're done."

"Yes sir," said Martinez.

Maury finished the call. "Did you catch all that?" he asked Ali.

The youth nodded.

"Expect a visit from one of my collegues from Narbonne, an officer called Martinez, in about an hour's time. Tell him all that you told me."

Ali nodded. "Merci Commandant," he said offering his hand in a gesture of appreciation and respect.

As he turned once more to the car, his phone buzzed and, to his surprise, he saw that the call was from Martinez. For a moment he feared that his aide may not be able to come and get the witness statements as promised.

"I forgot to say that there's a message from EDF about water samples," said Martinez apologetically.

"EDF?"

"Yes sir. Well, more exactly one of their laboratories." The centime dropped, the laboratory would have checked the water samples he'd asked the Rivesaltes' gendarmes to collect, "What does it say?"

The aide hesitated a moment, and Maury could hear him leafing through pages. "Two positive matches," he said at last.

"Two?"

"Yes sir, a spring and a swimming pool. I'll send the email onto the field office in Rivesaltes"

Maury's heart leapt, here at last was a decisive break, a solid line of inquiry had opened. "Thanks Martinez, I'll see you soon."

His reception at the Commissariat in Perpignan was cordial, the Desk Sergeant checked his credentials, and asked Maury to wait until he could inform Guillot of his arrival. The Captain, like Maury a stocky middle-aged man, duly arrived in person to collect him from the foyer, "Ah Commandant! To what do we owe the honour?"

"Maybe we could chat over coffee?" Maury suggested.

Guillot looked a little surprised and concerned, betrayed by a slight tightening of the jaw. "There's a canteen, a little bistro around the corner or an espresso machine in my office," he suggested.

"Your office sounds fine."

Guillot, dressed in his smart suit and Italian shoes, led Maury through a quiet squad room, detectives and uniformed officers were tapping at computer keyboards in air-conditioned comfort. Some looked up as they passed, but Maury recognised no-one. Guillot's end office was spacious and elegant, neatly set out as befitted a self-proclaimed pen-pusher. Maury installed himself in a comfortable leather chair, as the Captain passed to the coffee machine, fiddled a moment, and then closed the office door against the low murmur of the squad room. "It's this tribunal business isn't it?"

Maury nodded, "Yes, I'm afraid it is."

"I feared it would be," admitted the Captain, as he pressed a flashing button on the machine.

Neither men spoke, as Guillot saw to the hissing and gurgling coffee-maker and returned to the desk between them with two tiny cups of espresso, "Sugar?" he asked.

"Did you know, the Nassim family were intimidated in order to change their testimony?" asked Maury, taking a sugar lump and letting it dissolve in the crème of his drink.

"I read the reports," Guillot admitted glumly. "But I have to keep a professional distance."

"Verdier half-blinded a young kid."

"I know," conceded the Captain, looking down into his cup.

"I want him gone." said Maury.

"How?" Guillot asked, looking up in surprise.

"We're his line managers, we can deal with him in-house. We don't need a tribunal panel to do it."

"What do you suggest?"

"Put him back in uniform, let him control traffic somewhere," suggested Maury.

"Not that easy. I can't demote him without the approval of the panel."

"Then move him sideways, to somewhere where he can't harm anyone."

Guillot looked into space, then spoke an idea aloud, "I could put him in charge of CCTV monitoring."

Maury smiled and took a sip of the bittersweet brew, "My aide-de-camp is getting revised statements from the family, he'll be along with them soon...Now we need to talk about Babayan."

"Babayan? But I can't overrule the tribunal on this one. It's just not possible." Guillot protested.

Maury took another long and slow sip of coffee, then asked, "How well do you know your people Guillot?"

"Quite well," said Guillot. "But Babayan is a bit of a loner, she doesn't mix so well."

"Mm. Do you think, that's because she's got a family to look after?"

"Could be," admitted the Captain pensively. "She's good at her job though. I've never found fault."

"Did you know that her brother and sister-in-law work as front-line doctors, for Medecins Sans Frontiers?" asked Maury.

"Do they?" Guillot's tone betrayed a 'so what?' attitude.

"And Babayan looks after their children while they're on deployment?" continued Maury.

He could see the Captain grasping what this meant. Guillot almost choked on the espresso he was sipping, "Merde!" he muttered. "So, she's looking after her brother's kids..."

Maury took the conversation elsewhere, in order to save Guillot some embarrassment. "The Nassim family say they were pressured to change their testimony by this individual," said Maury reaching into his pocket, and extracting Dubois' business card. "Do you know him?"

Guillot nodded, "He's a junior lawyer at the Prefecture."

"Why would he lean on the family on Verdier's behalf?"

The Captain shrugged his shoulders, "I've no idea."

Maury took another sip of coffee and changed the subject again, "I'd like Babayan back on the case with me."

Guillot picked up his desk phone's handset, "Of course, I'll ring her straight away."

It pleased Maury to hear Guillot apologetically speaking to Babayan, he could hear her delight at being reinstated, and the Captain reassuring her that the Nassim affair would be dealt with through 'other channels', "I'm putting you back to work with Commandant Maury, if that's okay," said the Captain.

Lucine must have said something, Guillot looked up at Maury, "When? She needs to make childcare arrangements."

"Tomorrow will be fine. Tell her I'll meet her at Rivesaltes."

The message was conveyed and a pleased-looking Guillot replaced the receiver. "What about Verdier?" he asked.

"Let's call him back here, once my man Martinez has got the statements."

"Okay," agreed Guillot.

Maury wondered if having a bald head like Guillot was an advantage or disadvantage in the outdoor heat, as he rose and readied himself for the furnace. "Any restaurants in the area you can recommend?"

A couple of hours later, a sweating Martinez arrived in the Commissariat, with the revised statements from the Nassim family, they made shocking reading. The aide-de-camp had also thought to get corroborating evidence, from the doctors who had worked on

Mankour's injuries. Guillot perused them in turn and looked up at Maury, "If we deal with this in-house the boy won't get compensated."

Maury looked over his glasses at the Captain, "Then we'll have to formalise the thing over again. But we do need to make sure the Prefecture doesn't interfere."

"Internal Affairs?" suggested Guillot, doubtfully.

"I don't know, maybe we can deal with it as an internal matter" said Maury, an idea forming. Perhaps he could use this case to investigate the goings-on in Perpignan's Prefecture. "I'll get the Inspector General to authorise an Oversight investigation."

"Won't that reflect badly on me?" asked Guillot with some concern, knowing that Oversight investigations looked at systemic failures and problems.

"I don't know," admitted Maury with a shrug, "The Inspector General already has concerns, about how the Prefecture is handling police matters down here. You've read the papers. If anyone asks, it's you that blew the whistle on these irregularities."

Guillot looked a little more reassured.

Inspector General Lafitte, Maury's friend Pierre, heard him out as he explained developments at Perpignan. Maury also mentioned the seeming interference with Wittmeyer's investigations of Jimenez in France.

Agreeing that it smelled of 'cover up' Lafitte considered Maury's proposals for a moment before sighing heavily and making his decision, "Okay we'll use this Verdier situation to find out who in the Prefecture is interfering with police work. This situation is totally unacceptable though, and too important to be dealt with in-house. I am going to send a team from the IGPN down to Perpignan."

"Oh?" said Maury, with some trepidation, the Inspecteur Generale de la Police Nationale were hated, they were effectively the police of the police, and Maury realised that despite his reassurances, Guillot would probably find himself under the microscope after all. "But we've got Verdier coming back here for an interview," he explained.

"Very well, get Guillot to interview him. He can pass on the transcript to IGPN," Lafitte directed. "This affair shouldn't bother you Maury, you've still got those John Does to identify, haven't you?"

"Yeah," Maury admitted.

"Are you making any headway?"

"I've got some leads."

"Okay."

"Don't forget Marie-France's invitation to dinner," Maury reminded.

There was rustling, and Maury could imagine the Inspector General looking at his desk diary, "How about Friday?" he asked.

"Fine, we'll see you then," said Maury.

As he replaced the receiver, he saw that Guillot and Martinez were chatting in a corner of the squad room. He beckoned them back into Guillot's office. "The boss wants IGPN to investigate." Both men paled.

"Verdier will be back from Rivesaltes very shortly. I'd like you two to handle him. The boss wants the transcript passed onto IGPN when they arrive."

Maury decided to stay to see Verdier's reception, he had taken an instant dislike to the detective, and wanted to see the arrogant *couillon's* face when he had the rug pulled from under him. He knew he should remain professionally detached, but he arranged to watch through the one-way glass when they interviewed him.

When Verdier arrived, he was directed straight into the interview room by Guillot, who met him at the squad room door. Verdier nodded at some of the officers who looked up at him from their desks, but he was visibly wrong-footed, he had not expected this reception.

Guillot left the detective to stew for a few minutes, saying he'd return with paperwork. Verdier sat and stared at the one-way mirror as if trying to look through it to see if there were any observers.

Presently, Guillot, accompanied by Martinez, returned, and sat facing the disgraced detective. Guillot pressed buttons on the recording device, made the obligatory preamble and began, "Yesterday, a tribunal heard evidence from one of your colleagues, Lieutenant Lucine Babayan, about your assault of Mankour Nassim."

"The victim of this assault, Mankour Nassim, also testified on your behalf to the tribunal panel. Mr Nassim's testimony directly negated Detective Babayan's testimony. Without further evidence against you, the panel dismissed the allegations brought against you."

Now he knew what he was being questioned about, Verdier visibly relaxed, as if he seemed sure that the affair was closed. "Who's this?" Verdier demanded looking scornfully at Martinez.

"This is Gardien-de-la-Paix Martinez from Narbonne, he is assisting me with an investigation of your conduct," the Captain explained.

"Good luck. I've got nothing to answer for. I've been exonerated," was Verdier's cocky retort. He crossed his hands over his chest, his eyes boring into the Captain's.

"Yes, well, we have reason to believe that the tribunal was misled," Guillot continued.

"Misled? In what way?" asked Verdier with some exasperation.

Calmly Guillot continued, "Well, you, or should I say, your lawyer, submitted Babayan's personnel file as evidence and asserted that she lied about her status."

Verdier leaned forward, "Yeah, that's right she lied. She's a liar she is, that's what she is," protested Verdier with some venom. He sat back when the two men facing him were silent, cocking a snoot as if to say, "Put that in your pipe and smoke it."

Martinez made a show of passing Guillot Babayan's personnel file. The Captain opened it and slowly perused the first page, "Of course the tribunal was in no position, at that time, to check your allegations, and it took them at face value." The cocky snarl began to fade.

Martinez passed the Captain an official memo, who read aloud from its summary, "Subsequent investigations into the allegations against Lieutenant Babayan, conclude that Lieutenant Babayan has not lied about her status or made any fraudulent representation. In view of this particular officer's reputation for honesty and her record of exemplary conduct, we cannot dismiss her evidence against Lieutenant Verdier in this instance."

"But the boy himself told the tribunal that it was an accident," Verdier protested.

Martinez passed Guillot another file, he opened it and looked at it for several seconds, until Verdier started looking uncomfortable in his chair, before continuing to read from it, "Background investigations have concluded that Mankour Nassim was intimidated by Detective Lieutenant Verdier, or someone acting on Verdier's behalf, by falsely claiming that if he did not testify on Verdier's behalf, contrary to his previous sworn statement, he would be liable to pay the costs of the course of treatment he required, as a result of the injuries inflicted during the alleged incident. It has also been found that threats against his family were made to intimidate Mankour Nassim by Verdier, or someone acting on his behalf. Mankour Nassim's witness testimony to the tribunal is concluded to have been made under duress and should therefore be expunged and a truthful statement sought.

"Do you have anything to say Lieutenant?"

Verdier sat back in his chair, crossing his arms over his chest. Maury knew exactly what he was about to say. "I want to speak to my lawyer."

Again, Martinez went through the theatrics of passing Captain Guillot a wad of official documents. Taking his time, as a worried look came over Verdier's face, the interviewing officer leafed through the pages before speaking again, "I presume you mean Maître Dubois?" Verdier's jaw tightened. "I'm afraid that Maître Dubois has been implicated as complicit to your actions in our investigations into the Nassim affair. He cannot, therefore, represent you, there would be a clear conflict of interest."

Verdier continued to clamp his mouth shut.

Guillot administered the coup-de-grace, "Detective Lieutenant Yvan Verdier, I am formally informing you that your conduct will be investigated by the IGPN. You will be required to hand in your badge and firearm. You are to await their arrival here, or in the holding cells, your choice!"

Satisfied, Maury wiped his spectacles on his shirt before popping them into a case and pocketing them. Now that the wheels on this secondary investigation were rolling, he gathered his things and stepped back into the squad room. There were low whispers audible over the low hum of the air-conditioning, his colleagues turned concerned faces to look, as Guillot stepped from the interview room and gave the Commandant a silent nod.

Maury indicated with a swipe of the hand that he was leaving.

The Gendarmes, Pratt and Renaud, both raised eyebrows when Maury walked into the office alone. "Detective Verdier not with you then?"

"No," replied Maury with a sigh, "He's been side-lined by another investigation in Perpignan."

Pratt and Renaud looked at each other, then turned back to the detective, "What now then sir?" Renaud asked.

Maury crossed into the flow of cold air streaming from the air-conditioning installation, "Babayan will be back on the case with us tomorrow," he said, enjoying the cool on his head, shoulders and back.

"I've just received a file from Pamiers," said Pratt, tapping keys on his keyboard, his eyes scanning the computer screen. "It's all the stuff on that John Doe who jumped from the top of the castle at Roquefixade."

"Ah, good, print me a copy, would you? I hate looking at screens," instructed Maury.

While Pratt busied himself with loading his printer with a thick ream of paper, Renaud cleared his throat, "I hope you don't mind sir, but I took the liberty of contacting our colleagues in Figueres, to see if the Spanish police will allow you to interview Jimenez."

Maury admired the initiative of the two Gendarmes, "What did they say?"

"I got passed to a detective called Suarez, he gave me a direct number for you to call to make arrangements."

Maury nodded in satisfaction, sat at his desk, and thought about the courgettes in his garden, they were almost getting to be marrows, maybe he could make them into a jam or chutney.

Pratt placed a buff, freshly printed, file in front of him, "The stuff from Pamiers Sir."

There was little more detail on the circumstances of the apparent suicide in Roquefixade, but there were reams of technical and forensic information from the autopsy, that were beyond the Commandant's realm of expertise, he asked Pratt to forward them to the Coroner in Perpignan, as a matter of professional courtesy, before turning to the few witness statements in the file.

The incident happened on the morning of the 21st of June the previous year. The man was not seen arriving, although he was seen climbing the track leading from the village to the castle ruins. At dawn, he was seen standing high on the battlements of Roquefixade's ruined keep. The point at which he stood, was the first to be picked out by the rays of the rising sun. This seemed to be a signal for him to jump into the void. Witnesses say, he held his arms out from his sides in a cruciform position, and just tipped himself forward off the stonework. He fell head-first into the boulder field below the cliffs, on which the castle is perched. The police and the local mountain-rescue team recovered the body and took statements. The accompanying photos of the body in-situ were disturbing, only the man's extremities were recognisable. But the chemise and sandals he wore were familiar, similar or even identical, to those worn by the unfortunates at Périllos.

Pratt's desk phone rang, the young officer caught Maury's eye, "It's for you sir."

"Allo, Maury speaking."

He'd expected to hear Guillot's voice, instead he found himself speaking to Perpignan's Coroner, "I have some news for you Commandant."

"Ah?"

"Yes, that file on this chap who jumped off the cliffs at Roquefixade."

"You've already looked at it?"

"I thought you ought to know that there appears to be a strong DNA link with one of your Périllos victims...Of course, I've yet to officially confirm it, but it appears that this young man was the father of the unborn child in the Semite subject..."

At home, the boys were happily playing with their tractors, Marie-France had given them chores to do in the garden, moving over-ripe tomatoes and courgettes, from where she'd piled them in the furrows, to the compost heap. Sitting alone on the terrace nursing a glass of white wine, her eyes staring into space was Elisabeth. Maury looked at his wife, who ushered him silently to speak to his daughter, while she remained overseeing their grandsons in the vegetable plot. He deposited his briefcase, went to the kitchen, took the opened Chablis from the fridge, and took bottle and a glass to his daughter's side. He said nothing, he simply filled his own glass, refilled hers and sat down with her looking into nothingness. Presently Elisabeth spoke, "Can you have the boys while I go back home?"

"If your mum says it's okay, I don't see why not," Maury replied, "How long for?"

"A day or two," she said without explanation, and Maury guessed there was trouble at home.

Elisabeth sipped at her wine and looked about her at the Mas, "Its great here dad, and you and mum seem so happy."

"Yes, it did us good to come here," replied Maury.

A pregnant silence fell between them, though nothing was said, Maury was aware of his daughter's malaise, knew that she'd turn to her parents if she needed to. "Sometimes it's good to discuss things on neutral ground," said Maury.

Elisabeth's eyes slowly focussed, and she turned them onto her father, her expression quizzical. Maury held out his hand wondering if Elisabeth would take it, also wondering if Marie-France had managed to keep their little project a secret as he said, "Come with me a moment".

When she did take his hand, he led her, like the young trusting child she once and still remained, through the house and back garden toward the stand of Cedars, Umbrella Pines and Holm oaks that stood on the hillock behind the house. There was a gate in a dry-stone wall, which seemed to demarcate the property line, and beyond it a little-used track. There were ancient terraces, great broom bushes and wild herbs around them, above them in the canopy the cicadas scraped on their wing-cases in tuneless chorus. The place was magical, and taking to the track over the drifts of pine needles there appeared, hidden among the undergrowth, a Mazet, a small rustic dwelling in which winemakers, shepherds and farmers would shelter, or keep tools and equipment when working on the land. Elisabeth's eyes opened wide in wonder, when she saw the little building, with its rude little patio and veranda, "What is this place?" she asked.

"Our little hideaway. It came with the house and land," said Maury unlocking and opening the stable door, and letting his daughter step into the Mazet's simple interior, "We were doing it up, thinking of letting it out during the season, or for your family to have, so you have your own space when you visit."

Elisabeth, letting go of her father's hand, stepped onto the flagstone floor and looked around her at the Mazet's Spartan interior, its living area with farmhouse table and raffia chairs, the strikingly modern kitchen area, and the spiral staircase that led to the mezzanine. The space was deceptive, Velux windows in the roof let light into the lime-washed stone interior. Maury let her explore as he opened the windows and shutters to let more light, and air into the place, he heard her exclaim, when she found the wet room with its sleek shower and fittings.

When she descended from the mezzanine with its two bedrooms, one with bunkbeds for children, and the main one with its king-sized double and en-suite facilities, father and daughter stood together in the heart of the place. "It's amazing!" said Elisabeth.

"Your mum did the design work," Maury chuckled and held out the keys to the place, "Get Robert down here, we'll have the boys at the Mas, you two can have your own space for a bit. You're only a hundred or so metres from the main house, but the track leads in from the departmental road, so you can come and go as you please.

"Of course, you'll need to get food and drink, but there are a few tins and things here, and a few bottles..."

Half an hour later, they returned to the main house, where Marie-France was organising the boys to prepare vegetables in the kitchen, she nodded at Maury when she saw her daughter's mood had changed. Elisabeth passed her mother, pecking her cheek and tousling the hair of her two sons, as they sat absorbed with developing their paring knife skills, and went into the main body of the building to use her mobile phone.
"Is she calling Robert?" Marie-France mouthed.
Maury nodded, and sat at the table with his grandsons, "Making ratatouille, are we?" he asked. The youngest, Maurice, without looking up, nodded gravely.

Caedite Eos

With such a large Catholic army massed on the eastern border of Languedoc, Raymond, Count of Toulouse, reconsidered his options. He decided that this time the Catholics meant business, made his penance and swapped sides.

His actions left his fellow baron Trencavel, Count of Carcassonne, fatally exposed but, then again, Trencavel was more influenced by the Count of Barcelona than the house of Toulouse, so maybe, once the Catholics had wrought some vengeance upon the main centres of Catharism, all situated in Trencavel's lands, it would all be settled; the army would go home and Raymond would have negated the Spanish influence on his territories.

As the army, now bolstered by Raymond's knights, advanced along the Mediterranean coast, Trencavtel sued for peace, but his pleas fell on deaf ears. Trencavel now had little choice other than to retreat from Montpellier to his most formidable stronghold, the famous citadel of Carcassonne. His withdrawal left the town of Beziers sorely exposed, a town that he had sworn to defend, but could now not afford to.

Beziers is one of the oldest cities in France, dating from 575BC, it sits on a bluff above the river Orb, commanding a river crossing on the ancient Roman Via Domitia, a route connecting Italy to Spain. The lands around it have been important for its viniculture since Roman times, and the city walls were crowned by a glorious Catholic Cathedral dedicated to Saint Nazaire at the city's highest point.

The crusaders reached the outskirts of the town on 21 July 1209 and were met by the city's bishop, who tried to negotiate a peaceful settlement with the army's commanders. As the soldiers and squires pitched their tents, the bishop was sent back into the city with the message that its citizens would be spared, if they would hand over their heretics. The bishop had a list of 222 named individuals, mostly Cathars, but when these terms were discussed in a public debate, the citizens roundly rejected them. The bishop then asked the Cathars to leave the town voluntarily, but the citizens stood by their neighbours, in solidarity, and rejected that proposal too.

So, in the morning of 22 July the bishop returned, with some Cathars who were willing to forfeit their lives, to renegotiate terms with the commanders of the encircling army. As this discussion took place, some ill-disciplined militia, tired of all the talking, decided to take matters into their own hands. They ignored the orders of the attendant knights and entered the ill-defended city to begin wreaking havoc, while calling their hesitant fellows to arms. They were soon followed by the main body of troops, and together they embarked on an orgy of slaughter among the citizens of Beziers. The captains and officers rushed to Amaury for advice, "How do we tell Catholic from Cathar?" they asked.

Amaury is famously said to have replied, "Caedite eos. Novit enim Dominus qui sunt eius; Kill them all, the Lord will know his own."

By the day's end 20,000 citizens of Beziers, irrespective of their religion, rank, sex, or age had been put to the sword. Even Catholic clergymen clinging to the altars of their churches had been run through. As the sun set, there arose a great stench to heaven as the razed city burned, the great Cathedral of Saint Nazaire collapsing on the poor unfortunates who had sought sanctuary within its hallowed walls.

16th June

Elisabeth joined her parents at the breakfast table, enjoying the morning cool and sipping at an espresso, she was bright-eyed and excited, explaining that she would be collecting Robert, her husband, from the airport at Beziers later in the morning. "I told the boys I was going to see their dad; they think I'm going home to Orleans. They're only too happy to be staying here with you while I'm gone, they hate being in the car for hours."
Her mother covered her daughter's hand with her own, "I'll make the beds up and put a basket of things on the table for you."
She scolded Maury when he looked across at her, "Don't worry Commandant, I'll be gone before they get back!"
They'd agreed, in bed the previous evening, that Elisabeth and Robert should be left to it in the privacy of the Mazet, until they'd resolved whatever it was that had put their relationship in crisis.
Maury rose up from his chair, ready to make his way to Rivesaltes and walked around the table to put his arm over the shoulders of both his wife and daughter and to put his head between theirs, "I hope it goes well for you," he said pecking them both affectionately on the cheek. He straightened up, felt for the old Peugeot's keys in his trouser pocket and made his way to the drive.
"Merci papa," he heard Elisabeth call, as he opened the complaining door of the car, he smiled, waved and sat down and waited for the engine to pre-heat.

Lucine had beaten Maury to the Gendarmerie, she was poring over the incident board, paying particular attention to the suicide in Roquefixade. She looked around, as her superior entered and tapped her pen on the date, "The day he jumped was the Summer Solstice."
Relevant or not, Maury told her to note it. As she wrote on the board, Maury outlined the day, "I thought we'd interview Jimenez in Spain today."
The Lieutenant looked at the empty desks at which their two

gendarmes usually sat.

"They worked their normal duties over the weekend, I stood them down until Wednesday," Maury explained.

"My car today?" ventured Babayan, hers had air conditioning. Maury nodded, it was likely to be even hotter, on the Spanish side of the Pyrenees.

As he predicted, it was hotter on the Southern side of the mountains, by two or three degrees. They found the Police Station, a sleek white modern building, on the outskirts of Figueres. When they stepped from the car, it was like stepping into a blast furnace, there was not a breath of wind and the scorch from the sun was unremitting. They crossed quickly to the foyer, relieved to step into its cold air-conditioned comfort. They signed in, and were met at the reception by Suarez, a dark, thick-set man with a pock-marked face who spoke excellent French with a strong Catalan accent, "Jimenez has been charged for drug offences, supply and sale of cocaine. We can't touch him for much else, he's on remand until the magistrate hears his case in a week's time."

He led them to the cell block, uniformed Guardia nodded at the trio as they passed, the male eyes approving Lucine's trim form.

Presently, they were ushered into an interview room, where Jimenez, a tall handsome fellow in his forties, with deep-set green eyes, slicked down hairstyle, and designer goatee turned to watch them enter. Suarez made the introductions in Catalan, the default language of the region, "These detectives want to ask you some questions about your place in France."

Jimenez looked a little taken aback, "I thought my case was being dealt with by the Spanish authorities."

"This is about another matter Señor Jimenez," Maury politely explained, "This has nothing to do with Detective Suarez's investigations."

He motioned to the chair and invited the pimp to sit as he himself took a chair on one side of the table at the room's centre. He reached into a pocket and extracted the e-fits of the three victims, "Do you recognise any of these people?"

Jimenez looked at the e-fits carefully, "No." he said emphatically, "I don't know any of these people."

"What makes you so sure?" asked Maury.

"I have some black friends," Jimenez admitted, "But not many, and my girls are all white."

"Why is that?"

"It's a competitive business. My girls are white, other people have black and Arab girls or guys on their books," Jimenez explained. He looked up at Lucine who stood nearby, "It's not that I am racist or anything. In fact, I have a personal preference for petite middle-eastern girls."

Lucine looked unfazed, "So, all your girls are white Caucasian?" she observed.

Jimenez agreed, "From Eastern Europe."

"Okay," said Maury, knowing that Jimenez was probably telling them the truth, "Do you ever lend the Mas at Périllos to your friends or anything?"

Jimenez' answer was unequivocal, "No."

"What about your clients on the other side of the border?"

Jimenez looked puzzled, "No. Why?"

"It's just that there is a high chance that they were drowned in your pool,"

Jimenez's shock seemed genuine, "No, there's a state-of-the-art security system up there, nobody can get past the cameras without being recorded."

"Who checks the tapes?" Lucine asked.

"The housekeeper, Malit."

"How long are the tapes kept?"

Jimenez suddenly got angry, "My tapes have got nothing to do with you, and you have no jurisdiction."

"Do you trust your housekeeper?" asked Maury.

The pimp rose to his feet and turned to Suarez, "Take me back to my cell, I'm not answering any more of these frog's questions!"

"He's protecting his clientele," Suarez explained as he escorted the two French detectives back toward the front desk, "It's a bloody nightmare trying to run these cross-border investigations. I couldn't seize his CCTV footage or his hard-drives at the Mas either."

The Catalan opened the door into the foyer to let them pass, "Your colleague Wittmeyer couldn't get permission from the local Prosecutor's office, as he was based in Toulouse. Some idiot only allowed a Search Warrant, we couldn't seize anything. Even if we put Jimenez away for the drugs supply, he'll have his assets in France to return to when he comes out."

Again, interference from someone in Perpignan, Maury thought. And he wondered if Guillot and Martinez or the IGPN were any closer to finding out who was corrupt in the Procureur General's office.

"Well, apart from allowing us to eliminate him from our enquiries that was a bit of a waste of time," said Maury gloomily as they drove back towards France, "But I guess we could go and speak to Malit, the housekeeper at the Jimenez Mas, to see if he can tell us anything."

The Commandant watched Babayan drive, she was smooth, safe, and competent and he could safely doze until they turned off the motorway. The modern little Renault struggled on inclines, its three little cylinders roaring loudly but losing power, and although it had all the modern conveniences, he thought he'd trade air conditioning for the torque of his old diesel Peugeot.

They arrived at the Mas, to find Malit in the large garage polishing Jimenez's Ferrari, he stopped and walked towards them when the detectives alighted from Lucine's ticking car. Maury admired the shining red flanks of the supercar and pointed out a scrape on the rear left wheel arch, that spoiled its otherwise pristine coachwork, "Shame about that," he remarked, remembering to speak in English.

"There are a few places where it is damaged, but Señor Jimenez says that those things will be repaired when it next gets serviced. Can I help you detectives?" the housekeeper asked.

"Perhaps you can, "said Maury getting the e-fits out once more, "Do you recognise any of these individuals?"

Malit took the likenesses and studied them very carefully before returning them to the detective, "No, I have never seen these people before."

"Could they have come here when Señor Jimenez was away?" asked Babayan.

"No-one usually comes here when Señor Jimenez is away, it is just me and my family," said Malit.

"You've got CCTV," noted Maury looking up at one of the cameras, "Perhaps they came and used the pool?"

Malit's brow furrowed, "No Detective, I would have reported anyone trespassing when Señor Jimenez is absent from the house. He takes security very seriously."

"Maybe your wife or daughter might recognise these people?"

"I doubt it," said Malit, "Anyway, they are away right now."

"When will they return?" asked Babayan.

"In a few weeks. They've gone home to visit the family in the Philippines..."

"Could we look at the tapes?" Babayan suggested.

Malit suddenly looked stern, "No. That will not be possible. You would need to show me a Search Warrant."

"We should maybe look at the spring?" suggested Babayan.

It seemed a sensible suggestion, they were after all, in the vicinity of Périllos.

"The spring is nearly a kilometre from the road," observed Maury, "I doubt that they were killed in a remote spot and then dumped somewhere much more obvious. Still, maybe we should have a look while we're here."

They were loath to leave the cool of the car and step into the shadow-less glare of the garrigue. Lucine looked at the map, found the feature identified as 'la Caune', and pointed out a barely discernible path that led down the shallow slope into the rocky valley, "I think it's that way."

Maury walked ahead, stepping carefully so as not to turn an ankle on the stones. He paused every now again, to wipe the sweat that seemed to pour from his forehead and sting his eyes, and to check with Lucine that they had not inadvertently deviated from the path.

The sun beat down on their heads and shoulders, the sky was almost white, as if bleached by the unremitting sunshine. Once away from the road, the place felt lonely and eerily quiet, only grasshoppers clicked as they rose up from the low-lying vegetation as they brushed past. The ghost village of Périllos slipped out of sight, and only the path betrayed the presence of humans in this windblown landscape. Today though, not a breath of wind stirred to rustle the foliage or cool the surface of their sweating skin. Presently, the slope steepened, and the detectives found themselves picking their way down an increasingly difficult path. Thorns scratched at their clothing and exposed skin, and Lucine found herself agreeing with Maury's assessment, that the victims were unlikely to have met their demise at the spring.

Eventually they reached the bottom of a small ravine, bone dry, and there yawned a cave's mouth. They entered cautiously, glad of the cool in its interior, their eyes adjusting to the gloom. The floor descended steeply from the entrance, to a level floor of coarse sand which deadened the sound of their footfalls. The only noise was of trickling water from somewhere in the dark. The cave opened up into a cathedral-like space, and they could see the vestigial remains of stalagmites and stalactites. A crack in the rock, way above them, let a little light filter into the space. Now, they could see the spring, a slow trickle from a fissure in the rock-face at the back of the cave, at its foot, a small pool and darkened sand where the water soaked away into it. The pool could only be twenty-five centimetres deep at most, Maury looked into the clear water, and could see the bottom. "The entrance to the Netherworld..." he muttered.

"What's that?" asked Babayan.

"Ah. Well, according to our friend Vincent's leaflets, this is the doorway to Hades," Maury looked around himself at the cave, ten metres deep, five wide and five high, "I thought it might be a little more impressive than this..."

He put out a hand into the ice cool spring water, "And I always imagined the Styx to be a river!"

Lucine, hardly seemed to be listening, she was looking at the cave wall where a constellation of crosses or stars had been carved into the living rock. The pattern seemed familiar, she realised with a start that there was a remarkable resemblance to the patterns engraved on the reverse of the pendants they'd found with the bodies. She used her mobile phone to take photographs of the carvings, the flash lit the interior for brief moments and the detectives could see that there was more evidence of the cave's use, there was wax from where candles had been placed on ledges, and an altar-like outcrop covered in a dark stain that looked suspiciously like blood. There were also bare footprints in the sand of the floor.

While Babayan's camera documented the details of the scene, Maury scraped and dabbed with a small forensics kit at the stains on the altar. He felt suddenly cold, at the thought of what the rituals that had been performed may have been. He wanted to be out, to be back into the sunshine with its heat and light, but he made himself still to absorb the cave's dank atmosphere, to try to visualise their three victims here. He looked again at the pool, there was sand at its bottom, if they had been drowned here surely there would be sediment in their airways or clothes? Lucine, too pulled her shoulders together, as if feeling the cold. It was time to go, Maury raised his chin towards the entrance with a barely discernible tilt of the head and the Lieutenant led the way back up the slope towards daylight.

A raptor rose up from the valley floor, once they emerged into the sunshine, its great wings flapped, and it cawed in warning or alarm. Maury stopped for a moment and looked back at the cave's half-hidden entrance, "I don't think they were here," he said.

They sat in silence, poring over the evidence that had so far been gathered. On the office walls were photos of the gulley and its gruesome contents, the e-fits were headers to each individual's coroner's report. Their titles were depressingly anonymous; male one, female one, female two, infant one. All three had, so-far, unexplained pre-mortem injuries including fractures and burns, and all three adults had died by drowning in fresh water.

Babayan agreed with Maury's assessment that their best lead, up to now, was the link to the suicide in Roquefixade. The hand-made garments, footwear and Gema Abraxas confirmed the link to Ariege, and a high likelihood that there was also a quasi-Cathar element to be investigated.

Maury looked again at the notes posted to the walls of the incident room. Something still nagged, a feeling that there was still evidence to find in the vicinity of Périllos, and he knew better than to ignore that gnawing in his gut.

His musings were interrupted by Pratt who passed over a thick wad of reports he'd been compiling, "You might be interested in these Sir," the gendarme said, "Now that Jimenez is in custody, a lot of locals are coming forward with information about comings and goings at his Mas."

"We still need to establish where they drowned," said Lucine tapping the local map, "I doubt it's the spring at La Caune."

"That leaves Jimenez's pool," observed Maury, opening the file that Pratt had passed. He looked over a few lines of testimony, distinctively high-end cars going to and fro, strangers in evening wear, people – including dark-skinned foreigners - in costume. He looked up and addressed Renaud, "Get me the local magistrate on the line, I need a search and seize order for Jimenez's Mas and everything in it!"

Renaud nodded, "I'll get right on it, Sir," he said.

Now the senior detective turned to Pratt, who was looking at him expectantly, "That pimp's got a scarlet Ferrari, I want to know where the bastard's been seen in it, I want to know who's had dealings with him locally."

"I'm on it, Sir," said Pratt looking happy to have been given a more proactive task.

Renaud looked up, and held out his phone's receiver, "I have Maître Drouet, the local magistrate, on the phone for you sir."

Maury turned to Babayan as he crossed the room, "Tell the station commander we need his men for a raid on Jimenez's Mas."

Once again, the Jimenez Mas was crawling with police officers. Forensics men were removing pool filters, and putting various items into hermetically sealed bags. The pool itself look cool and inviting, especially to men to who had to don overalls in order to accomplish their work, but the heat could not detract them. Local gendarmes, including Renaud and Pratt, were scouring the outdoor areas while the two lead detectives, Maury and Babayan, were following a reluctant and distraught Irlo Malit towards the strong room that housed the CCTV and alarm systems. The Filipino caretaker had protested loudly when they'd arrived, and had refused entry, despite the search warrant being waved in his face, "Señor Jimenez will not be happy that I have allowed you access, he values his client's privacy, very much!"

He phoned his boss, while the two detectives and the team of gendarmes hovered, awaiting entry, even though they'd been at pains to point out that obstructing a police investigation could result in him being arrested. Despite the pimp's loud and furious protestations, from the inside of a Spanish jail there was little he could do but berate his caretaker and ask for the hand-piece to be passed to Maury, "Those fucking Africans have been nowhere near my place! Your bosses will be down on you like a ton of bricks if you go anywhere near the security videos. I've got protection!"

The Commandant merely shrugged and passed the phone back to Malit.

Now the Filipino pressed buttons on a keypad, to gain access to the security room. The door opened on a bewildering array of screens and recording devices that recorded CCTV feeds from cameras hidden away all over the property. As he stood there wondering where to start, Maury's mobile phone buzzed. Somehow, word of their raid on the Mas had leaked, it was his old friend Pierre, who made it clear that he speaking in his capacity as Inspector General, he was nonetheless apologetic, "I'm having my ears chewed off by some bigwigs down there in Roussillon, and they want you to suspend your search..."

"But I think there may be evidence here that connects this place to the case I'm presently working," Maury protested.

"You can't have anything from inside the house. Especially not the surveillance videos!" the Inspector General said, "On no account are they to be accessed or examined by you or any of your team. Seal the Mas off, the IGPN will take over from you. I'll request that, when they've reviewed the footage, anything relevant to your investigation will be forwarded.

"I'm sorry Maury, that's the best I can do."

Maury understood, there was probably a sensitive and high-powered clientele availing itself of Jimenez's services, including a link to someone in the Prefecture in Perpignan, he suspected. He conceded, not wanting to make things more awkward for his friend or have his own investigation completely halted, "Okay, we'll get the forensic evidence we need and call it a day."

From the corner of his eye he saw Babayan rolling her eyes in frustration.

"It doesn't matter," observed Maury, as they walked the team out of the Mas, "Getting the filters from the pool was more important."

"Won't they have been changed?" asked Babayan, her brow furrowing.

Renaud, who was walking alongside carrying an obviously heavy evidence bag, interjected, "No. It's a totally natural system up here. Rainwater is channelled into plant beds where it filters through organic matter before it goes to the pool. The re-filters are carbon and can last up to five years without being changed."

"So, what's in the bags you're carrying?" Lucine asked curiously.

"Organic matter," guessed Maury.

Renaud grinned and nodded.

There was little more to do, the evening was approaching, although it seemed to bring no relief from the heat. Maury looked on the limpid water of the pool, as the investigators packed their things away and returned to their vans and cars, and determined to take Marie-France and his grandsons to the beach for a cool dip on his return home.

"We'll take a little trip out to Ariege tomorrow," he told Lucine, "We'll have a good look at the Roquefixade case, and maybe we'll turn up something that will help us identify our own John Does."

Maury then turned to Renaud, "How long before the forensics team finish with the filters and stuff from the pool?"

"By the end of the week they reckon," the gendarme replied.

The End of Trencavel

Leaving the smouldering city of Beziers in their wake, the crusaders continued advancing west towards Trencavel's great stronghold, another ancient city, this time founded by the Visigoths in the fifth century, the heavily fortified Carcassonne. By this time, the city was overflowing with refugees driven from the eastern reaches of Languedoc before the advancing Papal army, including a large number of Cathars.

Six days after sacking Beziers, the crusaders appeared at the gates of the city and began assembling their frightening array of siege-engines. The mangonels, ballistas and trebuchets launched their missiles remorselessly at the city's towers, walls and gates, but it was not their salvoes that brought about the fall of the city. The act of cutting the over-populated city's water supply brought Trencavel out of his donjon to parley. Despite his white flag of truce, Trencavel was captured and imprisoned; parched and leaderless the city's defenders were forced to surrender after a relatively short two-week stand-off.

This time the citizens were spared their lives, they were instead forced to leave the city wearing and carrying nothing but the shirts on their backs.

Seeing the great citadel suffering such an inglorious defeat, the surrounding cities of Albi, Castelnaudary, Castres, Fanjeaux, Limoux, Lombers and Montreal all capitulated without a fight.

Some days later, a prisoner in his own donjon, Trencavel passed away in mysterious circumstances, some blamed dysentery, but more likely he was assassinated.

17th JUNE

Setting off early, after meeting up in Rivesaltes, the two detectives headed west, in Maury's old Peugeot, towards the constriction of the Roussillon plain into the valley of the Agly, the area known as the Fenouilledes. They rode in comfortable silence, Maury concentrated on driving, carefully matching gears to road speed and engine load, the engine throbbing and growling as he kept it in its power band. Their sinuous route gained steadily in altitude, taking them up through the Cotes de Roussillon Villages vineyards towards the Pyrenees proper, passing under the ancient 'Cathar' fortresses of Queribus and Puylaurens, before the road fell again, running alongside the white torrent of the Aude River, through the spectacular gorges of the Defile de Pierre-Lys, to the sleepy market town of Quillan.

The road then rose steeply, in a series of tight hairpins up to the Col de Ginoles, where the flora became distinctly less Mediterranean as the temperate influence of the Atlantic began to influence the climate. They continued on across the Plateau de Sault until, at the verdant oasis of Puivert, with its own astonishing castle overlooking the ancient village and its lake, the road rose again, before plummeting steeply into Ariege and levelled out again, on the run in to the old textile manufacturing town of Lavelanet.

As they journeyed, Babayan watched the scenery slip by, every bend and hill-crest opening yet another spectacular view of the Pyrenees, the vineyards being replaced by Box shrubs, then ever-bigger deciduous trees; Beech, Oak, Ash, Chestnut and Black Locust. The mountains became higher and broader, with occasional vistas of the very high snow-capped peaks to the south, that delineated the border of France and Spain. The ancient castles on their 'pogs', were a chain of sentinels, guarding the approaches to the valleys, perched impossibly on limestone spurs, rising ever higher on the mountainside until here, near Lavelanet - the last bastion of the Cathars, Montsegur, rose to giddy heights above the sombre Gorge de la Frau.

The Gendarmerie in Lavelanet looked like a school, a featureless concrete structure, on the main road that led towards Foix. Maury announced his arrival via the intercom box on the steel gate, and was told to enter, park up and they would be met. Presently a large, bald-headed but fully bearded man, in his late thirties, emerged from the building and crossed to the car. Both Maury and Babayan formally introduced themselves to the towering Officer Barthez, who spoke with the thick local accent, and had slow grey eyes under extremely bushy eyebrows. "I thought I'd ride with you up to Roquefixade, if that's okay."

Barthez was still a lowly corporal despite his long years of service. He freely admitted that he lacked ambition and had no desire for more responsibility. He spoke non-stop, once he sat in the front seat that Lucine had vacated, so that he could navigate them to Roquefixade. He told his life story, as the car left the main road and started climbing the single-track road, that snaked up to the mountain village. Maury said little as he drove, he preferred to concentrate on steering and selecting gears. Lucine didn't say much either, the old diesel car was noisy, especially when it laboured, she caught only snippets of the Gendarme's commentary, preferring to watch the road ahead, as it wound through dense forest towards their destination. But they both listened intently, when he at last got to the business that found them here. "We get our fair share of jumpers. Not usually at Roquefixade though, most go to finish themselves at Montsegur. I suppose because it's more famous. I can never understand why they make all that effort to climb up that slope just to jump. You'd think the view would inspire them to keep living, but no. Last year, we had nine jumpers at Montsegur and just the one here at Roquefixade..."

Their arrival at the village, interrupted Barthez, who bid them park near the track that led from the ochre and red tiled village to the castle teetering on the rocks above them.

Although it was cooler here than in the Pyrenees Orientales, due to its altitude, the high humidity made the heat even more oppressive. Barthez led the two detectives along the stony track that led up the mountain until, directly under the overhanging cliffs and the looming walls of the castle, he halted and pointed down at the scree slope below them. It was littered with stones, large, small, lumps of dressed masonry, boulders, and great slabs of eroded cliff. "That's where he fell. He must've hit the rocks, because he was pretty mashed-up," said Barthez, "Some witnesses, parked up where we left the car, saw him jump and called the Gendarmerie. We were up here pretty quick, but there were a couple of German ghouls with a video camera filming when we arrived, sick bastards!" The gendarme shook his head in disgust, "A right old mess it was."

"How did he get here in the first place?" asked Maury, knowing that the deceased would have had to have transport to reach this remote location.

"We asked around, but there were no cars, vans or bikes unaccounted for. That's what you're here for, is it? To find out who he was?"

"Yes," confirmed Maury, without expanding on his reply, even when the gendarme's brow furrowed in puzzlement, as he stood momentarily mute waiting for the detective to explain.

Maury looked down upon the scree, nothing now remained to indicate that someone's life had ended there, time and the elements had erased every stain and vestige. Nonetheless, he wanted to see the place for himself, before he and Babayan continued to Pamiers, to collect the pathetic personal effects that had been recovered from this slope.

Then, catching sight of Babayan taking longhand notes, Maury asked their guide if he himself kept a notebook.

"Yes, I do," replied Barthez, "But everything in it will have been transferred to the official report."

The Commandant was seasoned enough to know that the official report would have been sanitized, the notes taken at the time would be rich with the incidental detail a forensic investigation might need. "You've still got your notebook, haven't you?"

"It's at the Gendarmerie. My handwriting's awful, and there will be a lot of spelling and grammar mistakes," confirmed Barthez with some embarrassment.

"You'd be happy for us to have a copy of the pages you wrote at the time?" asked Maury.

Barthez nodded, "I suppose so. What do you want to do now?"

Maury looked up, "We might as well see where he jumped from."

Despite his age and his middle-age spread Maury, to his own great surprise, reached the ruined castle before his companions, and enjoyed the vista stretching before him while he caught his breath and waited for their arrival. The view was amazing, under a blue sky, that darkened in hue as it rose heavenward, stretched the forested flanks of mountains, atop which could be seen the still-snowy pistes of the Monts d'Olmes ski resorts. To the east Montsegur rose, prominent on its lonely spur, then to the west the valley ran away slowly down to the Ariege, unseen under the misty massifs that soared upward into the craggy peaks of the Pyrenees.

Babayan and Barthez arrived together, the big gendarme silenced by the exertion of the climb, she wide-eyed at the panorama. Already, Maury had realised, that to see where the man had actually jumped from, meant a dangerous climb along the crumbling walls, to a corner perched on the overhanging cliff. There was no room for two people atop the loose stones, the man had either deliberately jumped or fallen alone on the wrong side of the wall. Foul play could be discounted, "I think we'll give going up there a miss," said Maury pointing at the crumbling wall.

Barthez invited the detectives to take coffee in the Gendarmerie canteen, while he went to get the pages of his notebook photocopied. Lucine asked her boss for his thoughts, "Well," said Maury with a sigh, "By our reckoning, this guy was in a relationship with the Arab girl and she was carrying his baby. That would either make or break a man, depending on his state of mind or religion, I suppose."

Lucine nodded, "Or maybe he didn't know," she suggested.

"Do you think that maybe they had some sort of suicide pact?" Maury thought aloud, "You know, some sects commit suicide en-masse."

"Yes, but usually together and using the same method," Lucine replied.

Maury nodded in agreement, her observation was correct.

Barthez returned with the photocopied pages, "I hope they help."

Maury offered his hand in handshake, "Thanks for your help."

"Where are you off to now?" asked Barthez as the two detectives rose to leave.

"Pamiers," Maury told him.

The road to Pamiers led away from the higher mountains, into the foothills and the plains. The land became cultivated, and the endless forests were now managed woodlands. The town's administrative centre was easy to find, in such a low-lying place, Maury simply headed for the tallest structures, the communication aerials of the Gendarmerie Nationale. There, they found the station, and were met at the front desk by a thin, sallow looking sergeant with a brusque, efficient manner that saw him supplying the files and boxes of evidence that the detectives had requested, in just a few short minutes. "Want to check it over here?" he asked as he passed the things across the reception desk, nodding in the direction of a desk bathed in sunlight, washing in from the high lobby windows.

"No," replied Maury, "That's okay, we'll take it with us."

"Sign here," said the Sergeant, opening a ledger and offering a pen.

On the route out of Pamiers, Maury pulled the car into the parking area of a rustic little restaurant. The waiter who met the detectives at the door appraised Lucine, with a lingering look over her curves, then almost tutted at Maury before asking where they'd like to be seated. Maury asked for a large table on the covered terrace. The waiter asked if they were expecting others in their party and was exasperated when Maury replied in the negative and asked for a table tucked away in a corner. Then, the man actually tutted, pointed at a table in the otherwise empty restaurant, and went to fetch menus, as the police officers settled themselves into their chairs.

The panoramic view led the eye over fields of sunflowers, bordered by tall poplars, with forested foothills in the middle-distance and high mountains beyond. Clouds were bubbling up over the snowy peaks.

"Think it will storm soon?" asked Lucine.

Maury looked at the cumulus, it was white and puffy, and this area was famous for afternoon thunderstorms that might break the heatwave they were experiencing. He shrugged, "Perhaps."

The waiter came back, and asked if they wanted anything to drink. They both ordered sparkling water and Lucine looked over the menu as the waiter told them the day's special dishes. "I'll have the esclivada please," said Lucine decisively.

"Make that two," agreed Maury.

When the waiter nodded and left in the direction of the kitchen, Maury excused himself and followed the man off the terrace. He returned a few minutes later, to put the evidence folders and Barthez's notes from the car onto the table, he obviously meant this to be a working lunch.

While the Commandant looked through the official reports, Babayan looked over the gendarme's handwritten notes. The writing was scrappy, and the notes seemed unordered, and, as he'd freely admitted, Barthez's spelling and grammar were atrocious, but there was a clear narrative.

On arrival, the responding Gendarmes had been met in the car park by the witnesses who'd called the emergency services. The Gendarmes had beaten the Fire and Rescue Services to the scene. Barthez and his partner had gone ahead to secure the area. What met them was a gruesome scene, the unfortunate jumper had burst when he'd fallen onto the rocks of the scree slope. The officers were disgusted to discover that the scene was being filmed by a couple of German women, ('lesbian ghouls' he'd scribbled in the margin) who'd been asked to desist and return to the car park to await interview. When assistance, in the form of the local Mountain Rescue Team, arrived and took over, the gendarmes walked up to the castle, but found no-one there and no evidence of belongings or a note. The mountain rescuers had meantime documented the deceased's remains and had begun to clear away the carnage.

Maury had those photos in front of him, the returning waiter, catching sight of them, paled as he placed two glasses and a large bottle of sparkling water on the table, "Oh, you're police officers, then?"

"Yes," Babayan confirmed with a smile.

The man hovered, as if wanting to ask more, then decided that he'd better withdraw, "I'll let you get on then."

Lucine returned to the notes.

After leaving the Mountain Rescue team to their task, Barthez and his colleague returned to the village to interview the witnesses. First, there was the couple who'd called the incident in, they'd seen it from their breakfast table, under the awning stretched from their camper van.

Then, they'd found the German 'ghouls', who it seems, spoke very little French. They were alternative types travelling in a converted school bus, Barthez had scrawled 'hippies' near their contact details. They had also witnessed the fall from below the castle, so had only really seen the aftermath. The younger woman of the two kept mentioning seeing a woman jumping from the walls at Montsegur. This entry had been crossed out but was still visible.

The food arrived, and their study of the documents was interrupted. Maury asked for a glass of red to complement the dish, and they resumed studying as they ate. They forewent dessert, the main meal had been generous, and Maury settled the bill as Lucine gathered the documents together.

"We ought to get the video off the German women who filmed the body," thought Babayan aloud.

Maury looked puzzled, there was no mention of this fact in the official notes. Seeing that her boss was ignorant of this incidental fact that Barthez' notes had provided, Lucine explained.

When he nodded in understanding, Lucine tried the mobile number that had been given, several times, as her boss drove them back towards Perpignan, but to no avail. Feeling a little travel sick, Babayan decided that she'd better enjoy the journey, as they headed back east towards the Mediterranean.

Cabaret and Minerve

From their newly won prize of Carcassonne, the confident Catholic army wheeled north to deal with the defeated Trencavel's main ally, the lord of Cabaret. The crusaders advanced towards the Montagne Noire, to find themselves constricted into the deep valleys of the Orbeil and Gresilhou rivers where they found themselves under an impressive array of four castles that operated as a single entity. These four castles, known as Lastours, were built on a high rock wall, so the siege engines engines they were laboriously dragging with them, were next to useless in such a constricted area.

Nevertheless, the Catholics settled themselves in for a long siege, but every time they concentrated their efforts on one tower or another, they exposed their flanks to the defenders from the others. Frustrated, the crusaders kept at it for the whole of the late summer and autumn of 1209 hoping to succeed by attrition. But with the onset of winter they turned their attentions elsewhere. For now…

Reinforcements and fresh troops arrived to bolster the Crusader's ranks in the new year, and Simon de Montfort decided to take his thwarted army on an excursion east. In March 1210, the town of Bram capitulated after a short and easy siege. Buoyed by this success, the army's attention turned to nearby Minerve, known to be harbouring a number of displaced Cathars.

Minerve's fortifications and natural geography, meant that it could not be taken by storm, this was to be another war of attrition. Four trebuchet's were set up to pound away at the town's defences, three targeting the gates and the largest, known as Malvoisine, or 'bad neighbour', by the defenders, concentrated its fire on the town's known weak spot – the well.

After raining down missiles on the town's 200-strong garrison, its people and the Cathar refugees for six weeks, the

Crusaders succeeded in destroying the town's water source. The garrison commander raised the white flag of surrender and sallied forth to negotiate terms.

Simon de Montfort was inclined to be lenient, the town had suffered appalling damage, but his co-general, the Abbott Amaury, wanted blood. He agreed that the town's soldiers and townspeople should go free, but the Cathars they sheltered should be surrendered.

The Cathars were lined up, and Amaury offered them life if they should recant their faith, or death in flames should they refuse. He had fires lit to illustrate his point. One-by-one the Cathars made their choice, three women in their number chose life, the remaining 140, chose the fire, some even walking voluntarily into the flames without waiting for their executioners.

18th JUNE

Maury relished these little moments, sitting on the light-washed terrace of the Mas with his wife and a small coffee, as the sun rose. He could contemplate and muse, listening to his internal voices. He and Madame Maury had hardly had any of these moments since they'd agreed to look after Elisabeth's boys. No matter, despite her fatigue, Marie-France looked happy and was glowing with contentment. "I thought I'd take the boys to the water park at Saint Cyp' today," she said.

Maury nodded in approval, that was a great idea, "Any word from Elisabeth?" he asked.

"No, but their car is parked near the roadway."

"The boys won't see it will they?"

Marie-France shook her head, "No, I don't think so. You'd have to be looking for it."

Maury chuckled Marie-France had obviously been looking for it herself.

A Jay flew from one tree to another in an arc, its bright plumage sparkling against the shadow. They watched as it settled on a branch of an oak, then void itself in a great dollop, that landed with a splat on Maury's old Peugeot. Madame Maury laughed, and at this signal Maury rose, walked behind her and kissed the fragrant warmth of the top of her head, his arms falling to cradle her shoulders, "I'll see you tonight," he said, reluctant to leave.

The sound of the boys rising to meet the day galvanized him, he grabbed his keys and his mobile phone and headed off to work.

The little investigative team met up in their room in Rivesaltes, the sun had risen once more into a cloudless sky. The clouds that had bubbled up over the high Pyrenees had vaporised, without giving rain. Laid before them on a table, was the evidence that Maury and Babayan had collected from Ariege.

Maury turned first to Renaud, "I'd like you to turn over the physical evidence to the forensics people in Perpignan. You can chase up the results from those water samples, while you're there." Renaud nodded and made off with the hermetically sealed box, in which the articles were stored, he looked happy to have been given a task that took him away from the office.

Maury turned next to Babayan, "I'd like you, to keep trying to get hold of the Germans, for the video we talked about yesterday," Lucine nodded, but Maury continued, "I'd also like you to contact the other witnesses again, there might be details about the incident they might have since remembered."

"I'm on it," Lucine replied, consulting the list of numbers she'd noted.

Maury turned at last to Pratt, "You and I, will take another little trip out towards Périllos, to see if we missed anything."

Pratt looked surprised, "Want me to drive sir?"

The lead detective nodded, "If you like."

Once again, Maury found himself looking down into the deep culvert in which the remains had been found. He looked about himself, the road on which he stood, sloped up toward Périllos, and down toward the intersection with the Opoul-Vingrau road. Several metres away, were worn areas of verge where cars had pulled in off the road, the vegetation flattened by the passage of tyres. Reasoning that the unfortunate victims would have had to reach the area from the direction of either Opoul or Vingrau, rather than the dead end that led to Périllos, he began to walk down the slope. Pratt, sitting at the controls of his Gendarmerie van, slowly followed, grateful for the air-conditioning that moderated the sun's intense heat through the windscreen.

Maury continued walking without haste, looking about himself, as he went. There was couch grass on either side of the road, broom, heather, box, and privet but precious little else by way of flora. There was little evidence of the activities of man, except of course for small items of rubbish, but nothing to pique the detective's interest.

Eventually, sweating and his feet burning hot through the soles of his strong shoes, Maury reached the junction on the Opoul-Vingrau road. East the road would drop towards Opoul, Rivesaltes and the Mediterranean. West it rose towards a col, before dropping sharply down the side of a dramatic cirque towards Vingrau, Tautavel, Estagel, the Agly valley and (eventually) to Ariege. Pratt's van came alongside, and through its window the gendarme proffered a welcome bottle of water, "Which way sir?" he asked.

Maury guzzled greedily, wiped his mouth with the back of a hand and looked west, "Towards Vingrau I think," he replied.

Maury's head swam in the heat, like the mirage that floated over the super-heated tarmac, but he continued his walk regardless.

The first kilometre led him up the slope of a limestone plateau, on either side water had eroded small canyons in the soft grey stone, it was almost a moonscape. Again, there was little evidence of man, but Maury reasoned that is was along this route that the unfortunates had travelled, if indeed they had come from Ariege as they'd surmised. So, he continued, deciding that once he'd reached shade, he'd call the exercise off. At last the land rose faster than the road and the metalled surface converged with a canyon, where it constricted under grey bluffs.

It was here that Maury found shade, he sat drinking the remaining water from the bottle he carried, as Pratt parked up his van. He noticed that green shoots were sprouting from blackened earth on the other side of the gorge, and that the white-washed stones of the tightly contoured road's parapet were damaged by the glancing blows of passing traffic. No wonder Jimenez' Ferrari had sustained damage; such a wide car would find such roads almost impossible to negotiate. Someone had not been so lucky, in the rocks below the road lay the rusting hulk of a crashed car. Looking at the car, it was evident that here was the source of ignition that had caused the wildfire – the blackened earth on the opposite slope.

As he locked his van and alighted from it, Pratt wondered what the detective could be up to, he crossed to look down into the ravine. Maury was making his way down the slope, he'd obviously seen something of interest. The viewpoint changed as Pratt walked towards Maury, he could see that the detective was making his way to the burned-out shell of a car, caught between boulders on the slope below the road. Its alignment led the gendarme to conclude that its driver had lost control on the narrow and sinuous tarmac above. He too, made his way gingerly down the steep scree slope towards the wrecked car.

When Maury reached the car, he began looking carefully over it. Little remained, except the badly crumpled shell and its metal components, all traces of rubber or plastic had gone, it was hard to even identify the make or model.

Pratt wondered what Maury was looking for but realised quickly that he was trying to locate the VIN number, its unique identifier, stamped somewhere under the windscreen. He looked again at the wheels and the shape of the body, the heavy-duty build suggesting that it might be a German car. If it were a Volkswagen, the VIN was usually in the spare wheel-well.

Pratt told Maury so, and between them they managed to prize open the tailgate. While Maury held the tailgate open, Pratt used his mobile phone's camera to record the near-indistinct digits.

Both smeared with rust and ash, the policemen returned to their van, and Pratt extracted a pouch of wipes from the glove box. Grateful for the cooling and cleansing square of cloth, Maury thanked him.

When Babayan's eyes were turned toward him Maury felt self-conscious; his clothing was still sooty, rust-stained, and sweat-drenched from his excursion into the ravine. He noticed that Pratt had gone straight off to interrogate the Vehicle Database, to see if he could find out more on the crashed Volkswagen. But Lucine, once she'd heard about her superior's work, reported that she'd at last managed to contact some of the witnesses to the Roquefixade suicide, although she'd only been able to leave a message with the Germans, who were their main interest. None of the witnesses that she had managed to contact, had anything useful to add to the testimonies that Barthez and his colleague had gathered at the time.

By his absence, it was clear that Renaud had still not returned from his errands in Perpignan. But, nevertheless, both detectives agreed that at last their investigations seemed to be going somewhere.

Pratt soon looked up from the screen and reported his findings from the Vehicle Database, "The car is registered to a certain Monsieur Eric Tradot from Albi."

Another strange coincidence, thought Maury, the Cathars were also known as Albigenses because they were denounced as heretics at Albi, "And has anyone reported the car involved in an accident, missing or stolen?" he asked, "Or the man himself, for that matter?"

"It doesn't seem so, but I'll give the home number a call," replied Pratt, already pressing digits on his phone's keypad.

Babayan, meanwhile, was once again trying to contact the witnesses to the Roquefixade incident. Suddenly, she was speaking in English to someone and waving her superior over, "Hello, this is Lieutenant Babayan of the Police Nationale in Perpignan...No, nothing for you to worry about...We understand that you witnessed a suicide at Roquefixade last year...Yes...That's right...We wanted to speak to you further, if that's possible...Oh! Really?...Yes, I'm sure that something can be arranged...You had a video...You still have it?...Good...Okay, I'll speak to my colleague and I will ring you back presently to make arrangements...Thank you, speak to you soon."

Lucine looked up at her boss as she hung up, "That was one of the Germans who witnessed the suicide. Apparently, they are back in the area after a trip to Andorra, they reckon to be back in the Montsegur area tonight, so they suggest we could interview them there tomorrow morning."

Maury though for a moment, "Yes, get back to them, we'll visit them tomorrow morning. Find out exactly where, and suggest a time, so we can make arrangements."

Pratt interjected with more news, "I got hold of Monsieur Tradot, and he says his son is using the car. He wasn't aware that it had been stolen or crashed. He hasn't heard from his son either, but didn't sound concerned, says that they've been estranged since the death of the son's mother a couple of years ago."

Pratt flourished a note that the detective glanced at briefly, saw that it gave the son's name and date of birth, and handed back to the gendarme, "Find out what you can about this Sebastien Tradot."

"Yes sir," said Pratt tapping once more at the keyboard of his workstation.

Maury wondered if he had a clean shirt anywhere, when Babayan reported back, "We've a rendezvous at 10am tomorrow with the German people."

Maury nodded, then asked, "Where?"

"The Camping at Lavelanet."

"That's good, we'll make an early start from here tomorrow."

He'd only just sat at his desk and started opening drawers, to see if he'd thought to put a spare shirt there, when Pratt stood before him and put a sheaf of papers in front of him. Maury fanned the papers out, on them was everything that could be found on the driver of the crashed Volkswagen.

"It's not much," explained Pratt apologetically, "But there were some academic references to him that I printed out too."

Lucine rose from her own desk to pore over the paperwork from over Maury's shoulder. Maury hoped he didn't reek of body odour.

Sebastien Tradot was born in Albi twenty-six years ago. He studied Humanities at Paul Valery University in Montpelier, finishing his studies there about two years ago, around the time that his mother – a veterinarian – died, obtaining a well-regarded master's degree. Since then, nothing.

The young man's official photo showed an attractive, slim-shouldered young man, with green eyes and dark-blond hair. He was of average height, 174 cm, and had no distinguishing features.

Lucine reached down and put her finger on the description, "He could pass for our suicide at Roquefixade," she remarked.

Maury looked again at the picture of Tradot, "Mm, yes perhaps," Maury acknowledged.

Babayan was right, this man could well be the suicide at Roquefixade, so how did his car end up in a ravine at least three hours' drive away? "It's worth pursuing Lieutenant," he agreed, "Is Tradot's DNA on file?"

"No," Lucine replied.

Maury considered for a moment, "Make arrangements for the father to give us a comparative sample"

Babayan looked at the senior detective, as did the other occupants of the office, "Do you really think they might be connected?"

Maury shrugged, "We'll find out."

Lucine picked up a corner of the pile of papers that summarised Sebastien Tradot and his life, "Want me to give these a closer look?"

Maury nodded.

Renaud approached and passed a note to Maury, "If you're going to Lavelanet tomorrow, you might want to visit this place." On the paper was the address of a garage. "It's where Tradot's car had its last Controle Technique," the gendarme explained.

Termes and Terms

In August 1210, the crusading army marched to the south of Carcassonne to lay siege to the castle at Termes. They were harried en-route and upon their arrival by raiding parties sent out from Lastours, by the doggedly determined Cabaret.

Situated in the arid Corbieres mountains, the besieged castle, just like those of Carcassonne and Minerve, suffered from a shortage of water. Except this time the shortage was a natural occurrence rather than an act of war. The castle at Termes is protected on three sides by formidably deep gorges and so relied on water stored in man-made cisterns built atop the promontory upon which the castle sits. After an exceptionally dry summer and autumn, these water reserves were nigh on exhausted. So, the castle's custodian tentatively sued for terms.

However, when the crusaders went to possess the castle they were met by a defiant hail of arrows. A heavy overnight rainstorm had refilled the cisterns and the defenders had decided to hunker down and continue resisting, instead of surrendering.

The situation was at an impasse, the crusaders could not take the castle and its defenders could not break the siege. However, by November, after four months of resistance, the situation, due to disease and hunger, within the castle became untenable. So, under the veil of a night-time downpour the garrison, the villagers and their Cathars attempted to melt away, abandoning the castle, and tried to make good their escape. Unfortunately, their flight was discovered, the alarm was raised, the fugitives rounded up and put to death by soldiers of the encompassing army.

Such wanton bloodshed being inflicted, so cruelly, upon their kinsmen, and their subjects, as well as the Cathars, alienated several high-ranking lords of Languedoc, including Raymond of Toulouse who was excommunicated (again) for his dissent, so they decided, by the time the crusaders returned to the field in March 2011, to once again, change sides.

20th JUNE

Maury's hope of a cool start to the day evaporated, as the sun rose and warm light probed into the valleys that would normally preserve some cool and moisture from their rivers and dewfall. But even the deep valleys of Ariege seemed parched, the grass yellowing in the normally verdant emplacements of the Camping Municipal of Lavelanet.

Somehow Maury had expected the Germans they were to interview to be impoverished young hippies driving a converted bus. But the couple sitting at table under the awning of chrome and white behemoth of a campervan, were middle-aged, pink, prosperous and pampered. The thicker set one, Dianne, stood to introduce herself, and Maury guessed her to be around her middle forties; tall, filled-out, a paunch, grey shoulder length curls and glittering blue eyes. Her wife, Ilsa, was also tall, handsome, with John Lennon glasses and natural blonde hair worked into a long, thick plait, and enormous unfettered bosoms in a shapeless sky-blue dress.

They invited the detectives to partake in a coffee, an offer they were glad to accept after their long drive from Roussillon. Together, they sat at the table in the awning's shade, looking about them at the quiet pitches. The wooded slopes of the containing valley and the poplars that shaded the site were already autumnal with stress, under the inevitable blue and cloudless sky.

Forgoing any small talk, Maury got straight to it, remembering to speak in English, their common language, "We understand that you were witness to a suicide in Roquefixade, and that you may have a video of the incident? We were hoping it may help us to find out more about him."

"That was a horrible thing to see," admitted Dianne.

Ilsa nodded in agreement, her face grim.

"We did not expect it. We were on our way up to the castle, when the poor man fell. I was filming Ilsa, we were making a little film of our visits to the Cathar castles. Suddenly he was there, falling – like a bird – with his arms out, dressed in white. I couldn't help myself, I turned to watch and filmed him crashing onto the rocks!"

"Was there anyone else up at the castle?" Lucine asked.

"Oh, there were a few people in the village, but no, there didn't seem to be anyone up at the castle, just that man by himself."

"I can show you the film if you want," the German suggested, standing up from the table

Maury nodded, drained his espresso, and followed Dianne into the campervan. The detective was impressed with its size and its level of equipment, it was wider than he'd imagined and furnished like a caravan with deep, ghastly-patterned, upholstery. However, it was cluttered with knick-knacks – grotesque little ornaments – probably from their ports of call, and books. The reading was predictable; books on the Cathars, the Holy Grail, the Templars, and pulpy thrillers by best-selling authors.

Ilsa bid the two detectives sit side-by-side on one of the sofas, while her partner opened a cupboard full of DVDs, arranged in alphabetical order according to the handwritten covers. Once the correct disc had been found, it was inserted into the side of a neat display unit and the pertinent chapter selected. The quality of the picture was excellent, Dianne paused the playback and asked if she should continue.

Ilsa asked if she could be excused, "This is too awful to watch!" she explained.

"I'd rather you didn't," said Maury, "I may need you both to talk me through things the camera can't see," he explained.

A little dejected, Ilsa sat on a cushion and watched as Dianne restarted the film.

First, they watched the film in its entirety, the two detectives making notes.

The video began with Ilsa outside the camper van talking to camera, as she explained where they were. The camera panned up, towards the skeletal remains of the castle, above the path that snaked up from the parking, across the flank of the mountain. Cut.

Next, Ilsa was once again talking to camera, the stunning panorama as her backdrop. The video appeared to be recorded under the cliffs, unlike the mountains in the background, which were bathed in warm early morning light, Ilsa was in deep shadow, her form just a silhouette.

A scream, the camera pans suddenly and shakily upwards, and something white falls from the blurry rocks above the track. A sickening, thudding, tearing sound and the camera pans downwards, autofocusing onto a boulder field where the remains of Sebastien Tradot are strewn. A distressed cry from both the Germans, as they realise what they have witnessed, some words in German. Cut.

Figures on the scree, what they are regarding has blanched their faces. There are stains and viscera on the stones, bloodstained vestments on a bloody torso. Cut.

The video did indeed make harrowing watching, and Maury apologised to Ilsa for making her relive the episode again. The Commandant looked to his fellow detective, but Lucine silently shook her head, "I think the film speaks for itself. May we have a copy?"

"Of course," replied Dianne.

"Do you have the original uncut footage?" asked Babayan.

"Yes, on my laptop," the German admitted.

Babayan extracted a memory stick from her bag, "We'd prefer that, if possible."

"Of course," said Dianne, opening a drawer which converted ingeniously into a workstation.

"Do you have any idea who that man was?" asked Ilsa.

"That's what we're investigating," replied Maury.

"You don't think it was murder, do you?"

"Why do you ask?"

"Well, we thought maybe he was trying to do what the person in Montsegur did the year before."

"Oh?" said Maury, his interest piqued.

"Ah! It may not be real," interrupted Dianne, as she transferred files from one digital memory to another, "Most people who have seen it think it's a hoax!"

"Could I ask, what it is you're talking about?" asked the detective.

"Oh. Some video uploaded by a grail hunter last year on his blog. I can play it once I've done this," Dianne explained.

"Would you like another coffee?" asked Ilsa, her huge breasts almost escaping her dress as she rose from her seat.

Once she'd accessed the blog, Dianne scrolled down until she found the video. Then, satisfied that everyone had their eyes on the screen she double clicked the title "Esclarmonde at Montsegur?"
The camera pans to the pog of Montsegur, blurred then sharpening, as the autofocus responded to the light, the castle walls are silhouetted high on the outcrop. There is a female figure standing high on the battlements, brightly lit by the dawning sun on white clothing. The figure outstretches its arms and steps into space, plummeting from the castle walls towards the dark chasm of the gorge below. Then the figure's fall seems to slow, just as death seems inevitable, and it begins to soar like an angel in a wide arc to disappear from view, around the shoulder of the mountain.
"Isn't that just someone in a wingsuit?" asked Lucine aloud.
"Experts say not," said Dianne matter-of-factly.

As they made to leave, Lucine picked up a small item from a shelf, "You should have handed this to the police," she scolded.
Ilsa looked mortified as the detective held up a small gold pendant, seemingly identical to the ones worn by the Périllos trio.
"I wasn't sure it was his, I found it after everyone had gone," Ilsa explained.
"We'll need it for evidence," explained Maury, shaking his head at Babayan as a signal that she should make no more of it.

The garage that undertook the technical control on Tradot's Volkswagen was easy to find, situated almost opposite the Gendarmerie, on the main road that led back into the town centre. The detectives entered the reception area and introduced themselves to the branch manager, who was only too willing to access the garage database to give them the information they requested. However, Sebastien had given his home address as the family house in Albi, the car had failed its first test on a worn front wheel bearing, that had been repaired at the test centre. The manager shrugged, unable to assist further, "Unless," he said, "Jerome, the technician who fixed it, can remember anything."

"I'll call him in, shall I?" the manager suggested.

The mechanic, Jerome, a dark, thin, sullen, young man with dark ringlets entered, nervously wiping grease from his hands with a rag. The branch manager made introductions, then explained what it was the detectives wanted to know.

"Volkswagen Polo, front wheel bearings, SDI engine?"

"That's right," said the manager with a nod.

It was obvious that Jerome lived for cars, his demeanour lightened, "I remember the car. It was peppermint green, all original. I asked the guy if he wanted to sell it," he said, pocketing the rag in his overalls.

"Was this the man?" asked Lucine, proffering Sebastien Tradot's official photo.

Jerome looked at the likeness carefully, then back at Babayan, "Yeah, that's him. He hasn't done something wrong has he?"

"No," interjected Maury, "We are just tracking his movements."

"Well, I don't know exactly where the guy lived, but I do know where he parked his car most of the time," admitted Jerome.

Maury thought it typical that a mechanic would remember a car better than its owner, "And where was that?"

"Out towards Varilhes, near St Martin. At the end of a track, at the end of the village."

Lucine, pleased that she'd thought ahead, asked, "If I get a map from the car, could you show us where exactly?"

"What made you notice it?" Maury asked.

"I come that way to work," Jerome said distractedly, his eyes on Lucine's derrière as she exited the office.

Just then, Maury's phone vibrated. He made his excuses and stepped out to answer. It was Pratt, "The DNA tests were conclusive, the suicide is indeed Tradot. What's more, it seems that he was definitely the father of the Arab girl's unborn child."

Babayan, returning with the map registered Maury's shock. And looked grim when Maury finished the call and conveyed the news.

"We'll continue tracking Tradot's movements for now," the

Commandant said, holding the door open for Lucine.

The Lieutenant spread the map out on the customer service desk. Jerome pored over it for a few moments, then pointed decisively at a point where an unmade road intersected the departmental road D713, at a place called Rasigueres.

"Is it hard to find?" asked Maury.

"If you go this way," explained Jerome tracing a route with his finger, "It'll be on your right as you come out of the village."

The mechanic was right, it was relatively easy to find the track signposted as Rasigueres, but there was little around it on the mountainside but a long farmhouse, which they figured must be Rasigueres itself. They alighted from the car and Maury led Lucine towards it, their approach challenged by two yellow dogs, who left their slumber in the shadows to bay, with their hackles raised, at the approaching policemen. A woman came to the open doorway, her face wide and ruddy, clad in a shapeless pinafore, her strong arms covered in soap suds, "What do you want?" she growled.

"Bonjour Madame, detectives Maury and Babayan from the Police Nationale, would you give us a few moments?" asked Maury flashing his warrant card.

"I suppose," said the woman wiping suds into her apron, "What's it about?"

"We wondered if you might recognise any of these people," said Babayan, holding out a photo of Tradot and a printed sheet with the e-fits of the ditch victims.

Madame looked at them carefully, squinting her yellow-grey eyes, her mouth a severe line in her leathery face. "No. Don't recognise any of them," she said looking up from the pictures.

"We understand that one of them might have parked their car at the junction, a green Volkswagen?" ventured Babayan.

"Yeah. I know the car. It was parked for a while about a year or so ago," said Madame, but she didn't expound.

"Why would it park here?" asked Maury.

Madame shrugged her shoulders, "No business of mine. Probably broken down, it was here for a time, then, not. I really don't know."

"Perhaps someone else who lives here might know?" suggested Lucine.

"I doubt it, people round here tend to their own onions" said Madame, "Now, if you don't mind, I've got a floor to scrub."

"Do you think that Sebastien jumped, because his partner and his unborn child left him?" Lucine conjectured.

"Maybe," conceded Maury, "Or perhaps she left because he jumped. What do we know of the timeline?"

"Well, according to their autopsies, all of them died around the same time. With Tradot we can be exact, with the others we can only make a broad guess."

Maury, who drove, suggested that Babayan look over Sebastien Tradot's pendant, "Does it differ in any way from the others, or is it the same?"

Lucine examined the Gema Abraxas carefully, "It looks the same to the naked eye," she reported.

Silence fell upon the detectives once more, as the car growled up the gradients on the route back to Rivesaltes.

"What about the video, does that help us at all?" asked Maury, presently.

"I can't say I noticed anything on the video the German's took at Roquefixade. The other one is intriguing though. I already sent a link to Pratt and asked him to find out a bit more about it," replied Lucine.

Maury grunted in satisfaction; Babayan had made a good call.

Back at Rivesaltes, the detectives and gendarmes gathered around the incident board.

"Okay, here's what we've established so far," said Maury outlining the case, "Sebastien Tradot appears to have jumped from the battlements of Roquefixade castle in Ariege. At around the same time, his pregnant girlfriend and a pair of siblings, whose identities have yet to be established, end up drowned in a culvert on the road to Périllos.

"Three kilometres from their bodies we came across the wreck of

Tradot's green Volkswagen, a car we know was being used by Sebastien in Ariege at the time all this occurred.

"So, we need to figure why the car ended up where it was found. We need to establish a connection between Tradot and Périllos. With that in mind, Lieutenant Babayan and I will visit Tradot's father in Albi on Monday."

"I'd like you two," Maury looked at the two gendarmes, "to revisit Périllos and wave Sebastien Tradot's photo under a few noses, to see if we can jog someone's memory"

"With respect Sir," interrupted Lucine, "I don't think we can put off visiting Tradot's father until then. No-one's done the 'death knock' yet, he's had his DNA taken so he must know something's up, but he still doesn't know his son is dead."

Maury frowned and looked at Renaud and Pratt, "Is that true?"

"Yes Sir, until now we didn't know that the jumper was definitely Sebastien Tradot," replied Renaud.

"I could do tomorrow Sir," suggested Lucine, "Perhaps I can find out more about the type of person Sebastien was, and what sort of company he was likely to keep."

"Are you sure?" asked Maury, mindful that Babayan had a responsibility to her young charges.

"The grandparents have the children tomorrow," said Lucine, as if reading Maury's mind.

"Very well. Who's going with you?"

"We're both off-duty tomorrow," said Renaud looking at Pratt who nodded in solidarity.

Maury shrugged, "Alright Lieutenant, pick me up from my place on your way past, I'll go with you."

"I found out who posted the video of the jumper at Montsegur," said Pratt.

"That was quick," said an impressed Maury.

"The footage is genuine," continued the gendarme, "It was taken by a local history group, who were there to film the sunrise at the castle. They wanted to see if what they say about the alignment of the windows is true. Apparently, the sun shines through one set of windows on one side of the castle through the other side. They were using a telephoto lens from the mountainside, level with the castle. They weren't sure if it was just someone in a wingsuit, so the guy I spoke to posted it in his blog to see what others thought."

"Has he got the original footage?" asked Lucine, "If he has, it may be higher quality than what's online."

"He's already provided it. I sent it on to the technical department in Castelnaudary, who are seeing if it can be enhanced."

"Good work!" said Maury, in approval.

At the Mas, Marie-France was preparing food for the evening, she was being assisted by her grandsons who were watching her deft fingers prepare salads and other finger-foods, then seasoning and garnishing the exquisite little dishes with various herbs from the garden.

She directed Maury to get fresh cherry tomatoes from the garden, and for Maurice to assist his grandfather. So, hand-in-hand, the detective was led by the little boy into the vegetable patch, to become once again the montagnard peasant he really was at heart. He let his grandson choose the little tomatoes, while he checked on the other produce growing in the plot. When a small basket was filled with the sweet red fruits, grandfather and grandson returned to the kitchen.

After they'd prepared the table on the terrace together, and the feast that would be served, Maury, Marie-France and the boys awaited the arrival of their guests.

Presently, a large black Mercedes-Benz saloon crunched up the drive with the Lafittes – Pierre and Jeanette – stepping from it, to be greeted first by the boys, and then Maury and his wife.

The Lafittes had been family friends for a long time, Pierre had been a trainee detective with Maury, in fact he had courted Marie-France before Maury came on the scene, but had graciously given her up to his romantic rival, and even acted as best man at their wedding and later become Godfather to Elisabeth. Although Maury had shown greater promise as a detective, he lacked the political instinct of his friend who had rocketed through the ranks, while Maury languished in isolated Lozère, where promotion passed him by.

Pierre looked every inch the politician, he was tall, clean cut with steady hazel eyes, his white hair was styled in a military 'flat-top' and he wore tailored suits – except when socialising. Today he was in tailored shorts and a loud short-sleeved shirt.

Jeanette and Marie-France had been best friends right from primary school, they were both intelligent and pretty, and from the same little town in Lozère. Unlike Marie-France, who'd remained slim and shapely, Jeanette had thickened with age, probably because, as the wife of a high-ranking policeman she lived a more urbane lifestyle. She was immaculately coiffed, her hair dyed red, and wore stunning haute-couture clothing. Around her friend though, she became a laid-back, country girl with a heart of gold and a laugh like a drain.

Marie-France and Jeanette, as always, were delighted to catch up with each other and went off clucking like mother hens, as they rounded up the boys and headed towards the kitchen.

Once at the terrace, Pierre turned to Maury, "How's your case going? There's a lot of interest from upstairs. That article in the Midi-Libre certainly raised some hackles. We can't be seen to be racist in any way or manner."

"We're getting there," Maury reported, as he poured water over measures of Ricard for their aperitifs, "We had a break in the case which is leading our enquiry towards Ariege."

"Whatever resources you need are yours," said Pierre taking his glass of pastis from Maury, "we need this thing done and dusted. I want you to report your progress to that pet reporter of yours. What's her name? Oh yes, Petit."

Maury raised his eyebrows, "It's not like you to embrace the press Pierre."

"Well, it might take their eyes off this shitstorm going down in Perpignan."

"Oh?"

"The Procureur General is a bit pissed off to have the spotlight on his department. He got wind of what happened with Verdier and Maître Dubois, and decided it was time to clean house. He's a bit of a boy scout, wants his people to be beyond reproach. When he saw the list of high-brow people frequenting Jimenez's brothel it raised a few eyebrows. A load of public servants have strange sexual appetites, it seems. If anyone saw that list, the Pyrenees-Orientales would be without an administration!"

"So, what your remit?" asked Maury, directing his old friend towards a chair.

"I've got to oversee the Internal Affairs team and report to both the Procureur and the Minister. I also have to keep a lid on it, which is why we took over the Jimenez investigation from you."

"Isn't that case, the Spanish police's?"

"We're sharing jurisdiction again."

"Can I get what I need from you, if my investigation goes back that way?" asked Maury.

Pierre paused, as if gathering his thoughts. "If you come back with a compelling case, then I'll consider it," he said, looking over Maury's shoulder at two shadowy figures walking towards the Mas from the grounds. "Is that Elisabeth?" he asked.

Maury turned, to see his daughter hand-in-hand with her husband Robert, her head on his shoulder, their faces tired but beaming, eyes glittering in the twilight. They embraced in greeting, in typical fashion and Maury understood his daughter's grateful thanks from her warm kiss and a squeeze of his hand with hers. The boys emerged, whooping, from the house, elated to see their parents, gambolling like puppy-dogs for attention.

Marie-France and Jeanette came to the terrace to watch in silent delight at the family reunion, until the boys had spent some of their bubbly energy, and then made their greetings in turn.

After the boys had gone to bed, the adults sat on the terrace enjoying the moonrise and the chirp of crickets in the pines. They sat as couples in the half-light, enjoying the savour of the fine wine that Lafitte had brought as a table offering. Robert was sat with Elisabeth, snuggled together on a sofa, when at her unspoken prompting, he spoke, "We were wondering if we might stay on in the Mazet for a while?"

Maury looked at Marie-France's shining eyes and he spoke for the both of them, "Of course, have the place for as long as you like."

"No dad, we don't want to extend our holiday, we'd like to move down here permanently." Elisabeth explained.

With Marie-France's hand squeezing his, Maury expressed their shared delight.

"Have you thought about what you'll do?" asked Maury of Robert.

"We have savings and I'm hoping we can sell our place in Orleans quite quickly," replied Robert, who'd obviously being giving the idea serious consideration, "Then I was hoping to set up my own business down here."

"You're into systems analysis, aren't you?" asked Pierre, "I might be able to put some work your way."

Looking around at his companion's faces, Maury realised that he was the only person that had been caught by surprise at the news. Marie-France and Jeanette had no doubt plotted behind the scenes, as they had to make the Maury's own move to Aude from Lozère possible.

"Come on dad," said his daughter, her happy eyes sparkling as she reluctantly rose from her husband's side, "Let's make coffee."

To Lastours and Back

In March 1211, the crusaders were back in Languedoc with a particular score to settle against their thorn in the side, Cabaret, the lord of the castles of Lastours. This time, the attackers came in greater numbers, with siege engines more fitting for attacking the four-square towers.

Cabaret knew when to throw in the towel. He had a strong hand, in their previous year's sorties his raiders had managed to capture an important crusader knight, he used his prisoner as a bargaining chip, and surrendered his castles in return for freedom and lands near Beziers.

Next, in the crusader's sights was the place where Dominic had humiliatingly lost his discourse to Guilhabert de Castres, the little town of Montreal. To erase their failure in logical argument, once the town had fallen, they hanged the castle's lord, his senior knights and made a barbecue of several hundred Cathars.

In June Cassés, famous for its Cathar cross upon which Christ is depicted as triumphant - rather than suffering, forsaken and bleeding - also fell to the Catholic army.

After taking Montferrand, after a short siege, from Raymond of Toulouse's brother, Baldwin, their business in the area around Carcassonne appeared done. The crusaders could now turn their attentions to the defector Raymond's capital itself.

They began their siege of Toulouse's strong curtain walls but found that they needed much more in equipment and men against such a large, well-defended city. Simon de Montfort, realising that perhaps his army was over-extended, withdrew to Castelnaudary. Seeing his foe retreat, Raymond's army counter-attacked and laid siege to that town.

The shoe was suddenly on the other foot, the hunters had become the hunted. After several weeks of resistance, de Montfort managed a break-out with the bulk of his army, leaving Castelnaudary to fall. Raymond's counterattack went on to liberate over thirty towns, ending at Lastours where the year's campaigning had begun, nine months previously.

20ᵗʰ June

Beyond the starboard wingtip, the high peaks of the Pyrenees rose, as the plane fell towards the runway, at the edge of the sprawling city of Toulouse. Edward Mason nudged his wife Rosalee, who pulled her eye-shield up and looked at him with puzzled blue eyes. "We're landing, you need to buckle your seatbelt," he said.

Apart from the roar of the engines, the rush of air over the opening wing-flaps and the low murmur of French conversation in the interior of the descending aeroplane, it was quiet and calm. Eddy was glad to be back in the lush green of Europe, after the red aridity of the Arabian Desert, even if the trees looked to be yellowed and the grass bleached by drought.

They passed through customs and passport control without issue, and wheeled their suitcases towards the taxi rank, where Jean-Claude, the owner of the gardiennage that garaged their car, awaited them. He drove them quickly through the traffic to the compound, where he assured them that their own vehicle had been readied. He commented on the weather, and was pleased to hear that his assumption that it was as hot in the South of France as the Horn of Africa was correct. Presently, they arrived in the anonymous Industrial Estate where Jean-Claude kept rows of caravans, motorhomes and cars under sunshades that also doubled as solar panels.

It was a good business model, Eddy mused, as he took the keys to the valeted Dacia 4x4 that had been in the man's care for the last thirty months- he sold renewable energy from the sun and sold its shade too. The Frenchman assured them that the vehicle was in good mechanical shape, had its Controle Technique up to date, and pointed out the new cross-country tyres on which the car sat. He then helped Rosalee into the passenger's seat, loaded their bags into the tailgate and nodded approvingly at the wad of cash that the American pressed into his hand as payment. "Receipt?" he asked as he pocketed the Euros.

Eddy shook his head and shook the man's hand in thanks, "Have a great day."

They used the motorway to make quick headway to Pamiers, the drone of the off-road tyres on the asphalt sending the exhausted Rosalee back to sleep. Eddy was thrilled to see the Pyrenees as the backdrop to the road, rising and dropping in a tarmac ribbon into Ariege. In Pamiers, Rosalee stirred and woke, as Eddy parked the Dacia under plane trees at the centre of town. They alighted and made their way to the Post Office, to collect their mail, cancel the poste restante arrangement and withdraw cash. They returned to the car and while Rosalee, with her spectacles balanced on the end of her nose, sorted through the envelopes, Eddy drove to a large agricultural store on the outskirts of town.

* * *

Maury stirred as the car entered the outskirts of Albi, he still felt a little under the weather after the excesses of the previous night. Together they'd feted Elisabeth and Robert's new phase of life and watched a blood-red moon rise, before retiring. So, when Lucine's car had crunched over the gravel he'd simply fallen into it, and, confident in Lucine's ability as a driver, dozed on their journey north.

The big, red-brick cathedral dominated Albi's skyline as they navigated towards Tradot's address on the western side of the old city, past an otherwise unremarkable town. Turning into an avenue, they were fortunate to find shade under one of the pollarded plantains that leaned over the sidewalks, and parked in its relative cool.

The detectives adjusted themselves and steeled for the unwelcome task of delivering bad news to Sebastien Tradot's father. As they found the house and approached the front door, a small, wiry man in the attire of a golfer exited as they approached, tugging a rattling trolley of clubs over the threshold. He looked the approaching officers up and down and Maury hoped he didn't look as rough as he felt.

Lucine flashed her credentials, "Monsieur Tradot?"

The man nodded, Maury and Babayan glanced at one another, "May we come in?"

* * *

Having settled their outstanding account and loaded the car with the essentials needed for the commune to live in isolation for another few months, the Masons headed south-east, from Pamiers, towards home. Rosalee's hand settled on Eddy's as he changed gears, "It's good to come home. Let's agree not to leave it again."

Eddy knew what she meant, they both wore their three-score years well, but this last couple of years had tested them both, physically and mentally. Had it not been for the insistence of old friends in the Yemen, they had been quite happy to remain retired. But the trip had been worthwhile all the same, they'd accomplished a lot of work to alleviate that war-torn country's humanitarian troubles and earned a tidy sum, that would enable their little mountain community to flourish, without money worries, for a good few years. It was God's provision, they felt, so they'd faithfully heeded the call and left their little community in the hands of their disciple.

* * *

Tradot said little when the officers informed him of his son's death, but the colour drained from his face and his eyes welled.

Maury gave the man some moments before asking the inevitable question, "Do you think your son could have committed suicide?"

Tradot shook his head, "No. No, he was never an outwardly happy boy, but he was stable. Serious. You know what I mean. Inverted, but never desperate..."

"When did you last hear from him?"

"Some time ago. We had a row. He left. He took the car, it was his mother's anyway. Said he was going to find himself. October. He'd just finished University, he was unemployed. Listless. He was of age, it's natural for children to move on from their parents."

Lucine was looking around the room in which they were sat, her eyes settling on a stone-carved fleur-de-lys on the windowsill, "Do you know a Monsieur Jean-Baptiste Vincent in Opoul-Périllos?" she asked.

Tradot blinked in surprise and looked puzzled by her left-field question, "Yes. Yes, I do," he admitted.

"Did Sebastien know him?"

Tradot nodded, "Yes, he's the boy's godfather. A good friend of the family. We served in the army together...What's he got to do with my son's death?"

Babayan shook her head, "Probably nothing. But it was near there, that we found Sebastien's car."

"What? Near Jean-Baptiste's place?"

"Some distance away," Maury interjected, "Would Sebastien go there if he needed help?"

"I expect he would. But you say that Sebastien jumped from the walls of some castle in Ariege. That's some way from Périllos," Tradot remarked.

"We don't think that it was Sebastien who was on his way there..."

"Well, who then?" Tradot demanded to know.

"That's what we're trying to establish," Maury explained. "Did Sebastien ever mention a girlfriend?"

Tradot looked blank, "No. No, he never mentioned one. But we've not spoken for over two years." The sudden realisation that the gulf between himself and his dead son could never now be bridged hit him, his face crumpled, and his body heaved with a primal sob.

* * *

At last, they reached the end of the track that led to their isolated property on the mountain. Rosalee stepped out of the car, to unlock and open the gate to allow the Dacia to pass, she glimpsed the woman at the window of the Rasigueres Farm and raised a hand in acknowledgement, the woman barely nodded in response.

Soon, the car was scrabbling for grip on the pitted, barely discernible track that wound through trees, and emerged some four kilometres further, on the high pastures above the tree line.

Eddy drove carefully, glad that the going was dry. Come rain, the steep gradient and the slippery nature of the terrain would make vehicular access all but impossible. They could see the old Spanish roof-tiles of the Labaouse farm complex, the long-house and the outbuildings they'd renovated years previously, the duck pond and the new windmill. There were figures working the garden plots on the slopes above the house, who stopped and stood to watch the unfamiliar sight of a car wending its way to the gateway that guarded access to the walled boundaries of the domain.

* * *

As they drove away from Albi on the open road, Maury asked what had prompted Lucine to connect Tradot with Jean-Baptiste Vincent.

"The fleur-de-lys on his windowsill," she replied.

"The fleur-de-lys?"

"Yes. Vincent has the same ornament on his windowsill. It's an identification symbol." Lucine explained, "I think that they're monarchists. I suspect that they may be members of the Alliance Royale."

Maury was flabbergasted, "I would never have noticed," he admitted.

"I have an eye for such things," explained Babayan, "My people use peacock symbols to identify themselves."

"What, a statue or a carving?"

Lucine chuckled, "No, usually a picture in the hallway or a mosaic as you enter the house."

"So, who are your people?" asked Maury with genuine interest. He'd already guessed by her surname, "Armenians?"

Lucine took her dark eyes momentarily from the road and nodded, "Sort of..."

"My family is Yazidi. According to some we're Devil worshippers. We just follow mystic teachings..."

"A bit like the Cathars," observed Maury.

"Yes, I suppose so," Lucine conceded.

* * *

Antoine met them as they stepped from the car. The tall, slim Frenchman wore no top over his honed and tanned upper body but wore breeches for manual work, and a straw coolie hat to cover his long dark curls. A smile radiated from his brown, sun-kissed face as he greeted each American in turn, "It's so good to see you," he said, helping Rosalee with her bags, "Did you have a good journey?" His English was fluent yet heavily accented.

Eddy stood straight to ease his lower back from the shaking it had suffered on the way up the track, and looked over the place, noting that all seemed very shipshape and orderly, "It was fine thanks Antoine. There are some supplies in the car to unload. Are our rooms ready?"

"We'll go up, while you see to that stuff being put away, if you don't mind. Rosalee and I, will install ourselves and get changed."

"Let me take Rosalee's things for her. Then I shall see to the goods and put the car away," insisted Antoine, looking down at the small and obviously charmed Rosalee, "I expect you are hungry and thirsty, we eat soon, but there is a bottle of freshly drawn spring water in your room."

* * *

"Tradot seemed more affected by the death of his unborn grandchild than his son," Maury remarked.

Babayan nodded in agreement, her eyes scanning her mirrors as she prepared to overtake a slow-moving motorhome, "I think he half suspected that something had happened to Sebastien, after his DNA was taken for analysis."

Maury looked over the Leviathan as they passed, it had satellite dishes, bicycle racks, ladders and solar panels on its flanks and roof. The old couple piloting it looked inordinately small and frail to be in control of such a large machine. It brought the German's campervan to mind, and the macabre videos they had watched while sitting in its tasteless interior.

"We need to get that Montsegur video analysed," he said aloud, "And we also need to speak to our old friend Vincent up at Périllos, to see if he has been in touch with Sebastien at all, in the last few months. Why can't the damned man have a telephone or mobile, in this day and age?" he complained, then added somewhat philosophically, "Mind you, I wish sometimes I never had to have one either."

Lucine declined Maury's offer of lunch, she saw his extended family awaiting him on the terrace and felt that she'd be intruding on his family time. She waved an acknowledgement at Elisabeth who sat hand in hand with her husband and Marie-France who was arranging the table.

With a pang, she missed her own family – the gatherings around the table where conversation and love always seemed to be served with the food. She needed to phone her brother, to gather her own brood about her.

The Fall of Toulouse

After two years of crusade, the sponsors of the war being prosecuted against the Cathars were becoming nervous; they'd hoped for quick gains. What they had on their hands was a public relations disaster.

The Count of Barcelona, to Languedoc's south, who was championing the Christian cause against the Moors on his own southern border, was particularly concerned. He was outraged at the indiscriminate slaughter of Catholics along with heretics. An otherwise staunch ally of Pope Innocent III, he appealed for the pontiff to reign in the excesses of Simon de Montfort's crusading armies.

Even, King Phillip of France had concerns over the prosecution of the war. So far, his involvement had been distant, he had problems enough with the English to the north, and he, too, didn't want to be associated with the savage bloodletting of Simon's mercenaries. But, his crown had made gains in Languedoc at the expense of the defeated or displaced Languedoc knights whose lands had been so ravaged, because they were now under the control of de Montfort, who had pledged his allegiance and all his gains to the French King.

So, Innocent ordered a halt to the crusade, he feared that the Count of Barcelona, who was related by marriage to Raymond of Toulouse, might withdraw his support from the Catholic's continuing wars against Muslim forces in Iberia and the Holy Lands.

So, 1212 became a year of political posturing and wrangling, a relatively peaceful pause for the downtrodden people of Languedoc.

Despite Innocent's concerns, the Catholic clergymen who made up the Council of Lavaur, rejected the Count of Barcelona's petition to reinstate Raymond of Toulouse, they refused to absolve him, and insisted that the lands he controlled were a safe-haven for heretics.

As a result, the Count of Barcelona allied with Raymond to

stand against Simon de Montfort's crusaders. Innocent was enraged, he denounced his erstwhile favourite and ordered the crusade to recommence.

De Montfort's troops now mobilised against Toulouse, engaging with the Spanish army of the Count of Barcelona on 12 September 1213 at Muret, just south of the great city. Even though the crusaders were heavily outnumbered, they were battle-hardened and better led, they managed to outflank the Spanish cavalry, fatally wounding the Count of Barcelona in the fracas. His dismayed forces, aware that their esteemed leader had fallen, withdrew in confusion. With the field open, the crusaders pressed on, capturing and occupying a portion of the city of Toulouse.

It was a serious blow to the resistance, but things deteriorated further in 1214 when, unable to check the crusader's advance Raymond and his son were forced to flee to England and cede their great city to de Montfort. But the Catholic general lost no momentum, he continued his advance pressing on into the Perigord, to the banks of the Dordogne.

By 1215 the crusaders had solid control of the County of Toulouse, it seemed the battle was ended, little did anyone know that the war would rumble on for another fourteen years...

21st June

He was still seething with indignation and resentment as he parked the car, this was no way to feel with what he had in mind to accomplish. He took deep breaths of fresh air to calm himself and whispered scripture under his breath. *The angel of the Lord encampeth round about them that fear Him and delivereth them.* By the car's clock he had two hours before the sun was due to rise, time to make the climb and time to prepare himself before taking his leap of faith. He put the little canister of Cyproterone Acetate into the glove box, glad that at last he would have no further need of them. With that action, he increased in resolve and confidence, stepped from the car, locked it and placed the key, out of sight, on top of the rear wheel. *Surely he shall deliver me from the snare of the fowler, and from the noisome pestilence.*

The night would soon be morning, the starry sky was already lightening in the east, he paused to savour the moment, and looked up in wonder at the Milky Way. *He that dwelleth in the secret place of the most High shall abide under the shadow of the Almighty.* Below, in the dark valleys, streetlights twinkled and from somewhere reverberated the low barking of a farmyard dog.

Aside from the dark form of a small campervan, illegally parked to overnight in the parking area, there was no-one around as he pressed towards the castle entrance. *He shall cover thee with His feathers and under His wings shalt thou trust; His truth shall be thy shield and buckler.* He passed the ticket office, easily bypassing the barriers that were supposed to prevent unpaid entry to the monument and crossed the flat area beyond, passing by the monument to the Cathar dead there. And, although he could not read the inscription in the dark, he felt a certain solidarity with the martyrs whose death it commemorated. *A thousand shall fall at my side, and ten thousand at my right hand; but it shall not come nigh me.* In company with those long-gone ghosts he began the climb proper, up towards the castle on the spur's high peak. Box shrubs and gorse caught at his loose white garments as he passed. Like the crowds that had plucked at Jesus' hem as he passed, he thought. *There shall no evil befall me, neither shall any plague come nigh my dwelling.*

His anger had dissipated. He concentrated on his mission, driving himself upward on his strong legs over the loose shale of the rough pathway. Each step drove him upward, each step an ascent to heaven, each step one away from the surly bonds of earth, the Cyproterone Acetate, the vagaries of humanity, towards perfection. *And behold, I am with thee, and will keep thee in all the places whither thou goest.*

The devil spoke suddenly, a seed of doubt in the resolve of his mind. Are you really perfect? Yes, I hold to those promises, to what is written, to what I know deep in myself; I am perfect as my Father is perfect. *Because he has set His love upon me; therefore will He deliver me; He will set me on high, because He knows my name.*

"Get you behind me Satan," he rasped. By now the steepness of the slope, its relentless gradient, had him breathing hard. His legs burned with the effort. Why the rush? He asked himself and moderated his pace. *For He shall give His angels charge over me, to keep me in all my ways. They shall bear me up, lest I dash my foot against a stone.* His body was bathed in sweat, even night-time gave no relief from this unseasonal heat. He looked up, but the privet prevented anything other than the stony pathway and the sky above to be seen. *I shall not be afraid for the terror by night; nor for the arrow that flieth by day.* Again, he put himself to climbing, but at an easier pace that allowed his breathing to be less ragged. At a hairpin the panorama opened before him and he was able to see the streetlights of Lavelanet and Mirepoix below him and other neon lamps that lit the dispersed villages of Ariege's hinterland. *As the mountains are round about Jerusalem, so the Lord is round about His people from henceforth and forever.*

He pushed on, and then, in a gap in the shrubbery he saw the feet of the thick walls of the sacred castle that was his goal. The Cathars called this their safe place, "Montsegur", the secure mountain. That is why all but one of the Cathars that took sanctuary here perished in the fires of the Catholic armies that had besieged this place. But, they had erred, for earthly fortresses are no place of safety. *Because I have made the Lord, my refuge, even the Most High, my habitation.* One last push on his aching legs got him to the base of the castle walls. The great stone bastions seemed to be rooted in the very rock of the mountain, so that there was little distinction between the constructs of man or nature, other than the former being dressed to be straighter edged and uniform. *I shall call upon Him, and He will answer me. He will be with me in trouble; He will deliver me and honour me.*

Despite his faith, the pit of fear in his stomach yawned. He prayed for the strength to accomplish that which he felt compelled to do. He looked up to see that a ray of light lit the heavens, as if God were looking down and giving his approval – light in his darkness. He felt his way along the bottom of the great wall. Something slithered off between the stones as his sandaled feet disturbed them and a cold shiver of irrational fear made the hairs on the back of neck stand up. *I shall tread upon the lion and the adder; the young lion and the dragon shall I trample under feet.*

Now the entrance to the castle, a dark archway in its flank, appeared and after hoisting himself over the high threshold how found himself within the ancient enceinte. On the far wall a great stone staircase rose, like the proverbial stairway to heaven. He crossed to it and began making his final ascent, hugging the masonry to stay far away from the un-railed drop. When he reached the top of the great keep's walls his head swam with giddiness at its awful height. He looked about, balancing himself by minor adjustments of his centre of gravity, using his legs and arms until his head stopped spinning. The keep had slit windows like eyes, and he had read that on this day, on this sunrise they would align to the rising sun that he now awaited. The windows looked down sightlessly at him as he girded himself and trod gingerly over the uneven cappings of the wall, towards a lightning conductor spiking upward from the castle's highest point. He could not stop his fingers curling around the metal for safety. His whole body began to tremble, and it took all his determination to force his digits to release, so he could shuffle out to the quoin at the fortress' highest corner.

Far below him the Gorge de la Frau made a pitch black slot between this grey mountain and the next, the eastern sky was warming with yellow and the blue massif brooded at his back. Crows cawed and soared from the ledges of the ruins, catching updrafts under their rigid wings, their orange eyes bearing witness as he raised his arms to make his stance cruciform. *He shall cover thee with His feathers, under His wings shalt thou trust.*

A ray of sunlight lit him as the bright orb lifted itself above the far-off horizon. Swallowing all his fear, mustering all his faith he stepped out into the void. *I bare you on eagles' wings, and brought you unto myself.*

The wind rushed as he plummeted and within himself he heard a still small voice speaking. *Thou shalt not tempt the Lord thy God.*

* * *

They gathered around the board for the day's briefing. Lucine wrote succinct notes under Sebastien Tradot's portrait photo as she spoke, "Sebastien Tradot jumped from the battlements of the ruins at Roquefixade. He had been estranged from his family, his father, since the untimely death of his mother. He has no known history of depression or mental illness.

"What ties him to our three 'John Does' up at Périllos are his clothes, which are identical, his pendant and the fact that he was almost certainly the biological father of the unborn child that one of our deceased was carrying. Also, we have established that he was using the family car, a green Volkswagen Polo that was found in a ravine by the Vingrau-Périllos road. The evidence seems to indicate that the car was travelling in the direction of Périllos when it crashed. In Périllos lives one Jean-Baptiste Vincent, owner and operator of a cafe cum bookshop, who also happens to be Sebastien's godfather."

Maury, Pratt and Renaud nodded their heads in agreement at this summary. Lucine looked at the two gendarmes, "You did show the e-fits of our Jon Does to Monsieur Vincent?"

"Yes," confirmed Pratt, "He was adamant that he'd never seen any of them before."

"Okay," said Babayan, "So, Commandant Maury and I will be re-interviewing him this morning to see if Sebastien has made any sort of contact in the last two years.

"What we do know, is that Sebastian studied at Montpellier. I'd like you both to track down and speak to anyone who may have known him there. Start with his lecturers and his fellow students. Someone among them, might be able to tell us more about his state-of-mind, his interests and life beyond his family."

It amazed Maury, that cyclists still traversed the sun-baked roads of the area. The sun beat down on their arched backs and melted the tarmac under their wheels. Yet still they rode up the ochre slopes, slowly climbing the relentless gradient, a string of sinewy, ageing men, clad in the bright colours of a local club. He overtook them in a roar as he and Lucine drove once more towards Périllos.

The sky, which they were able to see stretching far and wide once they'd reached the col, was cloudless and bleached. The mountains were faded, as if the world had become an over-exposed photograph. Heat-haze danced over the metalled ribbon of the road. Presently, they reached the forsaken village and were surprised by the wind that moved the air around them, but just served to spread heat uniformly into the shelter that shadow normally affords, so it was as if they stepping into a fan-assisted oven.

Vincent came to the door, when Lucine rang the little bell that signalled the arrival of customers to the bookshop, he looked taken aback to see the two police detectives there on his doorstep. He waved down Maury's proffered credentials, "I remember you. How can I help you this time?"

"May we come in?" asked Maury looking towards the sun.

"Of course, of course. Can I get you a coffee?" Vincent asked, leading them into the shadows of the cafe.

Once sat, Maury slid a photograph of Sebastien Tradot onto the table, "Do you know this man?"

Vincent nodded, "Yes, that's my godson Sebastien. Why? Has something happened to him?"

"Yes," said Maury gravely, "I'm afraid he's dead."

The blood drained from Vincent's face, he gulped for air, "When?

How?"

"He jumped to his death, from the castle ruins at Roquefixade on the twenty-first of June last year. Precisely a year ago, today."

Vincent shook his head in disbelief, "No."

Maury tapped his finger down on Sebastien's photo to regain Vincent's attention, "When did you last see him?"

Jean-Baptiste sat back in his chair, his eyes glassy with welling tears, he swallowed, "Around Christmas last year. He passed by to collect some of the things he'd left here."

At Maury's expression, Vincent explained, "He stayed here, just after his mother died. He worked in the shop for a few weeks and we spent the evenings sat in the garden philosophising.

"He was searching for answers after his mother's passing, her death hit him very hard. He felt that he couldn't communicate with his father, so he came here. I've known him since he was a boy. Once he'd gathered himself together, he went off. Said he was going to travel the Pyrenees, something about Santiago de Compostella. He came by a few weeks later, said he'd found what he'd been looking for, went through his stuff, took what he needed and left again."

"Was he alone?"

Vincent nodded his head, "Yeah. Most of his stuff's still here, he left a lot of it, just took some books and some winter clothing, by the look of it."

"Can we see what he left?" asked Babayan.

"Of course," said Vincent, getting up from his chair unsteadily and leading the detectives deeper into the building. The place was simple with white-washed walls and heavy, old-fashioned mahogany furniture, the walls decorated here and there with little reproductions of classical paintings including the inevitable 'Shepherds of Arcadia' by Poussin and Tenier's 'Temptation of St. Anthony'. He led them up the rickety chestnut stairs to a small bedroom, and opened the tallboy next to a single neatly made bed, "His stuff is in here."

Under his watchful gaze the two detectives rifled through the clothing and articles that Sebastien had left in his godfather's safe keeping. There was little of interest, just brightly coloured t-shirts and shorts, some sweaters and trainers, the informal uniform that students tend to wear. Then, in the bottom of a suitcase, a ring-bound notebook, which Lucine passed to her superior. The Commandant quickly leafed through the pages of handwritten notes and doodles. "You don't mind if we take this?" asked Maury passing it back to Babayan, who placed it into a plastic bag and pocketed it.

Maury sat with Vincent for a while, nursing a coffee, saying little, aware that the poor man was obviously distressed by this turn of events, until Vincent asked, "Did Sebastien have anything to do with the three people they found in a ditch up the road?"

Maury considered his answer, this was an ongoing investigation, so he could not say too much, "Yes, it would seem that they're connected."

Vincent went back into himself, absorbing this news.

"Did you have a good relationship with Sebastien?" asked Maury.

"I like to think so," Vincent replied.

"Was there anyone else in his life, apart from you, to whom he could talk?"

Jean-Baptiste looked blank, "I don't know. The boy was sensitive and private, a bit of a dreamer. He liked to talk of esoterics, the wonders of the mind and soul. He had no time for ordinary conversation or gossip. He hated materialism and had ideals..."

Vincent's eyes welled again.

"Renaud messaged me to say that the water samples have been re-compared to what we took from Jimenez's swimming pool," said Lucine as they strode towards the car from Vincent's cafe.

"And?"

"Inconclusive. The water in all the places we tested is so similar that the lab can't be precise."

Maury thought for a moment, as he opened the driver's door to let the car's stifling interior heat escape, "So, Jimenez's pool isn't ruled out."

"No," admitted Lucine.

Something nagged at the back of the Commandant's mind, he felt sure that the pimp's high-class brothel, and its underground enterprise, was still somehow connected to the whole sorry affair. He cursed inwardly that such an avenue of investigation had been effectively closed off to him and his little team.

As they passed by the Jimenez Mas, they found the road blocked by a car transporter reversing into the drive, to collect the pimp's Ferrari. 'Carosseries Junot' was emblazoned on the truck's cab door – so, the Italian supercar was going off to have its bruised bodywork repaired. The truck driver was struggling to turn his long flat-bed lorry into alignment with the car, so Maury stepped out to assist. Lucine too, stepped from the car, and with a police officer to guide on either side, where mirrors could not, the lorry was soon in position. The driver dropped from his cab and thanked them both for their assistance.

"Taking it for repair, are you?" asked Maury in friendly small talk. The man nodded, admiring the thoroughbred's scarlet flanks. Only then did Maury look down at the damage that marred the bright red paintwork, the scarring on its wing. He beckoned Babayan to his side and pointed at the damage, her eyes opened wide at the sight of Peppermint Green paint on the red.

Once Pierre had heard Maury's request, the Inspector General was happy to release the Ferrari to the forensics team, who would undoubtedly confirm that, at some point, it had been in collision with Sebastien Tradot's little Volkswagen. What they now needed was to establish when this incident had happened, so it would narrow down a timeline of the events that led to the deaths of three unfortunates on the roadside.

"We could re-interview Jimenez," suggested Lucine.

"Mm," agreed Maury, wondering if it would be worthwhile. Then, looking around at where they were, he stepped towards the gateway of the Mas.

"Are we going to talk to the housekeeper?"

"Yes," grunted the senior detective, "He might know something."

Arlo Malit was not at all happy to see the police officers, he stood in the doorway and challenged them with some hostility, "You cannot come in here without a search warrant," he barked.

Maury paused, shifting his thoughts into English, he shook his head dismissively, "No, we have come to talk about something else."

Malit was looking past Maury at the Ferrari being off-loaded back onto the driveway, he shouted at the operator, "No! You take it to Carosseries Junot in Perpignan. It must be repaired!" His intervention was in heavily accented French. The recovery man shrugged, ignored the complaining housekeeper, and continued to winch the car off his truck.

"That's what we need to talk about," explained Maury to the flustered Filipino, "The car is going to be examined by our forensics people at the Police garage in Perpignan."

Malit looked at Maury and Lucine in confusion and anger, "But the car has already been examined by the Police."

"We need to look at it for something else," said Maury.

"The damage to the bodywork," explained Lucine in a soft voice, "We think Senor Jimenez may have been in a collision."

Malit looked taken aback, his eyes went wide, "Oh?" he said.

"Can you help us with that?" the Lieutenant asked.

Malit paused, as if weighing things in his mind, then stepped forward, pulling the farmhouse door closed behind him. He led the way to the garage, entered and went to a locker on the back wall. From one of its shelves, he withdrew a ledger, a logbook in which he'd made longhand entries. "I keep records," he explained as he thumbed through pages. He looked up, his finger on an entry, "The damage occurred sometime in June last year. I can't tell you exactly when, but I log all the weekly maintenance I do to the car when I wash it and check the levels."

"May I?" asked Lucine, beckoning for the book.

Malit passed the ledger with some reluctance. The detective identified the entry and photographed it with her mobile phone camera. Then she passed the book back to the Filipino with a smile, "Thank you, that's very helpful."

"Yes, thank you," echoed Maury.

"So, we are managing to put together some sort of timeline to explain the movements of our three victims," explained Lucine, transferring notes from her pad onto the incident board. "Sebastien Tradot jumped to his death on the morning of the twenty-first of June last year. Exactly one year ago.

"His green Volkswagen and the Ferrari of our friend Jimenez appear to have been in some sort of accident on the road between Vingrau and Périllos, in the week between the twenty-fifth of June and the first of July last year."

"That certainly narrows the window of our investigations," commented Maury, for the benefit of Renaud and Pratt, who sat at their desks while the two detectives got them up to speed with developments.

"How do we know it's in that week exactly?" asked Pratt.

"Because," explained Babayan, "Jimenez's housekeeper also looks after his car. Every week he cleans it, valets it, and checks its fluid levels. He keeps records of anything he finds. On the twenty-fifth of June there was no damage, on the first of July he noted damage to its rear wing." She held up her phone so they could see the photo of the entries Malit had made into the logbook.

Maury turned to the gendarmes, "How did you get on with finding people who knew Sebastien at university?"

Pratt looked down at his own notes and shrugged, "I managed to speak to some of his lecturers, but they don't seem to remember a lot about him, other than him being quiet and serious. He met his deadlines and annoyed the other students by asking questions."

"His fellow students say much the same thing," added Renaud, following on from his colleague, "They all say he was quiet, stayed in studying and didn't mix much. One girl admitted dating him, said he was shy and drippy. The relationship didn't last long."

"Did anyone say anything about his state of mind?"

The two gendarmes shook their heads.

Just then the phone rang, Lucine answered it, listened to the voice on the other end and then passed the device to Maury, "Sir, its Barthez from the Gendarmerie in Lavelanet, he wants to speak to you."

Maury took the handset, "Maury here, Barthez, what can I do for you?"

"Hello Commandant, I thought you ought to know that we had another jumper at Montsegur this morning. Apparently, all dressed in white like the one at Roquefixade."

When Maury replaced the telephone's receiver into its cradle, he told his little investigation team Barthez' news. "I think we need to get ourselves over there."

"What do you want us to do?" asked Renaud.

"I want the Gendarmerie's records revisited for the time period Lieutenant Babayan identified. I want Sebastien Tradot's photo and details sent to Mademoiselle Petit at the Midi-Libre, and tell her that his death is definitely linked to the three on the Périllos road. I want her to make an appeal to her readers, for information on any quasi-Cathar sects operating in Ariege who dress in white clothes, wear sandals and have gold pendants hanging around their necks. Someone, somewhere can make the connection for us."

"Is that wise Sir?" asked Lucine.

"I don't know," admitted Maury with a shrug, "But we need to give the tree a shake to see what falls out of it.

"But first of all, I want another interview arranged with Jimenez. We need to know all that he can tell us about his crash with Tradot's Volkswagen.

"So, Pratt will go with me to Montsegur. Renaud, you'll go with the Lieutenant to interview Jimenez, provided I can get permission from the Inspector General."

Pierre's permission given, the team reconfigured itself, with Maury and Pratt travelling west to Montsegur and Lucine travelling with Renaud, to interview Jimenez in the remand centre in Spain. Maury had worried about letting Lucine be exposed to such an unsavoury character, but she assured him that she'd be alright and that she was quite confident that she could get him to talk. Now he sat as a passenger in a Gendarmerie vehicle ably piloted by Pratt.

"Why should I help you?" asked Jimenez with a sneer, his eyes fixed on Babayan's breasts, in an effort to make her feel uncomfortable and intimidated.

"Because," said Lucine, slowly undoing the button of her blouse and leaning over the table to give him a better view of her cleavage, "You're being investigated by authorities on both sides of the border. It might go better for you, if you were to co-operate with the French police. We do you know you have a clientele among the rich and powerful of the Pyrenees Orientales, but the Justice Minister and the Procureur General have taken it into their heads to clean house. I don't think your so-called friends can afford you their normal protections."

As her words sank in the pimp's eyes rose from Babayan's exposed flesh to her face and held her gaze.

"Anyway," continued Lucine, sitting back in her chair, "I have not come here to talk to you about that business..."

Jimenez looked puzzled, as if wondering what other matter brought the two French police officers to visit. "Okay," he said, relaxing – the taut hostility of his body language easing.

The detective thumbed through her notes, "At some point between the twenty-fifth of June and the second of July last year, your Ferrari was in collision with another car on the road between your Mas and the village of Vingrau."

Jimenez' mouth dropped open, "You're here to question me about a minor scrape I had in my car? Unbelievable."

Lucine smiled coyly, "Can you remember that?"

Jimenez paused and thought, "It was only a scrape. If you've seen the damage, you'll know it wasn't a proper crash.

"If the people I hit need to make a claim, I can give you details of my insurance."

"So, you didn't report it then?"

"No," admitted Jimenez.

"Did you stop at the scene as required by French law?"

"We met on a hairpin bend, we barely touched. It's my car that will cost a fortune to fix!" the Spaniard complained. Then, it seemed to dawn on him that the situation might be more serious, "No-one was hurt, were they?"

Lucine ignored the question, "So you were in collision with another vehicle. What can you remember?"

"Well, it was dark. I was going around a corner when I met a car on the wrong side of the road. We both swerved, otherwise we'd have crashed head-on"

"Did you see anyone in the car?"

Jimenez shook his head, "I don't remember, I had enough to think about as it was."

Lucine was making scribbled notes, she nodded and continued, "Did you see the car crash, or leave the road?"

The colour drained from Jimenez' face, "No, I kept going," he admitted, "Was someone hurt?"

Again, Lucine ignored the pimp's question, "Why did you keep going rather than stop? After all, if what you're telling me is true, it will have been the other driver's fault."

Realisation dawned, "It's the people that were found in the ditch isn't it?" Jimenez was beginning to panic.

Lucine looked at the pimp, normally so cocksure and arrogant, he was getting worried. She didn't want him to clam up, "Their car left the road, but they seemed to have continued on foot. Are you sure you don't know them?"

Jimenez looked affronted, "I already said I don't."

Babayan changed tack and pressed him, "So, why didn't you stop?"

Jimenez seemed reluctant to answer, until Lucine's insistent gaze drew him to speak, "Because I was taking one of my girls, Mercedes, to the doctor's!"

The door opened and a sweating man in a wrinkled suit entered, "My client will not answer any more of your questions." He proffered a card, but their Spanish liaison Suarez introduced the intruder "This is Senor Jimenez's lawyer."

There was a helicopter circling the 'pog' on which the ancient ruins sat. The parking was full of sightseers' cars and responders' vehicles. The public who'd come to gawp had been ushered away from Montsegur's approaches and were congregated on the mountainside opposite, to get a better view of proceedings at the castle.

The gendarmes charged with perimeter duties directed Pratt to park alongside the track that led to the ticket office. There, four-wheel-drive vehicles of the Mountain Rescue teams had been drawn up, their neon-clad crews could be seen milling about at the foot of the castle walls.

Another vehicle parked nearby caught Maury's eye, it was a large silver panel van bristling with aerials and beside it, technicians were preparing a large camera-equipped drone for flight. When he left the car, Maury crossed to it and introduced himself, "Would you mind me sitting in to watch things from here?"

The two technicians looked at each other and shrugged, one pointed at the van's side door.

"I'll speak to the local guys," said Pratt, "to see if they need my help or can get us a coffee."

The Commandant liked the young gendarme's thinking, he nodded and pulled open the van's door on its runners. Inside, another technician in a gamer's chair looked up from an array of screens and removed his headset, "Can I help you?"

"Is this the command centre?"

The man shook his head, "No, the guy in charge is co-ordinating things from the helicopter. Who are you anyway?"

"Commandant Maury, a detective with the Police Nationale"

"Hang on," said the technician and proceeded to reattach his headset and address someone through its mouthpiece, "I've got a Commandant Maury here from the Police."

He listened intently to the reply before relaying it to the waiting detective, "Go to the flat area just beyond the entry office. Someone will meet you there."

Pratt met Maury, as he stepped away from the van, and passed him a Styrofoam cup of strong coffee and conveyed the same message as the technician.

The burly figure of Barthez awaited them by the spray-painted H on the ground, "My Captain's in charge of the scene. He's in the chopper monitoring the situation."

"What is the situation exactly?" asked Maury.

"Same as at Roquefixade. Some guy climbed up on the castle and jumped off when the sun rose."

"Is he dead?"

"We don't know."

"How far did he fall?"

"A long way. It seems he hit the rocks on the cliff, on the far side of the castle and got stuck in a crevice. He's not moving, but we can't get a proper view of him yet."

"Do we know who it is?"

"No. But witnesses say he was dressed in white."

"What witnesses?"

Barthez pointed at some young hippy types sitting on the grass by the side of a Gendarmerie van. Maury went to speak to them but Barthez' hand on his arm stopped him, "The helicopter's coming round for you."

Maury turned to Pratt, "Would you do the honours?"

Pratt smiled, nodded, and made off towards the witnesses, withdrawing his notebook and pen as he went.

The thump of the helicopter's rotary wings grew louder as the olive-drab machine banked and descended towards the makeshift landing area. The downdraught caught up dust and debris from the parched vegetation and the air became even hotter and stank of unburned kerosene from its turbine exhausts.

Barthez and Maury had to turn away to protect their eyes and bare skin from the whirlwind. Only when the turbines decelerated, with a lowering whine, did they dare to see that the helicopter had landed and a member of its aircrew, clad in khaki fatigues and wearing a white flying helmet, was approaching in a crouching run, "Commandant Maury?" he shouted. Maury nodded. "Follow me, keep your head low." He led the detective to the idling machine and helped him get aboard through its gaping side door. Almost immediately the turbines began re-accelerating. Maury was handed a headset, shown into a bucket seat, and strapped in by the crewman as the helicopter began to lift.

Opposite him a neatly uniformed Captain of the Gendarmerie leaned forward and offered his hand in greeting, "Captain Kerouac at your service. I thought you'd like to see the situation for yourself."

Maury nodded, acutely aware that the helicopter was leaving the ground with its fuselage door wide open. The crewman who'd seen him to the aircraft stood right next to the maw, nonchalantly watching the mountainside recede as the helicopter gained altitude.

"Our jumper is caught in some rocks below the castle. It's rather a difficult place to extract him from. The mountain rescue boys say they're going to try to put ground anchors in place and abseil down to him. Let's hope they manage it before it rains," explained Kerouac.

Maury looked at the sky, and saw that although still blue and cloudless here, a front was developing over the higher mountains of the range. The darkness below the massing cloud was ominous and threatening. Then Maury could see the rescuers on the mountain, they were insects against the high walls of the castle ruins and dwarfed even further by the height of the precipice on which the ancient fortress balanced. Pairs of men were driving spikes into the top of the pog with heavy sledgehammers. It must be exhausting work thought the detective, in this oppressive heat, after having climbed the steep pog under the weight of their equipment to get there.

Kerouac pointed to a feature of the cliff-face below the toiling men, "He's caught in those rocks there." Now that his eyes knew where to look, Maury was able to see an almost indiscernible point of white way below the rescuers. The fall from the castle walls was already high, perhaps three storeys, and the jumper seemed to have been caught in a fissure five storeys below that. Had he continued to plummet he'd have fallen another hundred metres before hitting the scree slope that dropped steeply to the torrent of the Lasset, even further below.

The helicopter circled impotently as the men on the pog continued their laborious tasks, until the pilot addressed the crew via the intercom, "We've only got fuel for another thirty minutes of flight time. What are your instructions, Captain?"

"Can you put us down on the field again?" asked Kerouac.

"Yes, Sir" Acknowledged the airman tickling his controls to bank the aircraft and commence a slow descent around the pog. Another fleck of white on the mountainside caught Maury's eye, a little below and around the limestone flank from where the present rescue was taking place, "What's that?"

Kerouac craned his neck to see, "Probably some rubbish or something. It seems to get everywhere. But maybe we can get the drone to have a look at it."

It was clear that the Captain was not going to delay the helicopter by ordering another pass. Maury was a little disappointed but understood the decision.

"So, who is this girl Mercedes, that Jimenez was taking for emergency treatment?" Renaud asked.

"Maybe one of our Spanish colleagues can help us with that, if we ask nicely," Lucine suggested as she re-buttoned her blouse.

Suarez, their liaison from the Garda shook his head when Babayan turned to him, "I work here in Figueres, you need to speak to someone in La Jonquera, that's who's most likely to know. Pop into the station there and ask for Benet, she works vice up there."

The two French police officers thanked the Spanish detective for his help and stepped from the cool detention centre into the heat and sunshine. Renaud looked across at the Pyrenees and pointed at the dark thunderclouds massing on the peaks, "Looks like we're going to have rain at last."

The helicopter landed, kicking up another cloud of dust and debris and roared off immediately the two senior officers had their feet on the ground. Maury followed Kerouac as the Captain led him down the slope to the silver van, he'd left just minutes ago. The uniformed officer slid open the van's door and ushered Maury inside, then slid it closed behind them when they'd entered. The lead technician, who was piloting the drone remotely, didn't look up from his screens, he simply told the two officers to take a seat. One of his colleagues, sat at another screen, pointed at a leather covered bench in the cramped control room, "You can see everything from there."

Maury watched the men's fingers make deft adjustments, as the drone was flown up over the gorse and box covered slopes of the pog. He understood that one was the pilot, and the other controlled the drone's high definition cameras. The images on the screens were remarkably sharp, the drone could fly in close proximity to the mountain, where the helicopter could not.

At last the great stone walls of the castle came into view. The garish dayglow outfits of the rescue team were bright against the darkening sky in the background. It appeared that they were preparing a man to abseil down the face of the mountain, to recover the jumper, they were uncoiling ropes and attaching carabiners to a bright alloy stretcher. The drone descended and presently they had a view of the person who had jumped, there was little to see, as he had fallen deep within two limestone outcrops, caught by the thorns that clung to life on the desolate cliff-face. The camera zoomed in, and a hand came into focus, blood dripped from the fingertips and the pinkie was bent to an impossible angle. What little clothing could be seen was bleached white linen, similar to that worn by the three victims in the ditch. The torso and head were out of sight in the shadow of broom sprigs that grew with the thorn. One leg could be seen, it was darkly tanned and hairy, so one could safely assume that the jumper was male, the foot was enclosed in a tan leather Roman type sandal.

The image started swinging, the pilot seemed to be having trouble keeping the drone stable, "The damned wind is getting up. It looks like they'll have someone lowered down to him soon. We're going to have to call it a day, if it gets gusty."

"Do you mind flying down diagonally right?" asked Maury, "I saw something from the helicopter. Is it possible to have a quick look?"

The camera panned out and the drone descended slowly, so that the cliff-face could be examined. Limestone crags, tawny coloured wounds on blue-grey rock all passed by the drone's gaze, but other than items of rubbish such as soft drinks cans and odd bits of plastic there appeared to be nothing. Nobody in the command van said anything, the drone hovered while the camera operator panned left to right, but there was still nothing to see. "Sorry," said the pilot,

"We'll have one more look at what the rescue team is doing and then we'll bring it home."

The drone gained altitude until the camera operator barked, "Stop!"

Right at the edge of the picture something off-white flapped in the rising wind. Between them, the pilot and the camera operator centred the image and began to focus in. A shred of ripped grey-white cloth flapped from the branches of a thorn, the tree was growing impossibly from an almost imperceptible ledge, its roots were somehow finding nutrients in the scree. It looked like nothing until Kerouac rose from his seat and went to the panoramic screen of the monitor, "What's that?" he asked, pointing at the stones behind the thorn.

All eyes in the control room turned to the screen and tried to interpret what was being relayed back by the remotely controlled aircraft. Maury's heart rose in his throat, "They're not stones, they're human vertebrae. It's another body!"

Figueres is famous for the Dali museum, otherwise the Catalan town has little to distinguish it. Its outskirts are industrialised and, mercifully, centred on the motorway and the bypass, rather than the Route Nationale that Lucine and Renaud were now taking to La Jonquera. To their left, as they travelled north, was the high-speed rail link from France, with its concrete scar spoiling otherwise pretty scenery. To their right were the foothills of the Spanish side of the Albères stretching east to Cadaques, the erstwhile haunt of Salvador Dali, and the Costa Brava. As they neared the lorry staging-post that is La Jonquera, they passed bronzed and bleached prostitutes parading themselves suggestively at the passing traffic. These girls were prettier than Lucine had imagined they might be, dressed in shockingly bright and skimpy attire, to draw the eye to their trim bodies, legs and breasts. Their presence jarred with the pastoral scene of a shepherd leading his dogs and his woolly charges to glean the common-land grasses of the verge.

When they reached the Service Stations and lorry parks of the town, these working girls seemed to be everywhere, flaunting themselves shamelessly to prospective clients as well as shopping families. Lucine wondered if Mercedes was one. Renaud was not immune to ogling one or two as they passed, but he concentrated on following Suarez's instructions to reach the police station situated in the quieter old quarter of the town.

Babayan and Renaud were soon at the station's reception asking for Detective Benet.

Benet, a thick-set redhead, in her mid-thirties, with a friendly face and yellow-green eyes invited them into her office. She spoke perfect French, heavily accented by her native Catalan pronunciation, , "How may I help you?"

"Detective Suarez said you may be able to find a working girl we know as Mercedes," explained Lucine

Benet tutted, "Who's she work for?"

"Jimenez," Lucine replied.

Benet shook her head, "Lots of girls use the name Mercedes as their alter-ego, it makes them sound up-market. And, if she works for Jimenez then that is certainly not her real name. He only uses Eastern European girls, it's hard to keep tabs on them."

"You know Jimenez?"

Benet laughed ironically, "El Pistolet, he calls himself. He's a scumbag like all pimps are, but he's one of the better ones."

"How do you mean?"

"His girls are clean. He won't use junkies or illegals and they're well looked after."

"Does he run a brothel here, or something?"

Benet laughed again, "His mother does."

"His mother?"

"Uh-huh," confirmed Benet, nodding her head. "She's got a hotel here in the old town. Now, her clientele is upmarket, she provides special services…"

"Like her son does in France?" asked Renaud.

"Uh-huh," agreed Benet with another nod of her head. "She was on the game herself, years ago. Set up her own place with her savings, wanted girls to be able to work in safety. The family charges them rent and food, then takes a percentage of their earnings."

"Why Eastern European girls?" Lucine asked.

"They're tall, slim, blonde," Benet replied, looking down at herself, "All the things I'm not.

"And they're only in it for the money, so they're not complicated. They usually work until they've got enough money saved, then off they go back to where they came from. So, it could also be that this Mercedes you're looking for has gone home by now."

"Did Jimenez take his girls from his mother's place to work across the border?" Renaud asked.

Benet look up at the questioner, giving Renaud a good look over, "It would seem that way," she replied.

"She'd have been working about a year ago. Any chance that she might be known at the Jimenez's hotel" Lucine asked.

"Well, we could try asking I suppose," said Benet getting up from her desk, "We can walk there, it's only two hundred metres away."

The temperature had fallen suddenly, the massif of the Monts d'Olmes was now a sombre brooding presence, under its cap of ominous black cloud. The wind had risen, and the threat of rain saw the ghoulish crowd of onlookers disperse. Only the gendarmes remained on station at the castle's official entrance. The technicians were frantically dismantling the landed drone and now, without eyes on, the two ranking officers were standing together at the back of one of the mountain rescue Land-Rovers monitoring radio communications with a rescue worker. The static was increasing as the approaching storm interfered with the magnetic field. But the expert's accustomed ear relayed the messages he was receiving from his colleagues high above them on the pog. "They're looking at him now."

A garbled cry over the speakers and the radio man asked for the message to be repeated, this time the message was clear, "He's alive! He's got horrific injuries and he's obviously unconscious, but we're going to have to move him. Any chance of getting the chopper back to lift him off the mountain?"

The radio operator looked at Kerouac, who nodded and got out his mobile phone. He made the call and turned back to the rescuer,

"It's on its way. It'll be here in fifteen minutes or so."

A rumble on the mountain signalled the storm's imminent approach, it was going to be a close-run thing.

"Where will he be taken from here?" Maury asked the Captain.

"Toulouse, I imagine," replied Kerouac after a moment's consideration, "It sounds like he'll be needing intensive care. If he survives extraction."

Benet entered the hotel lobby, the old lady sitting there recognised her and beckoned the three officers in, "Hola, detective. How can I help you today?"

Benet introduced her French counterparts, "This is Lieutenant Babayan and Gardien Renaud, and they're looking for a girl called Mercedes who may have worked for your son in France."

Senora Jimenez suddenly became a lot less welcoming, "We don't have a Mercedes here. Anyway, I wouldn't tell you if I did. What you French police are doing to my son, is disgusting!"

Lucine shrugged, "So is drug-running Senora," she stated.

"Drug running?" Senora Jimenez repeated in genuine shock and consternation "I don't believe it! Now, get out of my premises, I have nothing more to say to you."

"I'm sorry about that," apologised Benet as they stepped back into the street, "I don't know if I can do any more to help you."

"Give me your card." The Spanish detective said, addressing Renaud, "I'll keep asking around and let you know if anything turns up. Here's mine if you want to stay in touch."

The helicopter manoeuvred into position, rising and falling with the disturbed thermals and the winds that preceded the gathering storm. A winch lowered a crewman down out of its fuselage to descend out of sight behind the castle. Maury and Kerouac could now only follow what was happening, by monitoring the radio transmissions of the men above them. There were curt instructions and, finally, a pregnant pause. The helicopter began slowly climbing, reeling in the winchman and the stretcher containing the foil-wrapped casualty dangling below it. Kerouac breathed a sigh of relief and told the radioman to order everyone off the mountain, "Ask them to leave the ground anchors in place. There's another body up there that we'll have to recover once the weather improves again."

"I think Detective Benet liked you," teased Lucine as she and Renaud sat back in their car.

Renaud smiled wryly, and buckled his seatbelt, "Let's hope she can track down this Mercedes for us. I don't think Jimenez, or his family, will be likely to assist us in our enquiries anymore."

"No, I don't suppose they will," mused Lucine as Renaud started the car, "I wonder how things are going in Ariege."

Kerouac looked at the sky, dark and ominous, "We could try recovering the other remains tomorrow morning," he suggested, "If the rain holds off."

Even as he said this, rain fell in great sporadic spatters and thunder rumbled once more on the massif. "We can get you and your man lodgings in Lavelanet, if you like," he offered.

Maury thanked the Captain and motioned Pratt over, "Let's talk in the car."

The raindrops that fell were large and make a great dunk as they hit the car's bodywork, but it didn't yet rain with any force or persistence. "I think the cloud's lifting," Pratt remarked, looking at the clouds on the mountains through the windscreen.

"Can you get anyone on the car radio?" asked Maury, "I've got no mobile signal here."

"I should think so," answered Pratt, switching on the transmitter receiver, "Who do you need to talk to?"

"Get hold of Babayan or Pratt at Rivesaltes, they should be back there by now," instructed Maury watching the mountain rescue men's loading of equipment slow to a more sedate pace. Pratt was right, the cloud was lifting, the rain that had fallen had barely wetted the ground.

"Are you alright to stay the night, if we have to?" Maury asked the gendarme as he fiddled with the radio frequency controls.

Pratt looked up at the detective in surprise, but nodded to the affirmative, "As long as I get overtime and allowance for food and lodgings," he replied.

As it happened, Pratt was able to raise Renaud and Babayan directly, the teams had opted to take gendarmerie vehicles in both directions that day. Renaud reported that he and Babayan were stuck in motorway traffic, at the toll station in le Boulou.

Maury took the microphone and addressed Babayan first, "Lieutenant, they've lifted someone off the mountain who looks to be connected to our case. He's alive, and they're taking him off to hospital in Toulouse as we speak, I've asked for updates on his condition to be relayed to our Rivesaltes office. There's another body on the mountain that might be connected, so Pratt and I are staying here until tomorrow."

Lucine listened carefully, making notes, while Maury continued, "I need you to let the Inspector General know that the scope of our investigation has widened, and that we might have more unexplained deaths to investigate. I don't want this case going to the Gendarmerie in Lavelanet. He'll understand, I just need him to make me the official lead.

"And can you ring Marie-France and let her know I'm stuck here? I've got no signal and no phone charger."

"Of course, Sir" Lucine replied.

They were accommodated in rooms in Lavelanet's Gendarmerie, comfortable enough but basic. In clothes borrowed from lost property, the two colleagues decided to visit the town centre to find an open restaurant or bar in which to while away the evening.

It was quite a stroll along the arrow-straight high street to the centre, and the whole place was quiet now that day-time businesses had closed. Eventually though, they reached the roundabout around which the town was centred. There were a few eateries, all offering reasonably priced menus. The sky was orange-tinted by the setting sun staining the remaining cloud on the mountains, and so they chose a terraced restaurant where they could dine while witnessing nature's light show.

At first the little place was quiet, older couples dining well-spaced apart within and without, until cars and work vans arrived, spilling out boisterous locals who greeted each other with exuberance, and took over most of the other tables on the terrace. It became clear that these were local rugbymen, both by their build, and, of course, their loud conversation. As pastis and beer were imbibed, the language got coarser and louder, little tackles and rucks were demonstrated to loud approval, which served to bring other locals along to join the impromptu party.

It was great spectator sport for Maury and Pratt, who watched the good-natured tomfoolery with amusement as they consumed their meal and sat enjoying drinks of their own.

The night wore on and the rugbymen began to disperse in dribs and drabs, lurching off on jelly legs, roaring with laughter and bawdy songs. The genteel diners had long gone, and now only the sportsmen and police officers remained, but the effect of the alcohol had quietened them to drawled boasts full of drunken emotion. One sot caught sight of their amused audience and called over to the officer's table, "You into rugby or soccer, you two?" he demanded.

"Rugby," said Pratt diplomatically.

At first, Maury thought the young gendarme had said this to deflect any argument or aggression, but when the local pressed him for details, Pratt admitted that he played for the Rivesaltes-Bompas XV. The impressed local crossed over to their table, pulled up a chair and soon the two were immersed in earnest conversation about their shared passion for all things concerning the odd-shaped ball.

Meanwhile, the local transvestite arrived at the bar dressed outrageously in, over the top, sequinned gown, flamboyant feather boa and fishnet stockings. The application of thick make-up did nothing to disguise his masculine jawline or the bristles of five-o'clock-shadow, and the blonde wig he wore appeared to be made from fishing filament. Nevertheless, a couple of the drunkards decided to flirt suggestively, to the great amusement of their half-cut friends and the sober waiting staff.

Maury quietly settled the bill. The observant Pratt finished his conversation with the local man, and they left, after circulating to shake everyone's hand in goodbye as they went.

The Tide Turns

Under the nose of the new Count of Toulouse, Simon de Montfort, Raymond returned from England in company with his adult son Raymond junior, to his former lands and managed to raise a substantial army from the region's many disaffected. This army marched east to the city of Beaucaire, straddling the main route from the Rhone valley, through which the crusader's supplies and reinforcements would have to pass. After withstanding his siege for three months the city surrendered to its one-time lord. Realising this danger, de Montfort led his army to retake the strategic town, but his troops failed.

The crusaders were still in a dominant position, but the sudden death of Innocent III during this time, brought their whole endeavour into disarray. Overall command of the crusade passed to the ever-reluctant King Phillip of France, who was already embroiled in an epic struggle with the English in Normandy.

As his back was turned, the citizens of Toulouse decided to revolt against their new Count. Simon de Montfort decided that instead of pressing on with attacks against Beaucaire, he would march back west to crush this uprising, and another revolt taking place in Bigorre. Stretched by battle on two fronts, Simon's exhausted forces met with defeat at a battle near Lourdes in December 1216.

All looked settled, until an uprising in Foix, in the Summer of 1217 meant that the crusaders had, once again, to leave the protective curtain walls of Toulouse to put down the revolt. While he was distracted, the city's former Count, Raymond, retook Toulouse without a fight, the citizens throwing open the gates to welcome him back. The crusaders hurried back, but Simon's diminished armies could not retake the town before the arrival of winter, so they withdrew to Castelnaudary.

The new Pope, Honorius, called for the crusade to press on, so Simon de Montfort continued besieging Toulouse in the

Spring of 1218. Repulsing a sally from Raymond's cavalry in June, while under attack from the city's defensive artillery, said to be operated by women and girls, Simon de Montfort was struck in the head by a stone and killed. Toulouse was held and the crusaders driven back.

In 1219 King Phillip appointed his son, Prince Louis, who was as reluctant to get involved as his father, to take over his command of the crusade. So, Louis led an expeditionary force south through Poitou to join forces with a second army led by Simon de Montfort's son, Amaury de Montfort. These combined armies besieged Marmande, in June, as they advanced west along the valley of the Garonne, towards Toulouse. The town quickly fell, and all its occupants, excluding the commander and his retinue of knights, were massacred. After this brief pause, the armies continued towards Toulouse. After six weeks of siege, the French Prince tired of the adventure and withdrew his forces back north to the heartlands of France, leaving Amaury de Montfort with a much-depleted military force. Without, support he was unable to continue the siege or even to hold his hard-fought for gains. Pope Honorius called the debacle 'a miserable setback', but things were to get even worse.

From 1220 to 1225, under the leadership of the two Raymonds, the gains of the crusaders were gradually rolled back. Castelnaudary was retaken by a protracted siege of eight months, Montreal and Fanjeaux were recaptured, and by 1222 the old Counts of Toulouse had retaken all the lands that they had lost. At least the older Raymond lived long enough to see that victory, by the year's end he had died, and his son Raymond VII succeeded him.

In July 1223 King Phillip of France died too, and he was succeeded by his son, Louis VIII.

In 1224, the crusaders of Amaury de Montfort abandoned Carcassonne and Raymond reclaimed the area. In shame, Amaury ceded the lands around Beziers and Montpellier, all that remained of his late father's gains, to the new French monarch.

22nd June

The mountain Rescue team assembled early, in the yard of the Gendarmerie. After breakfasting in the canteen, Maury and Pratt joined the briefing, where rescuers were reminded of safety protocols and other technical information. The Commandant was introduced to the men, and he reminded them to treat the site where the body lay as a crime scene, stressing that they needed to catalogue everything they discovered with still photographs and video. The gathered men understood these constraints and were eager to get to work before the sun and the temperature both rose. So, Pratt joined their car to the end of the convoy that wound its way up to Montsegur to accomplish its grisly task.

Maury and Pratt climbed with the mountaineers to the top of the pog, even Pratt who was reasonably fit from his sport, could not keep up with the professionals who, even loaded with equipment, left both police officers in their wake. Maury brought up the rear and arrived to find that the ground anchors had been checked over and two overall-clad men were readying to abseil.

With little to do, other than wait, Maury explored the ruined remains of the castle. The views from every angle were commanding and he found it hard to imagine how such a stronghold could be besieged. But, it had, and he knew that many of the rounded stones at the feet of the mighty walls had been flung there by siege engines. The curtain walls were laid out in an unusual plan, seen from above the castle must be coffin-shaped, but with its high donjon adjoining it at its stern end, to Maury the layout was almost like that of a galleon. This comparison seemed apt, the donjon was almost like a vessel's bridge from which it was commanded, its elevation giving it oversight of the entire edifice.

Like on the previous day, clouds were once again forming on the massif of the Monts d'Olmes and a rumble of thunder rolled from the high mountains, out of sight under their blanket of darkening cumulonimbus.

As interesting as the ancient fortress was, Maury needed to see from where yesterday's casualty had jumped, so climbing down the metal stairway that gave access to the keep he returned into the castle's enceinte, via a small postern in its flank. There was evidence of recent campfires within the walls and Maury guessed that the hippy types who witnessed the traumatic event were probably here, passed out from the drink that their scattered empties had contained. A vestigial staircase rose to the wall's top, the only route to the crumbled battlements. The first steps, heavily eroded and loose, did nothing to instil confidence, but Maury ascended carefully, placing his feet methodically until, at last, he emerged atop the thick stone curtain. The height was giddying, so Maury stopped and looked around without looking down, a trick he'd learned during military service from aerial erectors. They'd said that if one ascended in stages, stopped to become accustomed to the height, the brain is fooled into thinking that this is now ground – like resetting its datum point.

It did work to a degree, but Maury nevertheless made his way, gingerly, to the lightning rod demarking the angle where the castle's walls kinked along the top of the precipice. Holding the thick metal spike, he dared to look over the wall's edge. His head swam with fright, the drop down to the gorges, in the valley below, was sheer. The road that climbed up from the depths was a narrow grey ribbon, a car climbing through its hairpins a mere toy. Just below was the ground anchor from which the mountaineers dangled precariously to go about their task. They were working well over to the left from the jumping point and had set up other anchorage points that diverted their ropes diagonally to the recovery site.

A voice hailed him by name, so Maury nervously looked down the vertical wall to see Pratt shaking a silver flask at him. He'd seen enough, anyway another coffee would help him control his thumping heart.

By the time that the recovery operation was complete, the cloud-base had thickened and descended onto the lower shoulders of the massif. Maury looked at the plastic crate full of bagged remnants of a curtailed life – bones, shards of fabric, strands of blonde hair, leathery skin, and a sightless skull. By its diminutive proportions, fine cheekbones, and lack of over-brow, Maury guessed that the remains were of a female, but only the experts could fully ascertain that.

"Did you find a pendant, or anything like that?" Maury asked the lead mountaineer.

The man nodded and reached into the crate and withdrew a small plastic bag and held it up for the detective to see. The pendant within was not what Maury had expected to see, instead of a gold Gema Abraxas, it was a small white enamel dove.

"Can you have all this sent to the Coroner in Perpignan," directed the Commandant.

Maury and Pratt took their leave of their Lavelanet based colleagues and headed back towards the Pyrenees Orientales. They descended through the gorges that sat below the castle, Pratt driving with his usual competence through the zig-zagging switchbacks. The thick cloud enveloped the massif and descended dark and threatening, on their heels.

With a loud crash of thunder, the onslaught of the promised rain began. Great droplets fell, leopard-spotting the road's surface ahead of them, slowly at first, then pelting faster and heavier until rain fell like proverbial stair-rods. The car's wipers could barely clear the screen, it had gone so dark, that Pratt had to illuminate the headlamps in order to navigate. Now, the rain appeared to rise from the ground's surfaces, the droplets hitting so hard that they ricocheted upward to atomise in a metre-thick layer of spray above the ground.

Pratt could not see at all, the yellow light of the halogen headlamps barely penetrated the falling sheets of water, and the wipers seemingly made no effect, other than flap uselessly across the windscreen. Taking the wise decision to stop and the idling engine quiet, the officers became aware of the great drumming the falling rain made as it bounced off the car's surfaces.

Maury watched the rain, wondering what a deluge like this might do to his garden if it was falling like this at home. Then he realised that the car was slowly creeping forward, he looked at Pratt about to tell him to reapply the brakes, but the young gendarme already had the handbrake fully applied, and his foot pressed down on the brake pedal. It was the sheer weight of water now running down the asphalt that was moving the vehicle. The water ran like a torrent from the mountainside and swirled down the road as if it were a watercourse. With the boiling water came mud, rocks, branches, and other debris that blocked any run-off and sent the water cascading off the mountain by the shortest route.

Now Maury understood how the three unfortunates might have met their deaths on the lonely road to Périllos. If they'd been caught in such a storm, it was nature itself that had assaulted them, disorientated them, and drowned them.

But then he noticed the road's apex, and saw that the water there was shallow and benign in comparison to the streams coursing either side of its domed surface, "Get the car into the centre of the road," he commanded. This action would normally be one of utmost folly, but now the vehicle's wheels found purchase on the tarmac and their frightening downward drift halted.

"It hasn't rained like this since last year," Pratt observed, "It should ease off soon."

The gendarme's remark piqued the detective's interest "Can you remember exactly when that was?" he asked.

In the Rivesaltes office, Babayan and Renaud were busy catching up with overdue paperwork, when the phone began frantically ringing. Babayan picked it up and when the voice at the other end asked for Maury, she offered to take a message, "It's the Urgences at Hospital Joseph Ducuing in Toulouse. Could you let your colleague know that the casualty from Montsegur, who arrived with us last night has been rushed to the Critical Care Unit."

"What's his condition?" Lucine asked.

The male voice considered a moment "It's too early to tell, his injuries are extensive. Ring in a few hours for an update, after he's been properly assessed."

"Thank you, we will," said Lucine, replacing the receiver. She turned to Renaud and told him the news, "I expect the Commandant and Pratt are on their way back."

Renaud looked up from the alert flashing on his computer screen, "They might be a while, there's a severe storm going on in the high mountains."

Lucine looked from the window over the sun-kissed roofs of Rivesaltes, and the arid slopes of the Corbières, at the purple-black overcast on the western horizon and wondered if rains might come to Roussillon.

According to Pratt, there had been several flash floods in the Rivesaltes area in the previous June. The valley of the Agly had been hardest hit, with roads inundated, bridges breached by the force of water, houses flooded and the lives of two unfortunates lost in the village of Tautavel. But, he couldn't be precise about the dates, and he pointed out that some storms were highly localised, "A few years ago there were massive floods in Tuchan, which is only on the other side of the mountain from Tautavel, but nothing in Tautavel itself. Last year, the rain fell on Tautavel and Estagel but didn't affect Tuchan."

"What about Périllos?" asked Maury.

Pratt shot the detective a sideways glance that signalled that he understood why the question had been put. "Yes," he replied, "Last year the rains fell on the eastern slopes, in the Fitou region. We caught it in Rivesaltes too, and Salses, so probably Périllos was affected. Thing is, not many people live up that way, so we don't know how bad it might've got."

Maury ruminated. Feeling sure about something didn't make it a fact. It may well be that the three unfortunates and an unborn child were overwhelmed by nature on that forsaken road up to Périllos. But their deaths were preceded by a chain of events that led to them being there. And, the fact remained that the investigation had still not determined who those poor souls were. So, they still had legwork to do, his little team had to continue digging into peripheral events and persons that may be connected in some way.

Maury hoped that Lucine and Renaud had returned from Spain with some useful lead, and that the poor wretch hauled off the slopes of Montsegur would make a full recovery.

The phone rang and once again Lucine lifted the receiver. The voice was familiar, the emergency consultant at the Hospital Joseph Ducuing, "I'm afraid I've got bad news," he cautioned, "We've had to put the casualty into an induced coma".
Lucine was shocked, and her disappointment silenced her.
"We don't know when, or even if, he'll come round," continued the doctor."
"Can you send anything you can to help us identify him please," requested Babayan. "We're conducting an investigation down here and have reason to believe that the person you're treating is of great interest to us."
"Very well," agreed the consultant, "We shall be in touch."

The journey back from Ariege took a lot longer than normal. The streets of Belesta and Quillan were deep with floodwater like rivers, and Pratt had to drive carefully to ensure that the bow-wave pushed by the car did not swamp the engine. The mountain roads were hazardous. Even though the rain had eased to intermittent showers, water still poured from overflowing drains, gateways and mountainsides, bringing down shallow-rooted trees, banks of mud and scree. But, once through the gorges and over the col where Aude bordered the Pyrenees Orientales the rain stopped, and the cloud base was broken. By the time they'd descended to Puylaurens the roads were dry, and they were re-emerging into sunshine and heat.
Pratt looked at the detective as they travelled through the village and vineyards of Maury, and asked a question he'd been aching to ask, "Are your family from around here?"
"Originally," conceded Maury, "But I was brought up in Fabrezan."
"Not too far away then," remarked Pratt, noting Maury's reluctance to talk about himself.

Back in the small incident room in Rivesaltes, Babayan made her report. Maury didn't seem surprised to hear that Jimenez had proved to be of limited use. But he had her write up 'Mercedes' as a possible lead.

But when she reported the news from the Urgences in Toulouse he swore aloud, "Merde! I was hoping we'd learn more about these damned Cathars, whose hobby it seems is to turn up dead!"

"Okay," he said with resignation, "So, what now?"

Babayan interjected, "I asked them to send us anything that could be used to identify him."

Maury nodded in approval and looked pleased, "Well done, we'll await their report.

"Alright, let me outline my thinking..." Maury explained how he thought the three main deaths they were investigating had come about. The other three officers listened quietly and tried to imagine the scenario.

"Our three deceased are travelling along the road, in Tradot's car, from Vingrau towards Périllos, probably on their way to see Monsieur Vincent. They are in a collision with Jimenez's car and forced off the road to crash in the ravine. The car catches fire, we do know the fuel tank was ruptured, but they managed to get back up onto the road. They continue, on foot towards Périllos, when a storm catches them. The flash flooding overcomes them, and they are swept into the culvert with all the other debris coming off the mountain."

"I'll get up the area reports for last year," said Pratt springing straight into action, their timeline's window of opportunity was now not quite so wide.

"I think your theory might be right," agreed Lucine, "The water from a flash flood would fill the culvert, Jimenez's pool and the Caune spring. It would be the same rainwater."

"We need to find this 'Mercedes'," reasoned Maury aloud, "We have to make a definite link between Tradot's car and our deceased. Until we have a witness, all we have is supposition."

"Oh yes," he added, "I forgot to say that they are shipping the body we found at Montsegur over to the Coroner in Perpignan. He'll call us when he has news."

The Mas, when he arrived back, was quiet without children or visitors, but Maury knew where he'd find his wife. He was right, she was tending the fruit and vegetables, her hair a sweaty mess, her face wet and rosy. "We really need rain," she remarked.

Maury began attaching a rose to the end of the garden hose so he could mist the plants as the sun set, "I got caught in some today," he said.

Marie-France stopped pruning, "Really?" she asked suspiciously, as if he were joking.

Maury nodded, "I was in Ariege. I've never seen a storm like it, the rain came down in buckets. I was actually glad to get back to the sunshine and heat."

Her eyes took on a faraway look, he wondered if she was thinking about rain or something else. He instinctively knew that she was missing their grandsons, "We'll pop over to see Elisabeth and the boys after we've finished here," he suggested.

The French Crown Commits

The Catholic Council of Bourges convened in November 1225 to discuss the future of the crusade against the Cathar heresy. The gathered bishops decided to excommunicate Raymond of Toulouse, like his father before him, for protecting the Cathars and foiling the success of the campaign so far. Gathering a thousand clergymen, the church authorized a 10% tithe on their annual incomes, in order to finance a new mobilisation.

Now King, and the problem of the English resolved, the once reluctant Louis VIII agreed to lead this phase of the crusade. He assembled an army at Bourges in May 1226, its exact number is unknown, but it would be safe to say that is was, by far, the largest crusading force yet gathered. In June he led his army south and quickly recaptured Beziers, Carcassonne and Beaucaire without encountering resistance. The only town to resist was Avignon which Louis set to besieging. After a month, in which frontal assaults were fiercely repulsed by its determined defenders, the town eventually surrendered. This time no killing or looting took place, the town had to pay reparations of 6,000 marks and dismantle its defensive walls.

When King Louis died of dysentery of his way back to Paris after this short and successful campaign, command of the crusade passed to his widow Queen Blanche, mother of the child King Louis IX.

Blanche sent the Constable of France, Humbert de Beaujeu, to lead the crusade on the French Crown's behalf. Under his command the fortresses that protected the eastern flanks and approaches, of the County of Toulouse, were taken; Labacede in 1227 and Vareilles in 1228.

The crusaders were now ready, once more, to assault the great walls of Toulouse. To underline their seriousness, the crusaders scorched the city's surrounding lands, uprooting crops and vines, burning farms and fields and slaughtering all the livestock. Raymond did not have the manpower to intervene, soon the city fell.

The French Crown had a different approach to that of the Pontiffs and the de Montforts, who had been commanding the crusade until now, instead of consigning Raymond to exile or the gallows, Blanche offered him a treaty which would see him reinstated as Count of Toulouse in return for turning over all his castles and strongholds to the French Crown, destroying the defences of Toulouse and fighting with the crusaders against the Cathars.

In April 1229 agreed to the terms and signed a binding treaty which effectively brought the military phase of the campaign against the Cathars to an end.

23rd June

As was their habit, Maury and Marie-France breakfasted together, enjoying the comparative cool of the dawn before the heat of the day began in earnest. The sky was another cloudless dome of azure, only paling where the rising sun bleached the sky. About them, in the stubby oaks Jays and woodpeckers went about their own daily business.

Today, the newspapers had been dropped early and Marie-France perused them, while Maury turned reluctantly to retrieve the emails that had no doubt stacked up during his absence from the Narbonne office.

There weren't as many as he thought, Martinez, his aide-de-camp, had obviously been deflecting as much business as possible. What remained was mostly routine and he had only to peruse them and acknowledge receipt. But there were a couple pertinent to the present investigation.

The first was from his old friend Pierre, in it the Inspector General outlined the progress the IGPN's investigation in Perpignan had so far made. There were no details, but the highlights made interesting reading. Detective Lieutenant Verdier had been demoted and, as Maury himself had once suggested, found himself in uniform working for the Municipal Police in Elne.

There had been fallout for Guillot too, he had not yet lost his rank or title but his days as Head Detective in Perpignan looked to be numbered, the investigators had concluded that his style of management had been too remote. That probably was the case, thought Maury, after all Guillot hadn't even known Babayan's personal circumstances.

But what was most pleasing to read was that the Police Nationale had agreed to settle affairs with the Nassim family by way of a generous financial settlement, and a small life-long pension for Mankour. The investigation's focus was now on the Procureur General's office and its links, among others to criminal operations in Roussillon.

The other email, of note, came from the Urgences in Toulouse. Not from the Consultant, but a lowly technician who had matched the casualty's fingerprints to a record on the Criminal Database. He'd responded to a 'flag' and followed protocol by informing the Police. Maury was genuinely excited at this unforeseen development; he had expected the members of a pious religious order to be squeaky clean. He wondered what the man's offence could possibly be, as he swallowed down his coffee.

"Going already?" asked Marie-France, looking over her paper at her husband as he closed the lid of his laptop.

"A break at last!" he said. "Want me to get anything while I'm out?" he asked.

"A few more bottles of that nice Fitou," his wife replied.

At Rivesaltes, Babayan and the two gendarmes were already busy. Pratt was working his way through log entries from Gendarmeries round about Rivesaltes, as well as the station's own. He had a map and was using pins to identify events reported by local officers in the week they'd identified.

Renaud, meanwhile, had the weather data for the same time period. He'd downloaded maps to show radar images of storms and cloud formations in the geographic areas concerned.

Lucine was typing up reports, transferring her longhand entries onto the computer logs.

Maury went straight to the incident board and wrote a name upon it – 'Antoine Mercier' – their attention gained he addressed the team "This is the name of the man who jumped at Montsegur. He has a Criminal Record apparently. Find out all you can about him, and print me out a file," he directed.

"I'm on it," said Renaud, who'd finished pinning the meteorological data to the board. Maury nodded in approval.

Lucine cleared her throat to get the Commandant's attention, "Sir, I've been thinking about something Jimenez said in his interview." She thumbed through her notebook, "He told us he was taking 'Mercedes' for medical attention..."

"So?"

"Well, he was going the wrong way. The nearest medical centre is in

Perpignan," Lucine pointed out.

"Perhaps, he was taking her to a local doctor," Maury suggested, "See who he's registered with. Good work Lieutenant."

Maury watched Pratt sticking his pins in the board, the gendarme had colour-coded them: red for incidents of violence, green for natural occurrences, blue for traffic violations and yellow for other incidents of interest. A lone yellow pin at Vingrau piqued his interest, he asked the gendarme what incident it related to. Pratt looked at his cross-index and chuckled as he recalled the event, "We busted the local boy-racer for drug possession."

"I remember reading it. Wasn't a retired doctor involved?"

Pratt checked the incident report again and nodded, "Yes Sir, you're right."

Maury turned to Babayan, "If you don't find Jimenez registered with any local doctor, you can bet your last sou, this chap in Vingrau is working under the counter," he had his finger on the yellow pin. Lucine nodded in acknowledgement and continued her research.

Maury continued to type up his own paperwork, until Renaud passed a print-out across his desk, the file he'd requested on Antoine Mercier. Renaud looked grim, Maury passed the file back and invited the gendarme to brief them on what he'd uncovered. So, Renaud crossed to the board and spoke as he wrote bullet points below Mercier's name. "Antoine Mercier, aged twenty-seven, registered at an address in Lens. No criminal record, although he is on the Sex Offenders Register."

The officers looked at each other in confusion. If Mercier had no convictions, how did he end up on the Register?

Renaud continued, "He is registered as a potential sex offender at his psychiatrist's recommendation. He spent some time institutionalised in his youth, but since his release he's kept a low profile…"

The gendarme paused, puzzled by what he was reading, "But his psychiatrist only put him on the Register in March last year!"

"Does it say what his potential offences might be?" asked Lucine.

"Potential to inflict sexual violence on women, it says here."

"That's a catch-all" remarked Maury, "Who's the psychiatrist?

Maybe we can get more information from him."

A wry smile crossed Renaud's face as he replied, "A certain Doctor Benhamine from Pamiers."

And there it was, the connection to Ariege once again.

"Right. I'll get onto this doctor," said Maury.

Dr Benhamine had a thick foreign accent, which made understanding some of what he was saying difficult. But the psychiatrist had no issue talking about his patient in general terms, after all Mercier was a registered Sex Offender, "He came to me and said that he was having sexually violent fantasies about one of his female friends. I wanted to offer him therapy, but he insisted on an immediate solution before he'd be tempted to act on his impulses.

"I told him that unless he was convicted and put on the Register, there was little I could do. He asked if it was possible for him to be put on it before committing an offence

"It is highly unusual, but such pre-emptive interventions have been made before. He wanted me to look at his history there and then. I won't go into it, as that would be unprofessional of me, but he suffered childhood abuse under a female member of his family. These things had clearly had an effect on him in the past, hence his incarceration in an establishment near his hometown of Lens.

"So, I acceded to his request, entered his name on the Register and prescribed him a rolling course of Cypretone Acetate…"

"What is that?" asked Maury.

"It's a form of chemical castration." The doctor replied.

"You're right," confirmed Babayan, "Jimenez is not registered with any local doctor or clinic."

Pratt had pre-empted this, he passed over a note with the retired doctor's name and address.

"What else do we know about him?" Maury asked.

"He used to practice medicine near Poitiers, retired five years ago and settled in Vingrau. Apparently, still licensed to practice…" said Pratt, who'd obviously done his homework, "Widowed three years ago and keeps himself to himself."

"Except for the odd abortion," said Maury sarcastically.

The drive to Vingrau from Rivesaltes is, at first, scenic as the road rises slowly from the plain, passing quarry entrances and villages shaded by Umbrella Pines in stands among the garrigue heathers. But, once the road gets to altitude the views become spectacular, the panorama opening as the road circumnavigates a cirque, a natural amphitheatre, so that the high mountains become a backdrop to the vineyards and crags of the Tautavel 'terroir'. Eventually, the road wends its way down to Vingrau, nestled at the foot of the cirque.

The village streets and roads were quiet, but for a few 'Senators', ancient locals, who sat out in clumps in the shade watching the world go by. Any through traffic had to negotiate the narrow streets to find a place to park that didn't impede other passers-through. Maury parked his car in the shade of a pretty, roofed market with filigree wrought iron detailing and marble floors and steps. Nearby, water gurgled through an unused lavoir and a flowered public space.

The villa they were seeking was easy to find, the place stood just off the main street that dissected the village centre. A brass nameplate on green gates confirmed their goal, 'Dr CLERGUE Paul, General Physician'. On the brick gatepost was a pushbutton bell that Maury pressed. The waiting detectives heard footsteps trotting and a jolly voice shouting, "I'm coming!" A key turned in the lock, and the gate was pulled open by a small pot-bellied man, dressed in shorts and flip-flops. The doctor had a bald head, intelligent eyes and a friendly demeanour, "Can I help you?" he asked.

Maury and Babayan flashed their credentials and made their formal introductions. Clergue didn't seem fazed, "Come on in," he invited, "I've just this moment sat down for an aperitif in the garden."

He led the detectives around to the back of the house, through a garden of date palms and succulents all overflowing their pots, to a flagged stone patio. Bees buzzed in the flower heads and the shade was delightfully cool, the music of Mozart echoed from the open door that allowed a glimpse of an untidy kitchen. The doctor bid the detectives sit with him at a metal patio set in front of a small bar, on which stood a selection of aperitif wines, a jug of iced water and the inevitable bottle of Ricard, "What's your poison?" he asked.

Lucine looked at Maury as if expecting him to decline the offer, but when he accepted a Ricard made long with the iced water, she asked for a Muscat.

Clergue poured the drinks and made a quick toast to health, "Santé," he wished, before sitting and asking what business brought the police knocking.

"Do you know a Senor Jimenez, who owns a Mas up near Périllos?" The doctor nodded, "Yes, I know him."

"Are you his doctor?"

"No," replied Clergue, "I'm just a friend."

This revelation surprised Maury, who wondered what the connection with his retired French doctor and the brash Spanish pimp might be.

"Okay," said the detective, "But have you ever been called upon to treat any of his..." Maury thought carefully about the word, "companions?"

"Yes, admitted Clergue, "Once or twice."

"Did you treat a girl called Mercedes around this time last year?" Clergue looked blank, as if the name meant nothing to him, "No-one called Mercedes. But I did treat one girl for some nasty injuries about this time last year. A broken Ulna, a broken jaw and a smashed eye-socket as I recall.

"I can consult my records and get you her full details if you wish," he offered, "She was Bulgarian, if memory serves me correctly. I administered First Aid and sent her off to hospital with Jimenez."

"Which hospital?" asked Lucine.

Clergue turned his attention to the petite detective and looked with unhidden admiration at her olive features and her trim form, "I do believe that he took her back to Spain. I gave her pain-killers and a sedative for the journey."

"Anything else you can remember?" asked Lucine, who now seemed to have the doctor's complete attention.

"It was late, around midnight, I think."

"Can you remember what the weather was like?"

"Oh?" said Clergue, it was not the question he was expecting, "Ah! Yes. It was dry when they arrived and absolutely pouring down when they left."

"Anything else?"

Clergue's eyes continued their appraisal of Lucine's figure and form, then he took a deep intake of breath, "The girl was pretty, tall, slim and spoke French fluently. Normally one finds that it's easier to communicate with Jimenez's...companions in English. She wasn't a natural blonde and she'd have been prettier if she'd just been her natural self." The words were meant to flatter the detective, "And, she was upset, of course, saying it was the last straw and other such things."

The doctor rose to his feet, "I'll get my records and I can give you exact details"

Lucine nodded and smiled, "Perfect," she purred.

Clergue looked happy and trotted off into the house. Babayan turned back to her superior officer, who sat back quietly observing everything as he sipped his pastis, "What other information do you want me to get?"

Maury chuckled, Lucine could probably have asked the good doctor anything, he seemed magnetised by her, "We're not here to investigate anything other than Jimenez and this Mercedes girl," he reminded her.

He looked around again, "Any secret symbols?" he asked.

Lucine smiled and turned her eyes down to the table, "Nothing out here," she observed.

When Doctor Clergue returned with his records, Lucine rose from her chair, "Do you mind if I use your bathroom?" she enquired.

"Oh, help yourself. Go through the kitchen into the hall, the rooms you are looking for are on your left," directed Clergue.

Lucine made for the house, feeling the doctor's eyes on her posterior she passed through the kitchen, untidy but clean, and entered the tiled hallway where a splendid spiral staircase curled up to the first floor. There were sideboards with pictures, and paintings on the walls. A framed photograph caught Lucine's eye, a picture of a younger Clergue cheek to cheek with a striking woman, who Lucine assumed was the man's late wife. Striking, because the wife was of obvious Persian descent, with the same noble features, dark eyes and blue-black locks as Babayan herself. He'd connected because he was reminded of his dead wife, a thought that saddened and impressed Lucine all at once. She freshened up in the bathroom, noting its awkward masculinity, the razor, the plain soap, the lonely toothbrush, and the fine layer of dust over everything, then returned to the garden.

The two men had left their seats in the shade and were chatting over their drinks next to a raised bed where melons and other gourd plants were being grown. When he caught sight of his colleague, Maury drained his glass and told the doctor that they appreciated his help and had to now take their leave.

Clergue pumped Maury's hand, "I think the Charentais type of melon would be perfect for you, they grow without any trouble. They're ideal for chutney, if you're into that sort of thing." He turned to Babayan and took her hand gently, "Goodbye detective, it was lovely to meet you."

Back at the car, Maury passed Babayan his notebook. In it he'd noted the date of the entry, the twenty-eighth of June and the girl's details; her name, date of birth, her address and, more importantly, her passport details. Lucine wondered how difficult Rada Dilov aka Mercedes would be to track down.

In fact, Rada Dilov took very little time to find, she'd registered with the French authorities and was now employed as a sales representative by a construction company developing flats and time-share apartments on the Cote Vermielle. Ringing ahead, she'd agreed to be visited at her place of work to help with the police enquiry.

So now Lucine and Maury were driving towards the Mediterranean, dark blue and sparkling in the sun. They passed by the outskirts of Perpignan using the fast roads that bypassed the old towns and villages of the plain, heading for the unsightly sprawl that seems to be the global pattern for seaside development. They reached a construction site situated on the spit of land between the salt sea and the etangs and pulled in by a mobile sales office. Today, the building work had ceased, but the cars of a few prospective buyers and the sales team were parked in the shade of a scraggy stand of bamboo that had yet to be razed for landscaping.

The offices were pleasantly cool, well-lit by natural daylight and humming to the sound of air-conditioners and low conversation. A young girl with too much foundation and severe lipstick smiled at the detectives in greeting and motioned them to a door when they asked for Rada.

Rada Dilov rose from the seat behind her desk when the investigators entered, regarding them with pale green eyes. Her hair was no longer bleached with peroxide, as the doctor had described, it was her natural auburn with tasteful blonde highlights cut into a professional bob. She was very tall and slim, dressed in a grey pencil skirt and silver silk blouse. Her long shapely legs were nylon clad despite the heat and ended with feet wrapped in expensive-looking stiletto shoes. Her smile was disarmingly wide and genuine, and her clever application of blusher and eye make-up minimised the asymmetry of her face, no doubt caused by the injury inflicted to her eye socket a year ago.

She shook the detective's hands, invited them both to sit, and closed the door for privacy, before retaking her place on the opposite side of the desk, "How may I be of any assistance?" she asked, in immaculate French.

"Our enquiry pertains to something that occurred on the twenty-eighth of June last year," explained Maury, knowing that she might find it uncomfortable to talk about her past. She nodded in understanding and sat back to listen carefully to Maury's questions.

"As we understand it, you suffered some injuries which were treated, in the first case, by a certain Doctor Clergue in Vingrau."

Rada nodded, "I don't remember the name of the place, but I do remember the doctor," she confirmed.

"Do you remember anything of your journey there? We understand that a certain Senor Jimenez took you there in his car."

She cast her mind back, "Yes, we almost had a crash with another car."

"Can you remember any details?"

Rada looked concerned, "No-one was hurt, were they?"

The two detectives remained silent, she looked at each in turn, trying to read their faces with concerned eyes. At last she continued, "It was a small green car. The driver was black. There was a black girl in the back seat. They looked frightened."

Lucine reached into her bag and slid the e-fits from it onto the desk for the Bulgarian to examine. Rada looked at the images carefully, "I don't know, it was dark, and I only caught sight of them for a moment...

"These are the people they found in the ditch up at Périllos aren't they?" Rada's face and demeanour became distressed.

Maury spoke in reassurance, "We only need to establish that they got there by car. Their deaths are nothing to do with you. Now, look at the likenesses again, and tell us if you think these people could have been who you saw in the car."

Rada wiped a tear from her welling-up eyes and looked at the e-fits again, she nodded, "Yes, I think they might have been."

"Good," said Maury, as Lucine put the photos away, "Thank you very much for your help," and he got to his feet.

"Do you know who they were?" asked Rada, her voice a little ragged with emotion.

"Sadly, no. Not yet," replied Maury with honest regret.

She offered her hand and gave the senior detective a firm handshake, then offered it again to Lucine who noticed the sparkling ring on her finger, "Oh! When's the big day?"

Rada flushed with pleasure, "In September," she replied.

"And who's the lucky man?" asked Maury. Lucine looked daggers at him, had he forgotten that Rada had been injured by a woman in her sex games?

"My boss, Andre," Rada gushed, "We're getting married in Nessebar, that's where my family are from."

"He's a lucky man," complimented the Commandant. "It's good to see that you're making something of your life. Good luck and best wishes."

Rada's wide smile returned and her eyes flashed, "And I wish you every success," she said.

"Oh!" exclaimed Maury, turning from the door to look at Rada directly, "Did you press charges against your assailant?"

She looked at the detective in surprise, her hand rising unbidden to her disfigured cheek.

"We understand from the housekeeper's family that you were assaulted."

She put her hand down and nodded, almost imperceptibly, "I was. But I didn't press charges."

"Why not?" Maury asked gently.

Rada looked down, as if in shame, then raised her eyes to look directly at the detective again, "El Pistolet told me it wouldn't be a good idea.

"Anyway, my assailant paid all my medical fees and some compensation."

Maury nodded, "Could you tell us who it was?" he asked, pressing her gently to say more.

Rada shook her head regretfully, "We were bound by a legal contract to keep silent about the clientele."

"Okay," said Maury with a sigh, "It was nice to meet you Mademoiselle."

Marie-France stepped out of the house when she saw Maury arrive and seemed pleased that he'd brought the wine as he promised, "I've got a surprise for you" she hinted mischievously. He wondered what that might be as he lifted the box of wine from the boot of the car. He half-expected visitors, but the house was its usual quiet self.

"I've got news," teased his wife.

Maury put the carton carefully on the kitchen table and saw that Marie-France had prepared food to be taken, in baskets and tubs.

"Are we off somewhere?" he guessed.

Marie-France's eyes flashed girlishly, and she nodded, "So, go and get changed into some nice smart casual wear."

Maury followed with the box of wine towards the Mazet, behind Marie-France who strutted happily ahead with a laden basket. They passed through the gate and were met by a whoop from the boys who, catching sight of their grandparent's arrival, ran from the terrace to meet them. Joel, the eldest, grabbed the handle of his grandmother's basket and helped her along like the young gentleman he was. The younger, Maurice, ran to Maury and unable to assist him with the box confided the secret, which Marie-France had been keeping, in a whisper, "Daddy's got a new job!"

Inquisition

Now that the lands of Languedoc had been politically and militarily pacified, an operation now began to root out heretics by Inquisition. Supported by troops, the Inquisition searched out and prosecuted Cathars.

Drawn from Friars of the Dominican Order, the Inquisition operated in Languedoc for nearly a century and a half, and it was this repressive tool that eventually succeeded in crushing Catharism.

The Inquisition's methods were straightforward:

First, the Inquisitors arrived at a place and declared that any heretic who wished to recant could do so immediately without penance. But those that did come forward were required to name all other heretics they knew or suspected of being heretics.

Second, these named people were called before the Inquisition to be questioned. A defendant could not call for witnesses or debate any point, he or she was there simply to answer the questions the Inquisitors asked.

If a heretic recanted, he or she underwent penance, ranging from fasting, pilgrimage, flogging or – most hated – the wearing of yellow crosses on outer garments to identify him or her as an ex-heretic.

If a defendant lapsed back into heresy, or refused to recant, he or she was passed over to the Friar's secular guard to be burned.

The people of Languedoc despised the Inquisition, the Dominicans were mostly strangers and were, effectively, the state police of the Church of Rome. The operations of the Inquisition drove most heretics underground or displaced them, south to the Pyrenees or north into Lombardy. Many were concentrated in the remote valleys and castles of Ariege, particularly in the region of Sabarthes, where the fortress of Montsegur became a magnet to those fleeing the Inquisition.

When a party of knights, sympathetic to the Cathar cause, descended from this remote bastion and executed four Inquisitors and their bodyguards in the small town of Avigonet, between Toulouse and Carcassonne, the incident brought down the wrath of the Catholic church on the concentration of Cathars at Montsegur.

The death of four Friars and their retinue was spun into a massacre, an outrage that led the Council of Beziers, sitting in 1243 to call for the eradication, once and for all, of the citadel and Cathars of Montsegur.

24th June

Maury conveyed news of Robert's appointment when he rang Pierre. The Inspector General was pleased, but didn't sound surprised, "That's good news for the family."

"Did you know something about this Pierre?" Maury asked, suspecting that he'd somehow been kept out of the loop in some conspiracy cooked up by their wives.

"Well, yes. I put in a good word for him. But that's the least I could do for my god-daughter's husband."

Maury, not one for small talk or chit-chat, moved the conversation on, "I need something from you Pierre."

"Well, tell me what it is, and I'll see what I can do"

"I need to know what happened at the Jimenez place on the night of the twenty-seventh of June last year. We know that one of Jimenez's girls was hurt and he took her off to see a doctor. I want to know if anyone else left the house at around the same time. I'm hoping we'll find other witnesses who saw our three victims on the road."

Lafitte did not answer right away, he was obviously weighing things in his mind, "I can't promise anything, but I'll see what I can do...Any new developments?"

"We've a few leads we're following up. I think we may be getting there."

"Alright, I'll give you another week, while the Perpignan station is under the microscope, then I'm going to have to get you back to Narbonne."

Lafitte hadn't meant to put any pressure on his friend, Maury knew that. But Maury felt he'd like to see this case through to its conclusion. Those three young faces in the e-fits and poor Sebastien Tradot haunted him.

He made a call to Toulouse, the status of the casualty was unchanged, but some rapid eye movement was evidently quite encouraging. Mercier was still in his induced coma but breathing without a ventilator. So, it wasn't all bad news, it was just a matter of patiently waiting.

As was their routine, Maury and Marie-France were enjoying the early morning cool, but today the sky was not the Cerulean shade to which they'd become accustomed, instead it was a high white cirrostratus. A sense of change permeated the atmosphere. Officially, the heatwave was over, at least according to the article on the page of the Midi-Libre Madame Maury was reading. But no rain had yet fallen on Roussillon, despite the heavy storms that had wrought havoc in the Midi-Pyrenees and Haute Languedoc.

But Maury was reflecting on family events, pleased yet worried for Robert, Elisabeth and the two boys who were making sea-changes in their lives. He realised too, that his own life was still undergoing substantial change. A short time ago he and Marie-France had moved from Lozère to be here, and that move had worked wonders for them personally and their marriage.

But, if he was honest, his promotion to Commandant had removed him from the investigative role he so enjoyed, now he was signing papers, attending seminars and shaking the hands of local dignitaries rather than doing 'real' police work.

"Would I be stupid to ask for a demotion?" he asked aloud, the question posed as much at himself as Marie-France, who stopped reading and looked at him over her paper

"What's the matter Commandant? Missing being a detective?" she asked perceptively.

"Mm," he said, a non-committal grumble that only wives can decode.

"They might need a lead detective at Perpignan soon," Maury mentioned.

"A demotion would affect your pension," Madame Maury pointed out.

"Mm," Maury grunted, acknowledging her insight.

He picked up his coffee and looked at the sky. Marie-France looked at her husband and considered their options.

Maury wasn't sure what the team should do today, he was toying with the idea of standing them down for a well-deserved break, contrary to his urge to keep working, when his mobile phone rang.

It was Babayan, "Bonjour Commandant, I wondered if I might have the day off today? My brother and sister-in-law are returning from Chad. I need to have the house and the children ready and pick them up from the airport."

It was decided. Maury was happy for Lucine, but more so for little Mikel and Samara whose sad eyes betrayed their need for their parents. So, he, of course, consented to her request, "How long do you need? Take all the time you want."

"Thank you, Sir. A day will suffice."

In the background he could hear the excited voices of the children, "Alright Lieutenant, I'll see you tomorrow."

"Oh! Before you go Sir…I spent the evening looking over Sebastien Tradot's notebook."

"Did you find anything of interest?" asked Maury, his ears pricked.

"Well…" Lucine hesitated, "Not really, but it did me some insight into his mind-set."

"Do you think he was likely to have committed suicide then?"

"No, I don't think so. He was a dreamer, and he felt that he didn't belong in this world. But he was a romantic too, there are little poems and things and they're full of…hope!"

"Ah!" said Maury, pensively, "Have a good day Lieutenant, I'll see you tomorrow."

So, how did a young man with hopes and dreams end up burst asunder on the rocks below an ancient castle? And why did a registered sex-offender attempt the same? Perhaps the video that had been sent to the technicians at Castelnaudary could provide some answers, after all that purported to show someone doing the same but flying instead of falling! Who else had flown from the battlements of Montsegur? And who was Esclarmonde?

Maury stood Renaud and Pratt down for the day and decided that he ought to do some research.

It was difficult to separate fact from fiction, the internet was mostly full of theories rather an hard historical fact, but then again, as

Maury trawled through websites he realised that romantic Disneyesque fables about the Cathars seemed to be more attractive to most people than their actual history. It was more dreamy, syrupy and hopeful to believe that the Cathars guarded the Holy Grail and had a mystic cathedral where astral power was focussed, namely Montsegur, than the real story of a people that would rather walk into a bonfire than recant their faith and bow the knee to a Catholic church, that they believed was run by Satan. Their actions to rational modern minds are simply beyond comprehension. So, the fanciful seems more believable than fact.

What he did establish though, was that there was indeed a Cathar called Esclarmonde, a high-born figure who became a cause-celebre of the gnostic movement. Somehow, time and imagination had transformed her into 'Great Esclarmonde' whose very name meant 'Light of the World' in Occitan. According to legend she was the guardian of the Cathar 'grail' and she was with the body of credentes (believers) that withstood a long siege by the Catholic forces sent to crusade against the Cathars in their last bastion – the secure mountain – Montsegur.

The story goes that when the ancient fortress finally succumbed to the besieging army, a white dove descended from the heavens and split the rock on which the castle stood, with its beak. Esclarmonde, high-priestess or Parfaite, placed the 'grail' into the cleft rock which then closed itself upon it. But Esclarmonde did not descend from the pog to the fiery stake to be burned as a heretic with the other Cathar defenders, she is said to have ascended to the battlements and transformed in a white dove which ascended from the mountain and flew off east.

The dove has since become a symbol for the Cathars, along with the Occitan Cross. Elements of which were all found in the Gema Abraxas worn around the necks of the disciples of some modern movement to which the three victims on the ditch, Tradot, Mercier and perhaps, even, the 'white dove' remains belonged.

It was a fanciful story, but it seemed to Maury that on the 'Esclarmonde' video it was this event being reconstructed.

He needed to see the cleaned-up video. He rang the technical department at Castelnaudary and pulled rank in order to prioritise its analysis. The supervisor promised that it would be back with the investigating team soon.

The Fall of Montsegur

In 1232 the Cathar, Guilhabert de Castres, who had prevailed in argument and discussion with Dominic and other Catholic legates seemed to sense a future need for protection from the threat of the Roman Church. He asked the castle's lord to ensure that Montsegur was equipped to protect its growing population of dispossessed souls. The castle's lord recruited Pierre-Raymond de Mirepoix, a professional knight, who provided around 100 men to protect the Cathars living in and around the castle.

The army assembled to assail the place in the summer of 1243, was around 10,000 strong and it marched under the leadership of the Archbishop of Narbonne and the King's man, the seneschal of Carcassonne, Pierre Amiel.

Situated high on its 'pog' or rocky spur at 1,207 metres of altitude, the castle stood above a series of serrated and forbidding crags above the village of Montsegur. The castle proved to be as impregnable as it appears, it withstood the unwanted attentions of the besiegers for nearly ten months. While most of these mountain-top castles succumbed through lack of water or food, Montsegur was resupplied by locals who knew every contour of the mountain. So, despite being populated by a garrison of 100, 207 Cathar perfecti and at least 131 others, the 435 inhabitants seemed secure against the vast army arrayed against them.

But just before Christmas a party of Gascon climbers managed to infiltrate a pill-box that protected the castle's approaches, slit the throats of the defenders, and provided a passageway for the invaders to the foot of the castle's walls.

Sensing that the end was near, two perfecti were charged with removing the legendary treasure that the castle contained, and they slipped past the sentinels of the besieging army undiscovered.

Around 21st February 1244 a bombardment of the castle began, mangonels launched stones weighing up to 80kgs apiece at the curtain walls. This attack was repulsed, but at the beginning of March Pierre-Roger de Mirepoix was compelled to sue for a two-week truce.

During this respite, the 205 perfecti prepared themselves for inevitable death. Something extraordinary happened as these Bonhommes prayed and fasted, twenty of the other inhabitants asked for the rite of 'consolation', where they would be inaugurated as full perfecti, knowing their fate too would be to be burned alive rather than turned over to the Inquisition to endure a lesser penance.

On the 16th March 1244, the truce was ended, the castle surrendered to the Archbishop and the seneschal, and its defenders filed down from their refuge. The Cathars went down to the lower slopes where a great pyre had been lit, but no stakes were needed, they ascended the burning faggots and volunteered themselves to the flames.

25th June

Maury arrived early at Rivesaltes to wait for his team and was pleased to find that the technicians at Castelnaudary had been as good as their word, sending the enhanced video of 'Esclarmonde' as an attachment to an apologetic email.

First through the door was Pratt, the reservist was surprised to see that his superior was already there, "Can I get you a coffee Sir?" he asked. Maury nodded, knowing that his mind and body would appreciate its usual caffeine hit.

Pratt was soon followed by Babayan and Renaud. Once Pratt had returned with his coffee, Maury outlined the day's task, "Castelnaudary have sent back that enhanced video. It's an attachment on an email I forwarded to each of you."

"The 'Esclarmonde' one?" asked Renaud, seeking clarity.

"That's right. And that got me thinking that maybe all these jumpers were copying the legend, or at least trying to.

"So, I want you to each look at the video carefully. There might be clues, some bystanders, or witnesses at the scene, who can tell us if it was a stunt staged for the YouTube generation or not. Because, these two poor sods Tradot and Mercier may have been copying a hoax!

"Excuse me," said Maury as his phone buzzed.

"Allo," he said, holding it to his ear, noting that the caller's number was withheld.

"Commandant Maury?" asked an unfamiliar male voice.

"Yes."

"My name is Dec, I'm a Captain in the IGPN. I've been requested to assist you in your enquiries regarding our mutual friend, Jimenez, up at Opoul-Périllos."

"Yes?"

"I've some video and a name. I'll send them as an attachment..." The call ended abruptly.

"IGPN have sent over a video and a name for us," explained Maury to the company, "Let's have a look, shall we? We'll get back to the other one later."

He pulled his laptop from its bag, opened the lid, and fired it up. A few moments later he had the email displayed on the screen.

Dec was as good as his word, it simply contained a name and a video attachment.

The name, Dubois, had a familiar ring, but Maury had to dig into his memory to connect it to Verdier's lawyer from the Procureur's office in Perpignan. It surprised him, wasn't Dubois a man?

The video, which seemed to be captured by a CCTV camera on the outside wall of Jimenez's garage, showed the roofs of several cars parked on the driveway. It was raining so heavily that the image was blurred by the refraction of the raindrops. A figure, under the protective shelter of an open umbrella appeared at the edge of shot and got into a silver car without the camera betraying any meaningful detail. The car reversed, its shape that of a large German-made coupe, and it turned, without the registration or the driver's face being visible, and left.

"It's an Audi" said Renaud, "that's about all I can make out."

"The timestamp says a quarter after midnight, which fits our timeframe nicely," observed Babayan.

"I think that here's a lawyer called Dubois, in the Prefecture in Perpignan, who may be connected," added Maury.

"How should we approach this?" Lucine asked, aware that it might be difficult to conduct their investigation alongside the IGPN's.

"Best check that this Dubois owns an Audi first," suggested Renaud.

"Won't that be difficult without the registration number?" cautioned Pratt, "Maybe we should find out something about Dubois from the Prefecture's website, or something first."

"Good idea," said Maury, "Pratt, you check the Prefecture's website. Renaud, you find out what cars the Prefecture runs in its fleet, if it's a pool car the registration won't matter anyway.

"Lieutenant, I need you to find out more about our Monsieur Mercier. There's got to be someone who can tell us more about him, a family member or friend."

"I'll try the hospital first," said Lucine, "They might know who his next of kin is, and they can give me an update on his condition."

"Sir," interjected Pratt, pensively approaching the detective's desk,

"I think we've got something on our board concerning a silver Audi on the night of twenty-eighth of June."

Maury looked up with interest, "Okay, what've you got?"

Pratt had the foresight to have a printout ready, "A silver Audi stuck in the flooded underpass that cuts under the railway on the D5B at Salses-le-Chateau. Flooded engine, causing catastrophic engine damage. The driver, a Mademoiselle Christine Dubois, Government Employee at the Prefecture de Perpignan. Home address, Chemin du Phare, Leucate-Plage. Attending officers called for assistance from Europcar, as the car was on a long-term lease to the Prefecture. A recovery vehicle arrived after a thirty-minute wait, bringing a replacement vehicle for Mademoiselle Dubois and it recovered the flooded Audi back to the Europcar compound, Polygone Nord, St. Esteve, Perpignan."

"Alright," said Maury, ready to act, "I want you and Renaud to go to Europcar in Perpignan, if the car was damaged, they'll have photographs and maybe even tracker information.

"The Lieutenant and I will see if we can catch this Christine Dubois at work."

Maury glanced at the green pin on the board the D5B was the departmental road that would take someone with local knowledge back to Leucate-Plage from Périllos.

The gendarmes were quickly away to the car hire depot.

Lucine tried to track down Dubois, by ringing the Prefecture's reception desk. Maury heard her conversing with an administrator and scribbling notes onto her pad. When she looked up from her call, he could see that she was puzzled, "There are two lawyers called Dubois working in the Procureur's office," she told him, "Eric and Christine."

That explained how Dubois could be another sex, "Are they related?"

"I didn't ask. Anyway, Eric's on administrative leave and Christine will be happy to see us before lunch."

"Did you speak to her?"

"No, I spoke to her Personal Assistant."

"She must be high-up in the place then," remarked Maury.

It was a quick drive from Rivesaltes to the Industrial Estate on which the Europcar depot was situated. The route skirted the runway of Perpignan's regional airport, around which light aircraft of a flying school were circling to practice take-offs and landings.

"Did you meet with that Spanish vice detective," asked Pratt.

Renaud, driving, smiled to himself but said nothing.

"Well?" insisted his partner.

Their arrival at Europcar saved Renaud from further interrogation. The gendarmes stepped from the car and saw the furtive looks of customers and staff. They adjusted their uniforms and stepped towards the office.

A severe looking middle-aged manager, with the deep eye creases and yellow fingers of the heavy smoker stepped to the counter to deal with them. "Can I be of assistance?" she asked, with a husky voice.

Renaud didn't ask for privacy, he simply pushed the incident report they were investigating across the desk. Pratt stood behind him appraising the customers who stood patiently waiting to be served. That the gendarmes had jumped the queue and made their business public was not really an act of arrogance, they acted as officers of the law who should be held in respectful fear.

Marie, the manager, according to her name tag, looked through the papers carefully, pursed her lips, and began tapping keys on her computer keyboard, "What do you need to know?" she asked.

"You've got tracking data, I assume. I'll need that and the damage report, with photos, of the car when it got returned," replied Renaud.

Marie nodded and continued tapping keys. She looked up, "They're big files," she warned.

Hearing her comment, the well-prepared Pratt opened his chest pocket and produced a flash-drive that he laid on the counter.

With a sour look, Marie took the drive in her long yellow fingers and continued tapping for a few seconds before inserting it into a port on her tower computer. Moments later, she withdrew it and put it back on the counter.

"Thanks for your help," said Renaud.

"Madame," added Pratt, as a courtesy.

"My pleasure," replied Marie without smiling.

Christine Dubois was in fact one the Procureur General's deputies. Maury and Babayan found themselves waiting for their appointment in the hushed sitting area, outside her office, to which they'd been ushered by her Personal Assistant. Maury got up to stretch his legs and helped himself to water from a dispenser, and looked out at Perpignan's boulevards from the windows. For a weekday, the city was remarkably quiet, but the Catalans did tend to do their shopping and chores either early or late to avoid the midday heat. Anyone in the streets remained, as much as possible in the shade of the pollarded Plantains in which the town's flocks of pigeons roosted. The risk of getting a dropping on one's head was high, but still preferable to being directly in the sun's rays. The sky was still white, and the sun had a halo around it.

Presently, the assistant's intercom buzzed, and she rose on tip-tapping heels to lead the detectives into her boss's office "Commandant Maury and Lieutenant Babayan of the Police Nationale to see you Maître," she announced.

Christine Dubois had mousey brown, shoulder length hair, pale skin, and a plain face with pale blue eyes behind her rimless spectacles. She wore a smart brown trouser suit, a cream blouse with a silver and turquoise brooch at her throat. Her hands were strong and square, as she extended them towards the chairs on which she wished her visitors to sit. Her mouth was small and miserly, she looked Maury and Babayan over as they entered, her look neutral, but obviously judging. "Pray sit," she said. She sounded like a schoolmistress, her words well pronounced and accentless, "How can I be of service?"

Maury fumbled in his pocket for his notebook and leafed through it as the lawyer waited, and then began, "On the twenty-eighth of June last year you were involved in an unfortunate incident, with your car, in floodwaters at Salses-le-Chateau..."

Maury paused until Dubois acknowledged, with a nod, that the information was correct. "It was very late at night, at around one 'o' clock in the morning when you contacted the emergency services..."

Again, the pause, a little agitated Christine Dubois agreed, "Yes."

Maury slowly withdrew a pen from his top pocket and found a blank page on which to write in his notebook, "Could you tell us what you were doing in that location, so late at night?"

"I was visiting some friends," Dubois quickly replied.

"Oh, they live nearby, do they?"

"In Salses," Dubois countered.

Maury looked at Babayan, "We can check that against the tracking data."

Lucine nodded as Maury turned back to Dubois, "Could you let me have your friends' name and address?"

Realising that she may have painted herself into a corner Dubois corrected herself, "It may have been other friends I was visiting."

Maury nodded, "I understand. It was foul weather that night, perhaps that would help you to remember the journey," he suggested.

"Does it matter where I was going, or who I saw? That's not really your business, anyway, is it?" Dubois said, with some irritation.

"Do you remember the journey?" Maury asked again.

"Why? What do you need to know?" Dubois was clearly irritated by the detective's questions and manner of asking them.

Maury closed his notebook, put both it and his pen back in their respective pockets, and then leaned forward to look Dubois directly in the eyes. "I want to know what happened in the time between you assaulting a girl at the Jimenez Mas and getting in your car at a quarter after midnight, to calling for assistance in Salses at One 'O' clock in the morning," was Maury's retort, spoken in the same clipped and well-pronounced tones that she had used.

A look of fear crossed Dubois' face, "Nothing happened. I drove from Jimenez's to Salses and got stuck in a flood."

Maury nodded at Lucine, who withdrew the e-fits from her bag and placed them before the lawyer.

"Think carefully, Maître," Maury cautioned, as Dubois looked at the likenesses "Did you see these three people on the road?"

Christine Dubois said nothing, collected the e-fits together and held them out for Lucine to take back, "No, I didn't. Now, I'd like you to leave."

Maury rose, "Well, thanks for your time Mademoiselle Dubois. Perhaps you'd like legal representation with you next time we speak. Here's my card, should you remember anything useful," he said, placing a dog-eared business car on the Deputy Procureur's desk.

Lucine thought about Maury's technique, his oblique questioning style and his manipulation of peoples' preconceptions, they were effective tools, except that she suspected he used them instinctively. They came away from the Prefecture knowing that Maître Christine Dubois was covering things up, or outrightly lying about the events of that fateful night. Maury's intimation that things might escalate if she weren't more forthcoming was clever, it put a slow-burning nag into the back of the Deputy Procureur's mind. If there was indeed, tracking data on the contract hire car she'd been using, Maury's remark about checking it, had implied that the investigators knew more than they were letting on. If there wasn't any data, there was no harm done. Maury had not lied, he'd just made it a possibility about which Dubois would fret, and if she had enough of a conscience, she might even tell the detectives what they needed to know. Maury's secret weapon, Lucine decided, was that he was underestimated.

Maury's mobile phone rang as he climbed the stairs after Babayan up to the Rivesaltes office and a familiar young voice addressed him, "Is that Commandant Maury?"

"Yes, that's right," Maury confirmed.

"This is Ali, Ali Nassim, Mankour's brother."

It was an unexpected development. Maury stopped on the landing and spoke warmly to the young man, "Hello Ali, how's your family?"

Ali sounded excited and happy, "It's fine, it's all great, man. You know we got a settlement from the Police, right? Yeah!"

"Yes, I heard. I hope it helps you out."

"And Mankour gets money for life!"

"It's what he deserves."

"Yeah. You're right man. But there must be some way that we can thank you…"

"There's no need for that…"

"No, that's why I'm ringing, see. Mankour says he'll do you a picture of something you like."

"There's no need…"

"Mankour wants to."

Maury decided not to object any more, to refuse the injured boy's generosity would amount to an insult, "Okay. Let me think about what I'd like him to paint. This is your number, right? I'll get back to you, once I've had a think."

"Cool man. I'll tell Mankour. Speak soon, yeah? Bye, Monsieur le Commandant."

Maury chuckled to himself as he pocketed his phone and entered the office.

"How did you get on?" Maury asked. The three others were poring over data displayed on a computer screen.

"We got everything we needed from Europcar," Renaud replied, "Tracking data and photos of the damage to the car."

"And what've you found?"

"You were right about the tracking data, Sir," confirmed Lucine, "Dubois took just over three quarters of an hour to go just twenty kilometres. We're getting more detail now."

Maury was impressed, he hadn't realised that a tracker would be so precise.

"And you might want to see the damage on the car," said Renaud, holding out a wad of printout images.

"Right," Maury said with some satisfaction, going to the clearest desk to lay the photos out. While Pratt and Babayan continued to retrieve the tracking data, Renaud helped the Commandant lay out the photos.

"She hit the water so hard that it tore off the front valance and engine undertray," Renaud started a commentary, as he laid out the pictures, "The water got sucked up into the air intake and hydro-locked the engine.

"Look how deep the water was, the foot-wells are full of water and it short-circuited the seat control circuits!"

Renaud was obviously a petrol-head, "But, this is the interesting bit Sir, look here…"

The photo to which Renaud was referring showed the bonnet and front-wing of the Audi "That," said the gendarme with excitement, his finger on dents and creases on the top of both body panels, "is not damage caused by hitting the water!"

"So, what do you think?" asked Maury, half-guessing the answer.

"It looks like she's hit something."

"Okay, let's send the photos to an expert and see what they make of them. Know anyone?"

Renaud smiled with self-satisfaction, "Yes, we have a Crash Investigation Team right here in the Gendarmerie. I could get them to have a look," he suggested.

Maury turned back to Pratt and Lucine as Renaud saw to getting the other Team's help, "How are you getting on?"

Lucine's look betrayed some disappointment, "The tracking data is not as detailed as we first thought. It only tracks the route of a journey, between long stops."

She went on to explain, "On the journey we're interested in, Dubois' car started its journey from the Jimenez Mas. It used the shortest route to get to Salses-le-Chateau. The tracking ends when the car gets stuck under the railway bridge. We don't know anything else about that journey, other than the time it took to take – forty-four minutes and one second."

"Okay," said Maury, "Now, she must have made that journey before. See how long those journeys took and you should be able to work out what type of driver she normally is. If we can figure out how long the journey takes in bad weather, then we'll be getting somewhere.

"Pratt, I could do with another set of eyes, if you don't mind. I think we ought to go over that 'Esclarmonde' video to see if it divulges any new clues."

The afternoon was spent in the little office, even with air-conditioning the confined space warmed with the heat of their bodies and the humming computers on which they worked. Outside, high lines of grey, like the lateral markings of a mackerel, formed under the stratospheric white of the sky. Uncomfortable as they were, they found the airless heat outside even more oppressive. When Maury went to get everyone a slice of gateau and a coffee from the local patisserie, he came back drenched in sweat.

When Renaud arrived back to the office, Maury decided that it might be time to debrief. He invited Renaud to start, with the findings of the crash investigation team.

Renaud had photographs of the damaged bonnet and wing, with measurements and labels superimposed, he put them up on the board to illustrate his points as he went. "This damage was definitely not caused when the car hit the water in Salses, and it was not old damage either. It would be consistent with the damage caused by a low-speed impact with something relatively soft. Whatever it was, the impact was glancing, rather than direct. If it had been direct, there would have been damage to the front bumper, headlamp or grille."

He put another photograph on the board, next to the first. It was a different car, but the damage was the same, "This damage is very similar, notice that neither bumper, headlamp nor grille are damaged. This car was in collision with an adult pedestrian..."

The three officers watching turned to each other and nodded with a shared sense of relief, but their low-key elation was short-lived. Renaud added another photograph of a car with the same damage, "And this was caused by the car colliding with a deer!"

Maury groaned with disappointment, he thought for a moment that they'd found the definitive evidence to explain the deaths they were investigating. He turned to Lucine, "Your turn Lieutenant"

Babayan spoke from her desk, turning the screen so they could see the workings out she'd made, "The data shows that Maître Dubois always sticks to the speed limit. She doesn't drive with any hard accelerations or heavy braking. In inclement weather her speed drops to around 80% of normal which points to her being even slower than usual on the night in question. But we do know that weather conditions were particularly awful that night, so that could account for this."

Maury bit his tongue, he wanted to swear, but made do with a grunt of disappointment, "And we haven't got good news either. The video was taken with the castle against the brightening sky. You've all seen it. Enhancing it doesn't really give us anything we couldn't see before.

"We don't get a clearer picture of the jumper either. But we do know that, according to experts, the footage is genuine.

"This really does show someone jumping off the walls of Montsegur and appearing to fly. There's no wires, no wingsuit and no safety net!"

Maury looked at the board, they'd gone down lots of avenues, but the investigation was still no nearer to establishing who the dead were, or even the actual manner of their deaths. The three young faces looked down at him, were these e-fits even accurate? Did Dubois collide with them and drive away? Did she see them at all? They had more questions than answers. It was possible that Dubois had been in an accident with them, but how could they prove it anyway, without an admission?

Then he looked at the picture of Sebastien Tradot, a dreamer, in the prime of life, with all to live for. A dad to be. Why on earth jump off a castle? Were you emulating Esclarmonde, did you think you'd fly rather than fall? What led you to believe that?

And, Antoine Mercier. You did the same. What possessed you? Were you driven by the same demons that caused you to want to commit depraved sexual acts and violence? Did you jump to escape them?

Maury addressed Renaud and Pratt, "Our lines of enquiry are drying up. Lieutenant Babayan and I will be visiting the Coroner tomorrow. "I'm afraid there's little for you to do unless there's a new development. You're going to have to return to your normal duties, for tomorrow at least"

The two gendarmes nodded, they both understood that if their manpower couldn't be justified, returning to duties for the Gendarmerie would be necessary, "Yes Sir," acknowledged Renaud for them both, "We're due a few days off, anyway."

"Oh, yes," admitted Maury guiltily, "You must be due some."

The stood down gendarmes left, leaving the two detectives alone in the office.

"You're alright for tomorrow, aren't you?" Maury asked"

"Yes," replied Babayan, she smiled a sad smile.

"Missing the children?"

Lucine nodded.

"Fancy a cold beer?" asked Maury.

The detectives sat in a shaded terrace in the quiet centre of Rivesaltes, which was just as well, as a soft rain pattered non-committally from saucer-shaped clouds high in the sky. They watched a flurry of activity, as shopkeepers ran to retrieve displays from the street, just in case the rain decided to get more serious about wetting the ground. It hadn't got much cooler though, but the petrichor made a pleasant change to the dusty scent to which they had become accustomed.

"So, how are things without the children?"

"Oh, you know, there is good and bad. I miss them like crazy, but I do have my own life back now," replied Lucine with a hint of regret.

"Will your brother and sister-in-law go off to work abroad again?"

Lucine shook her head, "No, I don't think so. It takes too much of a toll on the children."

"You look after them well enough."

"I try my best," admitted Lucine, "But I'm not their mum and dad."

"So, what are they going to do now?"

"They'll have some sort of holiday for a while, I expect. Then there's talk of resettling in Marseille."

"Marseille?"

"Yes, the suburbs there are crying out for doctors."

"You mean the immigrant quarters?"

"Yes," said Lucine, with a humourless laugh "It's not too different from what they were doing with Medecins Sans Frontiers."

"And what will you do?"

"I don't know, things got difficult for me in Perpignan."

"Mm, but Verdier has gone and Guillot will be moving on," revealed Maury.

Lucine looked at him, her eyebrows arching, "Really? I didn't hear anything"

"That's because you're working in the field with me," Maury observed, "Yes, Verdier is now a municipal policeman in Elne. And you'll be pleased to know that we've made things right with the Nassim family. Of course, we can't undo the damage that's been done to Mankour, but they've offered him a pension for life."

The news cheered Babayan, she shook her head in disbelief and smiled, "And what will happen to Guillot?"

"I expect he'll get moved to a post somewhere else, but I doubt he'll be in charge of detectives."

"That's a shame," said Lucine, "I quite liked him. Do you know who'll take his place?" She was thinking of the more ambitious detectives in the Perpignan pool, wondering who might put their hat into the ring.

"I'm thinking of going for the job myself," Maury revealed. "But I'd have to give up my rank and that would have a knock-on effect on my pension, so it's only an idea.

"This is strictly between ourselves," he cautioned.

Lucine felt honoured to be confided in by the Commandant, she knew that he tended to be an outsider to all, but his family. It would be nice for him to be her permanent boss, but to take a hit on his rank and pension would certainly make the possibility remote. Still, it cheered her to think that it might be a possibility.

"I'd like that," she admitted.

Maury's phone rang, "Marie-France," he told Lucine as he got up to speak privately before returning to swallow the last dregs of his beer, "I've got to go! The rain's stopped."

The rain had barely wet the ground.

Lucine thought about all that Maury had said as she drove home. The few days she'd spent on this case had been better than any in her two years at Perpignan as a detective. She felt less lonely at work now than she did at home, just days ago the opposite had been true.

What would she do if the Commandant's plan didn't materialise? She didn't fancy the ghetto of Marseille in the least, so relocating with her brother's family wasn't an option she'd seriously consider. But what would be here in Perpignan? The old jewellers, Monsieur and Madame Mayeur weren't her blood. Indeed, her brother was her only surviving full blood relative. She'd have to do something about this dreaded loneliness, she decided.

So, this was the place that Provencal S.A. had offered to house its new manager of CNC operations. It was a pleasant new build in the village of Espira de l'Agly, just a few kilometres from the marble processing plant, that produced stunning bespoke kitchen and bathroom fittings. It was very clean, and presentable, even if the generic furniture and fittings were devoid of personality.

Maury walked past the new company Renault and went to the back garden following the shrieks of joy that led him to the pool, where the boys were splashing about with their father. Through the French windows he could see Elisabeth and Marie-France planning how to make the place a home. The place had air-conditioning but it needed it, there were no trees to provide natural shade. It would be no good for growing vegetables thought Maury, but the little family seemed happy to have a new home.

The Cathar Treasure

History tells us that two Cathar perfecti slipped through the noose tightening around the castle of Montsegur, carrying off some sort of 'treasure'. What this treasure actually was, is a matter of great conjecture.

Contemporary records from the Inquisition that interrogated the defeated garrison and other survivors of the Montsegur siege, indicate that these two men escaped with the Cathar treasury: Money, gold and silver donated to their cause to maintain the Cathars hiding in the forests and caves of tucked-away places in Ariege and the Corbières.

Some commentators believe that the treasure was the symbolic meaning of Catharism itself, the perception that the enlightened spirit was the true treasure that Jesus and the prophets spoke of in numerous bible passages.

Matthew 19:21 Jesus said to him, "If you would be perfect, go, sell what you possess and give to the poor, and you will have treasure in heaven, and come follow me."

1 Timothy 6:17-19 As for the rich in this present age, charge them not to be haughty, nor to set their hopes on the uncertainty of riches, but on God, who richly provides us with everything to enjoy. They are to do good, be rich in good works, to be generous and ready to share, thus storing up treasure for themselves, as a good foundation for the future, so that they may take hold of that which is truly life.

Isaiah 45:3 I will give you treasures of darkness and hoards in secret places, that you may know that it is I, the LORD, the God of Israel, who calls you by your name.

James 5:3 Your gold and silver have corroded, and their corrosion will be evidence against you and will eat your flesh like fire. You have laid up a treasure in the last days.

In fact, these and many like scripture passages, reflect the doctrine of the Bonhommes, this was the exemplar life that they had lived among the peoples of Languedoc. The Cathars simply did not value their lives according to material norms, they were ready to move on to their promised 'mansions in heaven'.

Despite the impression given by the word 'crusade' and the fact that battles had been fought against them, there is no evidence that the committed Cathars ever fought back. The fighting that had taken place was between the lords and populace who protected them, and those sent to exterminate them. The Cathars had simply followed the biblical instruction in Matthew 10:23, When you are persecuted in one place, flee to another...

That their impact on the peoples of Languedoc was profound, is attested to by the amount of soldiery and citizens willing to lay their lives on the line to protect them. But when cornered, the Cathars submitted willingly to the consuming flame rather than protract the suffering of their protectors.

Somehow, the fabric of time and myth has woven another story into that of the Cathars, which rather embellishes it or utterly detracts from it, according to your point of view, the legend of the Holy Grail.

25th June

Marie-France was fussing from the moment she woke, looking through her clothes for the correct ensemble to be worn when shopping with Elisabeth, as Maury went to water the garden. When he returned to the house, she was still fussing, so he made a coffee, went out to the terrace and left her to it. There were puddles on the driveway, and house martins were enjoying them as if they were baths. Landing in the shallow water they spread their streamlined wings and shook droplets over themselves. Maury felt their elation, as little rain as it was that had fallen, it had given the parched natural world of Roussillon a refreshment it sorely needed.

A phone call from Martinez broke Maury's enjoyment of the moment, "Allo, Commandant. Thanks for actioning all the emails I forwarded to you."

"Thank you, for sorting through them first," replied Maury.

"There is a seminar for senior detectives in Toulon on the 1st July for two days, you've been invited to attend. Do I accept or decline?"

"Please decline"

"Very well Sir..."

"Is there something else you want to ask Martinez?" asked Maury, sensing that his aide-de-camp was reluctant to ask something.

"Your Citroen has had its software updated."

"Ah! So, you'd like me to come and pick it up?"

Martinez paused and carried on reluctantly, "It's gone to be used at the Commissariat in Beziers. And undercover want their old Peugeot back."

"Oh? Okay," said Maury with a little regret, "So, what am I getting in its stead?"

"The Inspector General has secured a sponsorship deal with a major importer. You've got to collect a new car from the Toyota franchise at Labege..."

"Labege? But, that's right up near Toulouse."

"Yes Sir, they're expecting you at around two 'o' clock tomorrow afternoon."

"And what do I do with the old one?"

"You leave it with them, it's due a service anyway, and someone will pick it up in due course."

It's a good job there are no red-hot leads to follow, thought Maury, what a waste of a day! "Okay, forward me the address and I'll see to it."

"When are we expecting you back Sir?"

"A few more days Martinez. The Inspector General said he wants me back at my desk soon."

Babayan met up with Maury at the Coroner's office, and they made their way down to the basement morgue. The Coroner was his usual officious self, as he greeted them and led them to the new body. "Quite interesting these remains. Not too much left of them, I think some sort of predation from birds or other animals has taken place. But, like all bones, they have a story to tell."

The pathetic fragments sat on a stainless-steel trolley. "I think you may have guessed that our deceased, in this case, is female. She appears to have died around two years ago from injuries received from a fall from height. I understand that she was retrieved from the mountain below Montsegur, is that right?"

"Yes," said Maury looking at the bones now free of the plastic bags in which they were contained when he last saw them.

"Very petite female," the Coroner waved to indicate Lucine, "Like our detective here. Around 160cm in height. Aged approximately 24 years. Like the others you brought in from Périllos, she was dressed in a white chemise." He pointed at grey rags in a bag and Maury wondered why they'd appeared so bright to him on the mountain.

"No underwear. That might be significant...

"A handmade enamel dove pendant with the initials AM on the reverse," he continued, holding up another evidence bag.

Now, he got to the skull. "As you can see, we still have some hair attached to the scalp. It's hard to tell from the dirt, but it's actually a very pale blonde and very long. It would have reached down to the small of her back."

"The teeth are the most interesting thing," the Coroner said, matter-of-factly, "There has been a lot of orthodontic work, right from childhood, all of it cosmetic. So, either she comes from a rather rich family or, as I surmised, she is American."

These quasi-Cathars seemed to have come from everywhere, Central African, North Africa, the South of France, the Pas de Calais and now, North America.

"Can we get dental records from the United States?" asked Babayan.

"Fortunately, yes." Said the Coroner without triumph, "But she's had no fillings, so no dental record. As I said, her orthodontic work was purely cosmetic, she'd have had a perfect smile."

"So, she could be French," mused Maury, "Or European, but from a rich family. Did you get DNA?"

"I did."

"What did that show?"

"That she's of mixed European heritage, Dutch or Belgian…"

"Flemish then?"

"Well, perhaps. But she almost definitely comes from America. There are traces of a hormone called melengestrol acetate, it's used for enhanced cattle growth in the United States, but it's banned here in Europe."

"So, she wasn't always a vegetarian then?"

"No."

They didn't leave the Coroner after he'd finished showing them the remains. Maury needed to pick his brains on the three that he'd previously examined, "Is it possible that one of the three, you looked at before, could have been injured in a low-speed collision with a car?" he asked, showing the Coroner the annotated photographs of Dubois' Audi's damaged wing and bonnet.

The Coroner went to a light and examined the photographs carefully, paying particular attention to the scale used to determine dimensions. Then he went to his computer.

While the detectives watched he called up high-definition photographs of bones, that the detectives assumed must be of the three Périllos bodies. He flicked through them, before settling on one particular image that he kept zooming in on. Then, he suddenly barked at his assistant as he put on protective apron, gloves and face-shield. The assistant listened to the Coroner's instructions attentively and went off into the morgue.

"I think there is evidence that the African male may have been struck by this car" the Coroner admitted. "But I can't confirm this until I have actually seen the signs I'm looking for, on the bones themselves."

The assistant returned wheeling a trolley on which was a body-bag which the Coroner unzipped, to reveal the skeleton in question. With loupe spectacles donned, the Coroner pulled the trolley directly under the array of surgical lights that hung from the centre of his working area. Under the glare he began making a careful examination in the hip area. He called his assistant over, conferred and, as the assistant started taking more high-resolution photographs, began removing his protective equipment as he turned to the waiting detectives.

"Yes, there is bruising to the upper, outer ilium. I put it down to how the bodies had lain together in the culvert. But, on re-examination, I'm prepared to say that the damage may well have been caused perimortem by a low-speed, glancing blow by a car similar to, or the same as the vehicle you have identified."

Maury admired how the Coroner hedged his bets, but he'd given them what they needed – a more definitive link between Dubois and the bodies in the ditch.

"I expect you'll need an e-fit for the body from Montsegur. I've already entered the data and you should have a rendering by this afternoon."

The slow traffic out of Perpignan gave the detectives' time to reflect on what the Coroner had said about 'White Dove', the moniker they'd decided to adopt for the unknown girl.

"If he's right about her being there for two years, then she might be our Esclarmonde," reasoned Lucine. She moved her legs from the hot sunlight streaming onto them and brushed one against Maury's.

"Yes, it doesn't look like she flew at all, just 'fell with style'," agreed Maury.

"Do you think the initials AM on the back of her enamel dove stand for Antoine Mercier?"

"In all likelihood," admitted Maury.

"Maybe he gave it to her as a memento," Lucine suggested.

"Can you access the Doe network to see if we've got any missing persons fitting the Coroner's description of White Dove?

"And inform Interpol and any other agency with a similar database. Let's see if anything gets back to us," directed Maury.

They were back in the incident room. Maury was writing up details, under the e-fit of White Dove that the Coroner had promised.

The board still didn't contain the answers they required and although they now knew that it was highly likely that Dubois had in some way been the agent of the Périllos Three's death, it could not be proved. The forensic evidence was non-existent, the Audi had been broken for parts, and a bruised bone actually meant very little without corroborating evidence. It was beginning to look as if Maury was going to return to his desk in Narbonne without closing the case.

Maury became aware of Babayan watching as he scanned the board. "We've reached a dead end, haven't we?"

Maury nodded, "We started with three to find names for, now we've got four. I don't think anyone murdered them. I'm not even sure there's been any foul play."

"Maybe not directly," agreed Lucine, "But, what if someone or something impelled them to jump, or to be on that road up to Périllos?"

"What are you suggesting?"

"Well, I was thinking about things last night.

"I was thinking that my brother and I are the last blood-relatives left in our family. And, now that he means to relocate, I somehow feel a strong obligation to join him, even though it would not be in my own interest. Because it's what's expected in family.

"What if some sort of control was being exerted over all these people?"

"A cult mentality?"

"Yes, I suppose you could call it that. These people were all looking for answers, they all wanted to belong to a movement, to be part of something good."

"Looking for religion?"

"No…Faith!"

"What's the difference?" asked Maury.

"Religious people say that they've arrived at their destination. People with faith say they're on a journey."

Maury pondered this difference. Hadn't his own Marie-France been a little religious before they'd moved from Lozère to Aude? She'd been unhappy, but she'd survived, using her religion as a crutch with all the window-dressings of piety. But she'd acted in faith, when she risked leaving all that behind to go off into the unknown, sure it would all work out in the end. Yes, there was a major difference thought Maury, the religious spirit is death, while faith is life.

"I say I'm a Yazidi, it's my heritage," continued Lucine, "But I'm not. Yet, I still feel obliged, impelled, by the memory of my dead parents and of a country, we left before I was even born, to buy a peacock for my mantelpiece."

"So, our jumpers were trying to prove their faith to a cause, while the other three were running away from it," suggested Maury, bringing the conversation round to their present conundrum. It made sense.

"Merde!" Maury suddenly exclaimed.

Lucine looked at him in surprise.

"How the hell did I miss it?" Maury's fists were clenched, and he seemed very angry at himself, "Of course the bitch did it!"

He'd changed the subject so abruptly, that Lucine found it hard to figure what had got into the lead detective. But she knew that the 'bitch' he was referring to was Dubois."

"I thought it was something to do with what was going on at Jimenez's. How didn't I see it before?"

"See what before, Sir?" asked Lucine, hoping that Maury would calm a little and explain his sudden frustration at himself.

"She closed us down!

"Remember the Procureur's Office closing down the investigation, saying they didn't have the resources to investigate?

"The Procureur General didn't do it, that bitch Dubois did when Guillot submitted his daily report!" Maury reasoned aloud.

Lucine's eyes widened, "Everyone thought that it was a race issue, that they didn't want to spend money on an investigation of the deaths of some illegal immigrants. Isn't that what the papers said?"

Maury nodded, "Yes, that's what the papers said."

"So, she's been trying to cover up her involvement all along?"

"Mm," grunted Maury, his thoughts already seemingly elsewhere.

"It doesn't change much. We still can't prove it."

"Maybe, we won't have to," replied Maury enigmatically.

On this visit to the Prefecture, Maury forewent the courtesy of booking ahead for an appointment. He flashed his credentials at Christine Dubois' Personal Assistant, ignored her attempts to stall, and marched straight into the Deputy Procureur's office.

Dubois seemed shocked to see him there, she looked up from papers she was sorting and objected to the manner of his entry, "You can't burst in unannounced or without an appointment. Need I remind you that I am a high-ranking public prosecutor?" Her eyes blazed with indignation.

"Do you remember these headlines?" asked Maury, throwing the Midi-Libre that called into question the systemic racism of the Procureur's office in Perpignan, before her.

Dubois looked at the article and paled.

"I'm sure your boss, the Procureur General, would love to know who sent these emails to the Commissariat to close down our investigation," continued Maury, as he placed copies of the missives on top of the newspaper.

Dubois gulped like a fish does for air, she was galled enough to shout at the detective, but her sense of self-preservation made her bridle the abuse that she wanted to pour upon the shabby man.

"Need I remind you Maître, that all I'm investigating is the death of three unfortunates? Not cover ups. Not debauched sexual violence. Not drug use. Not systemic racism or any other matter.

"How things go from here, is completely down to you. If you don't present yourself to the Gendarmerie in Rivesaltes within twenty-four hours, then we may have to widen the narrow scope of our investigation to include such things or pass our dossiers onto the IGPN."

Maury turned on his heel, "Sleep tight, Maître."

Maury had the Mas to himself when he got home. Marie-France and Elisabeth were probably still out shopping for the knick-knacks and sundries that would personalise the house at Espira. There was plenty to do, he dressed in old clothes, put on a straw hat and went to sort things in the garden.

Presently, tyres crunched on the unmade track and voices called out, announcing the shoppers' return. Elisabeth gave her father a peck on the cheek and the boys each gave him a cuddle before getting back into their car to return home. They'd deposited bags full of shopping, which Marie-France instructed him to help her bring into the house. The women had obviously found the giant outlet store at La Jonquera where the French stocked up on cheap Spanish alcohol and meat. He was pleased to see there were bottles of Ricard in the bags. He wondered how bruised their bank balance would be, when he saw that she'd also been buying herself shoes, clothes and lingerie.

As he was putting the bottles away, his phone rang. It was a call from a number he didn't recognise, "Allo?"

"Allo. Commandant Maury?"

"Speaking."

"Good evening Commandant, Doctor Tillier here from the ICU at Hospital Joseph Ducuing. I'm calling to let you know that Antoine Mercier is becoming more responsive. His sister came down from Lens today and when she spoke to him, we noticed eye movement. So, what we intend to do, is start giving him drugs that will bring him back to consciousness. There's no guarantee that he will come around. But I understand you'd need to speak to him, if he does. If the drugs work, he'll be regaining consciousness in about two hours' time."

"Okay," said Maury, considering what arrangements could be made.

"In any case, Commandant, Monsieur Mercier's sister would like to speak to someone investigating her brother's attempted suicide. She tells me that she needs to get back to her children in Lens early tomorrow."

"Understood Doctor, I'll be there as soon as I can."

Maury could deal with this alone, he'd quickly shower and change and get on the road with a sandwich and flask, "Don't cook for me," he called to his wife, "It looks like I'll be working tonight!"

Marie-France came to the top of the stairs, from the bedroom where she'd been busy stowing away her new purchases, "I'll be down to prepare you something to take away in a moment."

"I've got some stuff from the garden on the kitchen table, it needs sorting. I'm sorry, I've got to leave you to it."

Marie-France turned away from the bannister, calling over her shoulder, "It's fine. But, don't forget that you need to pick up that new car tomorrow!"

"Oh, merde!" Maury had forgotten about that, he swore under his breath, "Who wants a new car anyway?"

Montsegur and the Grail

The grail legend is strongly associated with Arthurian legend, which flourished during medieval times from the stories and sagas of troubadours. The epic, most associated to the grail with Montsegur and Catharism, is the work Parzival, a romance written in the first quarter of the 13th Century, by the German Knight, Wolfram von Eschenbach. The narrative centres around Parzival's long quest for the Holy Grail, which he eventually discovers in a grotto at the foot of a remote castle.

Eschenbach perceived the grail to be a rude drinking vessel, a hollowed-out stone, also known as Lapsit exellis, which in alchemy is the name of the Philosopher's Stone, a substance capable of turning base metals into gold or silver. It is also called the elixir of life, and it is the central symbol of perfection at its finest, enlightenment and heavenly bliss.

It was around this time that the Holy Grail myth became entwined with that of the Holy Chalice.

The connection was made between the Parzival's remote castle and the Cathar stronghold of Montsegur by the work of Otto Rahn, a researcher into Grail mythologies. In 1931 Rahn travelled to Ariege and Languedoc, and aided by the French mystic and historian, Antonin Gadal, argued a direct link between Eschenbach's Parzival and the Cathar 'treasure' mystery. He wrote two books on the subject, 'Crusade Against the Grail' in 1933 and 'Lucifer's Court' in 1937. The first of these works came to the attention of the occultist and Ariosophist, Reichsfuhrer Heinrich Himmler, head of the SS, who commissioned Rahn to continue his field studies. The leather-jacketed, fedora-hatted Rahn (supposedly the model for Spielberg's hero, Indiana Jones, who also goes on a Grail quest) returned to Montsegur and made fruitless archaeological digs and searches at its base.

The openly homosexual, anti-Nazi, Rahn lasted all of three years as an SS officer, before tendering his resignation in 1939.

Of course, he could not resign without consequence, and the Gestapo were instructed to hunt for him, after he turned down the 'honourable' option of committing suicide. On the 13th March 1939, Rahn was found frozen to death on the slopes of a mountain in Austria.

The myth of the Grail was further muddied by the fanciful writings of Englishman John Hardying in the 15th Century, when he parsed the Old French san-greal (holy grail) into sang-real, meaning royal blood. This entomology has since been commonly used by writers and fantasists who infer that the sang-real refers to Jesus' bloodline.

26th June

By the time he'd reached the hospital Maury did want a new car. The journey on the motorway revealed the old car's shortcomings, it vibrated at any speed above one hundred kilometres per hour and was so badly insulated that the drone of the engine and the drumming of the wind almost sent him deaf. So, it added insult to injury when some red lights illuminated on the dashboard, the power steering became heavy and the lights dimmed. He pulled over onto the hard shoulder and rang for assistance, "The fan belt's gone, I think."

Then, came a long wait for the breakdown man who waxed lyrical about the old car, but still cursed when he had to work in an impossibly small gap to fit the new belt.

Consequently, Maury was running late when he arrived at the ugly modern hospital, obviously designed by someone who stupidly thought Brutalist architecture apt for an old city. Inside though, it was clinically clean and sleekly ultra-modern. The receptionist directed him to the ICU and he was met by Doctor Tillier, who had been overseeing Mercier's transition back to consciousness.

Tillier, a young man with full beard and trendy hair-cut, did not look happy, "The signs looked positive at first, we had him reacting to stimulus, but he didn't come back to consciousness. So, we've just Cat-scanned again, I'm afraid that there's too much injury to his brain. We've even had to put him back on a ventilator."

"I'm sure you did your best. So, what are you going to do now?"

"I'm going to ask his sister to give me permission to stop providing life support."

"No hope then?"

Tillier shook his head, "Maybe you should wait somewhere while all this is going on. There's a kiosk in the reception area."

Maury looked at the clock, "Even at this time of night?"

"Oh yes, we, doctors need our caffeine twenty-four hours a day!"

So, do I, thought Maury, thanking the doctor, and making his way back by the way he had just come.

The body count had mounted, now he had six unexplained deaths to investigate. Surely, he couldn't be expected to return to desk duties in Narbonne, now?

Someone was gently shaking him awake, it took him a few moments to figure out where he was.

He was at a table in the cafeteria area of the hospital reception. The young woman shaking him awake had a long face, intense hazel eyes and dark hair pulled back into a ponytail. She wore those new jeans that look old, a printed t-shirt with the Clash's London Calling on it, and a denim jacket. From her ears dangled large hooped earrings, "Commandant Maury?"

"Yes," he replied groggily, "I'm sorry, I must have dozed off."

"I understand that you're investigating my brother's death?"

She'd got right to it. Her look was purposeful, and she was dry-eyed, considering that she'd just given permission to let her brother die, Mademoiselle Mercier seemed very on top of things.

"Yes, that's right," said Maury, coming fully awake. "I'm very sorry for your loss."

"Do you mind getting me a coffee, I've got to get to the railway station soon, to catch the TGV back to Lille I need to freshen up and call a taxi."

"I'll drop you. What time's your train?" offered Maury.

"At five to Seven. Are you sure that's alright?"

The detective got up and offered his hand in greeting, "Of course. How do you like your coffee?"

"Allongé, please. It's Julie, by the way."

So, saying, Julie trotted off towards the restrooms and Maury noticed her footwear, pink, studded Dr Marten's boots. She was tall and thin, pale skinned, like most people from the sunless north.

Maury ordered coffees and some freshly baked croissants, then returned to the table. When she returned, Julie had reapplied her make-up to accentuate her already dominant eyes. She sat and tucked into a croissant immediately. It was then that Maury noticed her pendant, an enamel image of Milou, (Snowy) Tintin's faithful white dog, hanging from a silver chain from her neck.

Julie noticed him looking, and took the little bauble in the fingers of her free hand, "Cute, isn't it? Antoine made it for me."

"He's something of a jeweller then?" this was Maury's chance to initiate a low-key interview.

"Yes, it's something he's done since school…" Julie went suddenly faraway and quiet.

A moment passed, then she took another bite of croissant, flaky bits of pastry going everywhere, but she ate without any sign of self-consciousness. Devouring the remainder, she wiped the crumbs from her lips and top with a paper serviette.

"Commandant, I might look as if I'm in control. But I'll be honest, the last thing I want to talk about to you, at the moment, is my brother.

"I can tell you this though, despite everything that's happened to him, and no matter how appearances may be, he was the sweetest, sweetest soul." Julie did well to hold in the tears that were welling in her eyes "I'll cry on the train," she said.

Maury nodded, he understood well enough, her brother's death was too raw. "Perhaps you can talk to me on the phone when you're ready?" he said.

"Are you going to eat that other croissant?" Julie asked.

Maury looked at the untouched pastry on his plate and pushed it across to Mercier's sister, "Help yourself."

Now, Maury felt to say nothing, just keep the grieving young woman company. He instinctively liked Julie Mercier, she was feisty, direct, and honest.

Her question, when it came, seemed to come out of nowhere, "What sort of person are you Commandant Maury?"

It seemed a strange question at first, but Maury guessed that she just wanted to know what sort of person was looking into the circumstances of her brother's death.

"I've been a policeman for a long time. I was in the army for a little while before that. I'm married and I have one daughter and two grandsons.

"I was raised on a farm, not far from here.

"But, in answer to your question. I'm not too emotional, I tend to investigate with an open mind and not rush to any judgement. I'm not ambitious, and I'm certainly no politician, if I was, I'd be a higher rank by now. I do care about the victims of crime and their families..."

Maury, as always, found it hard to describe himself, he felt as if he was a simple soul at heart, but when he began any sort of self-reflection he began to realise he was no such thing.

However, Julie seemed satisfied, "I can't help you until I feel stronger. But Antoine can..."

Maury didn't understand what she meant. How could her dead brother help?

"Antoine wrote to me, a lot. I've brought all his letters with me and you can have them. They're private though. They're in my bag. For your eyes only, understand?"

Maury agreed, "Okay."

Julie Mercier got to her feet and brushed the crumbs from her clothes and looked across at the reception's prominently placed clock, "I think we need to get to the station."

She was right, her train was due to leave in thirty-five minutes time. He could get her there with ten minutes to spare. If the car didn't break down!

After Maury had dropped Julie, he got snarled up in the big city's rush-hour traffic. On the seat that Julie had just vacated was the bundle of letters bound together with an elastic band. He decided he'd peruse them at his leisure, there would be time to kill before he was due to pick up the new car from the Toyota franchise at Labege.

He wondered why he should wait. Perhaps they'd let him have the car early? After all, he had barely got any sleep in the night, just three snatched hours at the table in the hospital's reception. He decided to take a chance and followed the crawling commuter traffic towards Toulouse's industrial outskirts.

The manager of the Toyota franchise could not be more accommodating, not at all fazed that Maury had presented himself early, "You have to sign some paperwork. I'll have the workshop finish the pre-delivery inspection and then we'll familiarise you with the car.

"I'll get you some refreshment. What would you like?"

Although he'd probably had enough caffeine for the day already, Maury opted for coffee when the manager had gone through the options. He looked at the paperwork and started filling in the boxes that the manager had thoughtfully marked with an 'X'.

"I've got an old Peugeot to hand over," said Maury, reaching in his pocket for the keys. "But there are a few things I need to get out."

"We'll do that shortly Commandant," said the manager, looking over the papers that Maury had completed.

The place and the people were slick and professional, the open-plan workstation doubled as a showroom, and shiny hybrids and SUVs sat on the wall-to-wall carpet. The manager was in his forties, at a guess, the name tag on his blue pinstripe suit proclaimed him to be 'Julien'. A pretty young receptionist, come secretary, sat at another workstation, busy tapping the keys on her computer keyboard.

Shortly, a coverall clad mechanic came through one of the doors marked for staff use and addressed Julien, "Monsieur le Commandant's car is ready. Do you want to go through the familiarisation or shall I?"

Julien turned to Maury, "Are you happy for our Workshop Manager, George, to run you through the car?"

"That's fine by me," replied Maury, getting up to follow the mechanic through the door he'd just entered by, marvelling at a mechanic's coveralls could be so immaculately clean.

George led him into a large workshop where cars were on lifts and attached to diagnostic machines. He pointed at a metallic white, four-wheel drive behemoth, "Here's your new car"

Maury was taken aback, he'd somehow expected a hatchback or saloon, not this.

"Top of the range, fully automatic, same as the Mountain Rescue services use. Leather, satellite navigation, all the bells and whistles!" George pointed out proudly.

He pointed at the silvery windscreen and window glass, "Heat reflecting, great for the type of weather we've been having…"

The tour continued. George had Maury sit in the driver's seat and adjusted it for fit using electrical switches, then pointed at the bewildering array of dashboard controls, "Just leave everything on 'auto' and the car will do it all for you. You can override but the car knows what it's doing. It'll go anywhere on any terrain."

Maury was impressed by the machine, but when the mechanic told him the engine capacity, he was glad that the State was footing the fuel bills.

The familiarisation with the new car took a little under an hour, George had paired his phone to the hands-free system just as its battery died, stowed the little stuff he'd left in the old Peugeot and saw him off.

Maury was soon on the motorway heading east back towards the Mediterranean. The car was tremendously powerful and felt, at the 130kph speed limit, that it was barely breaking into a sweat. The cruise control immediately became Maury's favourite feature, it held the car at a constant speed, taking it past all the traffic labouring up the ramps that bypassed Carcassonne. At Narbonne he left the motorway and found the car just as accomplished on the twisting old Route Nationale as the AutoRoute.

On the road that leads into Lavelanet from Belesta, Corporal Barthez was getting bored of pointing his radar gun at tractors and mopeds. He told his companion, a trainee gendarme, that they would put the contraption away and proceed slowly up through the Gorge de la Frau to Montsegur. The area needed a good look-over anyway, the recent storms had caused damage to property, and the local council workers always seemed to overlook the debris deposited on some stretches of road.

The delicate instrument safely stowed, the dark blue van began its slow wind along all the back roads towards the ancient castle at the far-off end of the valley.

The message left on Lucine's phone told her that Maury had been called to Mercier's bedside late in the night, so she did not expect him to be at Rivesaltes until later, if at all. She figured that she had time to run some errands, so she passed by the out of town shopping centre.

She wondered what the senior detective had done after he'd left the office on the previous afternoon. Maury had certainly seemed to have a bee in his bonnet, and she suspected that he'd gone to do something about the Dubois situation.

His message had left instructions for her to follow, she should follow up on the Nassim family and continue to try to find information on White Dove. For now, though, she was quite happy to potter around a craft and hobby shop.

The high seating position gave Maury a good view ahead, he could even see the otherwise hidden track to the Mazet, as he turned into Mas Maury.

As he turned onto the driveway, the reflecting light off a windscreen drew his attention to the black Mercedes-Benz sitting outside the house. His foot reacted before his brain, and he stepped down hard on the brakes to stop the car under the trees, as he turned from the road.

It was Pierre's car wasn't it? Maury's heart rose in his throat, as he suddenly realised what that meant.

"Shh!" said Marie-France breaking from Pierre's post-coital embrace, "I think I heard a car turn into the driveway!"

"I didn't hear anything," said Pierre watching her rise from the bed and pad to the window. Her suspender belt and stockings framed her pert bottom as she peered through the gap between the shutters. "There's a car stopped in the driveway!" she said in alarm.

"Do you recognise it?" asked Pierre.

Marie-France shook her head and watched the large white four-wheel-drive vehicle reverse back onto the road and continue its way along it.

"Who is it?" asked Pierre, "Anyone you know?"

"I didn't recognise the car."

"What about the driver?"

"It had those reflective windows."

"It's probably someone turning around. Come back to bed," Pierre reassured her.

She turned and he enjoyed the sight of her ripe, mature body. He pulled the covers off his lower body so she could see that he was ready for more.

But her eyes were troubled, her body quite tense when she climbed back into bed.

Barthez drove slowly up through the village of Montsegur, nestled at the foot of the pinnacle on which the old castle sat. Crime seldom happened here, especially out of season, but the Gendarmerie wanted its presence and authority to be seen in every rural corner. So, they slowly patrolled every street, stopping often to look up alleyways or simply to watch people going about their daily business.

At the Mairie, the Maire, Garaud, a stressed middle-aged man flagged the gendarmes down.

"Bonjour, Monsieur le Maire, how are things?" said Barthez in greeting.

"If you're going up towards the castle, can you move on the people who are camping with their vans on the parking area?"

"We're going up there shortly," Barthez told him. "Anything else to report?"

Garaud ran his fat fingers through his bristly grey crew-cut, "No. All quiet since that pantomime the other day. You recovered two bodies, didn't you? Why can't they find a place to kill themselves closer to home? Eh?"

Barthez shrugged his shoulders, Garaud was probably moaning about the cost of police operations to the village economy. But, without the castle, who would come to this off-the-beaten-track village? He raised his hand in a goodbye wave, let out the clutch and continued their snails' pace reconnaissance.

The intercom from the Gendarmerie's reception buzzed, so Babayan answered the call from the Desk Sergeant, "Hello

Lieutenant. There's a Maître Dubois here, she'd like to speak to someone."

For a moment Babayan was lost without Maury's lead, then she decided that she'd hear what Dubois had to say. She did need a witness though, "Are either Pratt or Renaud available?" she asked.

"No, but if you want someone to sit in an interview, I'll come up myself."

"Thank you, Sergeant, can you send her up?"

This was going to be an informal interview, Dubois had not been cautioned, so it could be done in the office. Lucine arranged chairs, so that they could all sit comfortably.

Presently, the smartly shirt-sleeved Desk Sergeant opened the door and bid the Maître enter. Christine Dubois looked tired and nervous, Lucine motioned to the chair opposite her own, at the desk. "Bonjour Maître," she said, attempting to make Dubois a little more at ease. Lucine was surprised to see that Dubois had come alone, she'd expected her to be accompanied by a lawyer. The Desk Sergeant pulled his chair away, so that he sat a little on the side-lines.

"What brings you here Maître Dubois?" Lucine asked.

"I wish to make a statement," said Dubois.

"You will need to dictate it to me. I'll copy it down and then I'll read it back to you, so you can make changes if you wish. Unless you have a prepared statement, that is?"

"No, that will be fine," confirmed Dubois.

Christine Dubois had not slept tight. After Maury had been by to see her she'd swallowed her anger at his impertinence and considered all he'd said, he was right of course, if the Procureur General got wind of her interference in the case there would be a lot of fall-out. Her plans for further advancement in her chosen career would suffer. She didn't worry too much at her involvement in drugs and sex games at Jimenez's Mas, after all, others in the administration had also been there, people much more powerful than her. She knew that the French are, in general, tolerant of their politician's and elite's personal appetites.

No, her mistake had been to close down the investigation. If she hadn't, Maury would have no leverage and the whole mess would have just gone away. So, she'd decided to come clean about the events of that night and to minimise, as much as she could, her actual involvement.

After clarifying dates, times and places, she began, "I was at a party at my friend Senor Jimenez's Mas near Périllos. I had an altercation with another woman which resulted in us both having to leave. Because my blood alcohol level was too high, according to my personal breathalyser, I had to wait until I was safe to drive. When I left, a little after midnight, I remember it was raining heavily. I got in my car and drove according to the conditions. On the way I passed three people dressed in white on the side of the road..."

"These people?" asked Lucine, for clarification, sliding the e-fits in front of Dubois.

"Yes, these people."

"Why didn't you stop?"

"They didn't appear to need assistance. So, I continued towards home."

Dubois appeared to have concluded her statement. Babayan read it back. Dubois made no corrections or additions.

"Are you sure you have nothing else to add Maître?" asked Lucine.

Dubois shook her head and beckoned for the statement, to sign it. Babayan asked the Desk Sergeant to countersign.

Maury's head was reeling with a mixture of thoughts. He drove on autopilot, not noticing any of the scenery slipping past.

How hadn't he suspected Pierre and Marie-France's infidelity before? Now that he'd seen Lafitte's car at the Mas, when he was supposed to be elsewhere, all the bits of the puzzle began to fit. The favours to the family, his appointment from Lozère to here, even his promotion to Commandant, the lingerie...Marie-France and Pierre had been pulling strings for a long time. When had their affair begun?

So, the religious spirit Marie-France had, was that due to good old-fashioned guilt? Or was it that she was trying to subjugate the carnal urges of her flesh? Had she been unhappy with him all along?

Was their new-found happiness a sham? Moments borrowed from Lafitte?

He felt angry, but not at the clandestine lovers, at himself, self-professed man of logic, who'd been blind to what was happening right under his nose.

There is never a good time for bad things to happen, he thought. His premonition of change had been correct.

Barthez cautioned the English people, who pretended not to be able to understand the 'Camping Interdit' sign, to decamp immediately. They did understand his wagging finger and "Non!" though. So, now he and his young protégé were watching the freeloaders move on.

There were other cars on the parking, but Barthez supposed that they belonged to people who'd gone to visit the castle or to walk elsewhere on the massif. But a white Dacia caught his eye. He was quite sure that it had been parked up a few days previously when the poor fellow had jumped from the castle's battlements.

"Can you check the registration details on this Dacia?" he called to the novice, who was returning to their van.

Just beyond the car something caught his eye one of those fangled pop-up tents, illegally pitched. Some bare legs protruded from the tent flap, "Hey! No wild camping here!"" he called out.

A scruffy teen, all skin, bone, spots, and dreadlocks put his head out and apologised, "Sorry, I didn't know."

"There are signs," said Barthez, cocking his head at the notice, in plain sight, just metres away, "Get your tent down and move on!"

His colleague walked up from the van to watch the youth trying, unsuccessfully, to get the tent to fold into its bag, "It's locally registered. Belongs to someone in the Pamiers postcode area. Must be English by the sound of the name."

"You've got to twist it!" Barthez shouted at the struggling boy. He turned back to the trainee "What's the name?"

"Miller, Edward from place called Labaouse."

"Never heard of it," shrugged Barthez. He called to the youth, "Yes, that's it!" then feeling a little sorry for the boy, he added, "They allow wild camping just below the village.

"Right. Well, if it's local I expect they're getting myrtle berries up on the mountain."

"What are myrtle berries?" asked his companion.

"Bit like blueberries. You pick 'em with a comb contraption. They make good eau-de-vie."

Barthez turned his attention back to the youth, who'd managed to put his tent and all his stuff into a supermarket's carrier bag. He pointed down the hill, "The wild camping's down there," he indicated.

As they made their way back to their van they passed the Dacia and something glinting on top of the rear wheel caught Barthez's eye, "That's a silly place to leave the keys!" he exclaimed. He looked at the fob, pressed a button and the car unlocked. "Let's see that he hasn't left anything important on show, or he's asking to have it broken into or nicked!"

At first there seemed nothing out of place or remotely interesting, the interior of the car was very clean and tidy, as if recently valeted. But, in the glovebox he found a drug canister, he read the label and with a start he saw that the drugs had been prescribed to Antoine Mercier.

"Oh merde!" he groaned.

"We need to secure the car and get onto Commandant Maury at the Rivesaltes Gendarmerie" he told his puzzled junior.

Maury was at the Gendarmerie in Rivesaltes, he'd driven himself there almost automatically. He sat for a moment, gathering his thoughts, it would be good to have his mind set on other things. His anger had abated, he felt rather a sense of hopelessness and shock.

Lucine's car was parked there, so he'd have to pull himself together before getting to the office. He left Antoine's letters where they were on the passenger's seat, he'd read them when his head was in the right place.

When he arrived in the incident room Babayan looked up at him with concern, "Are you alright, Sir?"

"Just tired that's all. What's the latest?" he asked, to deflect further enquiry.

"Christine Dubois popped in and made a statement."

"Oh, really?"

Lucine shook her head, "But, I don't think you'll like it Sir," she said passing the form across.

Maury read the few lines, and for a moment his blood ran cold.

"She didn't come clean. Those poor people were obviously in trouble, injured and burned in their car crash. No way didn't they try to flag her down for help. And there's the damage to the car and the body!" exclaimed Lucine, obviously upset at Dubois' omissions.

"She's trying to save her own skin," remarked Maury, "But she doesn't know what we know. Oh well! We've given her enough rope."

He crossed to his desk and opened his emails.

"What are you going to do?" asked Lucine.

"If we can't get her one way, we'll get her another. I'm going to send what we've got to the IGPN and Mademoiselle Petit at the Midi-Libre."

"But Sir!" Lucine protested, "If you inform the press, you'll just cause us more of a headache. You know how the powers that be feel about whistle-blowers!"

At this moment, I couldn't give a shit, thought Maury. But he heeded the Lieutenant's warning and pinged off everything they had on Dubois to Dec at the IGPN, the Procureur General himself and to Inspector General Lafitte who was still his boss, even if it made his blood boil just to see his name.

The die was cast, if the result was unsatisfactory, he'd have no qualms about sending the same material to Petit.

"You didn't send it to the Midi-Libre did you?" Babayan asked.

"No. Don't worry yourself yet."

"How did it go at Toulouse?" Babayan asked.

Maury sighed, "They couldn't get Mercier to come out of his coma. In fact, his condition worsened. They asked permission from his sister to take him off life support."

"He's dead then?" Lucine's eyes went wide with shock.

Maury was about to tell her more when his desk phone rang, it was

Barthez.

The Corporal told him about the Dacia found at Montsegur, "It appears that Mercier drove there in it. I found some prescription tablets."

"Cypretone Acetate?"

"Yes. What is that?"

"Apparently, a chemical castrator."

"Was this bloke a paedophile, or something then?"

"Not a convicted one."

"Anyway, the car's not his, it's registered to an American, a certain Edward Mason."

"I've never heard of him."

"Apparently he comes from a place called Labaouse. It's some sort of farm complex miles from anywhere."

"Did he report it stolen?"

"No."

"Okay. Then, I suppose we'd better visit this place. Are you, available tomorrow?"

"Yes, but you'd best clear it with Captain Kerouac first."

"I'll do that. Shall we meet you at this Labaouse place or pick you up from the Gendarmerie in Lavelanet?"

"Best you meet us there. The track starts at a place called Rasigueres..."

Memories flooded back it was the place where Tradot parked his car, the place with the miserable farmer's wife. "I know where that is," confirmed Maury, "We'll see you there tomorrow morning."

"What sort of time?"

"Say Nine?"

"That's fine by me. See you then," said Barthez ringing off.

"What's all that?" asked Lucine as Maury cradled the receiver.

"That was Barthez. He found the car that Mercier used to get to Montsegur. Apparently, it's registered to an American who lives near the place that Tradot parked his car. We'll meet him there tomorrow, be ready for an early start."

"Who's car?"

"Mine," replied Maury.

"You might as well call it a day," Maury told Lucine, as he picked up the phone, "I'll make arrangements for Barthez's Captain to release him for the day."

It was time to go home and face the music. His earlier anger and hopelessness had both gone, now he felt a numb nothingness. He drove slowly, this time taking in every aspect of the astonishing scenery of the Fitou region. He saw flamingos on the etangs, and an eagle circling in the thermals that rose over the red brick fortress of Salses.

Soon, he reached the end of the driveway from which he'd earlier roared away. He was glad to see no sign of any vehicle outside either the Mas or Mazet. He and Marie-France could have their showdown in private.

As he arrived, Marie-France appeared on the terrace and visibly paled when she recognised the new car. When Maury stepped down from it, she became distraught, her hands moving to her mouth to stifle her silent wail.

Any anger that Maury may have harboured evaporated when he saw her distress. It felt, as if it was he that had wronged her, rather than the other way around. When he saw her like this, he wanted to hold her. But, the spite at the back of his mind told him it was the least she deserved. Then, along came his logic, things like this don't just happen. Even if just a little, he did share some culpability. So, he obeyed his first instinct, went to her and embraced her.

Sobbing wracked her body, tears flowed, and she uttered, "Sorry, sorry, sorry," as she put her head on his shoulder.

A weird voice croaked, "If you want to be with him, you should go," it was Maury's own, the words had escaped his mouth before his mind had framed them.

Marie-France's distress increased, she pushed from his embrace and pummelled her fists on his chest, "Non, non et non!"

Three Esclarmondes

Esclarmonde de Foix, was the daughter of the prominent Roger Bernard I, the Count of Foix, and his spouse Cecile Trencavel, she was born around the year 1151. She married the Lord of l'Isle Jourdain and by him had six children. When she was widowed in October 1200, she sought comfort in religion and became an adherent to Catharism. Four years later, she received 'consolation' from Guilhabert de Castres, and so became a 'parfaite', a member of the Cathar laity, and dedicated her life to the peoples of Languedoc.

With other parfaites she ran a sort of low-key convent at Dun which also functioned as a girl's school and a retirement home for aged parfaites. Esclarmonde is also credited with opening hospitals, schools and convents – a pattern later adopted by the Roman Church as part of its effort to become an organisation of the people.

Esclarmonde de Foix is thought to have died circa 1215. That there is no record of a grave or a marker to commemorate her, despite her regional fame, is not unusual, Cathars buried their dead anonymously for fear that their enemies would violate their remains and prevent their resurrection at the end of time.

Our second Esclarmonde is also a Cathar, the sickly daughter of Montsegur's lord. Esclarmonde de Pereilha, was barely in her teens, and was probably given her unusual forename in honour of Esclarmonde de Foix, who was highly esteemed in the Ariege region. She, apparently, took ill during the protracted siege of Montsegur in 1244 and had to be carried down from the 'pog' on which the surrendered castle sat, to be thrown upon the pyre that awaited unrepentant Cathars at the foot of it.

Historians argue that the two Esclarmondes have merged together to become the Great Esclarmonde (Light of the World), Esclarmonde de Montsegur, the 'White Lady of

Montsegur', and it was she, who was the final guardian of the Cathar 'treasure'. This heroine, in the songs and fabled stories of the troubadours, is said to have prayed to the heavens as all seemed lost to the inhabitants of Montsegur, to have her petitions answered by a descending dove that split the top of the mountain under the castle's foundations with its beak. Into this miraculous rent in the rock, she cast the secret 'treasure' of the Cathars, which closed upon it, so that it should not fall into impure hands. Then, she transformed herself into dove, that rose from the battlements and flew off east.

In the village of Minerve, adjacent to the church is a small memorial stone dedicated to the 140 Cathars who were consumed by the flames of the pyre of the Catholic crusaders. At the top of this stone is carved the shape of an ascending dove, some think to be the symbol of the Holy Spirit. But that dove is usually depicted as descending, this is then is more likely the symbol of Esclarmonde, the White Dove that is now commonly a symbol of the Cathars.

27th June

The beeping of her mobile phone woke her, Babayan extended a hand from under the duvet and looked at the text. It was from Maury, it simply said, "Wear outdoor clothing. See you 0630 Rivesaltes."

Lucine looked at the time, it was not quite 3am.

No wonder Maury looked tired, she thought, the man doesn't sleep!

She hadn't expected the Commandant to be driving the large four-wheel-drive vehicle that drew up next to her in the Gendarmerie compound. The sky was grey, and it felt cooler this morning. She stowed her coat and bag in the Toyota's boot and climbed into the high cabin.

Maury, as she'd half-expected, looked tired, "Bonjour," he said, passing her a folder full of documents.

Then, they were off on the quiet roads that led them, once again, towards Ariege. As usual, Maury concentrated on driving and did not engage in conversation. That suited Lucine, she could sit, half-asleep, in the passenger seat watching the scenery slip beneath the wheels. At Quillan, the car squelched on tarmac, wet from overnight rain. Then, they rose into cloud cover and drizzle as the road climbed to Puivert. By the time they reached Lavelanet it was properly raining, and the outside temperature had fallen to 18°c.

Maury pulled up outside an open café in the centre of town, "Let's have breakfast," he said as he removed his seatbelt. "Bring those papers with you."

Lucine sat, shivering, while Maury ordered at the bar, he returned with four fresh croissants and two large cups of café crème. He sat and pointed at papers he withdrew from the file, "We are going to interview this man, Edward Mason, his wife Rosalee and his friend, who I only know so far as Johnny.

"I think, that between them, they can tell us an awful lot about our victims. Have you got the e-fits?"

Maury seemed particularly focused and business-like this morning.

Lucine rifled through her bag and found the images he'd requested. Maury took them from her and inserted them, with the papers from the table, back into the folder.

"You're going to have to bear with me today, Lucine," said Maury, looking out at the early shoppers hurrying by on the rainy streets, "I've had two sleepless nights."

She noticed that he'd called her by her forename, and the familiarity reassured her that his distant, preoccupied state of mind was nothing to do with anything that she had said or done. Lucine had worried that she should have challenged Dubois more forcibly.

"I'm going to lead the interviews, I need you to take notes," Maury told her.

She nodded in understanding and watched him wolf down a croissant and wash it down with gulps of his creamy drink. Lucine looked at her watch, they needed to press on, so she followed suit.

Barthez and his companion sat in their van, at the foot of the track that led up to Labaouse from Rasigueres, worrying that even with its four wheel drive the Gendarmerie van was not capable of a four kilometre climb up the rough track that led up the mountain. Had the track been dry they might make it, but the storms had been torrential, and the land was saturated.

The gendarme was relieved to see that it was Maury stepping from the Land Cruiser that pulled in next to them. "Are you going to ride with us?" asked the detective.

Once the gendarmes had transferred to the Toyota, Maury navigated the large vehicle up the track. As the mechanic George had told him, Maury only had to leave the vehicle's controls on 'auto' and it climbed, without drama, over seemingly insurmountable obstacles and up greasy slopes.

When, at last, the buildings of the Labaouse farm complex appeared, Maury pulled up to brief the officers, "Corporal Barthez, if you and your colleague could process everyone we find there, Lieutenant Babayan and myself want to interview three people in particular; Edward Mason, his wife Rosalee and someone we know only as Johnny. If you get their all their details checked, I'll instruct you further once we've processed our witnesses."

"No problem," said Barthez.

Maury engaged gears and continued, on to the gateway that gave entry into the walled complex. Curious people appeared at the windows and doors of some of the buildings, and a white-clad, barrel-chested man stepped forward to challenge the new arrivals, "This is private land, what do you want?" From his accent, he was obviously American.

When they stepped out of the Toyota, it was clear that the visitors were official, the gendarmes were resplendent in their blue uniforms and the detectives both wore bright red police armbands. Nevertheless, Maury flashed his credentials, "Commandant Maury, Lieutenant Babayan of the Police Nationale, and two of our colleagues from the Gendarmerie in Lavelanet. Could we please speak to Mister Edward Mason?"

"That's me," said the man, "What's this about?"

"Is there somewhere private we could talk?" Maury asked.

"We can talk here, if it's all the same to you," said Mason, obstructively.

"It's a delicate matter we've come to discuss. It would not be appropriate to go into it here, unless you'd prefer to be interviewed at the Gendarmerie?" challenged Maury.

"In any case," continued Maury, "The gendarmes here want to run a control on everyone that lives here. Have you somewhere dry, for them to work?"

"You've no right!" protested Mason.

The burly Barthez intervened, "I think you'll find we do."

For a moment Babayan thought Mason would continue to be obstructive, but he signalled for the police officers to follow him into the courtyard.

Along one side of the complex was the traditional longhouse of the region with tawny, rendered walls, pale blue-grey woodwork and shallow Spanish tiled roof. Along two sides were single storey barns and stables, with recently renovated double-glazed windows which looked to serve as dwellings for the residents who had come to the windows and doors to gawp at the visitors.

The commune seemed to have attracted young people in the main, and a minority of more aged men and women. All were dressed in the white that the six victims had worn, but sandals had been replaced by rubber clogs, and anyone outside in the rain wore normal wet weather clothing over their vestments.

Mason pointed at the large buildings on the last side of the complex, "The gendarmes can use the workshops and meeting room," he said, addressing the group. He looked at Maury and pointed at the house, "We can talk in the kitchen."

"Johnny!" he called out in English, "Can you get the gendarmes settled into the hall? Tell everyone, that they want to see their papers!"

Johnny detached himself from a doorway, he was a fit looking man with a bald head but full, white, beard. Maury looked at him and gesticulated, "I'll need to see you in the kitchen too, when you're done." The man's bright blue eyes betrayed a hint of worry, but he nodded.

While Johnny led the gendarmes one way, the detectives followed Mason another. They entered the house, directly into a sooty smelling kitchen. Mason moved chairs around so that they could all be seated around the substantial oak table that dominated the room. "I'll need you wife Rosalee to be here," Maury told him, "Our business here concerns her too."

While Edward Mason went off to fetch his wife and Maury settled himself at the table with his file before him, Lucine looked around the room. The walls were bare stone, pointed with beige mortar and the floor was made of large stone flags. The two large stoves at the far end of the room were old-fashioned wood fired items and the work surfaces were hand-hewn solid wood. There were dressers and cupboards, all rustically styled, with pots pans and other kitchen utensils hanging from the chestnut beams. The sink was an industrial concrete affair, served by one tap on the end of a nylon tube. There were garlics, bunches of dried herbs lending their pungency to the woody smell. But, apart from the soot on the ceiling above the stoves, the place was utilitarian and clean.

Presently, Johnny returned from outside and Mason led his wife

Rosalee in through an internal door. Maury waved to the chairs, "Can you all please take a seat. My colleague, Detective Lieutenant Babayan here will be taking informal notes of our conversation. Are you alright with me continuing in French, or would you prefer me to use my, very bad, English?"

Edward Mason spoke for the three, "French is fine. Now, could you tell us what this is all about?"

"What is this place," asked Maury, looking about himself, "Is it a type of religious community?"

"That's right," affirmed Mason.

"You are sort of Cathars aren't you?"

"Sort of," agreed Mason, "We want to live simple, spiritual lives in harmony with nature."

"Are you Dualists, like the Cathars?"

Mason looked surprised at the question, "If you mean, do we believe that God is the author of both good and evil, then no. God is entirely good"

"But you do believe in good and evil."

"Oh yes, most definitely," agreed Mason

"What of the world, of the material world, is that a corrupt creation?"

Mason paused before answering, "Are these questions relevant Commandant?"

"I think they are. Please answer."

"Yes, the world and the spirit are at odds with each other. The material world is evil while the spirit is good."

Maury nodded, "And what of the flesh, does that war against the spirit?"

"Yes," agreed Mason, "I believe that it does."

"What is your profession Monsieur Mason?"

"I am the founder of a foundation, a charity that works in the worlds trouble spots to provide food, both actual and spiritual, to the needy and oppressed."

Maury looked at Rosalee. "My wife is my co-founder. In actual fact, we only came back from a thirty-month mission to the Yemen, Somalia and Eritrea a few days ago. It's been our life's work, but we hope to retire and settle to a quiet life of reflection here," said Mason on his wife's behalf.

"And you?" asked Maury of Johnny.

Johnny shrugged, "I was a software engineer in Welwyn Garden City, England. I got early retirement for health issues."

Maury's brow furrowed, to him, Johnny looked the epitome of fitness for his age.

Johnny tapped his temple with a finger. "Mental health issues," he explained.

"How long have you lived here at Labaouse?"

"Twenty-one years?" ventured Mason, looking to his wife who nodded in conformation.

"And you Mister Johnny?"

Johnny quickly answered, "Twenty-one years, like them."

"I'd like to see your passports please?" Maury asked.

Johnny rummaged in a leather man-bag hanging from his shoulder. Rosalee got up to retrieve her husband's and hers from an old ammunition box on top of one of the kitchen cupboards. The detectives could now see her properly for the first time.

She, like the men, seemed to be in her middle sixties, lean to the point of being skeletal, her cheekbones sharp, her eyes sunken and her grey-red hair unkempt. While the men's eyes were bright and quick hers were dull and lacklustre. She placed two US passports on the table in front of Maury.

Maury looked at the documents carefully, both Americans' were stamped with visas from throughout the Middle East and East Africa. Johnny's was British and almost out of date. Maury wryly observed this, and Johnny apologised, saying it was something he meant to attend to soon. Johnny's full name was Jonathan David Oates. Maury passed the passports to Lucine for safe-keeping and returned to the interview.

"You own a white Dacia Duster, don't you?"

"Yes," replied Mason, "A friend is borrowing it."

"A friend. Could you tell me his name?"

"Of course, it's Antoine Mercier, he lives here in the community, with us."

"Do you know where he might have gone?" asked Maury.

"We had a bit of a falling out. He's probably gone to see his family or something..."

"And, do you know where that might be?"

Mason looked to Rosalee and then Johnny who both looked blank, then shook his head.

Maury pulled Antoine's photo from the file and turned it so his audience could see it, "This is Antoine Mercier, correct?" All three nodded.

"And this is your Dacia?" Barthez had provided a photo of the abandoned car, which Maury showed.

"Yes, has he had an accident or something?" asked the increasingly concerned American.

"I'm afraid Antoine Mercier is dead," replied Maury.

The three quasi-Cathars looked at each other in obvious shock. "How?" asked Mason.

Maury looked carefully at them as he told them, "He jumped from the walls of the castle at Montsegur on the morning of the Summer Solstice, the twenty-first." The Americans looked at each other in dismay, as Maury guessed, to the Briton the news did not come as a complete shock. "When did you last see Antoine?"

"The day we returned from Africa, wasn't it?" Rosalee said, to prompt her husband.

"Yes, that's right. But I'm afraid that he and I had a falling out," admitted Mason.

"And you?" Maury asked Johnny.

Johnny stroked his beard, "Must've been at the evening meeting. We have a praise and prayer meeting every evening."

"Was your falling out before or after the meeting?" Maury asked Mason.

"After, we had a discussion after the meeting."

"What did you fall out about?"

Mason sighed heavily, "Rosalee and I have been away from here for thirty months or so. We left Antoine and Johnny in charge. When we got back, they'd made changes that I really didn't agree with."

"Why wasn't Johnny at this meeting, if it concerned changes, they'd both made?"

Edward Mason looked down over his simple white attire, "You see how we dress. There's no outward show, we have no icons, no symbols. But when we returned everyone here was wearing pendants."

Maury dug into his file again and produced an image of one of the Gema Abraxas, "Like this?"

Mason nodded, "It may seem a minor matter, but to us it's still idolatry."

Hardly, thought Maury, "So, you had it out with Antoine because he was the one who designed and made these, wasn't he?"

Mason looked up from the photo in surprise, "Yes, that's right."

"So, you had an argument with him, and he left. Did you think he was upset enough to do something stupid, or out of character?"

"Well, yes, he was upset." Mason admitted, "But not upset enough to kill himself."

"And what do you think Johnny. Would he have jumped or done something stupid?" Asked Maury, turning his attention back to the Briton.

"Why are you asking me? I wasn't there when they argued," Johnny protested.

Maury ignored the protests, he pulled out another photo and laid it before them. "I don't think you'll know who this is Monsieur Mason, but I think Johnny might…"

Johnny looked at the image, "That's Sebastien," he muttered, "Sebastien Tradot."

Maury nodded, "He jumped from the castle at Roquefixade on the morning of the Summer Solstice, on the twenty-first of June last year.

"He was a member of this community while you away on your travels Monsieur Mason. He was here for around nine months, I think." Maury looked at Johnny for confirmation.

Johnny nodded his bald head and looked grim. The atmosphere could be cut with a knife, the three quasi-Cathars all fearful of Maury's next revelation.

Maury looked over his spectacles at the Masons who were visibly upset, they held tight onto each other's hands. Johnny looked stony-faced and was obviously deep in thought. Maury wondered how they'd react to seeing the next images.

One by one, he laid the e-fits of the Perillos Three on the table. Mason gasped and immediately held his wife, who blanched and screamed out in horror. Even Johnny looked upset at seeing those three young faces looking up at them.

Rosalee could not be consoled.

Mason kept trying to calm his wife, who kept looking over his shoulder at the e-fits and wailing in deep distress.

Maury decided it might be appropriate to let them sort themselves out privately. He beckoned to Lucine and both detectives went outside into the courtyard. It was still raining, but it was easing slowly into drizzle. To escape it the detectives stayed close to the farmhouse wall and stood in the shelter of the overhanging eaves.

"How do you know so much about what's been happening here," Lucine asked.

"Antoine Mercier wrote to his sister regularly. She gave me the letters when I went up to the hospital in Toulouse. I read them last night, they shone a light on everything," Maury explained.

"So, who are the Perillos Three?"

"I'm not sure, I know a little about them, but I think we are going to find out in a moment." Maury cocked his ear, Rosalee's wailing had ceased. "Shall we go back in?"

When they went back into the kitchen, they found all three huddled over the images. Maury sat opposite them and put his finger down on the three e-fits, one after the other, "So, who are they?"

"Are they dead?" croaked Rosalee.

Maury nodded, "Unfortunately, yes."

"How did they die?"

Maury put aside that question, "I'll come to that. Can you please tell me who they are?"

Again, Edward Mason took charge, he put his finger on the first face, "This is Godfrey, that is Faith his sister, and that is Fatima."

Maury looked at Mason hoping that the American would break the silence with a further revelation, but his mouth was closed tight in a reluctant line.

The silence was broken by his wife, Rosalee who seemed frustrated at her husband's reticence. "They're our adopted children!" she blurted.

Maury looked across at Babayan at this unexpected development, his look said, 'this is news to me too'.

"Have you got their papers?" asked Maury, looking towards the ammunition tin.

Rosalee crossed her arms, shook her head and lowered it in shame. The men too, were avoiding eye contact.

"Anything at all? Papers of adoption?"

Again, Rosalee shook her head. Then her husband raised his eyes and broke his silence, "We don't have anything official for them."

Maury was puzzled, "What do you mean?"

"We brought them back from Africa and the Middle East from the orphanages we were working in. Godfrey and Faith from Chad and Fatima from Syria," Mason admitted.

"You mean you smuggled them into France?" Maury was incredulous. Here were bastions of goodness, who had willingly circumvented the law.

Husband and wife looked at each other and nodded.

"How old would they be today?" asked Maury.

Rosalee answered, "Godfrey and Faith would be twenty-four, they were twins. Fatima would be twenty-one."

Maury sat back and digested what he'd just heard. No wonder they couldn't be identified, they had never officially existed.

"How were they to function without papers?" Maury asked.

Mason and his wife looked uncomfortable, "We were going to get them false identities," Mason admitted.

Maury shook his head, "Mon Dieu," he muttered under his breath. Then he continued with another question, "Let's move on from that. So, Godfrey, Faith and Fatima have lived here since you brought them from Chad and Syria?"

Mason nodded.

"But I suppose they never went to school or anything like that?"

"We wanted them to be pure!" blurted out Rosalee, "We wanted them to be untainted by the world..."

Maury nodded, "They were innocents."

"How did they die?" Rosalee pleaded.

"Maury breathed in, the breathed out slowly, "They drowned..."

The three quasi-Cathars looked puzzled.

"They were caught in a storm. They drowned in a culvert."

"What's a culvert?" asked Rosalee.

"A ditch,"" answered her husband.

Maury was not sure that Rosalee should go through more, the bluntness of her husband's reply had made her distraught once again. "Madame Mason," he said, gently, "Perhaps you need some time to compose yourself. If your presence is at all needed, I shall send your husband to collect you."

Snivelling, Rosalee retired to her chambers, they could hear her padding away through the house.

Maury turned to the men, "I'm going to temporarily suspend this interview. We shall resume, once I have informed my superiors of developments and I have liaised with my colleagues from the Gendarmerie."

Maury beckoned for Lucine to follow him into the quadrant and cross into the meeting hall where Barthez and his colleague were processing the other people of the commune.

The hall was a high space with high windows and pews. In fact, thought Maury except for the large table with benches around which the gendarmes and the calm and quietly compliant people milled, it would pass as an austere chapel.

All faces turned as the two detectives entered.

"How's it going Corporal?" Maury asked.

The gendarmes had identity cards and passports in front of them.

"Everything seems to be in order, so far," replied Barthez, "There are fourteen people here in addition to the three with you in the house."

"Where are they from?" asked Lucine, curiously.

"Six Germans, one Dane, two Italians and five French," said Barthez, sorting the passports, "What do you want us to do with them?"

Maury thought for a moment, "Let me talk to Mason and I'll come back with instructions."

Maury took Lucine aside for a quiet word, "Are you getting all this? I think we're going to have to send them all away..."

Lucine looked worried, "Won't that look bad, like we're suppressing a religious minority?"

Maury nodded, "Yes, that's why I need to speak to Mason. Go back into the house and send him out to me for a private word. Keep an eye on Johnny for me too."

Lucine did as Maury directed, presently the ashen, suddenly-old-for-his-age, Mason appeared in the house doorway. He caught sight of the detective sheltering from the drizzle under the eaves of a lean-to shed in which agricultural tools were stored and crossed to him.

"You've quite a place here," observed Maury.

Mason nodded and looked up to watch a small murmuration of starlings, flit across the sky. "A lot happened while you were away on your mission. The young people here need a leader who can protect them."

Mason nodded in agreement, watched a lagging starling catch up with its fellows, then turned to look Maury in the eyes, "You think they're vulnerable without me?"

Maury barely nodded, "Several dead, all in the prime of their lives. Something went very wrong here..." he paused before adding, "Smuggling people into France is a grave offence."

Mason's blue eyes clouded as he understood what Maury was implying. A custodial sentence was likely, and he'd have to leave the community in someone else's care once again. "What do you want me to do?" he asked.

"I need you to send everyone home. We will arrange for the Gendarmerie to send transport to get them to Pamiers, and from there to their homes."

Mason sank even deeper into himself, "Everyone?"

"Except for your friend Johnny."

Maury walked with Mason to the meeting hall. Every community member there looked at Mason expectantly for news. They'd probably heard Rosalee's wailing and distress and were wondering what the detectives could possibly want with the community's elders. Barthez looked like he too was wondering what was going on.

Mason clapped his hands three times as a signal for their attention, "Brothers and Sisters, I'm afraid that we are going to close the community for the foreseeable future." He smiled sadly, "So, I want you all to get your things and get ready to go home."

His adherents looked at each other in shock and began murmuring amongst themselves. Mason clapped his hands to silence them again, "You need to change into your ordinary clothes, get your things together and come back here to the hall. The gendarmes will brief you about what happens next in due course. I am very sorry..."

Reluctantly, the people began moving off to do as Mason had directed. Nevertheless, their compliance was impressive.

Barthez came over to Maury and the American, "Sending everyone home? Yes, that's probably a good idea."

"I'll make arrangements with our bosses," said Maury, "And I'll brief you as soon as I can."

"Yes Sir," said Barthez with a respectful salute.

While the Corporal went to speak with his trainee, Maury turned back to Mason, "Please, go to your wife and comfort her. When I'm ready we'll resume our interview in the house."

Mason looked incredulous, "You mean that there is more?"

"Yes," said Maury sadly, "I'm afraid there is."

He'd been dreading this, but he had no choice, he had to speak to Lafitte.

Feeling sick, he called the Inspector General's number.

"Allo, Inspector General Lafitte speaking."

"It's Maury."

Pierre Lafitte fell silent.

Maury grasped the mettle and spoke, "I'm in Ariege at a place called Labaouse. Get me the Gendarmerie at Pamiers to send transport for fourteen people and their belongings. The nearest place for access is called Rasigueres," he spelled it out and gave the co-ordinates, "Make it soon, these people will be on their way down with two Gendarmes I commandeered from Lavelanet.

"These people have done nothing wrong. I just want to make sure that they all get safely home.

"I'm dealing with a few things here. I'll be in touch again shortly."

Maury's hand was shaking, but he had to control his fingers to confirm the location and co-ordinates in a text. He hadn't let Lafitte get a word in.

Now he had to continue interviewing Mason and Johnny, to get to the bottom of all that had happened in this green idyll.

He walked back to the hall as his phone beeped with a quick reply from Lafitte, "All arranged. One hour at Rasigueres."

Maury briefed Barthez, "I'm afraid you're going to have to march these people down the mountain. I've asked for transport to be at the bottom of the track in an hour."

Barthez grinned, the weather did not seem to put him off, "That's how they got here anyway. I could do with a walk."

"At least they'll be travelling light," observed Maury sarcastically, "I doubt they'll have much material things to carry."

The policemen shook hands, "Thanks for your help Barthez."

Maury returned to the house, now there were only the Americans and the Englishman left to worry about.

When he stepped into the kitchen, Maury was pleased to smell coffee. Lucine had prepared everyone a drink. Maury suspected that the quasi-Cathars would have opted for some insipid herbal infusion. Mason and Johnny were sat silently and morosely at the table awaiting his arrival.

"How is Madame Mason?" Maury enquired.

"She is resting," said Mason.

"What's going on outside?" asked Johnny, aware of voices in the quadrant.

"The others are preparing to leave," Maury explained.

"You can't do that. You can't send them away, it's religious repression..."

"I sent them away," said Mason. His words stopped any further protest from the Briton.

A pregnant silence fell, Maury reached into his file and pulled the last e-fit for Mason and Johnny to see. "Do you recognise this young woman?"

The two men looked at the image and they both slowly recognised whose face they were seeing. It was Johnny's turn to get upset, he swallowed down a sob and wiped tears from his eyes.

Mason just shook his head in disbelief, "That's Kirsty...Kirsty Vandenbosch from Bluefield, West Virginia, my niece."

Johnny reached into his bag and placed a dog-eared United States passport in front of Maury. Mason looked at his friend with a confounded look, "Why, have you got that?"

Maury opened the passport to see a very apple-pie pretty girl looking back. Kirstin Ann Vandenbosch, she'd be twenty-five, if she were still alive. "We retrieved her body from the cliffs below Montsegur a few days ago," explained Maury.

Johnny became very agitated, opening and closing his hands into fists.

"We think she jumped off the castle walls just over two years ago," Maury continued.

"But she wasn't the type to get depressed or suicidal," protested Mason, shaking his head in disbelief, "When were you going to tell me Johnny?"

"You've not heard from her family of anyone then?" asked Maury.

"No," said Mason, turning his attention back to the detective, "She's estranged from them. That's why she came here to Labaouse."

"So, we have six young people from this community who have died in strange circumstances over the past two years. The first was this young lady, Kirsty.

"Did you know that before she came here from the United States, she was a member of the House of the Lord Jesus in Matoaka, a church famous for handling live venomous snakes? Their doctrine is that if a believer truly has the Holy Spirit within them, they should be able to handle all sorts of venomous serpents and drink poison without ill-effect. I expect you know the scriptures."

"Yes," acknowledged Mason, "And these signs shall follow them that believe. In my name they shall cast out devils, they shall speak with new tongues. They shall take up serpents, and if they drink any deadly thing, it shall not hurt them; they shall lay hands on the sick and they shall recover."

"That's right," said Maury, "So, when you and your wife went off on your mission, Kirtsy told the congregants here about the practice. They were cynical, until Johnny here captured two live vipers in the woods. You can imagine how greatly impressed everyone was when Kirsty handled these snakes without fear. A pretty little American girl and the symbolic form of Satan subject to her Holy power…"

Mason glared at Johnny, who wriggled uncomfortably, "Is this true Johnny?"

Maury gave Johnny no chance to answer, he continued his story, "Particularly impressed were two young men, Antoine and Sebastien, who were brave enough to handle the serpents along with Kirsty.

"Oh! It's an attractive doctrine, is it not, that signs and wonders will follow those who believe? So, if snakes can be safely handled, what else can you do? I understand that you already lay hands on the sick?"

Mason cautioned Maury, "That's different!"

"Yes," agreed Maury, "Jesus never said it was his hands that gave healing, he said 'your faith has made you whole'."

Mason nodded, "That's right."

"So, here in the mix we have a pretty young American girl who believes in signs and wonders, two young Frenchmen who are eager to experience some sort of 'rapture' and an older Englishman who is deeply influenced by Cathar mythology. He tells his eager young disciples about the Grail and the Perfecti, particularly Esclarmonde."

Mason looked at Johnny in disbelief, "Is this true Johnny?"

"It was only stories Eddy. But we started looking into other scriptures too, like Enoch, and Elijah who was taken up by chariots of fire and we thought there might be a transcendent path…"

Mason shook his head.

Maury continued, "So, they get fixed with the idea of becoming Perfecti, they decided to renounce all worldliness, become vegetarian and avoid all sexual impurity. The four decided to become the elite, the Perfecti of Labaouse.

"Johnny here, quoted scriptures, laid on hands and asked the Holy Spirit to dwell in them. So, they now thought of themselves as trans-material, as semi-angels."

Maury looked into space, "Of course, the real Cathar Perfecti only became that in extreme old age or on their death-beds, when the normal appetites of the flesh became weak. It was a recipe for disaster with such young and virile disciples. Antoine, in particular, struggled with his romantic and sexual desire for Kirsty, who he secretly loved. So much so that he visited a psychiatrist to have himself chemically castrated."

His audience looked at Maury in horror.

"The Summer Solstice came, so up the mountain they all went, Kirsty, Antoine, Sebastien and Johnny to the Cathar's holy place. You see, Kirsty identified with the Great Esclarmonde, and she felt sure that between them, she and the others had unlocked the secret of the Grail. The Grail to them was neither a cup nor a bloodline, the vessel in which the blood and life of Christ resides is the pure Perfecti. Who better to put words and ideas into action than our fearless little American? She went to the battlements of Montsegur castle and threw herself from them as the sun rose, sure that she would be transformed, as Esclarmonde was, into a soaring dove.

"To our witnesses' great astonishment, just as it seemed she was doomed she rose up and flew out of sight around the mountain.

"But she'd been caught in an updraft which caught her for a moment and then deposited her out of sight on the flank of the mountain. There she died of her terrible wounds, while the three men celebrated her transcendence and returned here to Labaouse to peddle their message of signs and wonders to their little congregation."

Maury noticed his forgotten coffee and gulped it down. Mason glared once again at Johnny who squirmed under the American's fierce scrutiny.

"Then the three of them analysed what had happened. Could Kirsty's transcendence be replicated? So, they planned to repeat the episode, but found that Montsegur was undergoing repair, so they had to consider changing the venue. They argued over this, Johnny was adamant that Montsegur was the only place that such a transformation could occur. The younger men weren't quite so sure. They felt it was the purity of the Perfecti that was more important than the place, after all, isn't God an omnipresent being, couldn't his blessing and care descend even to the depths of Hell?

Sebastien offered himself as the next candidate and it was decided that Roquefixade, the nearest Cathar fortress to Montsegur should be the venue for his transcendence. However, Sebastien had fallen madly and deeply in love with a young woman in the community, your adopted daughter Fatima. According to Cathar teachings sexual entanglements defile the spirit. But scriptures also say that love is pure and that it overcomes all. So, Sebastien was in a quandary.

"Antoine, who was so deeply influenced and affected by Kirsty, argued that the Cathars were right. After all, he was supressing his own sexuality with chemicals. If he acknowledged that love negated even sexual sin, it would compound his loss. His own beloved had already gone.

"Johnny though, understood romance and the deep connection a shared love can make between people. He also knew its purity. Don't forget that according to the legends that he was now espousing as gospel, that Jesus himself was married to Mary Magdalene. So, he gave Sebastien his blessing.

On the morning of the Summer Solstice, exactly one year after Kirsty's apparent flight from the walls of Montsegur, Sebastien went to a corner of the old walls of the ruined castle at Roquefixade and jumped into space. This time there was no sudden updraft to lift him or divert his fall, he plummeted headlong to his death on the scree slopes far below.

Antoine and Johnny, who'd gone to lend spiritual support and administer ritual washings, fled. They'd come up the other side of the mountain by foot, from Rapy, where they'd parked Sebastien's car. When they returned here to Labaouse, they tried to figure out what had gone wrong. Was it the wrong place, or had Sebastien's purity been compromised by his relationship with Fatima?

Antoine was certain it was Sebastien's sexual sin that had compromised his purity. Johnny was unsure, but he suggested that if Roquefixade were a holy place surely the Cathars would have mentioned it. So, between them they decided that it was a combination of both, but the main lesson to be learned was that the Cathars were right about human relationships being worldly and material, no matter how loving they may seem to be. The flesh wars against the spirit. So, they preached against the immorality of relationships and sexual sin to the commune.

You can imagine how Fatima felt about this. She had lost her lover, and their love was the reason he'd perished. Not only that, known only to herself, she was carrying Sebastien's child. She only knew that she could not stay. She turned to the only family she knew, Faith and Godfrey, to take her away from this place. They took Sebastien's car and went to find help with Sebastien's godfather. Sadly, they never made it, they crashed into a ravine, and when they managed to get themselves free of the wrecked car they were caught in a storm. But injured and desperate, they continued walking towards sanctuary until, in the rain and flood, they were forced from the road by an approaching car. The torrent in the drains overcame them and they were swept into the ditch where they drowned."

Maury's tone quietened, "No-one at Labaouse knew what had become of them and because they were illegals they could not inform the authorities anyway, and, because you see communications technology as part of the world's material evil, neither could they contact you. So, they assumed that they were all three together and they were safe. So, life returned to normal."

Mason swallowed and wiped a tear from the corner of his eye.

Johnny had visibly wizened, his pride had been broken and his eyes were yellowed and desperate.

"That brings us to Antoine," said Maury. "Poor Antoine, who you came across panning for gold in St Girons, an intense and talented young man who was an eager student and able worker for the fledgling commune of Labaouse. He worked alongside you both, fixing up the place, organising your agriculture, digging the well and listening attentively to your teachings. When you left, he was honoured to be given the opportunity to prove himself worthy of your trust.

You, Monsieur Mason, were his father-figure, but without your influence he turned to Johnny for guidance and, as you are already aware, he was too young and gullible to sort the truth from myth. He had talents, that young man, he was a metal-worker and jeweller. He had made Kristy a little enamel pendant and after her apparent transformation he wanted to honour her by smelting the gold he'd panned from the Ariege at St Girons. He produced nine little Gema Abraxas of his own design from that gold. On the back of each, what we originally thought to be a constellation of stars, is actually a map of the Cathar castles, with a dove to mark out Montsegur as the pre-eminent place. Only Sebastien's differed, the dove on his marked out Roquefixade.

But Antoine was having his doubts, Sebastien's death haunted him, and he did not want to continue supressing his nature with chemicals. He was looking forward to your return, when he could tell you everything and seek your guidance.

But, it seems, on your return all you wanted to do was chastise him for having used his God-given talents to produce little hand-crafted pendants that you condemned as idols. He would have been deeply upset to have his love-gift so condemned.

You know what happened next, he went to Montsegur, as his beloved Kirsty had done, and launched himself off the walls at sunrise. But poor Antoine did not die quickly as Sebastien had done. He was retrieved alive, but horribly injured, from the mountain and died later, in hospital, when his sister permitted the machines that were keeping him alive to be switched off."

Maury sighed with deep regret and looked at Johnny, "It deeply saddens me that you, the main architect of all this loss and tragedy, have committed no legal offence for which the law can prosecute or punish you. I hope it is punishment enough for you to know that you have fallen so short of the perfection which you hoped to attain, and to know that these young deaths are, in no small way, upon your head. As it is written: No-one is perfect, no not one…"

Johnny started blubbing, Mason looked at him in scorn, "Please…please Eddy, forgive me," he pled, reaching out to the American.

Mason turned his face away from his old friend, "Get your things and go!" he spat, "I'll forgive you when you're gone…"

Johnny looked at Mason with incredulity, "You want me to go Eddy? You mean it?"

Mason turned back to face Johnny and spoke through his gritted teeth, "I told you to go! Get your stuff and get off my land!"

Maury rang ahead, again he had to communicate with Lafitte. Again, his heart rose into his throat as the call connected.

"Lafitte."

Maury began, "I've got two American citizens here that admit to people smuggling. Those three bodies we found up near Périllos were illegals they'd brought into France as kids. I'm going to have to take them back to Rivesaltes to process."

"Who are they?"

Maury gave Lafitte as much information as he could from the passports, he had in front of him.

"Okay. I've got all that."

"We'll be on our way shortly. They just need to lock down the place. Have the others we sent away been picked up?"

"Yes," confirmed Lafitte, "They are being processed from the Gendarmerie at Pamiers."

"Okay."

Maury was about to terminate the call when Lafitte cleared his throat, "Maury?"

Maury said nothing, he waited for Lafitte to continue.

"I'm sorry," Lafitte said quietly, "It should never have happened."

By 'it', Maury supposed that the Inspector General meant his affair with Marie-France.

"No, it shouldn't," agreed Maury.

He let Lafitte digest the terse statement, then spoke again, "You're my boss, we've got to work together, so our dealings are going to have to remain professional. But I want to make this very clear. I don't want you anywhere near my family again, ever. Do you understand?"

Lafitte was silent for a few moments, then quietly agreed, "I understand."

Maury terminated the call.

The detectives helped the Masons to lock the Labaouse complex up. They closed shutters, locked doors and ensured everything was properly stowed.

Mason had changed from his white vestments into normal clothes, in his jeans, shirt and leather jacket, he had transformed from a pious religious figure into a worried looking man who was resigned to his fate.

Rosalee, now clad in jeans and a long-sleeved purple tee, looked like a care-worn housewife. She was being looked after by Lucine who had made her a drink and helped her throw away any perishable foodstuffs. After all, no-one knew when it would be that they would be returning.

Maury was glad that the Masons were prepared to face the music together. They'd both been equally involved with smuggling their adopted children across numerous borders. They needed each other at this time of grief and of uncertain future.

Despite their utter stupidity in bringing children from abroad illegally, Maury found that there was much to admire in the demure Americans, they were courteous, kind and obviously dedicated to one another and their cause. And he reflected on the role parents have with their children – it seems better to equip your children for the world than to insulate them from it, but it's of paramount importance to be there for them in their hour of need.

He felt hungry and hoped they'd reach Lavelanet before lunch stopped being served.

"Is this the way that Godfrey, Faith and Fatima would have gone?" asked Rosalee, as the Toyota headed eastward towards Rivesaltes from Quillan. They'd passed Johnny on the road between Rasigueres and Lavelanet, a pathetic figure still wearing his muddy white robe under his cape. Maury had not stopped to offer a lift. So far the Americans had said little, after eating at Lavelanet, Maury had driven in silence as was his wont and Lucine had been liaising with the Gendarmerie at Rivesaltes for a prosecutor to take over the case from the detectives once they'd deposited the Masons and made their report.

"I expect so," said Maury.

"Can you show us where they died?" Rosalee asked.

The two detectives looked at one another and with the slightest of nods a silent agreement was reached, they'd make a detour to accommodate the request. After all, these people needed closure.

As usual, the weather had improved on their journey east. By the time they had passed under the ramparts of Puylaurens castle, the sun was baking the vines and cypresses of Roussillon. Soon they were on the road that climbed up to Périllos from Vingrau, a thin strip of tarmac that wound with the contours. At the bend where Godfrey had lost control of Sebastien Tradot's car, Maury pulled onto the side of the road.

"This is where they crashed. The car is still in the ravine down there," said Maury, pointing into the boulder-strewn gorge. He noticed the scorched earth that had resulted from the vehicle's fire was still obvious on the far bank.

The Masons alighted from the Toyota and went to the white-painted concrete blocks that marked the side of the road and looked down at the rusted shell of the little Volkswagen, their sadness palpable.

"What do you think will happen to them?" asked Lucine.

"I honestly don't know," admitted Maury.

The Americans climbed back into the rear seats and Maury drove on, "They'd have walked this way."

He followed their route, going left onto the road that led to Périllos and stopped on an anonymous stretch of road.

"This is where they were found," Maury pointed at the deep culvert.

It really was a God-forsaken place to die. It was hard to imagine, in this hot sunlight, what the conditions were like on the night when the three injured youngsters were trying to get to Jean-Baptiste Vincent's place. What had they thought when they saw the headlamps of Christine Dubois' car approaching through the downpour? Here was someone to aid them? Maury could imagine Godfrey trying to flag the car down, but the car does not slow or deviate. The lawyer at its wheel is probably in a world of her own, high on coke and the masochistic pleasure she'd got from inflicting pain on Rada Dilov. The Audi strikes Godfrey, a glancing blow which spins him into the raging waters cascading down the side of the road. His sister Faith and Fatima try desperately to pull him from the flood, but their wounds and fatigue make them succumb to the elements, and the three are dragged by the current into the frothing sump.

The Americans stepped once more from the car and looked at the benign-looking drainage ditches, shaking their heads and clinging to one another as if they themselves were caught in a similar storm.

Maury's phone rang, the number was unrecognised, the voice unfamiliar, "Allo, Commandant Maury?"

"Yes, speaking. How can I help?"

"Bonjour Commandant, Prefet Dusablon speaking, are you free to talk?"

"Give me a moment Monsieur le Prefet," said Maury.

He turned to Lucine, "Can you see to the Masons, until this call is over, please?" he asked.

Lucine nodded, stepped out of the car, and engaged with the Americans.

"Pray continue Sir," said Maury to the Prefet.

"Lots of developments today Maury. I hear you've got Edward and Rosalee Mason with you, is that right?"

"Yes, Sir."

"Very good. Where are you now Commandant?"

"Up near Périllos Sir, the Masons wanted to see where their

adopted children died."

"Oh yes! I quite understand. It's a terrible tragedy, terrible. Anyway...I want you to go to Perpignan airport rather than the Gendarmerie at Rivesaltes, if that's okay. I'll meet you there to brief you in say...half an hour?"

"Perfect Sir."

"Alright, at the Helipad, not the main terminal. See you then."

The Prefet sounded upbeat and friendly, although Maury had never personally met the man. He pressed the button to quit the call and signalled to Lucine that she could now return the Masons to the car when they were ready.

Maury wondered why the Prefet had suddenly become involved and what he had meant by developments. He hoped it was good news regarding Christine Dubois, after all Maury's email must have landed on his desk, and he'd hardly conversed with Lafitte to get his thoughts. And why the airport?

Still, his was not to reason why...

Once the Masons were back aboard the Toyota, they clung to together, weeping in the back seat. Maury turned the big vehicle around and headed towards the airport as directed.

"I thought you were taking us to the Gendarmerie in Rivesaltes," remarked Mason, as Maury bypassed the little town and continued towards Perpignan.

"I've had instructions to take you to the airport instead," Maury told him, "The Prefet has asked us to meet with him there."

Mason looked puzzled but sat back and held Rosalee's hand.

Lucine leaned towards Maury, "What's going on?"

"I don't know. The Prefet said there have been developments, whatever that means," replied Maury.

"Do you think you may be in trouble?"

"What for?" asked Maury, wracking his brain for whatever his transgression may have been.

"Your email about Dubois?"

"We'll find out soon enough," said Maury, looking past Lucine at the airport's perimeter fence flitting past her window and the runway with its terminal buildings just beyond.

He pulled into the helicopter area that served the small regional airport onto a hardstanding reserved for private flights. On the ground was a jet with an N-prefix registration, there were two large Audis and a huddle of figures in the shadow of one of its wings. Maury drew up and two figures detached themselves from the plane's shadow, one a trim woman in a blue trouser suit in her forties, at a guess, with dark hair pulled into a ponytail and the Prefet, of similar age, gangly-thin with neat haircut and clean-cut features.

"Bonjour, Commandant Maury!" exclaimed the Prefet, "Can I introduce Vice-Consul Urban from the United States Consulate in Barcelona," he said, as he shook Maury's hand and went to help Rosalee step down out of the high Toyota.

Vice-Consul Urban took Maury's hand in a firm grip. "Looks like you've been off-road," she remarked, looking at Maury's mud-spattered vehicle. Her French was good, oddly though it had a slight Spanish lilt, "Thank you for getting the Masons here safely." Then she too moved on to greet her fellow Americans.

As the Americans conversed, the Prefet beckoned for the two detectives to step aside to talk with him. When he saw Lucine, the wolf could be seen beneath his lamb's façade, "Lieutenant Babayan, I'm so pleased to meet you."

"So, what's going on?" asked Maury, he suspected that some backroom deal had been brokered and the Masons would not be facing French justice.

"Monsieur and Madame Mason are being deported from France and being repatriated to the United States," explained Prefet Dusablon, "Via Spain, in this instance.

"Because of their humanitarian work in the Third World, it might not reflect well on France if we prosecute them for a lapse of judgement. Also, because they ran a religious sect, we could be perceived as persecutors of free religion. It's not ideal, but they become someone else's problem, and their little sect is forgotten."

"What about their adopted children?" Lucine asked.

"Well, you'll be pleased to know that Christine Dubois finally admitted that she did run into them with her car. She's been suspended, along with a number of other officials from the Administration, for their involvement in the unsavoury activities of a certain Senor Jimenez. We've yet to formalise charges, but we will prosecute her, you can be sure of that.

"The IGPN investigation has led us to have a reshuffle in both the Prefecture and the Procureur's offices. The Minister and I are most keen to see that the house is properly put in order in the wake of this affair."

"And what of systemic racism?" asked Maury, half-sarcastically.

"Oh, the other Dubois and a few other minor officials have been fired. As has your colleague Verdier and a few other officers in the Police Commissariat of Perpignan."

Lucine frowned, "I thought he'd gone on to work for the Police Municipal in Elne."

"So, did he. No, we had to be seen to clean up our act. We're under a lot of scrutiny..."

"What about Captain Guillot?"

Dusablon seemed happy to be engaged by Babayan, "Oh! Yes, he's going to fly a desk in Narbonne."

At the mention of Narbonne, Maury realised that Guillot would be part of his own team there. He was about to protest when Dusablon raised his hand to halt the conversation, the American Vice-Consul had finished talking to the Masons and had come over to the three French officials.

"I think we're about done here. The Masons understand their situation and are happy to voluntarily leave the territories of France. They also understand that should they return they may face prosecution," the Vice-Consul looked to Maury, "I understand that you have their passports."

Lucine responded on Maury's behalf, "They're in the car, I'll get them."

As Babayan went back to the car, Urban continued speaking to Maury, "The Masons said they were well-treated by you, and they're particularly grateful for you making a detour to put their minds at rest."

Maury nodded, he could see that two of the people waiting under the wing had come forward to see the Masons onto the waiting plane, a steward and stewardess of some private airline. He noticed that the Masons now trod instead of striding, they had prematurely aged and were leaving France shadows of the people they once were. "Wish them well from me," said Maury. "Their things are in the back of the car," he added.

Urban waved to gain the steward's attention and directed him to see to getting the Masons few belongings aboard the plane. Then, she shook one hand after another in goodbye finishing with Maury, "Thank you for your discretion." She said.

The engines started whining, the last remaining figure sheltering under the aircraft's wing came over to the Prefet's side to watch the Americans clamber up the gantry and enter the fuselage. Groundcrew removed chocks and stairway, the engines roared, and the jet began its slow taxi towards the airstrip.

Once the jet's take-off noise had abated, and the gleaming white aeroplane was out of sight the Prefet turned once more to the detectives. He gestured towards the unintroduced stranger, "This is Captain Monvoisin, he's going to take over from Guillot as head of detectives in Perpignan."

Lucine's heart fell, Monvoisin looked to be a dullard, he was in his late thirties, was more overweight than Maury, had receding sandy-coloured hair and a very ruddy complexion. Monvoisin smiled as he took first Maury's hand and then Lucine's pumping them and saying an earnest, "Bonjour," to each. My first impressions might be wrong, hoped Lucine, there's a first time for everything.

The Prefet continued, "Now that the IGPN have finished their investigation, Captain Monvoisin will be working closely with the Procureur's office to ensure that our next cohort of prosecutors are fit for their posts.

"I hear that you'd hoped to fill Guillot's shoes yourself Maury, is that right?"

Maury was wrong-footed by the Prefet's rhetorical question,

whatever or whoever had given the Prefet that idea? He'd mentioned that possibility to only two people – Marie-France and Lucine. Somehow, he doubted that Lucine would have said something to filter to someone as highly placed as the Prefet. That left Marie-France. Merde! That means it was probably pillow talk she'd shared with that 'couillon' Lafitte!

But, the Prefet was oblivious of Maury's response, he continued speaking anyway, "You know what the Region of Occitanie needs is to have is a flying squad of detectives that can work across Departmental boundaries. I mentioned the idea to my fellow Prefets in Aude and Ariege and we think it would be good to have a task force that can work on such cases in the eastern end of the Pyrenees. We haven't got a working title for it yet, but we'd like you to get it off the ground, straight away. It'll be based in Narbonne, that seems sensible, and it will work directly under the Regional Controleur General de Police, so it will have a very high degree of independence."

At light speed, Maury had to forget who had said what and done what to get in the Prefet's ear and concentrate instead on what the man was proposing. It sounded a very sensible idea and Maury told him so.

The Prefet clapped the Commandant on the shoulder, "Good, I'm glad you agree. What do you think it needs to make it work?"

"The team needs to be composed of detectives from the Police Nationale and some members of the local Gendarmeries," he replied, "The detectives need to be supported by colleagues with good local knowledge."

"Alright, think about who should be included in your team and submit your proposal to the Controleur General, we need a concrete plan at your earliest opportunity."

Had he heard right, had he somehow got himself a new job? "I'll speak to him tomorrow Sir."

"Good. I'm afraid we can't give you much of a promotion though, more a sideways move. You'll be working through different channels and reporting directly to the Controleur General, and the Prefets rather than the Procureurs. All this will be made official in due course, you'll go up one spine point in pay and hold the rank of Commandant Divisoire."

At Maury's astonished look the Prefet jibed, "That's if you want the job of course."

They drove back towards Rivesaltes, Lucine was excited about the remit of the proposed peripatetic task force, "Who would you have on the team? You mentioned Gendarmes from each of the three Departments. How about Renaud or Pratt from here? They've both been excellent. Barthez from Ariege, or that Desk Sergeant, the efficient one, from Pamiers? I bet he'd keep everyone in order. But I don't know the Aude lot so well..."

Maury was quite happy for Lucine to let her imagination run wild; she was actually making some very good suggestions. But he was wondering if Lafitte was the puppet master behind this promotion, once again, and whether he should take it at all. Wouldn't that make Marie-France some sort of whore, who sold herself for her cuckolded husband's, and therefore her own, advancement? But, on the other hand, it would mean that Lafitte was no longer his line-manager, their paths would seldom have to cross. He'd have to think about it.

"Do you mind if we take a little detour?" Maury asked, "We ought to get Renaud and Pratt a little something to say, 'thank you'."

He drove past Rivesaltes and Espira, turning off the main road to cross the Agly river by an unmade road and an old trestle bridge. He drew up in front of a neat brick-built manor house; the signage proclaimed it to be Chateau Jau, a wine domain known for its excellent cuvees. He alighted from the car and made towards the little on-site vintner's outlet that sold the nectar directly to passers-by and connoisseurs. Lucine followed him into its cool, dark interior where the bottles produced, were displayed under tasteful downlighting. Maury browsed and settled upon a gold-medal winning red, buying each gendarme a crate of six bottles.

"What can I get you Lucine?" he asked.

Lucine was intrigued by another award-winning wine, a white Cotes Catalans which Maury insisted they taste before purchase. He seemed suddenly carefree, the usually gruff, cynical detective forgotten, as he tried the white with her, and approving of her choice ordered her a crate from the attendant.

Just as suddenly, his mood went sombre, "It doesn't bring them back though," he whispered to himself as he placed his empty glass back onto the counter. He was looking through the door at the sun-drenched slopes. Lucine knew what he was thinking, she was too, of those poor young souls who had perished so needlessly on these mountainsides.

Lucine put her hand on Maury's forearm and brought her mouth close to his ear, "It wasn't me that told anyone that you might be interested in the Perpignan job. You looked a bit put out when the Prefet mentioned it..."

He could smell the sweetness of Lucine's breath and could see the genuine concern reflected in her sparkling dark eyes.

"It doesn't matter," he said, "It may have worked out for the best."

He knew who had betrayed his trust, but he could work it to his advantage. "How do you feel about joining me on the task force?" he asked.

Lucine was shocked and obviously thrilled to be asked. But Maury did not wait for her answer, "Shall we try the Rosé?" he asked.

The two detectives met up with the gendarmes and the station chief to wrap things up in the Incident Room. Renaud and Pratt deserved to know all that had transpired in the tail end of the investigation. They listened carefully to Maury and Babayan's debrief, shocked to hear that unless the connection to Tradot's car had been made they'd probably have never ascertained whose bodies had been found in the ditch. When Lucine told them about the community at Labaouse they were intrigued to hear that someone had actually tried to emulate the Cathars.

"But, we don't really know that much about them except what's been handed down by their oppressors and mythology," remarked Pratt, "What we do know though, is that they never hid themselves away in some holy huddle, they were among the people doing good works, not reading fairy-tales in a hermitage!

"All this signs and wonders stuff always seems a bit dodgy to me. And, this Mason fellow getting all uptight about a trinket being an idol, it's hardly a golden calf that they worshipped is it?"

Despite his mood, Pratt's remarks made Maury chuckle. "No," he agreed, "By your works you are known."

With the Station Chief's blessing Renaud and Pratt were stood down and allowed to accept Maury's invite to go for a little beer to celebrate the end of the investigation. Maury hoped to talk to them there, away from their place of work, about the peripatetic task force he was to assemble.

Once they'd changed out of their uniforms, the four police officers found the same café terrace that Maury and Lucine had sat within to watch the rain. Maury bought a round and watched his colleagues unwind.

Lucine and Pratt were ribbing Renaud mercilessly about a date he'd set up with the Spanish detective Benet, all very louche and amusing, until Maury tapped his glass for attention.

"Here's to a job well done," he said, raising his glass, "Well done everyone. Salut!"

He hadn't done yet, he told the gendarmes about the Prefet's plan to set up a flying squad of investigators and he asked them all to seriously consider joining it, if they felt they could.

Lucine and Renaud had no doubts, they rose to the new challenge without hesitation, while Pratt remained quiet and thoughtful.

The sun was setting, casting an orange light on the predominantly ochre houses of the old town, making them look like they were radiating heat back to the sinking disc. It was time to go, Maury could not put off facing Marie-France any longer. He got up and made his excuses. Lucine looked at him as he rose, "Don't forget about meeting up tomorrow," she reminded him.

"I won't," promised Maury, stepping out into the street.

As he was walking back towards the Gendarmerie, he heard hurried footfalls behind him, he turned to see Pratt, who made it clear that he wanted a private word.

"I will give your offer serious consideration, Sir. It's just that I'd hoped to continue my studies before settling into a career," he explained.

The young gendarme looked a little ashamed of his own reticence. Maury reassured him, "It'll be a good opportunity to progress in your police role, should you want to come on board. But I think you'll do well in whatever you choose to do...

"Let me know what you decide."

Pratt shook Maury's hand, "Thank you, Sir."

Mas Maury was silent, except for the cicadas scraping away their relentless songs from the trees. A note on the table looked ominous. But, when Maury read it, it explained that Marie-France had been commandeered by Elisabeth to babysit the grandsons, while she and Robert formally fraternised with his new employers at a company 'do'. Marie-France would be returned to him some at some point tomorrow.

Maury wondered if he should ring her, but decided against it, such intimate business as they had should take place face-to-face. But he did text message her, "Got your message. Kiss the boys for me. Maury x."

He found a prepared meal in the fridge, he reheated it and ate once he'd watered the garden. The house felt big and empty behind him, as he sat on the veranda digesting his food with a few glasses of wine. He watched the stars appear, heard Scops owls in the wooded mountainsides and glimpsed gekkos scuttling from their hidey-holes to wait on impossible surfaces for their insect prey, then he retired to bed.

Despite his fatigue he barely slept without his wife's body next to his and the soft lullaby of her snoring. Is this the bed where the marriage vows had been defiled? Had Lafitte entered this holiest of holies and worshipped at Maury's altar?

The End of the Cathars

After the fall of Montsegur, the remaining adherents of Catharism practiced their religion in secret. They dispersed when they could, but in the Languedoc and Ariege, the Inquisition continued to search them out and prosecute them. But the remaining Cathars were adept at concealing themselves, even when the Inquisitors turned to torture, only a minority were found out.

The activities of the Inquisition were limited by its funding, but after the new overlord of Languedoc, King Philip IV of France visited the region in 1303 and became alarmed at the anti-royal sentiments of the people, he decided to remove the Inquisition's financial restrictions.

A final push against the remnants of the 'good men' began under the organised and determined Inquisitor of Toulouse, the Dominican Bernard Gui from 1308. By 1350, all known remnants of the movement had been extinguished.

From the crusade's beginnings in 1209 to the last Inquistions in 1350, the Catholic Church had managed to send up to 1,000,000 fellow Christians to their deaths.

28th June

Birdsong woke him, Maury dressed and went to the terrace with his coffee. He sat and contemplated his surroundings as the dawn sun painted gold in the sheltering trees. A soft cooing caught his attention, a pair of turtle doves were perched on a branch of an umbrella pine, the cock-bird vocal and demonstrative, his hen quiet but attentive to her beloved's advances. They mated for life didn't they, these mild-mannered birds? You'd think that they'd sit in happy and silent contentment, but no, every so often the cock-bird re-courted his mate, perhaps reinforcing their bond with his cooing and his fussing over her. Perhaps that's where I've gone wrong, thought Maury.

Then he dismissed the whimsical thought and returned to the house to collect Julie Mercier's letters from her brother. He bound them together with an elastic band and put them into a large, strong envelope and reminded himself that he must post them, as he marked the label with her name and address.

Next, he felt he should pay his new boss, the Controleur General based in Toulouse, the courtesy of a call. Emile Franck, his new boss, had a reputation for being blunt and aloof, yet Maury found the Controleur General to be direct, succinct and willing to let his subordinates work with a high degree of autonomy. He listened to Maury's thoughts, agreed to attach Martinez as Maury's aide-de-camp and to attach Lucine, with promotion to full Lieutenant from Lieutenant Intern. He suggested some candidates from the Gendarmerie and they broadly agreed terms for the new task force's operations, "I have quite a caseload for you, which I will have sent to your office in Narbonne. When do you wish to start?"

"I'll assemble the team and we'll start as soon as I think we are ready," said Maury, hedging his bets. He'd expected to be given forty-eight hours, instead Franck gave him a full week, "I appreciate that Sir."

It was creeping towards midday by the time Maury had made calls to the various personnel that he wished to recruit into his new project. There had been some rejections, but those candidates had always made sound suggestions for others in their stead. By the time noon arrived he had the bones of an organisation sorted, he had to hurry, if he was to make it in time for his picnic with Lucine.

When Maury arrived, he parked his Toyota next to Lucine's Renault in the shade of a cork oak. She was already sat, informally dressed in jeans and a strappy white top which revealed her golden skin and more of her sublime figure than usual. Her hair was free of its ponytail and her blue-black curls cascaded over her shoulders. She removed the sunglasses that covered her sparkling eyes and she smiled at Maury as he approached the picnic bench laden with a bottle of Chateau Jau wine and a mixed salad, fresh from his garden. They embraced in typical southern fashion with triple kisses to the cheek, and Maury placed his items down on the table with her home-made falafels and Persian sweetmeats.

Maury opened and poured the wine, raised his glass and proposed a toast, "Here's to the future…We're now officially a mobile task force. Congratulations, Lucine, on your immediate promotion to full Lieutenant!"

Lucine almost spilled her wine in delight, she beamed from ear to ear and chinked her glass against Maury's, as he said, "Santé!"

They supped and looked about them at the spectacular view. "It's amazing here," said Lucine, in wonder. They were at the picnic area halfway up the cirque from Vingrau, the sky was rippled with soft clouds and the temperature was a much more comfortable 27°c, but they were still glad of the shade afforded by the maritime pines and Holme oaks.

A figure sat under one of the trees, where the view was uninterrupted. When Maury caught sight of him, he asked Lucine if they were now ready to eat. At her affirmative nod he crossed from the table to the boy busy daubing brightly coloured acrylic paint onto his canvas. "How are things Mankour?" Maury asked.

Mankour turned to the detective and smiled a wide, disarming smile, he wore an eye patch over his dead eye, it made him look like a corsair with his curly hair and dark features, "Bonjour

Commandant!" he said, in greeting and leaned back so that Maury could see his painting. His landscape was astonishing, combining vivid fauvism, inspired cubism for the rocky forms and buildings, and a fast impressionist style for the background. Maury was overawed by the young artist's natural ability, "Is it finished?"

"Almost," said Mankour, "Do you like it?"

"It's fantastic!" enthused Maury.

There was still no-one at the Mas, so Maury decided that he'd potter about in the garden. He collected tomatoes and harvested courgettes, then decided that he ought to make a cane frame for the peas and beans. He set to the task but found the earth so dry and hard that he decided to first water the ground to soften it to enable the canes to be driven in.

He was still working in the twilight, when he felt hands on his waist. He jumped in surprise at Marie-France's touch and managed to slice deeply into the index finger of his left hand with the trusty Opinel knife he was using to trim cord. He turned to his wife who looked at him with imploring and tearful eyes.

Yet, when she saw blood pouring from his wound, she held his hands in hers and began pouring kisses down upon them. Her beautiful head was bowed in shame, her shoulders rising and falling with her silent sobs. Her auburn hair stroked and tickled the skin of his hands and her lips felt like butterflies on his palms, making his inward parts tingle. Her tears mingled with his blood and fell in great drops to the earth and Maury thought that this was an apt way for the soil of Languedoc to receive life-giving sustenance.

Printed in Great Britain
by Amazon